Seven Rooms   (Assorted materials from

If *Hotel* itself were a concrete edifice, it would be more like *Fear and Loathing in Las Vegas*' Circus-Circus than the Grand Budapest, despite its tasteful, clean exterior. Its commitment to 'new approaches to fiction, non-fiction and poetry' promises all manner of havoc. It is not the only journal committed to literary innovation, but it is among the best.
 — Camille Ralphs, *Times Literary Supplement*

[*Hotel*] is a part of the renaissance of UK literary journals.
 — Nicholas Royle, *The Guardian*

Assiduously [chasing] the literary equivalent of a top-quality Tripadvisor review.
 — Dostoyevsky Wannabe

This hotel has coincidental resonance. At this moment I am fabricating scenes in a Parisian hotel, booked with a chance extravagance, and at the same time I am remembering a weekend in a Bristol hotel that was beyond our means, its trace evident now as we replaced our bed linen with Egyptian cotton. These facts come to the fore as Dominic asks if I will write a few words in response to the book in which you are at reception waiting to receive the keys to the reading rooms.

Once a magazine, now an anthology, a selection, a condensing, a celebration, a feast, call it what you will, for this volume takes on different forms in the eyes of each reader. Each generation should build their own edifices, whether hotels, factories or pleasure domes, places in which they gather their interests and ideas so that they can hand them forward. Each editor must have a burning desire to research and draw from precursors and move with contemporaries, find a dialogue, or ideally a community and make it public, a way to share, to offer as a gift the work that one finds valuable and that one would like others to consider.

I want to be made aware of that ongoing dialogue. I want something personal from its editor, an intimacy you might call it. This hotel started as a series of dialogues in seven issues of a magazine. Now it is re-edited to found a new dialogue, drawing from the series to make a fresh whole. Today technology allows us to use it to work with art, illustrations and markings to bind with the texts, helping the volume to gain its own rhythm. For me, there's added interest in this volume with its global reach, with foreign works to thread through the weave. And further, many of the texts are shaped with referencing other writings, and thus further weaves. And yet, though the fabric shows such diversity and span in its contributions, there is a sense of intimacy overall.

This anthology has acquired its own presence. And like any anthology of worth it makes me want to read more, to follow up various writers, people new, people who I've known about but who have slipped my net, too many to name, many in fact. This anthology does that, with panache. I love it. And as I re-read, seeking what I intend to follow through, I am listening to John Cale in concert making 'Heartbreak Hotel' his own.
 – Paul Buck

A hotel is defined by its inhabitants

15	Forethoughts	Dominic J. Jaeckle & Jess Chandler
33	Notes on the Pink Hotel	Jess Cotton
43	St. Joan in Idaho	Rebecca Tamás
51	Light Space / Diary Entries for Giuseppe Penone's Felled Tree	Stephen Watts
65	Idlewild	Helen Cammock
71	At night the rustle of many fountains comes…	Salvador Espriu (& Lucy Mercer)
75	Dear Messiah	Lucy Sante
79	Karuizawa	Ryūnosuke Akutagawa translated from the Japanese by Ryan Choi
85	Fortunes, Favourite Sayings, & Assorted Sundries	John Yau
89	The Rope Barrier	Nicolette Polek
93	No Show	Chris Petit
97	Five Columns	Sascha Macht translated from the German by Amanda DeMarco
107	Black Rabbit	Mark Lanegan
111	Chirologia & Phantasias	Lucy Mercer
115	come (A Poem for Two Voices)	Vala Thorodds & Richard Scott
119	Nine Notes (from a Diary)	Joshua Cohen
125	Butterfield	Hannah Regel
129	New York City, New York	Nick Cave

133	throttle song & nothingness is the scene of wild activity	Daisy Lafarge
137	this big bit cradle	Holly Pester
141	Rooms	Matthew Gregory
155	Notes on Happiness	Emmanuel Iduma
163	Sumari astral / Astral Summary	Joan Brossa translated from the Catalan by Cameron Griffiths
173	two types of the same return & moss	Imogen Cassels
177	Quantum Leap	Hisham Bustani translated from the Arabic by maia tabet
183	Menu of the Future	Raúl Guerrero
197	The Way Ahead is Spring	Velimir Khlebnikov translated from the Russian by Natasha Randall
201	white dog & an eight horse sun	Edwina Attlee
205	Timeshare	Aidan Moffat
211	Waiting for the Ferry, Lousay	Lesley Harrison

[INTERMISSION: James Hugunin]

217	A Working Week	Oliver Bancroft
227	Greenery	Will Eaves
243	(Verbal Translations of) Two Photographs	James Hugunin
247	Initiator	Aram Saroyan
261	The Hare	Glykeria Patramani

265	The Splendour and Effluence of the Motorway	Lauren de Sá Naylor
275	Three Pages (from Assorted Notebooks)	Will Oldham
283	The Heirs are Grateful	Antonio Tabucchi translated from the Italian by Elizabeth Harris
295	Yellow Fragments	Nina Mingya Powles
299	Spirit Human & The Future Tense Expresses a State that Does Not Yet Exist	Isabel Galleymore
303	Cameron's Dream (Super Barrio Shroud)	Jeffrey Vallance
311	Debt Night	Preti Taneja
317	We Have Come to Let You Out (Searching for Brion Gysin in the Last Museum)	Stanley Schtinter
341	The Gracious Ones (A Philosophical Ballet)	Sophie Seita
355	Ode	Cass McCombs
359	Travelling Alone is My Favourite Sickness	Ralf Webb
363	[elegant toplessness stoned in stairwell]	Wayne Koestenbaum
377	Prompt Note & Animal Bones	Iain Sinclair & SJ Fowler
385	Good night the pleasure was ours	David Grubbs
395	That's It	Agustín Fernández Mallo & Pere Joan translated from the Spanish by Thomas Bunstead

[CODA: John Divola]

419　Some Rooms: Dimensions of Dialogue　　Gareth Evans
　　　(An Afterword)

430　Notes on these texts

432　Hotel's History

434　Notes on these images:
　　　　Aram Saroyan (pp. 5, 182);
　　　　Mario Dondero, & the Hotel Roma, Turin, Italy (p. 12);
　　　　Erica Baum (pp. 14, 28, 128);
　　　　c/o Jules Verne (p. 24);
　　　　c/o the King Edward Hotel, Toronto, Canada (p. 30);
　　　　Dominic J. Jaeckle (pp. 42, 92, 196, 210);
　　　　Raúl Guerrero (pp. 50, 84);
　　　　Olivier Castel (p. 74);
　　　　c/o the Correios de Portugal (p. 96);
　　　　c/o *Augenblick*, by way of Samuel Kilcoyne (p. 106);
　　　　Jason Shulman (pp. 110, 204);
　　　　Georgia May Jaeckle (pp. 114, 298);
　　　　Jonathan Chandler (pp. 118, 282, 315, 358; 394);
　　　　Sandro Miller (p. 123);
　　　　James Hugunin (p. 124);
　　　　Matthew Shaw (p. 132);
　　　　Jeffrey Vallance (pp. 136, 140, 176, 242, 246, 264, 302, 310);
　　　　Levina van Winden (p. 172);
　　　　Lucy Sante (p. 216);
　　　　Yasmine Seale (pp. 226, 260);
　　　　Cass McCombs (p. 274);
　　　　Wayne Koestenbaum (p. 362);
　　　　c/o the El Capitan Hotel, Van Horn, Texas (p. 429);
　　　　& Adrian Bridget (p. 433).

436　Biographies

The 'Paper Hotel' (2016 to 2021) – born out of a conversation in Café Crema, London – was an anthology series that provided temporary accommodation for literary experiment.

Over the course of its wingspan, the project was edited and run by Dominic J. Jaeckle (*matchbook*), Jon Auman (*linens*), Thomas Chadwick (*kitchen*), John Dunn (*minibar*), and Niall Reynolds (*Gideons*).

~~elastic,~~

inelastic

Forethoughts   Dominic J. Jaeckle & Jess Chandler

A
Jaeckle, 'Neither Helena nor Oliver
had seen the Green Ray'

SOME CRESTING THOUGHTS ON A PAPER HOTEL: Across the seven issues of the 'paper hotel' (2016 to 2021), a persistent effort was made to never write an editorial nor preface for each of the seven instalments in the series. There was ever a keenness for the work to speak for itself; to rest on the page without any attendant road map for the astrology of ideas or constellation of concerns as each number in the series would accommodate. As such, the following remarks represent a reflection on a palmful of the ideas as underpinned *Hotel*'s curation, its project, and the kernel of argument as informs *Seven Rooms*.

This is a book that Chandler and I have deigned as more of an ancestor to *Hotel*'s activities; it is more a paper sculpture underwritten by the human and animal evidence as left in the room than any permanent record of a building's architecture. *Hotel* was intended to be a carnival of subjectivities, a prism for conversation. Likewise, *Seven Rooms* is a paean to the authority and practice of dialogue as a means of stretching the limits of literature's activity. *Hotel* is – and was – a 'paper plane' of a project; an undertaking dedicated to the practice of (to borrow a line from Edward Albee) our 'taking the wits for a walk.' *Seven Rooms*, in counterpoint, is that same paper plane now cresting on a line of thought.

*

*I do not take any
calls except from
the century we are in
when there is no bible in my hotel room
it makes me sad to have no place to put
my filthy poems for future guests
it is important to let them know*
– CA Conrad, 'Acclimating to Discomfort
of the System Breaking Beneath Us'

*

ON OUR INSTRUMENTS (PIANO & CLARINET): Thomas Bernhard, in his 1983 novel, *The Loser*, delivers the following instruction to his reader: 'Naturally, we want to have a practical relationship with the things that fascinate us, [...] because a theoretical relationship isn't enough.'

The Loser, if you were to boil the book down to the bare bones of its argument and indication, is a book about the conditions of (and commitment to) a sanguine engagement with the lived experience of creativity. It is a book about playing the piano, in the main, but equally the ways in which our elected preoccupations serve to tickle our own ivories and adjust the architectonics of the spirit and skeleton. How a sincere relationship with any given instrument serves as means to manipulate body and mind; to conjure up a contractual sense of dedication to something. The musician, for Bernhard, is a means with which to examine commitment; commitment to a practice, or craft, rather than to the more professionalist aurora and vapour trail of any theory of success as follows creative enterprise. 'A theoretical relationship' with the things that preoccupy us is ever deficient, for Bernhard, without its axiomatic 'practical' activity kept in mind. *Hotel*, borne out of such a sentiment, was always about the practice of creativity, of criticality, and the narrative drive of doing.

Such an idea constellates around myriad efforts to crystallise and portray creativity as an activity as we shuttle from the twentieth century to the terms and conditions of the twenty-first.

We look over our shoulder at Robert Stone for instance, who – in his own screen adaptation of his 1967 novel *A Hall of Mirrors*, Stuart Rosenberg's film *WUSA* (1970) – would riff on this very idea as a form of 'gratuitous grace.' In his case, the want to levy practical engagement over theoretical insight alone is figured as a life and death scenario. Stone envisages a clarinettist who, having '[fallen] off his life,' describes the high stakes of creative pursuit. Played by Paul Newman, our clarinettist coils around Stone's prose. An adaptive soul is key in 'an imperfect world,' Newman murmurs – 'take me to water and I'll grow gills and disappear into a flurry of fins' – but there is a sense of urgency that the clarinettist felt defined his need to play. Grace in gratuity. 'Gratuitous grace.' Such a sense of grace needs be 'wrangled,' it needs be ridden; if the horse isn't shoed, so to speak, such a grace comports a kind of poison, says Newman, sipping ice water in New Orleans. That grace can kill you, Stone suggests, if it's not given over to a practice.

We want to have a practical relationship with the things that fascinate us, because a theoretical relationship isn't enough.

Bernhard's piano and Stone's clarinet are instruments akin to those that sound out the way in *Hotel*'s orchestra of words and works; the ideas that play on as the vital organs within this project.

In *The Loser*, Bernhard antagonises a want and desire to play the piano; in Stone's *Mirrors*, the author describes the ways in which the clarinet itself plays the clarinettist. *Hotel* wanted to assemble works that rest in-between these two extremities. To consider works that were in conversation with a world and its contexts rather than contextually rendered subordinate to the world beyond the Hotel itself.

'A short story is narrower than a room in a cheap hotel,' writes Jack Spicer in his poem 'The Scrollwork on the Casket.' In *Hotel*'s contexts, this was a claim that required a little investigation. The narrowness of a story against the breadth of a room feels a way of picturing exactly the form of creativity that *Hotel* hoped marshal, champion, and accommodate. It was a publication defined by the simple idea that the room was ever big enough to afford myriad forms of telling, a multimodal form of tale, and all you needed do was decide to put a 'room' to purpose. To give it a job. To consider a practical relationship with a theoretical object of enquiry in a place designed for those aiming to 'pass on through.'

*

Two dogs named Ted and Fred do everything the opposite of each other. They go to the mountains and get rooms in a small hotel. The big dog gets a bed that's too small and the little dog one that's too big. Neither of them can sleep. The next day a bird suggests to them they trade rooms. Both dogs go back to sleep for the rest of the day. That is all there is of that story.
—Bernadette Mayer, 'Big Dog, Little Dog'

*

ONE BIG UNION: The 'hotel' was a practical metaphor first borne out in a South London eatery where I'd worked for some eight or so years in the kitchen to supplement the hourly costs of the city with the demands of hourly pay.*

In the kitchen, we'd occasionally loop on the idea of a union, of working in union – of 'one big union' – and a kitchen is always a beautiful place to think on the harmonics of working collectively. This gave birth to an ongoing conversation on and around collaboration; how such a public place as a café invariably hides the people that serve to scaffold it, as though secreting away a tattoo just above a hemline; how the best work is that which goes unnoticed. A hotel, a notable cliché in literary works of myriad vintage, holds its own easy, symbolic vernacular; the night-time; the illegitimate; the decadent; the runaway; of disappearing or (of standing on the brink of)

---

* With eternal gratitude to Daniel 'Red Man' Hughes of the Bluebrick Café for his example, his fraternity, and his friendship.

disappearance; but how a hotel shapeshifts was of interest. 'A hotel is defined by its inhabitants,' was the lead line on our masthead; the structure remains the same; the building is recharged, reformed, redressed by whomever may stake a room on any given night.

We set ourselves up to envisage the project of building such a 'hotel' that could (and would) present itself as a building willing itself to change shape on a regular basis. A proverbial run of rooms for occasional works, the idea that each cell would spill and inform the whole was fundamental. One big union.

*

The rose load falls silently from the walls,
and ground shines through the carpet.
    —Ingeborg Bachmann, 'Hôtel de la Paix'

*

ON DEVOTION: Conversations concerning the first Hotel broadly occurred in a garden, amidst the ducks and chickens behind Café Crema—a now shuttered coffeehouse on the New Cross Road—and it is to those birds to whom this book is dedicated.

*

He's talking
to the sky its finger
and walking bridge.
the mummers disappear
my city sounds.
dance crumples to

the archive sky of fela.
    —Fred Moten, 'tonk and waterfront, black line fade,
        unbuilt hotel, that union hall'

*

TO UNFOLD A MAP OF THE WORLD IN THE RAIN (I): Over the course of its life, *Hotel*'s construction owes to the following lines of longitude and latitude: 51.5072° N, 0.1276° W; 51.4545° N, 2.5879° W; 51.0500° N, 3.7303° E; 38.7223° N, 9.1393° W; 40.7128° N, 74.0060° W; and, however briefly, 37.7749° N, 122.4194° W.

Whilst we aimed provide a fleeting surveillance of a 'practical relationship' with literature, a relationship with London in end itself proved fleeting, and so a number of houses and cities were drawn into the mix. A little journeying serves as a footnote to *Hotel*'s dedication to communion, collectivity, and to conversation, but the circumstances of authorial and editorial play in our contemporary moment demanded serious engagement with internationalism from the outset.

Hotel #1 was published on the summer solstice, 2016, and launched on the summer eve of the BREXIT referendum in a room above a pub in Somers Town. The effects of this evening on any theory of 'conversation' from an English standpoint proved undeniable and immeasurable but – in line with *Hotel*'s efforts to facilitate a sense of direction – it made certain that internationalism would remain a given in any assembly of works as would lobby in this imagined building.

Hotel was a project indebted to the porousness of paper; it was a project that aimed actively ignore the borderlines between ideas; to repudiate any definitive sense of discipline; to encourage the making-public of a 'work-in-progress' as a talismanic stand-in for a 'practical relationship' with literary enterprise. Such aims were rendered all the more challenging in an eternal return of predicaments; be they mercantile, financialist – be it the rising price of paper or the soaring costs of accommodation – our circumstances gifted something to the idea of the publication of each instalment of *Hotel* as a temporary home for homeless ideas, and that knowing need that the swing doors that'd twirl about its spine needed remain eternally oiled and permanently open. Our argument itself needed its practical avenue.

Hotel was unfunded, with each issue in its seven-volume run seeded and set to scale solely by pre-orders and managed voluntarily throughout the project's duration. The project was defined by care, rather than capital, and – accordingly – *Seven Rooms* is dedicated to the hours spent and subdivided willingly on the works that formed *Hotel*'s ever-changing foundation. To the effort to advent lasting things when time is a semi-precious stone set at a high rate of tax.

Following *Hotel*'s lead, *Seven Rooms* is thus a compendium of conceptual rhymes. A paean to the forms of conversation, enthusiasm, and generous criticality as scaffolded the *Hotel* project and – in tribute to such a philosophy – it presents itself as an associative thread of broken couplets that roll on – in and out of the terms of argument – ever breaking and extending the reach of each rhyme, to present a collectivised dialogue.

It is a conversation eternally on the make; on the lamb; running; bleeding; growing, in terms both organic and artificial, and self-modifying as it goes.

Hotel was, somewhat deliberately, never a specifically or explicitly political forum – nor was it an effort to antagonise or analyse the drift of creativity when the odds are so stacked against creativity itself. To quote Joan Brossa (by way of a single line poem that retrospectively became something of a manifesto or mantra for *Hotel*'s activities), *Hotel* was a seven-storey effort 'To unfold a map of the world in the rain,' or – as ee cummings would put it – 'to eat flowers and not be afraid.'

*
You ordered
the wrong
thing but it's ok we can
come back
to this
restaurant
another time
      – The epigram to *Hotel* #1, excerpted from
      Mat Riviere's 'Accident Book,' circa 2016

*

Rather than any logbook or register of *Hotel*'s itinerant cohort, *Seven Rooms* is an effort to render a history of *Hotel*'s changing shape over the course of its seven years of operation.

    The anthology begins with the final entry in the first *Hotel* and works its way through to the closing pages of the final instalment in the series, *Hotel* #7. The collation of works is neither completist nor concrete – indeed, the book could have taken many a different shape – and, in its collection, it endeavours to underscore the degree of editorial accident as underpinned the project's curation. By accident, I am not implying that *Hotel* was a haphazard or unthinking enterprise – far from it – but the 'accident' of our enquiry serves as a means of situating the kind of experimental work in (and on) literature and culture we'd hoped to support. Conversation and collectivity was the main; openness, generosity, and a keenness to counter the forms of isolation that circle a more prosaic and 'garretted' form of artistry the project hoped to repudiate. An openness to ideas was fundamental, and a want for each idea to redirect and refract any light that'd shine on its predecessor equally so.

*

I can see the blank wall
I can see the silhouette in the window
He's talking
I'm not interested in
what he's talkin' about
I am only interested in the fact
That it's the last hotel
The last hotel
Ghosts in my bed
Goats are bled
The last hotel
   —Jack Kerouac, 'The Last Hotel
   & Some of Dharma'

*

ON CRAQUELURE: For those who work in heritage, in conservation and in museum cultures, 'craquelure' is a form of damage that marks the history of a painting and assists in the adjudication of its value. A term for the network of fine cracks that appear in the varnish of an oil painting over time, the morphology of these cracks displays the dynamics of history on the surface of a canvas, effecting an image with a new set of desire lines, with distortions — a kind of pictorial crow's feet that delineate a painting's age and antiquity — and these fissures or fault lines explicitly show how every surface gives way to tension, in end. Is changed by virtue of a subjection to its environments. A painting's decay can delineate a form of signature; the association of a work with a given school, with a given time. It's a signal of authenticity; a kind of lighthouse for those looking to identify whether a work is fraudulent or no; and a means of ascertaining how time effects a work of art.*

In some cases, craquelure is a hallmark of history; in others, the impact of accident. For example, if a layer of paint is applied over a wet surface, it causes what has been referred to as 'youth' craquelure. Alternatively, mix two types of chemical compounds in two varieties of paint that shouldn't meet — bitumen or asphaltum, for instance — and you've wide depressions in the paint layer, known as 'alligatoring.'

The work that *Hotel* sought to afford space for arguably bears more in common with craquelure than it does the practice of painting itself. Herein, we've the work of some seventy-five makers (of the five hundred or so who have thus far contributed to *Hotel*'s train of thought to date, across the project's various wings), engaging a

---

*   The metaphorical purchase of 'craquelure' is an idea that I owe (with thanks) to Chloe Aridjis.

practical effort to 'alligator' any fixed image of the *Hotel* as an edifice and to examine the cracks, crevices, and new symmetries that emerge.

*

ON SHAKY GROUND: In a building such as an imaginary hotel, as of knowingly and willingly fluid foundations, a nod to the work of the termite is appropriate here.

Critic Manny Farber, and his sense of a 'termite art' as in counterpoint to the work of the 'white elephants' of the twentieth century, was a signal post for our building the first *Hotel*. The 'elephants,' for Farber, are progenitors of humidor-like projects that showcase a 'drive to break out of tradition while, irrationally, hewing to the square, boxed in shape and gemlike inertia of the old, densely wrought masterpiece.' In sum, works that err toward a want to build themselves on the shoulders of a history of accepted experimentation and, in formal terms, mollify an audience with a satisfied understanding of what such an experiment is for – what it should be, in narratological or argumentative terms – and how such an experiment should look and feel.

At war with the emotive elephants of false experiment (or of an experiment set about with its results already in the mind's eye), Farber argues that we should side, instead, with the 'termite.' A critical quality he opines as akin to 'moss' or 'fungus' – Farber alludes to a kind of creativity that 'goes always forward eating its own boundaries, [...] termite-like, it feels its way through the walls of particularisation' to eat away 'the immediate boundaries of [an] art, and [turn] these boundaries or limitations into the conditions of a next achievement.'

In typifying his termite, picturing his termite at work, Farber is not presenting any limited view of story or of genre convention. The idea of resolution, for example, is not the enemy. If you write the story of a housefire, that the building burns to the ground is not necessarily a keystone to the telling, but it is obviously intrinsic to the work at hand. In this sense, Farber doesn't flag the gratification of a rhyming couplet nor the traditional *ends-and-means* of a story as any indicator that there's an 'elephant' in the room. He cites John Wayne's 'bitter-amused' performance in John Ford's *The Man Who Shot Liberty Vallance* as emblematic of such a train of thought for its 'intramural' qualities. Rather, to focus on the 'termite' is to think on the fragility of accepted structures, to consider how – by virtue of a subtle redirection of light – you can demonstrate such fragility and, in so doing, generate new and unexpected ideas.

*

TO UNFOLD A MAP OF THE WORLD IN THE RAIN (II): A favoured metaphor for the kind of creativity Hotel aimed to champion owes to Jules Verne's 1882 novel, *Le rayon vert / The Green Ray*. An unusual entry in Verne's escapist arsenal, here we've a more personal counterpoint.

Helena, besotted by the apparently revelatory, revolutionary effects that a meteorological phenomenon can have on our outlook, sets out for Scotland in the hopes of seeing the 'green ray' – an optical illusion, a green band that thumbs its way above a setting sun, in the right weather conditions, separating the declining light into distinct limbs of an apparently clear, green light. Helena's 'ray' is sought as a means of securing her interiority; she hopes that the split sun will provide a source of illumination for the darker corners of her own outlook.

Over the course of their journeying along the coastline, countless obstacles abstract the horizon as each day closes. Clouds, seabirds, *et cetera*. When the conditions hit their zenith, those clouds clear and the gulls alight, the light begins to subdivide; Helena and her compatriot – Oliver – are lost in conversation.

To miss the light for the sake of an exchange – to co-convene and co-conspire on a *tête-à-tête*, in spite of the authority and determinism of any weather system, the glow of a god light, or a metaphorical meteorology of distractions... This was the constant aim throughout the duration of *Hotel*'s seven-year run – a scrutiny thereof, *Hotel*'s hopeful wheelhouse – and it is an active effort to miss the light for the sake and privilege of conversation that runs through these pages.

*

Neither Oliver nor Helena had seen the Green Ray.

Page 306.

B
Chandler, 'The Inhabitants'

Now with a key in my hand, I'm surveying the foundations of the hotel I was for many years a regular inhabitant of. I remember clearly the excitement surrounding its original appearance, as though somebody had overheard our conversations and pleas for a new kind of creative accommodation, and suddenly there it was – welcoming us in, without asking for anything in return; 'a temporary home for homeless ideas.' *Hotel* was a magazine 'redefined by its inhabitants,' but constructed with a rigour, intelligence and vision which was invisible yet vital – formative in ways that its driving spirit of generosity and collaboration never chose to foreground, but which this volume shows so clearly.

When *Hotel* first appeared, I was running Test Centre, a small press co-founded in 2011 with my friend Will Shutes, releasing spoken word records and cassettes, poetry and fiction books, and eight issues of a fiction and poetry magazine based on the DIY approach of the magazines of the New York Mimeograph Revolution of the 1960s and '70s. Our first guest invitation came via Jen Calleja, who wanted to interview us for the *Hotel Archive* (an online counterpoint to the 'paper hotel'). We'd recently published her first poetry book, *Serious Justice*, and I've since published her short story collection and debut novel at Prototype – an ongoing collaboration that has been vital for us both. In her introduction to the interview, Jen wrote: 'I find great satisfaction and joy supporting the independent publishers I have the opportunity to work with through writing and translating, and I like to think of Jess and Will not as "my publisher" but as two new friends who I collaborated with to make a book. I feel proud of them and to be associated with them.' This is the spirit that has sustained us, and which adds meaning to the work within these pages, and to the work of its contributors that has followed. *Hotel* provided a space for so many reflective and interrogative conversations, and countless fictional lives were conceived within its rooms. Crucially, it wasn't just writers who found a home there, but editors and publishers too, and it became central to a small press ecology dependent on acts of generosity and collaboration.

Hotel came into being at a time (still ongoing) of exploration and experimentation in independent publishing, and looking back through its archive, it's clear how crucial a moment it captured, and nurtured. So many of the writers published in its pages, and reproduced here, along with the publishers who first discovered them, now lead the way – both as growing independents, and as recognised leaders in a much wider, and dare I say commercial, literary landscape. But this trajectory towards more mainstream publishing – as a way of becoming sustainable – was by no means predetermined, or even desired, and *Hotel* helped support a growing ambition to establish a means of allowing bold and innovative work to exist and thrive in the margins, with a quiet confidence in its importance and influence, confirmed by the strength of the community it built and sustained.

In his preface to *A Secret Location on The Lower East Side*, a document / catalogue / checklist of an incredibly influential era in countercultural American literary history, Jerome Rothenberg describes that crucial New York scene 'as mainstream and margin both, [representing] our underground economy as poets, the grey market for our spiritual / corporeal exchanges.'* It was on the edges but also absolutely central, mapping out a future culture. As with most movements, it emerged in response to a growing need for alternatives, as '[w]riters who sought new ways & languages took charge of their own publication.'** It was self-generated and unfinanced, with writers often doubling as publishers, making the operation of publishing itself central to the creative process, resulting in works in which form and content were truly aligned, the printed object inseparable from the written word.

In New York, location was vital, and the scene of those decades can be retrospectively mapped along specific topographies; collaboration was key, bringing with it an internal economy for the generation and distribution of work which kept it alive. *Hotel* kept the centrality of physical space and cohabitation alive, but as an imagined location, removing the walls in doing so, allowing individuals their own space within a shared community of web- or printed pages where nobody would ever be alone. Though London may have been its focus at times, any connection to one geographical place soon disappeared, and the magazine became distinctly international, and even more so as BREXIT tried its best to shrink the world around us. Just as the networks of the city once allowed, the networks of online communication and support grew and strengthened, and continue to reinforce the foundations we walk on now.

As a magazine 'redefined by its inhabitants,' *Hotel* remained in a state of energetic flux, reshaped by each new entry. By foregrounding the occupier over the building, it was vitally opposed to forces of ownership and division. As indie publishers in search of readers, and determined to give our authors the exposure we so strongly

---

*   Jerome Rothenberg, 'Preface', in *A Secret Location on the Lower East Side: adventures in writing, 1960–1980: a sourcebook of information*, by Steven Clay and Rodney Phillips (New York: The New York Public Library, 1998), p.9.
**   Ibid., p.10.

believed they deserved, *Hotel* opened its doors and formed its own audience, offering, as Jaeckle says, shelter to otherwise homeless things. It's no coincidence that interdisciplinary work was so strongly supported in its pages, and its editorial approach was an act of curation, filling the growing gallery space with work which over time took shape as something coherent, giving permanence to transient things.

Paul Buck, editor of the seminal 1970s magazine *Curtains*, and both a Test Centre and Prototype author, conceived of the magazine as a form of 'public notebook,' allowing a 'dialogue between contemporaries.' As the magazine evolves and develops, new ideas emerge; it starts to create its own afterlife. In his introduction to *Disappearing Curtains (a journal)*, Buck also asserts the importance of editorial conviction and courage, writing that 'when we create, when we edit, we shouldn't care to think in terms of a wide readership, we have to focus on what we need to explore, and to explode, and even to exploit, without fear of failure or going so far that we fall into the abyss.'*

So what does it mean to be publishing this book? Is it an archive of a moment, or an attempt to build something permanent from something designed to remain unfinished? There's no doubt that we're all on our own trajectories, and that the need to live, to adapt to rising costs and pressures, often requires us to either let things fade, or try to strengthen them into structures that can keep us more secure. This collection shows how crucial and influential the work of indie publishing can be; how important the foundations we've built are when the developers come in and acquire our land. And perhaps that's a process we should embrace, as long as it's acknowledged, and our work supported, so that we are able to continue it. Our fragility is our strength and our freedom, and with it we've built these seven rooms.

---

*   Paul Buck, 'Notes in & out of the disappearing mist,' in *Disappearing Curtains (a journal)*, ed. Paul Buck (London: Slimvolume, 2016), p.10.

In the vast, still-streaming house of windows, children in mourning looked at marvellous pictures. / A door slammed, and on the village square, the child waved his arms, understood by vanes and weathercocks everywhere, in the dazzling shower. / Madame xxx established a piano in the Alps. Mass and first communions were celebrated at the cathedral's hundred thousand altars. / The caravans left and the Splendide Hôtel was built amid the tangled heap of ice floes and the polar night. / Since then, the Moon has heard jackals cheeping in thyme deserts, – and eclogues in wooden shoes grumbling in the orchard.
 —Arthur Rimbaud

Every room is lonely / Blue Hotel
 —Chris Isaak

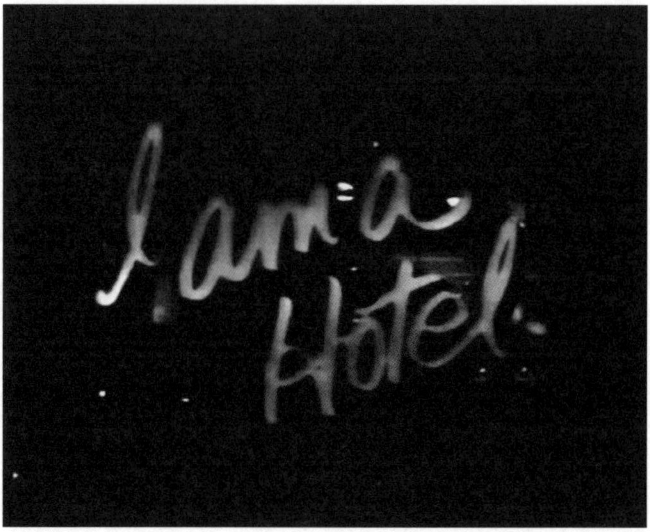
I am a
Hotel

Notes on the Pink Hotel   Jess Cotton

Room 1

I

WE TAKE LEAVE TO RETURN. The leave-taking
should justify the homecoming, or at least the
time, the expense. But sometimes other homes
present themselves along the way; or the ones
we had no longer fit. 'Goodbye to all that,' Joan
Didion says to the brightest city of them all, in
a story about moving to New York, which is also
a vindication for returning to the dry state.

II

I THINK OF VIJA CELMINS STRETCHING HER
CANVAS which is print which is water as she
wrenches her Californian sea from its bed, dry
pointing the ocean into its own still life.

III

IF YOU DIDN'T GROW UP HUNGRY FOR BRIGHT
LIGHTS, there can be a certain inevitability to cit-
ies, the way Cheever describes his affinity to water:
'less a pleasure, it seemed, than the resumption
of a natural condition,' which might be another
way of talking about homelessness.

IV

HOMES CAN MAKE US FEEL WHOLE, but they
also point up the holes in our habits of living,
especially when we want to feel fractional; to
pack several lives, or bottomless suitcases, into
one.

V

DIDION CALLS THIS UNHOUSED CLARITY,
the lurid *mare nostrum, weightlessness,* or the safer
mode of living.

VI

PENELOPE FITZGERALD, WHO BUILT HOMES IN UNEXPECTED PLACES, was always thinking about homelessness, or home-looseness. 'The child is an exile who must make the best of his way home,' she writes in a collection of essays, *A House of Air*, though her characters remain, in some way or another, resolutely (though that is the last word they would use) lost. In her fiction, not having a home is not so much a mode of living as a means of survival.

VII

THE ABILITY TO TRAVEL ANYWHERE, VIRTUALLY AT WILL, says David Rieff of Susan Sontag, DID NOT MAKE HER LESS OF A STUDENT of fluidity, nor her will (which is almost never virtual) less of a virtue.

VIII

RESTLESS AFTER THREE YEARS ON THE SUSSEX COAST and at her wits' end with a husband she was losing to drink, Fitzgerald set up house on a riverboat on the Thames. It was not an obvious choice, but it seems that choices were not something Fitzgerald was willing to make, yielding, as all vessels at anchor must, to the ebb and flow of the tide.

IX

A HOME [flat / room / bed / couch / boat] IS SPACE where the self *familiarises* its contours; and when a self sprawls out of that frame (when we do more for the home than the home does for us), that home is created by exclusion – in space that has yet to be *conquered*, as Sontag says – or, as I prefer, *known*.

X

    We claim a country by birthright, but we approach a city as an (un)invited guest, and we adopt her by overstaying our welcome.

XI

    Fitzgerald objected to translations of *Offshore* that implied 'far from the shore'. The intent was in the drift, in the unsteady nature of a craft anchored a stone's throw from the city's shore.

XII

    'Most of us who use the English language,' D.H. Lawrence writes in his essay on Melville's water-borne tale *Typee*, are 'water-people, sea-derived'. Inland, we duly source some life aquatic.

XIII

    LS LOWRY, WHO IS KNOWN FOR HIS NORTHERN INDUSTRIAL LANDSCAPES, populated by peculiar spartan men, had on occasion such an urge to see the sea, he would take a taxi some 140 miles from where he worked as a rent collector in Pendlebury to Sunderland, in whose etiolated waters his own cityscapes can be found.

XIV

    I THINK OF TACITA DEAN's air-crisp voice searching for the greenness of her exposure, not daring to imagine how green the splash will be, or when it will have scened.

XV

BORGES' NARRATOR, WHO EMBARKS ON A
QUEST TO REACH THE CITY OF IMMORTALITY,
HAS CONFUSED DREAMS of a labyrinth at whose
centre lies a well, which, though visible, remains
eternally out of reach, and of home, in which the
memory of the city of his birth merges with the
village of the barbarians. Later, having reached
the city, though having little memory of it, he surmises that our urge to hurtle frantically around
the globe must come from the knowledge that if
there is a river that grants immortality, there
must also be one that takes it away.

XVI

BUENO ES SABER QUE LOS VASOS / NOS SIRVEN
PARA BEBER, says Antonio Machado, for whom
there is no highway, only cool wakes upon the sea
in which, for Alejandra Pizarnik, *sea* (as in *Que tu
cuerpo sea siempre / un amado espacio de revelaciones*)
is its own sea, the blue velvet rinse of implacable
dreams.

XVII

WHEN DANTE'S TRAVELLERS EMERGE FROM
THE WOOD OF SHADOWS where the harpies
lay their nests, they find themselves on a plain
of scorched red sand onto which instead of rain
there falls fire-like snow.

    In the snow-like fire of Richard Misrach's
saline stage sets, fire's theft is sublime opalescent
baked rust, and the sea is only where it shouldn't,
giving the sky back to itself violet-blue.

XVIII

    I THINK OF RIMBAUD, far from his soft city rain, arriving at the *Grand Hotel de l'Univers* at the barren heart of the empire, weaving his *bateau ivre* through the sulphurous desert, trafficking in personas that multiply and divide on the red plateau of the *Forbidden City*, as he tacks back into *Une Saison en Enfer*.

IXX

    THE PHOENICIANS, Herodotus says, EMERGED FROM THE RED SEA, which is both a sea onto itself and that which flows beyond the pillars of Heracles into the Atlantic, though it is not always clear he is talking of the same Phoenicians.

XX

    AT NIGHTFALL, BAS JAN ADER, the gravitational star ever falling, SETS SAIL (in his locker *The Strange Last Voyage of Donald Crowhurst*) *In Search of the Miraculous* sadness of the smallest of crafts disappearing off the edge of the bottomless shore.

XXI

    I THINK OF ELIZABETH BISHOP's bays which take more than they give and how no matter how she pictures the *belle isle*, she can't keep the burnt matchsticks (the amputated years) from creeping back into the aching frame.

XXII

IN ANTONIONI's *Red Desert*, there is water, but it has lost its blue – or what we think of blue. For there is blue in Monica Vitti's cornflower-arched eyes and Arnolfini coat and in the ultramarine of the unmanned boat in the story she untells her son, which vanishes as silently as it appears. And there's fading blue (the colour of documentary) in Richard Harris's map of South America which they pore over, tracing the thin blue line to the delta-less fall into the ocean, knowing they will never depart, knowing that like the birds, they will only learn to circumnavigate the sulphuric bursts of the deep chasm by turning the screen inside out.

XXIII

AT THE PORTAL OF JOSEPH CORNELL'S BLUEAILLE, spectators of the eclipse guard the gates to Rose's indigo.

XXIV

FOR BRODSKY, Venice is a woman with yellow eyes, *like Greta Garbo swimming* (a glimpse of her in her private pool in her secluded garden), a city whose liquid depths so unsettle the principle of living on the surface of things that to be sidetracked is a matter of course, for to inhabit a city of reflections is to be aware of all the scenes it has born in its choric depths, and now holds on the brink of this static interlude. When we're in love, cautions Sontag, the other is always Garbo.

XXV

IN BILL VIOLA'S REFLECTING POOL, a man emerges into the squareness of the paragon frame, segments of sound impress themselves on the water's surface, and retreats as silently into the wood from whence he comes, leaving only the pool in its double sides.

XXVI
    TO BE A WATCHER, Anne Carson says, is not a choice, for unlike the swimmer who can just walk out one evening into the water, there is no way, nowhere, to get away from this watching. But what if swimming were its own form of watching, a way of keeping things that can't be housed out in the open?

XXVII
    I'M A PERFORMANCE SWIMMER says the underside of Eileen Myles's postcard,

> SLOWLY MOVING EAST,
> LET'S HOPE THIS GETS THERE FIRST!

XXVIII
    BACK TO SURFACES, she said, re-surfacing, to Plath growing numb in the Amazon of her New York hotel bathtub, steering nothing, least of all herself, against the pull of the city, thinking of transgressions and of Europe, of the little white Alp at the back of her eye.

XXIX
>   **THE DIORAMA OF OUR DIMINISHED DWELLING** is how Walter Benjamin classes his hotel. I tend to think of it as a silken gash keeping her revolving ache ajar

XXX
>   **THE BETTER THINGS ARE DONE IN SLEEP**, says Renata Adler, from the dingy hotel above the movie theatre, where scores are never kept.

XXXI
>   **WE TAKE LEAVE OF ELENA MCMAHON** (or does she take leave of us) at her Intercon loose ends, arriving at the Olympic shallows of the Surfrider, where time is a pool that leads inexorably from Hotel Colonial to the nameless Island and into Didion's second take of the old men in the pink hotel in the storm.

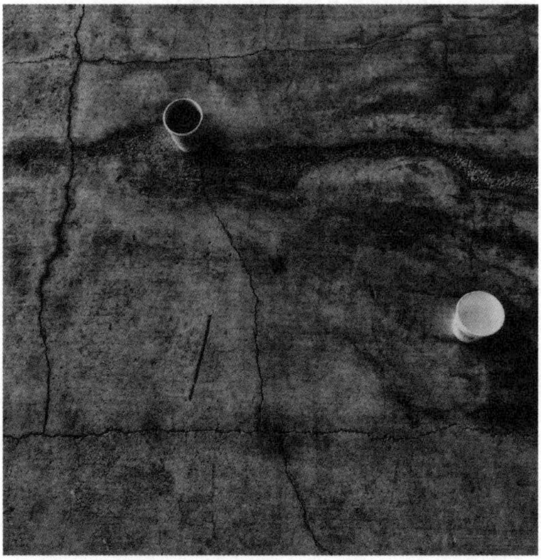

St. Joan in Idaho   Rebecca Tamás

Room 2

The light has pecked me full of holes,
I'm part space now, I float

On the motorway I hear God's voice:
keep moving   do whatever you want

I'm shouting over the traffic,
God's circuit board, his amplifier:

that milk on the stoop is God

that tank top

that colander

that tyre

that cherryade

that cling film

sacred sacred sacred world

The cat screaming along with the washing machine knows,
the rumble underneath knows, as I make my way along the hard
    shoulder,
presses in deep like a kiss at the back of your mouth

Neon knows, adorable ice-cream slash of God,
the strip lit cores of his eyes

At the roadside café is a man in checked shorts,
thighs pressed into the chair's plastic grooves,
God's flesh finding its spaces, caressing itself

He listens or smokes,
the core of his heart is a filigree I could lick,

he has been told of God as he spits saliva back to earth,
he is God's mouth
his eyes are closed
he says nothing

Light on the horizon knows, moves upwards,
lilac with half a cut of moon coming through

children are playing outside the shopping mall
their mother's shirt is so white, like a gleam of bone
burning through to the wide flat fields

the children keep falling over but not crying
they know
their teeth are rattling: God God God
they want to pee
God has his hand on their bladders,
their pleated lotus bulb insides

God's bar has a broken window
and blue and pink lights,
his music is playing

the car exhaust is thick
like the fog from the beginning of time
out of which we crawled,
whooping hooded blue

a few people are smoking out front
under the part light from office blocks
and 24-hour drugstores

Look (I say to them)
here is the holy land
here is Jerusalem
its brickwork showing,
alarms going off in God's name
here is paradise all around you
hot perfume you can taste on the wind
the swoop in your stomach at her wide,
perfect face, God's wishing when the fruit comes out,
those long roads and long rivers,
and your blessed movement along them
thick, candied, heaven brewing
under your feet
and above, God in a bird
licking the sky's iris clean

~

They drink up, and they are quiet and look away

a man stumbles toward me to say it's getting late
(it is late)
the man puts his hand in my hand,
he thinks he's lost money, his friend Joe,
a pair of red skates with silver flicks on,
but I know he hasn't really
can't lose,
the energy rebounds,
explodes with light,
returns, more room than ever,
more God, more brightness,
more goodness, more blessed,
Joe and money and his skates
glowing, fat with light like
scooped honey
holy ice-cold sweetness
waiting for his open palms,

so I tell him that

I hold his damp head in my hands
and tell him that we are warriors,
but that the hard fight is over
for both of us,

that even God has his pauses
where the vacuum shudders
and he takes in a breath,
that there has to be a rest
in this great glory
there has to be sleep in gold shining

don't think it means silence

when none of you are listening anymore
he is still listening
he is still singing one huge God note
under your ears
he is holding you more tenderly than you can imagine
the greatest, softly brushing gentle kindness
that knows the click at the latch inside of you,
how you are very good and nice and afraid,
and he likes all of that

and he likes the sound when you finish crying
and take in a breath, look around you,
that clarified, gorgeous view
where you can see him really well

and know that all the ugly things you bought
to forget him
are him

~

The street is very late now,
a young woman is leaning out of a window,
her long hair is love's diagram

Hello God (I shout)
as she puts her head back in

It begins to rain,
the cuffs of my jeans get wet

God wipes himself clean on the city's holy ground
light on water on light

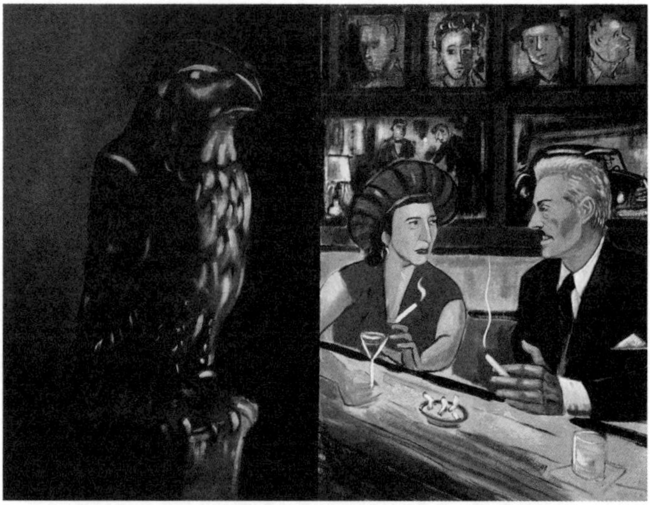

Light Space / Diary Entries Stephen Watts
for Giuseppe Penone's Felled Tree

Room 3

1

A mountain larch : felled & horizontal.

Giuseppe Penone's taken a larch, melted wax around its growth year & in-filled it with bronze-leaf. In this sculpture – the only one I know where this is possible – you can place your head inside a tree. Where else might that be possible? And inside the tree what you *hear* is silence.

This hollowed tree is full of light.

When you look along its laid-out length, it appears to be filled from within with sunlight, such is the effect of the golden bronze. Holes from the cut-off branches dapple inside : a whorl of gold time. Penone has taken a tree, filled it with light & breath & laid it out horizontally.

2

The tree has been cut into eight segments / sections.

Each segment with a gap of (breath) air space just wide enough for a person to bend halfway over & look into the tree, along its stretch. Its vertical-made-horizontal stretch.

You look along the tree's inside in the direction of its stump : you see the street outside.

You look 'north' toward the top of the tree & a path whirls round a thin passage in brown-gold. This is both calm breath & memory as the fracturing of time, the breakage of human breath.

You can put your head inside a tree ! Where else is this possible ? To see inside a tree !

And inside the tree – because the whole is segmented – you can see what is outside. Your eyes see beyond the segment they are looking into toward the whorl of lesser branches spinning off the next segment. You are inside the tree & outside it at the same time.

Never, perhaps, has a tree been so un-violently disembowelled, so un-damagedly turned inside out : golden wax of ancient sunlight.

In the Whitechapel Gallery setting the tree is 'felled' roughly south-north. Looking south down the tree you see the street, looking north toward the 'tree-top' you see rich abrupted memory.

The room the tree is in was formerly the main building of the Whitechapel Library. A hollowed yet entirely vibrant tree has replaced the space once inhabited by books made from paper.

*attempt to describe a pine
against the white of the snow*

3

The Whitechapel Library was closed down on August 6th 2006.

The closure was archived & the Gallery invited various artists to archive the closure. The work done by Rachel Lichtenstein & Alan Dein for instance : elaborate on this.

The poem written by Bernard Kops 'Whitechapel Library, Aldgate East' ... Where Penone's tree now is covers a line between the 'in' & 'out' space where the Librarians dealt with lent & returned books & the shelves covering various poetries of Bengal & elsewhere. Penone's tree is talking to us now in tree-language, engaging the past of Bangla & Somali & Yiddish. Penone's tree is talking to us now in the larch-language of the pre-Alps, with all the socio-political upheaval that felling involves. Felling, though, not just of a single tree, but rather of whole decades of human memory & migration. Felling of whole communities. Landslides of memory loss. Penone's tree once stood straight up from a hillside toward a sky.

Here, in felled segments, it is still beautiful.

4

For many years Kanai Datta was the Bengali Librarian at Whitechapel Library.

I recall many conversations with him about Subhas Mukhopadhyay, Saratchandra, Manik Bandhopadhyay, the Padma River Boatmen. You see I don't mention Tagore, Kobi Nazrul.

Purabi Datta, who was married to Kanai, was a language teacher in local Primary-Junior schools : I often worked with her & other colleagues as a poet-in-residence. There is a whole history here to be unravelled. My little book *Houses & Fish: A Book of Writing-with-Drawing by 4 & 5 Year-Olds* was launched in this Gallery – though quite not in this Penone-tree space – by Jenni Lomax when she was Education Officer at the Whitechapel Gallery. Astonishing drawings-with-words by very young children & done in their years before quite writing & drawing are so violently ripped apart. Remember the great Romanian poet Lucian Blaga – who did not utter a word until he was four & then started out with fully formed sentences of intricate language. Remember my niece Caoirsdaith (i.e., Kirsty in Gaelic) who when I asked her a colour's name when she was three answered me almost scathingly 'carmine.' As if I didn't know what her older brothers were about doing, burning barns. All the havocs & creations of soldier fallout & suicide bridges in the whit-burns of speech. She who now cutting edge researches the chemas of cancer in Cambridge.

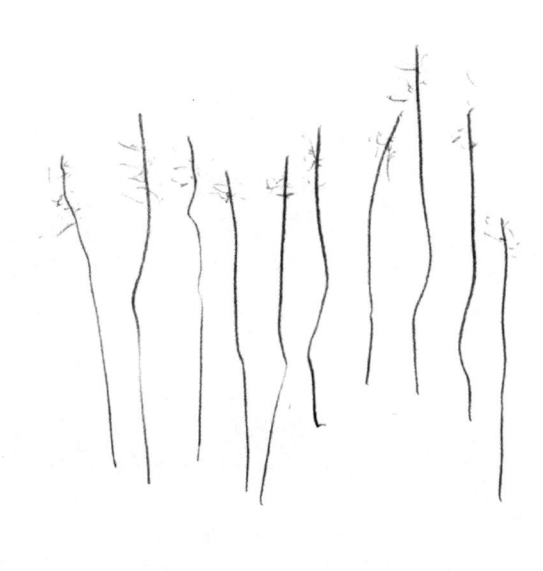

5

November 4th

We read Tonino Guerra's poetry before Penone's tree.
What did that feel like? It felt ....
We read Tonino Guerra in Italian & Romagnolo & English
& it felt very good, it felt just right.

It felt just right there beside Penone's tree, Cristina Viti in Italian
& me in our spliced English.

6

Each segment of the tree resembles an insect marching. An ant of life. Love's labour.

7

When I stand outside the only bar in Precasaglio looking over at the larch & spruce & fir. When I remember my grandfather there in the same spot exactly listening to the wind talk. When I realise that Gadda stood just precisely there too in the diary of his war-days.

When I surmise my mother getting out of Fulvia's car to go talk with her surviving cousin. When I archive in the entrails of my memory the snow-burst appendix of Bortolo Longhi. When I think of the forests of the Black Isle seen close up or across the Alness water. When I don't know where to go : Wapping or Toynbee or Bow or Precasaglio or Pirli ! When I ever, but never, manage to finish one of these brief archives of snow !

8

Some parts of this diary I wrote on the back of an envelope containing a letter refusing me Housing Benefit from LBTH. It seemed somehow appropriate. Or maybe it was the only clear paper to hand. I fought the decision. The Benefit Office admitted to having lost my papers & thus to coming to a false decision. I forced them to reconsider my application. They eventually determined that I had been entitled to Housing Benefit & even backdated it. I am glad : I can still live here. But maybe, homeless here, I would have moved back to the mountains ? Nonetheless the time & energies consumed by righting the false decision left me shattered & less able to work.

Elsewhere I have written a 'Little History of Migrant Denials' detailing such historic refusals.

9

Process / progression. Structure.

Or rather : passage & structure. And light.

The eight segments of the Penone tree resemble ancient insects. The passage (progress) of ancient insects. The progression of huge ants. The knowing & unknowing of such ants, such insects. And at the same time each segment resembles how life might be well on into the future, at a time when those such as we, as human beings, are long gone & probably bid good riddance to.

And at the same time again, each segment resembles a basic, complex structure.

Both what might be seen & what might be hidden (pieces of a backbone), what might be seen under a microscope, either as living creature or as enlarged atom (so, brought to life). They are the shapes also that march or shift laterally beneath closed eyes, on the screen inside our shut eyelids.

Does it help to say any of this ? Who knows whether it does or doesn't.

10

Penone positioned the tree just a half degree or so off 90 degrees.

The tree's aligned from the back of the gallery that once was the Public Library towards the door that leads through towards an exit and the road outside. But if the tree had been aligned exactly at 90 degrees, the view of the road from the hollowed-out trunk segments would have been mostly blocked by the two wooden median spars of the doorway. So he shifted the alignment very slightly, precisely so as to allow a view of the main roadway outside. Thus, we can look down the hollowed trunk of a horizontal tree and see people passing by on the pavement, vehicles (cars, buses, vans, lorries, bicycles) passing on the road.

Thus, from a former Library we can view – through a hollowed tree, a tree that might have been cut down and used to prepare or make or facilitate paper and books and printed language – people & vehicles passing by outside this space. They (vehicles & people) are beyond our reach or influence, we are far from theirs : in fact (especially the vehicles) we are unknown to them, outside their zone of power, they have no idea we are in this space regarding their outside passage through a tree.

Visitors, adults as much as children, smile as they enter this ludic space & see the Penone tree.

(uncertainty as to whether a tree is a person or vice versa, or not at all)

There are two small roof windows in the gallery that allow in sunlight.

Because the tree is laid horizontally along the middle of the gallery from one end (north) to the other (south) & the two windows are both quite small & to the sides, no sunlight falls directly onto the tree, as far as I can know, at any time of the year of its stay. Sunlight does fall in small patches quite close to the tree, but never directly onto its surface.

Nonetheless the tree is – inside its bark – lit up golden in part.

This is both because a small amount of sunlight does enter the room (gallery space), because there is artificial light within the gallery space, because the trunk has been hollowed and its insides coated with a sort of gold-coloured crust (the bark is as if inverted, turned within the tree), but also because the artist has sawn off a number of branches at their interconnect with the trunk and left the empty spaces intact, thus allowing light to enter within through a series of holes. Therefore, whatever light there is interacts with the gold veneer and lights up the hollow inside of the tree. If we look up (or down) the three larger segments of the hollowed trunk there is light & expanse. If we look along the narrower sections dark gains space and we seem to be looking into a spiral going toward darkness, though never reaching an entirely dark point. It is akin to the view & feeling we get when walking, in the autumn perhaps, along a path that narrows into denser woods, or that seems to.

There is thus perspective held within the hollowed tree. But also there are other physics. There is spiral & kaleidoscope. There is atomic model & breath crystal. There is knot & void.

There is substance & nothing. Light. Dark. Nullus. Nowt.

All of this because, from childhood & before, Penone has understood trees & because he continues experimenting in order to understand more & to know that understanding is innately limited :

> In 1881 Giovanni Battista Penone bought, on the 25th day of September, a plot of land sited in Garesio Borgo Ponte in the district of Vall'organa from Marco Antonio Campero. This plot was cultivated by Giovanni Battista Penone with vines; between each row he planted potatoes and wheat in a cycle of alternating years. All the work was done by hand. The plot was divided into four parts by low drywalls. The purchase price was 400 lire. In 1969 Pasquale Penone was still cultivating this land according to the same system. The physical structure of the plot had changed in that the rows of vines were gone. Each year a hundred & sixty or a hundred seventy hours of work are sunk into the land. In eighty-eight years that comes to about fourteen thousand five hundred & twenty hours of work. Can the accumulation of animal force make it that, with a further eleven thousand one hundred & sixty work hours, this land is able to assimilate and give expression to what is [it means to be] human ?*

---

*   A translation of the opening page of Penone's *Rovesciare gli occhi* (Einaudi, 1977), translated from the Italian by Cristina Viti and Stephen Watts.

(from) Idlewild   Helen Cammock

Room 4

Thread pile Meccanno bolted loft Full to itself wound With tightly Folded
stories Spines and edges of stuttering stacked casings of text Managers
manual to fast thinking Subtitle Of what? 35mm slides Of frames and
shapes and shadows Daylight fading Tracing through grey leaf blown sky
Fly suspended as Box file contents On a spiders string Singular web line
Swings to the rhythm Of draft streams Two boxes say 'A Mock Up' another
says 'fragments' So I sit with the mock up and the fragments and my head
and still waiting for the chasm that needs to fall sharply into somewhere
dark or somewhere cold or somewhere palpably wet or is it dusted and dry
- somewhere plants can't grow but ideas can A germination as stomach
tightens, chest relaxes, shifting synapses or is it something different
for you? I must stand and walk or sit and stare…is it the same for you?

And this morning the heat is strong
Thin heat
With a strong shafting A fly lies in light On desk A beautiful corpse Leg
flicks
And I realise it's the 'not-dead' fly I tried to let out last night
But it couldn't find the door
And I couldn't find the patience For the endless
Window Door Collisions
And so this not quite dead corpse With one leg flicking
I carry outside to live Or to die
In that shafting Damp Bright Fresh light Of
Nov
ember

A tree rises from wet earth Yellow through russet And it settles on the Tone of my skin When it's warm It punctures cloud And the leaves gently Caress the bones Of a smaller perhaps more urgent But commanding tree behind The wind aids the connection And I catch sight of the leaves on the architects model It is a world of ambition Perspex Encasement Plywood Base Screws hold the foundation Like the lugs in the meccanno of this loft Modern dry Older frieze blocked Concrete path Gravel Dirt road mud bath Tress and wood so much wood If I listen hard I can Hear the noise of scraping chair Feel the breath on my neck of a frustrated sigh Traces Yet something will come it always does

Chip on my windscreen Large car fast too fast Red, yellow Russets springs then Sound of rustle blast rain Memories of country living Shiver and shake me I feel the wet slide Down my wrist bones And prickle my elbow I stroke my hands On my lips Soft skin Ridges And remember how it Feels to kiss Gravel under foot Satisfying sounds Of chipped stone crackle I'm waiting for a flow that is already here

And
maybe Jonny Mercer didn't know the extent of what he'd ingested -
what he admired so much was so undermined by what those words
perpetuated - - lazy black man who lay under a tree, well fed, clean
clothes and straw hat… sleeping the day away…fingers grass sliced,
burnt soil, heatstroke, snake bite, whip, no sleep, gnawing hunger…
plantation to farm hand to dustbowl disaster; project to
projects..the space for the irresponsible lazy black person never
fades…

But the plantation owner…the landowner - the person owner…the
knighted landed peer - the Tory MP with business interests that
belong to him but are never worked by him..which came
And maybe Jonny Mercer didn't know the extent of what he'd ingested -
what he admired so much was so undermined by what those words
perpetuated - - lazy black man who lay under a tree, well fed, clean
clothes and straw hat… sleeping the day away…fingers grass sliced,
burnt soil, heatstroke, snake bite, whip, no sleep, gnawing hunger…
plantation to farm hand to to him at birth, who believes in nothing
but the furtherment of this entitled existence is of course the
faithful lazybones who needs the slave, the indentured labourer, the
child in the Congo, the disabled parent, the projects, the council
estate, immigrants all to hide their own laziness…to ensure they can
live off the Labour of others, the impoverishment of others, while
all the time hiding their own parasitic embodiment through the
projection of the lazy in all those who keep him or her there…head of
the straw chewing, toe bouncing, shade grabbing tree of betterment.
(PAUSE)

So is it in the activeness in doing nothing, not the passiveness in
working without question, that we should site our song…lilting jazz
melodies in a world of 'frozen step' bodies and dawn breaking
cleaning jobs

                                                                    Fingers
                                                                    tingle
                                                                    from
                                                                    cold
                                                                    School
                                                                    voice
                                                                    serenade
downstairs in action Action and sound Envelope marked Unknown slides
Drawing colour face of mind They click through my own Sequence
Unsequential Unknown slide is unremembered moment Day Movement Drawer
Painting We are all forgotten one day

Lazy Bones sleeping in the Sun when you gonna get your days work done You won't get your days work done Sleeping in the midday sun Lazy Bones sleeping in the Sun when you gonna get your days work done You won't get your days work done Sleeping in the midday sun Lazy Bones sleeping in the Sun when you gonna get your days work done You won't get your days work done Sleeping in the midday sun Lazy Bones sleeping in the Sun when you gonna get your days work done You won't get your days work done Sleeping in the midday sun Lazy Bones sleeping in the Sun when you gonna get your days work done You won't get your days work done Sleeping in the midday sun Lazy Bones sleeping in the Sun when you gonna get your days work done You won't get your days work done Sleeping in the midday sun Lazy Bones sleeping in the Sun when you gonna get your days work done You won't get your days work done Sleeping in the midday sun Lazy Bones sleeping in the Sun when you gonna get your days work done You won't get your days work done Sleeping in the midday sun Lazy Bones sleeping in the Sun when you gonna get your days work done You won't get your days work done Sleeping in the midday sun Lazy Bones sleeping in the Sun when you gonna get your days work done You won't get your days work done Sleeping in the midday sun

Lazy Bones sleeping in the Sun when you gonna get your days work done You won't get your days work done Sleeping in the midday sun Lazy Bones sleeping in the Sun when you gonna get your days work done You won't get your days work done Sleeping in the midday sun Lazy Bones sleeping in the Sun when you gonna get your days work done You won't get your days work done Sleeping in the midday sun Lazy Bones sleeping in the Sun when you gonna get your days work done You won't get your days work done Sleeping in the midday sun Lazy Bones sleeping in the Sun when you gonna get your days work done You won't get your days work done Sleeping in the midday sun Lazy Bones sleeping in the Sun when you gonna get your days work done You won't get your days work done Sleeping in the midday sun Lazy Bones sleeping in the Sun when you gonna get your days work done You won't get your days work done Sleeping in the midday sun Lazy Bones sleeping in the Sun when you gonna get your days work done You won't get your days work done Sleeping in the midday sun Lazy Bones sleeping in the Sun when you gonna get your days work done You won't get your days work done Sleeping in the midday sun Lazy Bones sleeping in the Sun when you gonna get your days work done You won't get your days work done Sleeping in the midday sun

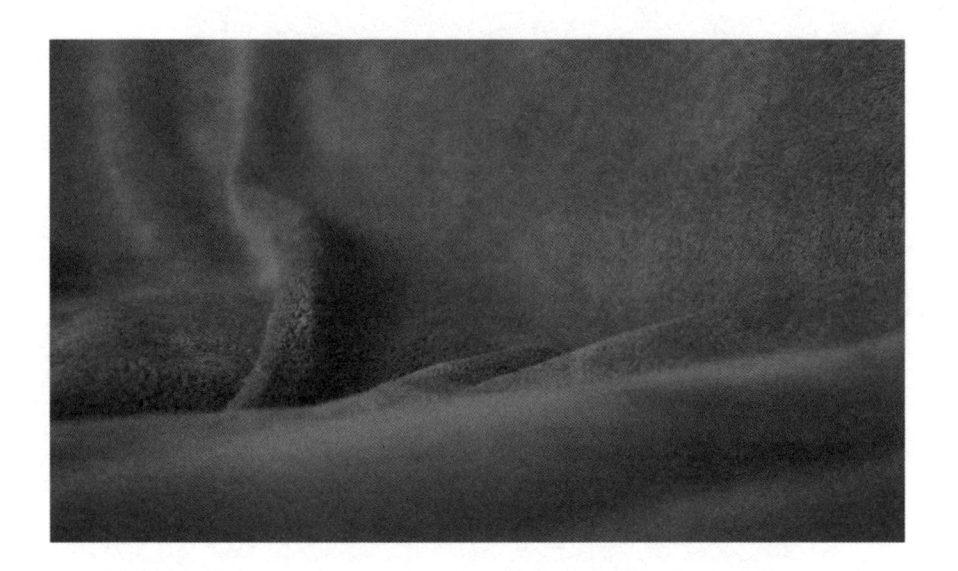

So the struggle to justify actively doing nothing - and the
problematics and bind of the labour cascade are murmurs then echoes
then shouted assaults and yet still we must hunt like the tracker in
search of the glade, for that light shaft of nothing-ness in order
for something-ness to scratch the back of the mind and tingle the
senses and then whoever we are and whatever the hunger….something
something will come. |

At night the rustle of many fountains comes...   Salvador Espriu (& Lucy Mercer)

Room 5

We shall speak
the truth,
without end,
for the honour of
serving,
under the foot
of all.

We loathe
great bellies
and great words,
the obscene showiness
of gold,
the poorly dealt
cards of luck,
and the thick smoke
of incense
set before the powerful.
Now the land
of the mighty
is vile and
grovels in hatred
like a dog,
barking far off,
nearby enduring
the stick, beyond
the mire
pursuing paths of death.

With a song,
in the dark
we erect tall
dream walls
to protect us
from the uproar.

At night the rustle
of many fountains comes:
we are closing
the doors on fear.*

---

*   A variation on the subtitles to Salvador Espriu's contribution to the first edition of the 'Popular Festival of Catalan Poetry' held at the Gran Price Theatre (Barcelona, 1970); an event organised in solidarity with political prisoners incarcerated under Franco's regime. The festival was captured on film by Pere Portabella in his work *Poetes Catalans / Catalan Poets* (1970).

as we're standing
outside the mansion
its honeycombed
windows glowing like
a mary barnes painting
for many nights now
like our nightmares
we can squash
our faces against them
frighten the occupants
you do not need
eyes or ears to know
that quantification
is tied to conflagration
as by the flaming
plow. this is reading
but not as they know
it, as we know it,
as in a dark screen.
a lilac ferris wheel
is turning with ever-
increasing numbers
among the marquees
so we press our faces
into the glass
like the softest pillow
they can see us now
they are afraid
of us. as many of us
as leaves or droplets
or tiny hailstones
falling into fountains
that in the world
to come will be
symbols of the in-
definable, like rain.

Mentx... les — el tiempo de los animales
                                        jauzten pen
... les   'ensuel violet plentier   le grand ... n de minuit
                                              verdiko pauma
impregnable
        Según la teoría de la supernovena
posses...
       cada particula en el universo
       ... tiene ... hablado dominante
                           un nuevo nombre
El armario   (spit out by the sun)   más pesado
está llena ... ... baby the ... of the ... merodeando en medio de los página
   ... por veces que extraño y claro el alma,
Piensa en nieve ...   ... eguzkia ... ragozi...iteke
... que todas las ... son!
... de las ...   .tenko
Le champ ...   ... realidades ...
todo el tiempo. ...   ...
    Cuando hables con una persona y ...
       o te des... cuenta dans l'âme
                 conversación es una ray ...
a High energy bar   ...
    ... the ... thickness of a nerve
              holiday ...   ...
   ... the ...   ...   bois rose
The fat ... rude of living in matter, minuscule ...
                ... wonderfully enough
¿ Qué sería de ... ...   Zubia garai...
  sin la ayuda de las cosas   ...
                       no existen?   ...
        the lives of images
     desiring images
        two bodies, 1 desiring & affecting the other —
          a body desiring another body —   un rêve — weave
                                                 revêtir
Bi hankatara jarritako zakurrak,   les perspectives qu...
Zenbatek lo egiten dute animaliak jugando cloak ...adierazi!
                         + zenbatek ... diren animaliak
                                  mer

Dear Messiah   Lucy Sante

Room 6

Dear Messiah,*

You were born in Houston to a 14-year-old single mother. You were the surviving child of twins born to an affluent family. Your mother was a former slave. A sensitive and sickly child, 'vague and dreamy,' you were often taken to be mentally retarded, and were beaten regularly at school by your teachers and at home by your father. You began singing at a young age and soon became a sports-car journalist and test driver for your own car-racing magazine, *Auto Pop*. You began experiencing fainting spells at age nine and people took your sleepwalking as evidence of secret powers. While still a schoolboy you began to reject the Talmud. You underwent what was interchangeably described as 'the benediction,' 'the immensity,' 'the sacredness,' 'the vastness' and, most often, 'the otherness.' Beginning in your youth you were uncomfortable with sexuality, especially your own.

After service in the Red Army, you settled in Minusinsk. You worked as a traffic policeman before losing your job in 1989. You were convicted of practising pharmacy without a licence and fined 200,000 yen. On 28 August 1974, you were arrested in Harlingen, Texas, for stealing credit cards. You took over the identity of your deceased predecessor, and in so doing completely erased your own. You had a son named Imperator. You had four children: Osiris, Isis, Iris, Hypatia. You asserted that your marriage was never physically consummated. You asserted that though you lay 'naked with virgins,' when the virgins asked you for sex, you refused. You were commanded to take a 'wife of whoredom' as the first symbolic act of your calling. You spent your days wandering the streets of Council Bluffs wearing a long white robe and became a local oddity. You exhibited a '666' tattoo on your forearm. Witnesses stated that you had nail marks in your hands. You felt compelled to eat non-kosher food and speak the forbidden name of God. You gained notoriety for the many Rolls-Royces bought for your use, eventually numbering 93. Your status as a rock singer was very localised.

You spoke to an estimated 10,000 in a spacious former casino. Your speech was often peppered with words of your own invention, such as 'physicalating' and 'tangiblated.' Robed in white, you stood behind the curtain, and the light brought out in full relief the gilt letters of the Tetragrammaton, which you had placed upon your breast. In the estimated presence of one to five hundred people, you announced the end of the world and ordered the extermination of sixteen enemy families. You claimed that you could slay 10,000 men

---

*   It's worth noting here that this text is entirely lifted from Wikipedia entries, with some rewriting to shoehorn them into the rhetorical format.
     L.S.

by hitting your left hand with your right. You addressed tablets to the kings and rulers of the world asking them to accept your revelation, renounce their material possessions, work together to settle disputes, and endeavour toward the betterment of the world and its peoples. You wrote a book which you said was dictated to you by angels. You dictated three books under the influence of nitrous oxide administered to you by your private dentist. You inscribed messianic formulas on your hands, and corrected Isaiah 45:1 to include yourself. You wrote your beliefs on a piece of paper and had it read aloud, but due to the clamour among the people, it could not be heard.

In a spiritual vision you were shown a plot of land containing the graves of such members of your community as are destined to be in heaven. The prophet Elijah appeared to you in a dream and led you to a beautiful garden, where you saw the pious of all ages, in the form of birds, flying through the garden and studying the Mishnah. You employed mystic prayers of your own composition to call upon the names of angels not accepted by the church canon. You claimed to have led a convoy of rocketships to Earth from the extinct planet Neophrates. You taught that dissatisfaction and evil among Blacks caused a major explosion to happen on Earth 66 trillion years ago, creating the current moon that orbits the planet. You asserted that a network of drug companies, banks, and psychiatrists were conspiring against you in a bid to take over the world. You threatened to drive the Christians into the sea, and you launched a major military offensive with your 1,500 Dervishes, equipped with twenty modern rifles. You said, 'I am' – at which point the high priest tore his own robe in anger and accused you of blasphemy. You declared the founding of the 'Heavenly Kingdom of Transcendent Peace' on 11 January 1851.

The total volume of your works is more than seventy times the size of the Qur'an and more than fifteen times the size of the Old and New Testaments of the Bible. You claimed that you discovered a mathematical code in the text of the Qur'an involving the number 19. You changed granite into sugar candy, changed water into gasoline, produced objects on demand, changed the colour of your gown while wearing it, multiplied food, healed acute and chronic diseases, appeared in visions and dreams, made different fruits appear on actual stems on any tree, controlled the weather, physically transformed into various deities, and physically emitted brilliant light. You authorised the burning of lists of pedigrees and books of law and theology because of their association with the old regime. You will lead the Ten Lost Tribes back to the Holy Land while riding on a lion with a seven-headed dragon in its jaws. Your face will be visible on the moon, the sun, and the Black Stone in Mecca. You will reign over the whole world with two legitimate authorities, not only religious but also political. After your Judgment you will throw the corrupt into the Fire.

The Kingdom of Heaven began to collapse in 1880, when both of your children died of diphtheria. Your son was suddenly killed at the age of twenty-two when he fell through a skylight while pacing back and forth in prayer and meditation. The departure of your disciples weakened, demoralised, and angered you, and it was at this juncture that you composed your most famous poem, 'The Tree of Bad Counsel.' During a meal, you predicted that one of your disciples would betray you. Followed by your disciples, you rode a donkey to the edge of the bluffs, whereupon you leaped off the edge. In 1706 you were killed by your nephew during a discussion about money matters. You died in Chatsworth, California, on 10 December 1958 in a suicide bombing instigated by two disgruntled former followers. In June 1934 you left Detroit for Chicago and disappeared without a trace. You suddenly disappeared and the extravagant hopes of your followers came to an end. Your remaining disciples tore your bloody shirt from your body and divided it up for relics. Your remains were dumped outside the gates of the town to be eaten by animals. There were many among your followers who did not accept your demise and expected your imminent return. You are said to have descended from the higher planes and manifested a physical body in early 1977 in the Himalayas, then on 19 July 1977 to have taken a commercial airplane flight from Pakistan to England.

Karuizawa   Ryūnosuke Akutagawa
             translated from the Japanese
             by Ryan Choi

Room 7

黒馬に風景が映(うつ)ってゐる。

　　　　　×

朝のパンを石竹(せきちく)の花と一しよに食はう。

　　　　　×

この一群(ひとむれ)の天使たちは蓄音機(ちくおんき)のレコオドを翼にしてゐる。

　　　　　×

町はづれに栗の木が一本。その下にインクがこぼれてゐる。

　　　　　×

青い山をひつ掻いて見給へ。石鹸(せつけん)が幾つもころげ出すだらう。

※ か

　　　　　×

英字新聞には黄瓜(かぼちや)を包め。

　　　　　×

誰かあのホテルに蜂蜜を塗つてゐる。

　　　　　×

M夫人――舌の上に蝶(てふ)が眠つてゐる。

　　　　　×

Fさん――額(ひたひ)の毛が乞食(こじき)をしてゐる。

　　　　　×

Oさん――あの口髭(くちひげ)は駝鳥(だてう)の羽根だらう。

　　　　　×

詩人S・Mの言葉――芒(すすき)の穂は毛皮だね。

Landscape mirrored in the flank of a black mare.

    ×

Breakfast: toast with blooms of *rainbow pink*.

    ×

Flocks of angels crafting gramophone vinyl wings.

    ×

Outside town, ink runs over the roots of the chestnut tree.

    ×

Scrabbling up the green hill crust. Soap bars go tumbling.

    ×

Cucumbers bundled in the English weeklies.

    ×

Who smeared honey on the walls of the inn?

    ×

Madame M. – Butterfly dreams on the tongue.

    ×

Mr. F., again, with his ratty bangs.

    ×

Mr. O.'s moustache flutters like ostrich wings.

    ×

The poet S. M. – *'Tips of the pampas stitch themselves into a pelt.'*

　　　　　×
或牧師の顔──臍（へそ）！

　　　　　×

レエスやナブキンの中へずり落ちる道。

　　　　　×

碓（うすひ）氷山上の月、──月にもかすかに苔（こけ）が生えてゐる。

　　　　　×

H老夫人の死、──霧は仏蘭西（フランス）の幽霊に似てゐる。

　　　　　×

馬蠅（うまばへ）は水星にも群（むらが）つて行つた。

　　　　　×

ハムモツクを額に感じるうるささ。

　　　　　×

雷（かみなり）は胡椒（こせう）よりも辛（から）い。

　　　　　×

「巨人（きよじん）の椅子（いす）」と云ふ岩のある山、──瞬（またた）かない顔が一つ見える。

　　　　　×

あの家は桃色の歯齦（はぐき）をしてゐる。

　　　　　×

羊の肉には羊歯（しだ）の葉を添へ給へ。

　　　　　×

さやうなら。手風琴（てふうきん）の町、さようなら、僕の抒情詩（ぢよじやうし）時代。

　　　　　　　　　　　　（大正十四年稿）

×

Face of the priest – then, his navel!

×

The slippery path that ends in napkins and lace.

×

Moon above Usui Pass: growing whitish moss.

×

Death of Madame H. – French phantoms in the fog.

×

Gadflies lumped all over Mercury.

×

Annoyance – Hammock against my forehead.

×

Thunder is even spicier than pepper.

×

In the mountains, on a crag known as 'The Giant's Seat,' I see the unblinking face of a man climbing alone.

×

Everyone in the family has pink gums.

×

'Sheep steak garnished with fern leaves, please.'

×

Goodbye, accordion town. Goodbye, lyric days.

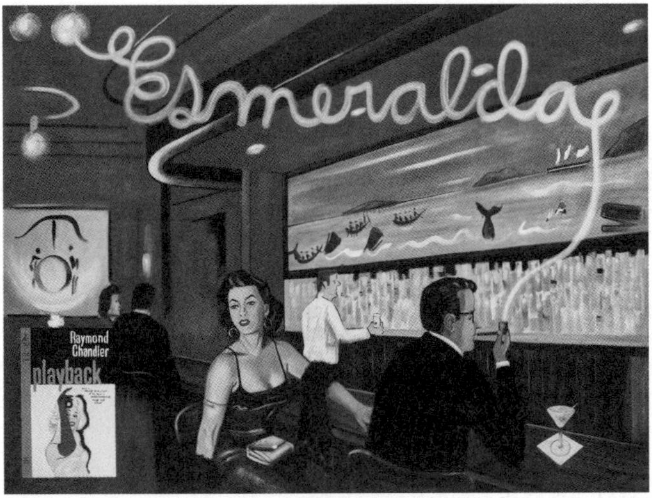
Esmeralda
Raymond
Chandler
playback

Fortunes, Favourite Sayings,   John Yau
& Assorted Sundries
(from a Blacke Calendar)

Room 8

1
Dust drifts across elliptical sky.

2
This is my biography. It tells the story of someone I never met.

3
This bayonet star is key ring swirl in renewable cup, night's unwinding bowl, silvery drops licked off dead stars for bullion and gumption, juice injected into a journey undertaken long ago, before you were deposited on a forsaken rock, another cloud of questions stirring air's blackened shadows.

4
You hear yourself talking and walking toward precincts of sky that remain closed to you, having banished you, staining the ovals of black and amber air again, as you sally forth from kingdom of craven knaves, dismal whiffs scudding across ceiling, doors banging in the wind.

What are you saying, you say to yourself.

Where will this talking take you?

5
Once a voice leaves a room, it cannot be caught.

6
Stop and enter a moment's quivering: what does breathing steal from you with each breath? Are you any more than a debilitating sequence walking down a posh street in collapsed underwear, always dependably expendable, poor imitations of a scream passing through your illuminated skin and inked parchment?

7
A sign in the window of a toy store: what is the poet's place on the totem of the tribe? We will let you decide.

Might not this question about one's place in the cosmos be a problem?

8
There is no way you can cross the border with confiscated photographs locked inside your head – glossy drifts behind rheumy eyes. The body is a spitting stump that defecates by side of road, an added passage, an acrostic that does not add up, ghost of listening to the antique dead rewrites a dream inviting you back to life, its daily carnage delivered in upturned caps.

Please adjust this channel in the future, which shivers at your approach.

9
How has your capacity for sympathetic murmurs extended your coexistence quotient?

Have you dialled into a member of a crying species yet?
Or have you put that encounter on hold?

Have you locked your horns of plenty so that no music is lost?

How can you spare time when your shopping cart is full?

10
You hear a voice behind you say: The promise was not made, nor was it kept.

11
When nothing you wear moves you closer to heaven's boat, time flies into the wind and does not return, a bird with a note pinned to its burlap throat.

12
In the dream, you file proper documents, leave dulled body behind. Thrill moves you up the chain, turns water into swine, the kind you eat only when your mouth is full of tiny wings.

13
What will you do with this pile of broken boxes, these dried flowers, this shoe nailed to the wall? I will live in them until they split apart.

14
The mirror is an oval, an empty eye. The rain finds you crouched in a corner, singing songs you never heard until now, old songs, they must have been waiting for you to fetch them from the sky.

The shadow of a passing bird stays printed on your face and hands.

15
One of us rents a room on a street known for its buckets of glass eyes, bad tunes to fill in the black holes when daylight absconds with the conversation between us suspended until further notice.

16
I used to live not so far from here. I don't remember where it is.

17
The light coming from the stars is full of death.

18
The bird looks in the mirror and falls asleep.

The Rope Barrier   Nicolette Polek

Room 9

The woman invested in a rope barrier, with a green velvet rope, that she carried around in her backpack like a tripod.

She assembled it when she sat down on the subway. She assembled it at work when she responded to emails. She placed it beside her when she visited the cemetery, and in front of the shower when she washed. Her husband sometimes stood on the other side of the rope, and watched her rest in bed.

When driving in the mountains she assembled it across her lap like a second seat belt. There were lynx and black widow spiders in the forests nearby, so she assembled the rope barrier while she birdwatched. She heard somewhere to 'never turn your back on mother earth,' but it felt okay to do it this way.

Eventually the woman and her family moved into a brick house with a turret and a gargoyle. The woman began to feel an occasional presence, like a heavy judgement, or a fallen angel, so she assembled the rope barrier whenever she felt a chill creep up.

Her friends called it the 'meditation median,' 'despair wall,' 'uncrossing the line.' Her niece called it 'the slinky barrier.' For birthdays she occasionally received replacement ropes from her family, in novelty colours, like *glow-in-the-dark*, or snakeskin.

The woman brought the rope barrier to functions. If she was seated next to someone whom she didn't like, she put it between their chairs. When she ignored phone calls, she assembled it, as a symbolic gesture.

The woman's sneaky distrust of things grew. Her sister moved to the other side of the country, started practising mindfulness and seeing a therapist. The sister sent happy letters, and the woman enviously read them in bed while her husband watched.

After a while, the woman still used her rope barrier, but it no longer protected her. Her hands shook when she hooked the rope onto the posts. The rope twisted and frayed. The colours faded.

She placed the rope barrier between her baby son and dessert until his vegetables were eaten. He still didn't listen. A man at the airport tried to steal it when she rummaged through her bag. Members of the mafia moved two houses down. The woman put the rope barrier across the porch steps, but the mailman or the wind would knock it down. Termites infested the walls of her house, and what was she supposed to do about that?

The woman both despised the rope barrier and hissed at those who approached it. She felt singled out and angry at the things that were bigger than her. It felt, now, as if she was forced to put herself on sides of things she encountered, and that she often chose the wrong side.

She wanted a rope barrier for her rope barrier, or a long rope that coiled against her body. No, she didn't want ropes: she wanted curtains, and blockades and stacked tires, and legal representation.

She became irritable and violent. She went into the garden with an axe and started knocking the heads off the sunflowers. She swung it at an ancient oak tree. She tried splitting a rock. She imagined the sound of rustling in the distant hedges and pursued the sound with passion. When she saw the rope barrier she brought the blade down, again and again.

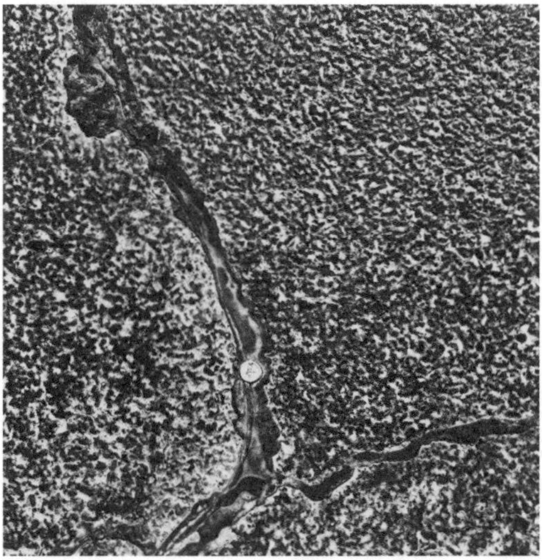

No Show   Chris Petit

Room 10

Maybe I don't know
in a time of such free-floating anxiety
and bad political hair
with everything running on empty
it's hard not to think of anything
in terms of show
or no show
it's not cultural pessimism exactly
more holding one's breath
waiting when it's too late
and anyway, it is a very grey-days winter
not conducive
to doing anything
and I feel I am making
connections of the wrong sort
not ones that turn out well in the long run
I spent the year buried in words
distracting from other things
more important but harder to deal with
we live in an age of distraction (and apology) screens actual and
    psychological
a screened world
and I am reminded of when adults used to say to children in exasper-
ation: you drive me to distraction (which no one says anymore)
and anyway perhaps because of all this bad political hair and
    rambunctiousness
I find myself thinking about an image of
an entertainer dead now but with perfect hair – an accidental image
    taken
from a frame fragment of an old movie though not old in my head
and the detail on the right of the frame
shows the back of his head in a mirror
and I don't know why but it is the only image I have seen in a long
time which has aroused my curiosity and everyone I show it to agrees
and they don't know why
maybe it seems right
for a particular moment
this man with perfect hair
turning his back on the world
face to the wall
and maybe also the fact that the image is
not original but a copy of a copy and
though it is obviously him

(or pretty obviously)
there is always a chance it is not
but an impersonator or a double or a fake
or someone else who fell to earth
and this fake / real image of a fake / real man seems to please people in
a way that also makes them a bit anxious
maybe even a little nostalgic for a time when it was still possible to
have such perfect hair and look to the future and still turn one's back
    on the world
and in one way it's like he's never been gone into these blue skies
    turning to black
and maybe for all these reasons it's the image I want to show you

Five Columns Sascha Macht
translated from the German
by Amanda DeMarco

Room 11

From late 2018 to early 2019, Sascha Macht was the writer-in-residence at a castle in the German city of Beeskow. As part of his appointment, Macht was required to write a weekly column for the *Märkische Oderzeitung*, a regional newspaper in eastern Brandenburg. *Märkische Oderzeitung*, in turn, was required to print whatever he sent them.

Renate Kanter

I finally visited Renate Kanter, in a nursing home at the edge of Bad Saarow, where she has lived for some years. Her room is small, and her treasures are stacked on two sets of shelves in the corner: colourfully printed boxes, each of them filled with maps, dice, meeple, instructions, and tiny tokens. Renate Kanter is the *grande dame* of complex conflict simulation, in which historical or fictional military operations can be experienced in the form of a board game on your living-room table. For more than forty years she's done nothing but develop these games, some of which have become classics with a limited but enthusiastic following, e.g. 'Storming St. Egidien,' 'Courland Isn't Answering,' 'The Tank with the Blue Eyes,' and 'Red Moon over Samarkand.'

There's coffee, pretzel sticks, and poppyseed cake as I sit with her on the sofa. Renate Kanter doesn't speak, at least not to other people. Her language has always been that of war and games, a challenging combination, which confronts us in every part of her simulations, in the relationship between intelligence and morality, strategy and decision, coincidence and luck, victory and defeat.

On the coffee table, she's spread out the prototypes for her new, yet unnamed work, perhaps her last. She must have worked on the concept for months and calculated thousands of possible moves. She painted and glued together her cardboard and wooden materials with the help of her nurse Jonas. I observe: a gigantic map with a dark centre, perhaps depicting Eastern Europe and a part of Central Asia. The instructions, written up on a typewriter, reveal: Every player takes on the role of a tiny national entity, which has recently declared its independence from a powerful central government. Now the goal is to strengthen your own economy, fight corruption, form alliances, and rebuff the attacks of the former motherland together. However, it is conceivable that one player could secretly make a pact with the central government, in order to gain military and economic advantages for themselves over their competitors. A sinister, quiet game, consisting of street fighting, industrialisation, organised crime, and the intrigues of secret services. Renate Kanter shrugs when I ask her when it will be finished.

On the drive back to Beeskow, I think over what title I would give to this work. 'Rise and Fall of the Soviet Empire'? 'Steppe and Shadows'? 'Wolves Eat the Dogs'? 'Death and Rebirth'? Through games, we understand the world. Dark and rain-swept is the country I am currently driving through in my car.

Some Things that Don't Exist

A FILM THAT WAS NEVER MADE
The World as Will and Imagination. A man thinks that he is a door and falls in love with a woman who thinks she's a window. The two moves into a house together, where they realise that their new abode is actually a group of people, friends who believe that they are a house. A great hubbub. At the end, Kevin Costner appears in the form of a revivalist preacher who claims to be a river and explains that all of the proceedings depicted in the film are based on a true story.

A BOARD GAME NEVER PLAYED
Kicking Up a Fuss in Heinzmannsdorf. When, in the titular locality, the lights go out, the players, in the form of a band of imps, begin to make all sorts of rude mischief in the lanes. No one wins or loses at the end of the match, because when the time comes, all of them have long been sitting in complete confusion around the board, which is buried under hundreds of figures, discs, marbles, dice, coins, and cards. What a surly lot of fun!

A BOOK THAT WAS NEVER WRITTEN
A Novel Without People. Nothing but extensive descriptions of natural events, animals, uninhabited architecture, ownerless things. A masterpiece of poetic contemplation and a coup against the psychologising outgrowths of a literature that constantly pushes the individual and their little problems to the centre of the narrative. Only a bit tiring now and again.

AN OBJECT NEVER USED
Are you in the possession of a wooden töftel? If so: good for you! I've heard that if you lay this small, round thing over the bridge of your nose, all sadness vanishes. Sadly, I haven't been able to try it out myself – wooden töftel are hard to come by nowadays.

A COMIC NEVER DRAWN
The Danish Lantern is about the courier Aksel Hansen, who, after a collision with an enchanted traffic light, develops the ability to turn into a living-room floor-lamp. Together with his best friend, the talking raccoon dog Thomas, he gets wise to the scheme of the avaricious orthodontist Dr. Nørregård, who wants to put overpriced braces on all of the children of Copenhagen.

A GOD NO ONE BELIEVES IN

Let's call him Bob. He's the patron saint of gravel, mayflies, and party hats – an inconspicuous, friendly fellow who spends his free time looking through the trash for bottles with refundable deposits. It's said that in a few forgotten corners of the world there are a few befuddled old birds, drinkers, handbag snatchers, and daydreamers who direct their prayers to him before they go to sleep, but that's nothing more than a rumour.

Märkische Heide

Steam rises between the lemon trees. The ponds and canals are clear but toxic. The salamanders, water sprites, and snails in them speak an incomprehensible dialect. At night, the glowing coaches of international caravans rumble past. Those who enter on foot via the road from the north-east must pay a toll: a haunch of venison. Many villages here were built on posts in the bog. The larger cities are woven with dense networks of steam pipes, ropeways, and pulley systems. In summer drunken wastrels stroll through the sparse birch groves.

A writing wayfarer once spoke of how this country is like the board of a game played with dice made from frozen blood.

The remote farms, mobile home courts, Rundlings, and garden cities bear names such as 'Strg Alt Del Golm,' 'Terrortal,' 'Stalinhüttenstadt,' 'Neu Tokio,' 'Bad Golfplatz,' 'Superzelle,' 'Preußisch Blau,' or 'Drehdichweg.' A former biogas plant is a karaoke bar today, gold panners doze on a bench in front of the German Unity Bar and Hotel, a pack of childlike ghosts have just taken up residence in an abandoned roadside service area, and music festivals, weddings, and court proceedings take place on the military parade grounds. If you come from the south-west on the magnetic monorail, you'll ride once around a forested shield volcano with a smouldering crater known as 'Old Boss.' At the beginning of spring, the Soviet combat tanks thaw in the asparagus fields.

Calendars haven't caught on here, and so the dreadful question poses itself: what time do we find ourselves in? A cautious answer: perhaps just before the end of the world, perhaps 2019 BC, perhaps at the end of the midday nap.

Manor houses are found throughout the country, erected by an extraterrestrial civilisation from the furthest edge of the Milky Way. On the shore of the flooded gravel pit, a motorcycle gang suns itself in the grass. Around the afternoon coffee hour, a trio disguised as sunflowers hold up the branch savings bank on the market square. If you take a close look, from the highest garbage heap at the scrapyard, you can make out two moons in the night sky: the one as if soaked in schnapps, the other the eye of the divine chinchilla. The lie was born in this country just as the truth was, poverty as well as wealth, wholehearted nonsense as well as dangerous monkey business, sorrow as well as mirth. Large dogs are sometimes treated with more dignity here than certain old persons.

Flat, vast, barren, narrow, blossoming landscapes. Day-care centres. Saw works. Zoos for local fauna. Crashed spaceships. Supermarkets. A few truly beautiful gardens inhabited by werewolves.

Von der Stille

I'm being followed. Recently while walking through the city, I thought I saw a figure from the corner of my eye, in the narrow lane between St. Mary's Church and Breite Straße.

I call him Dietrich von der Stille, sometimes also 'The Cyclops.' What he calls himself and what others call him, I don't know. Where he comes from, why he does whatever – a mystery.

But I know that he subsists on sniffing mumia, a substance made from the ground remains of ancient Egyptian mummies, Chinese corpses mummified in honey, or northern European bog bodies, used as a remedy into the twentieth century. I also know that in the winter of 1944, he was in attendance at the castle of the vampiric Vom Stein family in southern Hungary, together with a few nefarious German doctors, in order to decipher the secret of immortality. Additionally, to be found in my notes is the information that Axl Rose – frontman of the hard-rock band Guns N' Roses – once expressed the grotesque wish to be the commander of an army in the depths of the rainforests of Guatemala – I'm certain that Dietrich von der Stille really was such a commander, who hunted members of the indigenous Ixil population during the Guatemalan civil war.

It's not just writers, underworld bosses, and chimney sweeps, but every person is surrounded by dark, indeterminate things, signs, and occurrences: fear, conflict, misfortune, sadness. Poetry's significant advantage lies in its revealing of the unknown in plain view. It allows us to have dealings with it.

Once I wrote of a flying carpet that brought me to the peak of a mountain, where I hoped to discover the visage of evil, but there was nothing at all on the mountain, and so I looked down, dumbstruck, at the wide world lying below me.

Once I dreamed that I was lost in an endless vault under the earth. Through narrow windows, light fell into the passageways and chambers, but I couldn't manage to reach their filth-smeared panes. I was carrying a burning candle, my only comfort. I walked further and further, steadfast in the thought of eventually getting out. Only when the flame went out did I once again find myself on the shore of a black lake under a grey sky.

Once Dietrich von der Stille called me on my phone. He said that our entire universe was located in a single drop of sweat falling from the bodies of two wrestling and simultaneously copulating Titans. As I hung up, my heart was full of tender fright.

Dreams and Relations

In 1857, the poet Charles Baudelaire described the world as 'an oasis of horror in a desert of boredom.' The writer Roberto Bolaño took this sentence as a motto to preface his novel collection *2666*, that massive, winding panorama of literature, madness, love, and the unfathomable criminality resulting from the drug war on the Mexican-American border. What do Baudelaire's words mean? That reality is no joke – nor is literature.

In the literary universe of the horror writer H. P. Lovecraft, unknown evil gods from the icy depths of the cosmos determine the destiny of time and space. The ninety-nine rooms in the Paris apartment building on rue Simon-Crubellier, whose contents the writer and Holocaust survivor Georges Perec describes in detail in his novel *Life: A User's Manual*, are filled with the fates of their still-living or long-dead inhabitants. In Bolaño's text 'A Stroll through Literature,' he says: 'I dreamt that Earth was finished. And the only human being to contemplate the end was Franz Kafka. In heaven, the Titans were fighting to the death. From a wrought-iron seat in Central Park, Kafka was watching the world burn.' When Lovecraft died in 1937, Perec had just turned two. The science fiction writer Philip K. Dick died on 2 March 1982, Perec a day later after a long stay in Brisbane, the actor John Belushi two days later. On 3 March 1982, the day of Perec's death, the future actress Jessica Biel was born in Ely, Minnesota. Franz Kafka is still alive today, a tiny 135-year-old man, hidden in the back room of a shop for sports apparel in Alice Springs, in the middle of dried-out nowhere, Australia. 2666 minus 1982 is 684: the meagre remains of the never-completed submarine U-684, commissioned by the German navy in 1941, were sunk in the harbour of Hamburg a few days before the capitulation of the Third Reich.

Literature dreams. It dreams of life and of death, of life without death, and of the endlessness of death. It dreams of the beginning, the progression, and the end of time. In the dream of literature only two people attain immortality: its author and its reader, both lost in the desert on a cold, lonely planet between the stars.

Roberto Bolaño, who has been dead since 2003, writes: 'I dreamt that Georges Perec was three years old and visiting my house. I was hugging him, kissing him, saying what a sweet boy he was.'

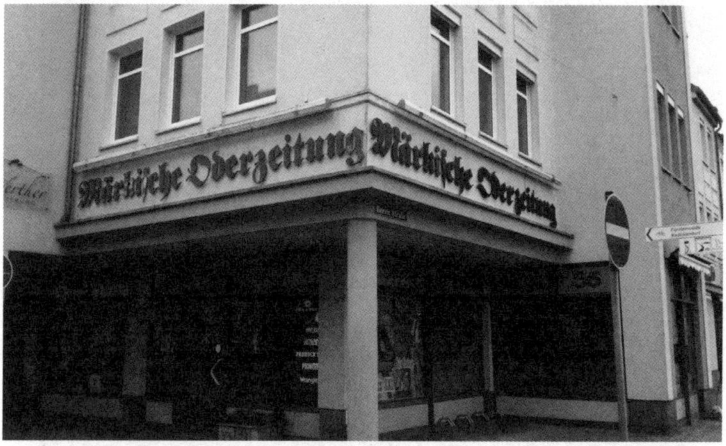
Märkische Oderzeitung
Märkische Oderzeitung

Black Rabbit   Mark Lanegan

Room 12

I was visited in a dream
by a wild black rabbit.
The Amami or Ryukyu
of Japan

Sometimes called the living fossil
because his lineage stretches back into antiquity.
I was at home with this creature
and wanted him to stay forever

Don't go the way of the Tasmanian tiger,
hunted and then neglected to death, I said.

Don't go down like the Irish elk or the grey wolf, I need you here
      with me, my friend!
      Please don't die off like the Carolina parakeet or the Cape lion...
half the animals of Africa are nearly extinct!

I'm sorry, but I'm afraid I might be soon as well, he said.
The mongoose is killing us, and industry has taken over our lands,
our numbers are dwindling and eventually everything must die.
Do not be sad, he said,
your species is dying too,
because there are those among you who strive to make it so
and all things have to move in this direction
in the end,
that is the way of the lonely world.

But I can't lose you, I've only just found you! I cried.

I will stay until you sleep again, said my friend, the black rabbit,
until you are finally at peace and the dreaming is done.

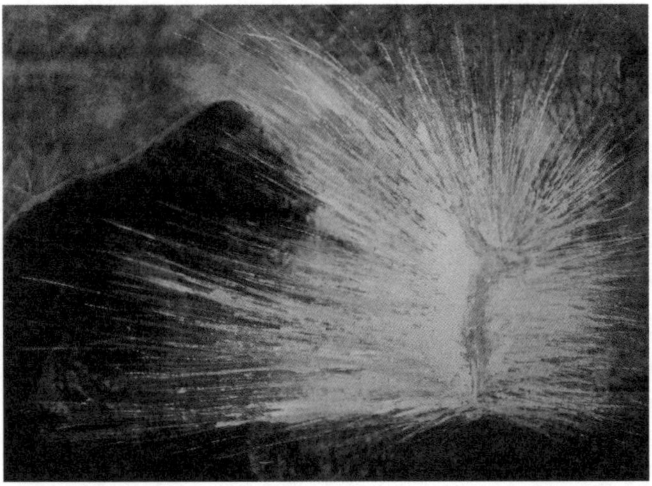

Chirologia & Phantasias   Lucy Mercer

Room 13

Chirologia

Climbing the stairs, I see no neighbours' lights
and the son is still sleeping before his first day.
There's a rainstorm outside, quieting the city.

Whatever's here is turning its face away.
Like when you anticipate a fly's path, John –
and with your hand vibrate the air,
so the fly feeling it then travels past.

I lie in my dark stage bed and remember.
I. *Recommendo*, one hand underneath the other;
G. *Confido*, one palm pressed upon another's back
both drooping down with shared knowledge;
O. *Adoro*, they are to the lips;

In this remembering,
the sensation of difference between hands,
two frightened butterflies, becomes unhinged.

O carpenters, like the window against the wind,
the language of hands is indifferent to resistance.

Phantasias

I sense you in the dank underpass
of the live chauvette cave that rebuses
in ruches, bubbles and lumps when I
slip past the figures so unintent
on their work, past the line-ladder of study
a line-ladder of shadow where the bracket
rises untethered like me as I am here
in the poem too its rings of rock so carefully
winding through one another. It is not hard
to get here when the sun is looking hard
through any window when the ground
is moving like *so* when the rain comes
and the trees are watery reflections
little fleshy waves coaxed by the unbearable
promise of living in the world we are supposed
to know, its fatal arrogance notwithstanding.
How quickly the restraining hand appears
across my sight scribbling you away
like a child's impatience with its drawing,
not wanting to leave what it had shown.

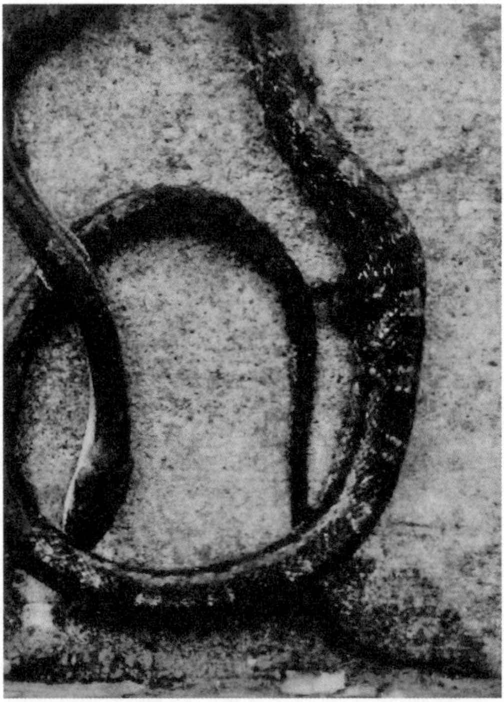

come   Vala Thorodds & Richard Scott
(A Poem for Two Voices)

after Paul Verlaine

Room 14

                    give me your body
                    in the context
                    of your body

     oh my god my beautiful   creasing inward and over
      peach-freckled luminous   you spill into the world
   bone and blue-lit from within   blind but conscious

                    without narrative
                    I see you only
                    as flesh

   and what of your meat-violence   the folds beginning
      spouting hot clear boy-tears   and ending nowhere
           all musk and muscle   hinting at the bits of you that matter

                    beneath
               a remnant of instinct
              mysterious and unruly

                your red   hair that
   opening from which I came   knows nothing of direction
           cat-soft stinking   of gravity
         of electronic flowers   or sunlight

                    it does not look
                    it does not need
                    to look

       girl boy I don't care I   remember your tongue
      climb onto you like you're   drying like cum

                    a raft

       envious of a hand   spread over the seafront
            skin like a sunset   and everything is possible

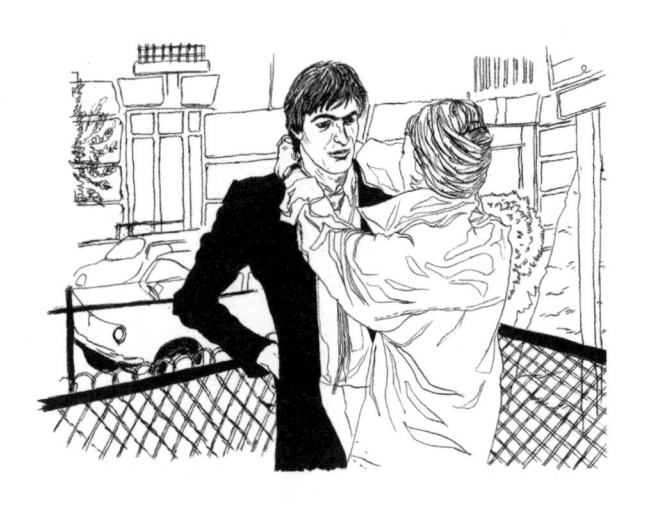

Nine Notes (from a Diary)   Joshua Cohen

Room 15

I   Navajo Reservation

A portrait of a horse painted on horsehide with a horsehair brush. I'd like to write a book like that, but *where* – or *what* – or *who* – is my horse?

II   Medium Thoreau

One generation abandons the enterprises
of another like stranded vessels

There is an incessant influx of novelty in the world,
and yet we tolerate incredible dullness...

   – H. D. Thoreau, *Walden*

>   MEDIUM / One generation abandons novelty, another enterprises the dullness of vessels. Tolerate the incessant yet stranded world.

III   Conversation Summary   *Next Table*

A woman recounts a dream in which she had sex with a celebrity. Her boyfriend, or husband, gets angry. The woman says it was only a dream. Her boyfriend, or husband, gets up from the table. The woman, getting up too and following him, says it means nothing not just because it was only a dream, but also because the celebrity was dead. (As for me, my Polish is so bad I wasn't quite able to determine whether the celebrity had been alive in her dream or she'd been dreaming of necrophilia – another shameful admission: I still can't quite accept the existence of such things as Polish celebrities.)

IV   Why I've Never Had Sex in Hungary

Mom calls me in Budapest:

> *Bring me back that paprika paste...*
> *the kind in the squeeze tube...*
> *Aren't all the women beautiful?...*
> *Don't they all look like me?*

V   Four Facts I Learned in a Bar on Staten Island

In 1992, tuition at NYU was $15,620 / year. In 1996, the starting salary of an associate at Lehman Brothers was $72,580 / year. Since 2008, Budweiser has been owned by the Belgians. No one hires bankers over forty.

VI   A Successful Man in Chicago is
Complimented on His Suit

'This thing? This is the seventeenth suit I've ever owned!'

VII   Museum Fact (Rijeka)

The shape of the anchor derives from the shape of the arrow.
An anchor is an arrow shot into the sea.

VIII   The Only Caravaggio in Russia

B keeps insisting that this painting at the Odessa Museum is the only Caravaggio in Russia, though Odessa isn't in Russia and the painting's not a Caravaggio.

IX   My Friend's Estimation of his Grandfather,
a Forgotten Hungarian Painter

'It was like he'd only seen, seen and misunderstood, one Cubist painting in all of his life – one day, as if by accident, in Paris – before returning directly to Budapest and attempting to imitate it. Rather, before returning directly to Budapest and attempting to nationalise it. To make Cubism Hungarian. For him that was enough.'

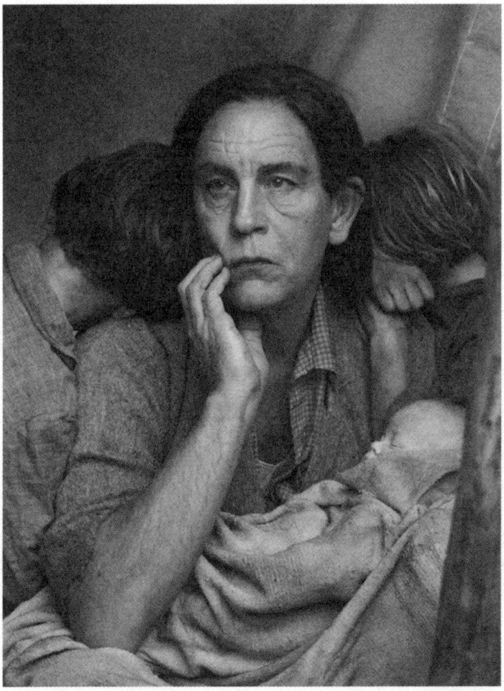

Argument Against Idea Art

For a period of one year this girl and I
carried on a conceptual (objectless) romance.
She was in Freiburg, Germany studying philosophy;
I was in California, U.S.A. trying to be an artist.
We exchanged documents, maps, and photographs in
lieu of corporeal interaction, ie. concept usurped
object. No matter to what extent we exchanged ideas
we both felt an overwhelming need for each others'
bodies. Could this be analogous to the relation
between artist and society?

Butterfield   Hannah Regel

Room 16

No one being able to recognise a door
we crack our noses and discard the shell
the night blows a dust into our skulls
writing our middle-years backwards
          Wake up to the engine of shoulders, perfect lips
            and my stomach kissing your back all big and full of wine
Can you do 7 days, 2 doubles? I mean I'd rather do nothing ever
just exist as scattered images already applauded, But Sure
when can I start? I'll need the money for raising horses
and building catapults for more permanent acts
define permanence, define catapult
pay all my bills, compost, what else
being gorgeously useless and full of it
          she said: I Am the Most Important Artist of My Generation
          then later, amended: Female Artist
She was wearing a big fashionable white shirt with a window for her
bra in the back
spilt wine all over it and was talking loudly and I wanted to be her
I want to be the person that spills wine all over their shirt
and still says things to the party like: I Am the Most Important Artist
to do what I want which is real
Elizabeth Taylor's posture
now that is a big Fuck You question mark
her curling shoulders, they just mean it
like Whiskey. Steal a mink
write No Sale on the big mirror
I wish
Sure, it was me that stuck the finger in but How Dare He:
with the grit fist of his rightness make a hole in our boat
the calloused hand of honesty
cringes in the raft
getting salt in the pact.
She goes back to him, Liz
and besides I love him
I wash my feet in the leaks eating sorry toffee
I would never punch a hole in a wall because there is no evil inside me
A lie. There is plenty.

Example: I would never punch a hole in a wall
I am too vain to move my body in ways that make it animal
this is a kind of evil because I am an animal. I am. See:
just yesterday I dropped a fish finger on the floor
because no one was there to see it fall I put it on his plate not mine:
my animality
it sits in its avoidance, in making other people dirty
there is a kind of pleasure

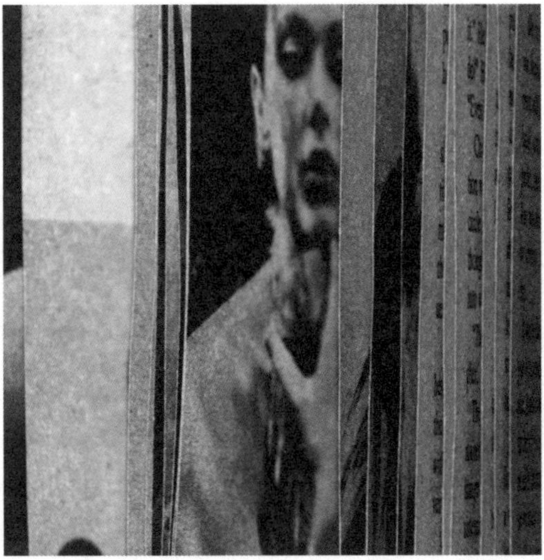

New York City, New York   Nick Cave

Room 17

There are those who work so they can stop.
Stopping is the *why* of work.
There are those who stop so they can work.
Working is the *why* of work.

~

I lie on my bed, in the Bowery Hotel, New York City
My Muse's decollated head, nestled in my lap,
Going lap, lap, lap, while I think of Sharon Olds,
Who wrote the best fellatio poems ever put to the page.
She writes lots of other great things as well.
Leonard Cohen had a shot in 'Chelsea Hotel' and of course,
Lou's 'Sister Ray' and Auden's porn-yawn, 'The Platonic Blow,'
But none comes close to the dazzling Sharon Olds.
This is how the night unfolds. I peer through the crack
In Sharon Olds' closet with my sick bag song ready to blow.
I could only say that it was nice and I told my Muse so.

~

Later, I throw my Bowery window wide.
Up in the far-right corner of the sky,
A rain cloud shaped like Elvis' severed head,
Cries its salt. And all across New York City
It pours beaded curtains of dewdrop jewels,
And rivers of ordinary love songs wash down
The gutters and fill the birdbaths and fountains
And the swimming pools. And from the bar below,
Nina Simone pounds the elephant ivory,
The Canadian maple and the strangling wire,
While up and down the hotel halls, the singing skeleton
Of Karen Carpenter glides and calls.
And as Roy Orbison deeply mines for cut diamonds
Of sorrowed sound, we begin to see a ghastly pattern!
Karen Dalton dangles from the rings of Saturn.
Hank Williams tilts to the side in the back
Of a powder-blue Cadillac, and Lou Reed's face
Appears on a napkin in a bar in Lower Manhattan.

Let the world know they worked to the end with love.
For there are those, poor things, who never start.
Let the world know they knew the why of goodbye,
That in love we often must depart.

Yes, in love we often must depart.
We will drown, poor things, in tears tonight,
But I've got to get an early start,
To Detroit on a Delta flight.

FROM ONE CAME THREE AND THE MANY
THROUGH SPLIT TIME EXPOSURE
REVEALING LAYERS OF ETERNITY
WHERE PERMANENCE DID LIVE
IN SHIFTING SANDS OF MIND

    *

RHUBARD
ANISEED
BLACK BEER
ZINC IRON
    M.S.

throttle song & nothingness is   Daisy Lafarge
the scene of wild activity

Room 18

throttle song

'she wants' to be more like moonlight
or a sky filled with porcelain
as it cracks under skittish weight
and bleeds the rosy milk of planets

'she wants' the old song with dirty words
and dirty, old-sung hands
that orbit her throat
as she barks red and white
at the sky, 'does she?'

nothingness is the scene of wild activity   *after Karen Barad*

I

the electron
touch not yrself!
lest you reabsorb the energy of yr own photon, with silky caress
o that is immoral! says the male physicist, 'and yet the electron does it'
eyeing a particular pleasure w/globular disdain
there is no void, unless the gesture towards the self is empty
a vacuum sac of touch & go *cul!*
'the electron touches itself, ∴ touches everyone' says the physicienne
'batshit!' says the audience member
who does not like to be touched
by so fertile a substance

II

as we have seen
repulsion is the core of attraction
the thing 'touched' is the thing
closest, pushed away;
noli me –
kin and bedmates
polarised

BIGFOOT 1   1994   Jeffry Vallance

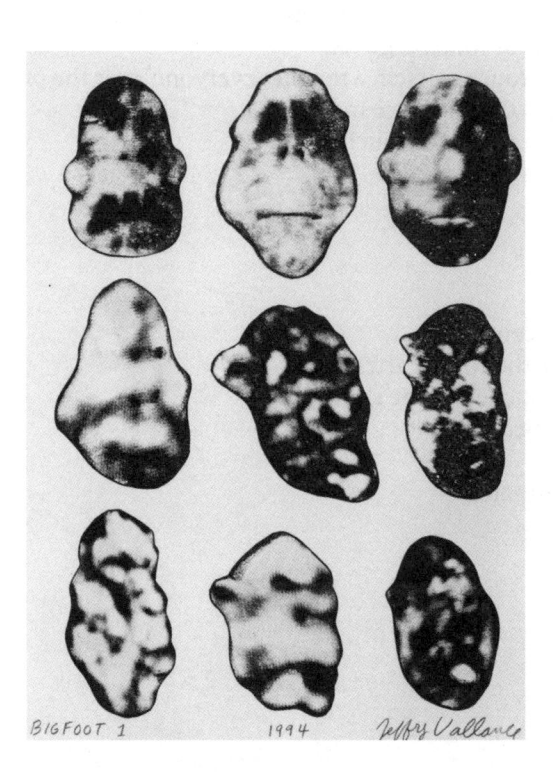

this big bit cradle   Holly Pester

Room 19

I made you, you nix, baby-hoofed punk   I stored
fit gunk, strung a bow with my nerves
to pluck hush   bled cats
flooted energies, brung and trained fluid   I fought
over that time   raved in pig halls, cooled down and made you
there is space in here in the
I settled it O
exhausted snagg belly   I rubbed my back on a bell to fix the time
crapped in that
and that   I boxed up cars , scraped pollen off race horses , bought a
contraption online that sucks and bites
my nipples for me . 8 hours a day under loose fitting clothing . It's
corrective of something   and arrived in the same box as a Kathy Acker book

lubber love relax extract hours from my spit
nothing like this mood you bring to bed   too late to rat cuddle
dont go mad dont get comfort from the
fucker-tight-blanket

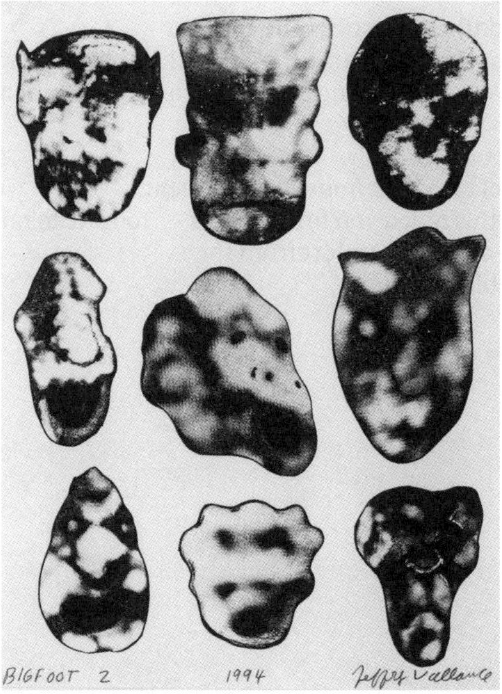
BIGFOOT 2
1994
Jeffry Vallance

Rooms   Matthew Gregory

Room 20

A Room in Paris, 1855*

An alchemist's gas lamp
reaches shakily into one corner,
some paintings nobody
has a particular opinion on
are nailed over
rose ballroom wallpaper.

And on the long bed
the middle-aged poet,
Gérard de Nerval.

He would appear restful
if it wasn't for his eyebrows meeting
like two dark horses
in the middle of his forehead.
He is dreaming of the beautiful apple
he palmed only a few days before
on Ile Saint Louis
and the grief of a wormhole
in the thing perfected.

He wakes all of a sudden.
He takes his collection
Les Chimères
down from its cramped shelf
and cuts it in half at the spine
with a knife.
He will clean
every sentence.

---

* Gérard de Nerval, Symbolist poet who died on the banks of the river Seine, in the winter of 1855.

A Room at the Grand Hôtel des Roches Noires, 1971*

Madame likes to air the double she takes for eight weeks
on the sea-facing east wing.

She has written twelve postcards to Brussels in a month.

Her tone — *La mer est jolie* — is light and blasé though
she counts six instances of the word
                                          ténèbres.

Arthritis has touched her best hand. Outside the sea
glances her way with distance

where once everything in the world was a man
asking her to dance.

On one shelf in ribbons, her empty hatbox deepens

into deeper hatboxes that collapse slowly
                          into the green pinochle halls
                              of the pinochle men she knew.

---

*   The Grand Hôtel des Roches Noires, in Normandy. The hotel, which can be translated as the 'Grand Hotel of the Black Rocks,' was a glamorous hub for the gambling and sporting sets in the early part of the twentieth century, falling into decline years later.

Madame dreams in the window chair

and sees her postcards
from the Roches Noires
fly lightly down
                              over the swathe of sea
                              from the undercarriage
                              of an albatross.

The ocean bird migrating   but so everything seems
at this point

                        the cad with a tall white grin
                        throwing double sixes at midnight
                        fresh oysters with their slight cologne
                        in the backseats of young France

The concierge is calling her
—*Madame. Madame?*

An old albatross the scuffed white of lobby magazines.

An old albatross, but content as she wanders off the edge
of the continent.

A Room on the *Capitaine Paul-Lemerle*, 1941*

Yesterday a deckhand confused the new land
with a cloudbank and its own flocks and shepherds
and white houses in the cloud's country.

The sea is green at night
                          a violent blue by day
and wider and deeper than the dreams of André Breton.
André Breton is aboard the *Capitaine*.

He is writing to someone, one a.m. His bunk wobbles
in the rough passage and his gaslamp swings.
On his wrists the eczema has come up again.

His yellow sleeve is spotted with ink as he spills
his hand across the page. He is writing to his wife
or to Nadja but won't decide who until he signs off.

He is describing the luminescence that rises
through the ocean at night and follows the *Capitaine*.

First there is only a pulse, the propeller turning
up green sparks, stirring them with its long ladles
before the lighted halls of plankton appear.

It follows us, Dearest, disappearing for days
then returning in waves like the mind to a place.

In every light shoal he sees something he remembers.

In every hall an empty lectern and shipment papers.

André Breton walks a Sorbonne in his head
and goes from room to room, to look for the lights
left flickering.

He writes how the crew saw
                          a manta rise in the glow
with its dark studies under one arm of its cloak,
circle once then wing slowly out of their surveillance.

---

*   The *Capitaine Paul-Lemerle* was a transatlantic vessel that smuggled a number of intellectuals and artists out of Vichy-controlled France in the 1940s. Among them were André Breton and Claude Levi-Strauss.

A Room in the Pacific Palisades, 1979*

*well here's something I never did like Tolstoy awful much
dontcha know Betty Beverly hell I mean Brenda*
the old novelist was saying as he thumped the tablecloth
just missing the silver goblets and service plates
steaming in drifts before him.
                              Bald and small he sat
across from the young actress he wrote to habitually
praising in his endless beautiful trains
and clauses that led often now
                              to great tiredness.
Against the one amber lampshade they were profiled
a grey king and confidante. Where the sitting room dimmed
at the periphery, characters from his years abroad stepped
out of dark friezes and spoke –
                              a lush with remarkable tattoos
needled like varicose, an ancient 'legionnaire,' the beautiful boy
leading a wolfhound by the reins, and young Jean Genet who
no, no, he'd not met Jean Genet.
                              On Montmartre he'd loved
so many whores. In the young actress opposite
he sometimes saw them play across her features:
an eyebrow arched back fifty years, the nose upturned
or lengthened in the dark, a mole drew itself on her cheek.

Thérèse, Sylvie, or Margot, was it, who sat with him now
with the fifty, one hundred, one thousand
who seemed to be there, leaning on an elbow, listening
brightly, always just across from him, in the other chair.

---

*   The writer is the novelist Henry Miller.

A Room in Taiwan, 2010*

And how many desert miles of the web
has she crossed tonight searching
for the home address of Mastroianni.

Mastroianni is no longer among us.
She doesn't know this so continues
her drift from one ruined domain

to the next one, signing herself in
to empty guestbooks as she goes.
I would like to write to Mr Marcello Mastroianni

please if anyone know where he is.
I dream us in light of stars and great city Rome.
I want to be like kiss of Anita Ekberg.

Mastroianni whose thousand pictures
in these forums lose him on pages
like palimpsests of man on top of man

where this girl, at her tropical desk,
who lists for his deep, romantic heart
touches a hit-counter, once, in the dark.

---

*   Marcello Mastroianni, Italian actor, famous for his role in
Fellini's *La Dolce Vita* and *8 1/2*.

A Room in Platinum, 1994*

thinking how simian he was
the singer
ate waffles and sat
in his observatory at dawn

watching the willows
come round like longhairs
in the mist

but he felt cold among them
and fudged the television on
to himself sleepwalking
part of the tour
inchoate somehow but there
how various to see himself

nobody would enter the house
he might not leave his couch again
the singer using
one room out of fifteen

sat on the floor of the whale
like Jonah and stirred
his pot of beans

---

*   The singer in the poem is Kurt Cobain, in the last year of his life.

A Room at the Oregon Coast Aquarium, 1992

the young keepers come   with their steadies to smoke
in the white recesses   of the observation bay
for a long moment   nothing   then the tiniest fraction
of him slivers the surface   his dorsal melted over
those beautiful clouds   patched around his eyes
woah   the girls are lost   in him the first time
he breaches out   turns whiteside   then spews
a beachball   some metres   above the tank
they'll watch   a while longer   then he's alone
until morning   a teenage whale   listening   to the deep
convolutions   sounding   inside his head
the intimate sea   mixed up with   human ordinance
Keiko at the glass   his dark eye on   the dome complex
in the starlight   empty except   many strange forms
of life   the whale   on his back   gazing up
at the horse   the scorpion   the implements
certain other   mythic shapes   more his size
he relaxes his flippers   he will fall backwards
                    into the sky

A Room at the Sasquatch Symposium, Montana, 1993

Raymond L. Wallace keeps his schtum.
Feels sadder than he has for ages.
1967 and his monkey suit shambling
out of focus and into the hungry tract
      of the American imagination.

A Room in Pëtkwo*

An observatory for the antics of remote weather.
Waterspouts and cyclones spinning up
on the furthest oceans. And an eye
watching over it all. The blurring vanes
of the anemometers high on the dome,
the dome, its curvilinear sides and funnels,
the fins and aerials, of an inoperative flying machine.
The century, here, an inoperative machine.
And the man who is charged with all this
watches dials and oscillating nibs
tighten their circles to the mad dense scream
of something enormous coming
into consciousness and moving on the sea.
It is impressive. You can impress someone
telling them you're guardian of the weather –
like the only personable woman in this town.
Often on the flimsy pier, pale Miss Zwida
in her straw hat, drawing beautifully
the faint taxonomies of seashells.
Shells in their complicated frequencies.
Or one time – a long line of hotel palms
leaning into wind like a stranded company
of islanders, ready to leave Pëtkwo
for time far away. But this was rare.
The day before, he surprised Miss Zwida
on her wicker chair, as a new front
darkened its interest a few leagues out.
Pointing to where the registers scribbled
continuously under the observatory dome
he said *it's like receiving a secret letter*
from one of the world's great authors
but late, into the night, you realise how
cold and far from us his brilliance has come.

---

*   Pëtkwo, a coastal town in Italo Calvino's novel *If on a winter's night a traveller.*

A Room in Florence, 1266*

More of a dog extended in all directions
over the thin rug, in the stone-wall cloister
the man begins to kick and whimper
while his gut, in good voice, escapes his belt.

The sleeping face is moist and flavourful
intensified by the little bursts of lightning
in purples across his cheeks and nose.
Mist. Then a kind of softish light. Certain tropes

of lyric poems pass into the scene where
the friar, this Loderingo, snores in deep chords
triumphantly out for all his sermons
and petitions. Marshes beyond the city walls

thicken with lowlife and schismatic
but the friar is dreaming, vague transactions
and soft flatteries, on an ideal balcony.
He has toothache in one molar but his dream

fills the space where the throb should be
with a pale horse, clip-clopping on cobbles.
His head is full of hoofbeats as the horse trots
through Florence without a rider or cause.

*   Loderingo degli Andalò, one of the profligate 'Jovial Friars,' as found among the hypocrites in the Eighth Circle of Dante's *Inferno*.

A Room in the Crystal Palace, New Year's Eve, 1853

'...inside Iguanodon a select party
          dine on turbot and mock turtle
till cognac and the humours
          send them, hats in hand, to bed
tiny formal spectres of men
          moving across the crescent lawns
of the starlit palace grounds
          the sculptor, a Mr Benjamin Watkins
alone at last, nurses his head
          in his hands before it can fall
forwards like a glass of water
          into wild surmises of the hour
then steps from the hollow cast
          scene of 'a most unmatchable dinner'
down from the rutted girth
          to look his model in the eye
the eye chipped into the skull
          the same whorl he'd grafted onto
Ichthyosaurus and Megalosaurus
          but dull recognition then
the gaze less a giant reptile's
          gaze than the bulbous fixéd
one of his creationist friend
          the venerable Sir Richard Owen...'

A Room in the Republic, (Capua), 73BC*

[FRAGMENT]

it's forty degrees when the sun really means it
moving light columns
        through the dark ludus

 overhead the white villa is empty

the menials, culinarians, gone
    leaving

        walls glancing with lizards
                a few mountain acanthus
    petrified in their pots

                the house treasures
    looted or shattered through the corridors

morning after morning from the low foothills
        daylight

a madness returning to a mind
        barely restored

    ~~*nihil semper restituit*~~

    nothing will ever be restored

inside the complex   barefoot, living on

    last pomegranates and dust

domina watches petals blow through the baths

---

*   The ludus is that of Lentulus Batiatus, ill-fated dominus of Spartacus.

Notes on Happiness   Emmanuel Iduma

Room 21

A school on the Island, the online newspaper reported, where a few devoted men, not more than seven each term, studied the god of water. How he turns water into wine, divides its onrush to reveal land; how he is dipped in it to fulfil or reveal righteousness; how it flows when he is pierced on the side; how it can't take the weight of a man, yet Peter walked afloat. Most of all, devotion: daily exercise of looking at the sea, writing notes compelled by it, or placing feet in it. One with it: obsessed with immensity. How God is in expanse. He is curious about the men. He goes to the Island certain of nothing but to seek the sight of those who place their bodies in water, as worship.

Last night he returned to the city. This morning he walks to the church at the other end of his street. His back aches, a tiny knot that stays put even if he bends his back and presses a knuckle against it while guessing the spot. He considers the length of the street and how tired he is. What outweighs what? God or fatigue, body or spirit.

Then he sleeps a little. Can't remember, but once awake, alert and with reprieve, he knows he had spoken with his mother sometime earlier. He calls to confirm. You don't remember? No, I don't, he says. 'You told me you would come this evening. Mind yourself and come here, or else.' She laughs. He closes his eyes when he hears her laugh. The thrill he feels is as sharp and instant, as giving and ephemeral, as whatever happiness has come over her.

He drives, and there is unexpected traffic on the street abutting Ikorodu Road. As he waits to turn the bend, he hears man whistle a tune, and he can swear it is Amadou. Am I sure of this, he wonders, not bothering to turn his face to the origin of the sound. Am I sure? Amadou had never whispered in his hearing. How does he attribute this sound to him – as though to trace in a crowd whose breath smells pleasant or foul, precise and peculiar, no margin of error.

Had he been to church, his mother asks. Yes. 'It's good that you went even though you are tired.' He takes the plate from her hand and sits. She tells him of her dream from the night before. Once she is finished, she asks him of the Island. 'Did you enjoy yourself?' He shakes his head, a kind of ambivalence, and checks for the knot in his lower back. Come here, his mother says, ready to hold him, so he stands. In all this time he hasn't touched the food.

He sees in her eyes all the traces of her magnanimity towards him, lines of daily worry, how he may be moored. She is his mother, and this cannot simply be broached as the fact that she is a woman. In her tired eyes it is possible to imagine a distinction as such, woman and mother. Not always, not necessarily. But right now.

Driving back, another go-slow. He looks at the car beside his, a couple and their little girl. She has an iPad, playing a game, dodging underwater monsters, cruising her little fish. He sees this and feels as happy as he can manage today. But just as he smiles her mother grabs the iPad, mouths a warning. His face relaxes, surly.

An image of large water forms in his mind at once, and ah, yes, from his mother's dream. It is an after-effect, a rendering of slow, broken time.

The Islanders haul Amadou's body from the sea. Those who look at the face, braised until bruised, rinsed in timeless salt, are hard-pressed to tell with their intent scrutiny in what belly he has undergone this passage. No one calls his name. They make an arc as they stand, gasping or grunting or howling. Once the arc is formed it stays sacrosanct, just as a grave for one is never marked for many. Those who eventually speak his name aloud have returned from the borderline of sea and land, where they saw his body. They sit two or more, or one, especially one, in distress over the long night, mesmerised by finality, and stunned by how, all along, they have been impervious to the faint dash separating is and was.

It's 3:45am when he wakes, and he is unable to fall back asleep. At least an hour passes. It's dread, not dream, a hovering. It's his life and Amadou's distinguished as memory, yet memory not past, as it leaps into what he has no other word for but now. Daily broken time. There is no innocence in dreams. Even benign ones – those in which he writes an email, speaks on the phone, throws a shirt in the laundry basket, grabs a mug – occur with sly purpose. These are not tentative moments, but final. In a dream he is spectator and protagonist. He is, at once, freed from responsibility for any action, and implicated in its consequence.

> *This morning you called my name. A male voice, yes – brother, friend, or father – but whose? A voice of my many childhoods and adulthoods, neither of which has run its course. It seems to me not a question of having heard you call me, but of all the voices that have spoken my name and have placed emphasis on the first two syllables. At the moment I hear you I am overtaken by sleep, by my benumbed body. Now I rise. Have you returned? What I miss most is what you might miss, me loving you. And so, whoever you are, bring me into this certainty: when I hear you I cannot mistake you for another.*

His sister is on the phone. 'I heard you came to the house.' Oh, yes. 'You couldn't wait to see me. See your big head.' There is a pause, like a clearing, right where his laugh could have landed. 'Are you okay?' He utters a remedial chortle, and her voice is back to normal. She tells him of a certain man, what he may or may not do with her, what she may or may not do to him, all this desire. He is back in his house, on the bed. He listens and thinks of how he loves her, if that how can be measured right, and what manner of love is in need of being measured.

The image of large water remains in his mind, this time from watching men who surfed on the Island, their bodies like songs. He tells his sister right then that one day she must see this, those men: I must return with you. Aww, you're sweet, she replies, and he begins to weep.

Sometime early the next morning, just as he wakes and picks up his phone, he reads an essay by a man who describes himself as 'hopelessly optimistic.' Not, in fact, the full essay. A short blurb in an email linked to the essay. He perceives he would carry those words in his mind, be interrupted in the middle of his banal day to check in on a mere phrase. Why optimism, why hopeless. Why qualify the future.

Now he has tightened his necktie and picked up his keys. Now he has turned the ignition, now he is pedalling gently. Now he is waving to a woman walking her boy to school. Now he arrives at a car park, now he climbs up the stairs. Now he stares at a blinking cursor, an Excel spreadsheet, and a beaucoup of numbers. Life is so. He sinks into banality.

On the Island, he sees a man singing to a tree. He has recalled that moment many times, and at no time does he feel in danger of hyperbole. Of course, a man sings to a tree, holding a lonely trunk in embrace. 'May peace be multiplied to you, my friend, whether you go or stay.' He does not dare interrupt the man, cannot dare put a languid word in that unerring image.

The day goes on. At the staff canteen he high-fives a coworker, then approaches an unoccupied table. His sister has sent a text, somehow hitting send thrice. 'I want to see you. I want to see you. I want to see you.' The light has gone off. In the darkened moment before the generator comes on, he sees the coworker he high-fived approach. He knows she will come with a question, and if he responds well, might tell a story.

One man in her story is Amadou in everything but name. He has devoted his adult life to one mission; incurious as far as money is concerned; loved by all but held in suspicion by those in power; never eager to dispel the half-truths attributed to him, however unsparing they may be. And so he is distracted when she comes full-circle with her tale, as if he has held on to a lifebuoy and missed the rescue ship. She slaps the back of his palm. 'What's on your mind?'

He drives his coworker to her home, two streets away from his. Before she leaves the car she hugs him, saying take care, and he rests an awkward hand on her neck. She remains sitting and speaks of the feel of his hands. Lingering and hesitant, drawing close even if gradual, just enough for the tickle to turn warm. He replies that she makes too much of a small gesture. 'I didn't touch you for long.' She stares at him hard and sad. And he feels the knot in his lower back, like an intuition never tested.

His sister insists on sleeping over. She sings to him one of her songs in progress, humming provisional notes. It's almost complete, she says. Every time there is a 'you' in the lyrics, she looks at the spot in his chest where there is a birthmark, where his unbidden anxieties thrive, or so she feels she imagines. He closes his eyes once the song is finished, and she sits beside him and holds his hand. In no other way could she prove her music as unfinished.

Why are you sad, his sister asks him, standing over the bed the next morning. There is a how, and a why. Of course, he can say how, the lingering distaste for anything remotely promising to spark a smile. Why? Amadou had shown him the exact point in the water where he could dip a foot and get some warmth. Only a foot, better even a toe. At the moment they stood together it was proven and true. Never when he went there without Amadou. And why? And how, if he wishes, can he return? And what memory does the water hold of a body bruised and braised? He stirs from the bed and reaches towards her to pull him up.

How this. Not how long, how much, or how ever. Maybe how however. I don't want how as grammar or mere word. I want how for how, how for how much of love. How as how, how how. I want to place it in front of God, how God, how of expanse. I want how in repetition. How how. How how how. How.

Today he can bear it no longer. He seeks out his coworker as soon as he sees she is at her desk and asks if she has a moment. They stand in front of the stairs, and he places a firm hand on the rail. There, then, he tells her about Amadou. 'He died.' It is the first time he says this to anyone outside the Island. She says something to him. He'd heard, 'How can I hold you?' But he doubts that. And once she brings him to herself, at first in a half embrace, and then with her hand on his nape, he wonders how to match what she might say or do with what he has seen or felt. 'Hold me like this,' he says.

All this desire. For, even before he left for the Island, when it was clear to him that, however repressed, his mind harboured affection for her, maybe lifelong, he hoped she would speak of those feelings first. She'd said, 'I like us like this, complicated.' He'd think nothing of it until now: in the time it takes for him to say more than a mere declaration. Yes, Amadou died. Now he must unknot that word for her, unfurl a main story of grief, not one where he is cast in one of several subplots.

He recalls a woman who sits beside him as the airplane leaves the Island. He pulls down the blind of the window. He despises the sensation of looking at the mottled world below. But she asks him if he can pull it back up, her tone near vicious, desperate. He obliges. Perhaps it is his hesitation – but she apologises. 'It is my first time flying. I am fifty-three, and I have never left this Island.' He feels close to pity, if not solidarity. Would she mind if he sits where she sits, he asks? Would he mind, she asks? One view of the world is exchanged for another.

He has heard of all those regions of the world in which the sun stayed months without giving a shine. Intermediate light; light as potential. Amadou once said that to not dream must be the kindest form of torture: what do you do with all that darkness shut up in your eyes? He'd had no dream since his return.

His coworker insists on driving him home. In order to beat the traffic on Ikorodu Road, they must leave at sundown. With her hand on the knob, she looks at the sky. She says nothing about it and enters the car. He sees in her demeanor that gold, this expanse, how God. Now that he has told her of Amadou, he hopes she might serve as counterpoint for his feelings. To reflect through her how the world goes on, shrugs off absence.

She insists on sleeping over. While she holds ajar his refrigerator, he weighs from the firmness in her voice how grave his loss seems for her and concludes there is no way to know—days from the Island lead here, days after the Island make a turn from here.

Sumari astral / Astral Summary   Joan Brossa
                                  translated from the Catalan
                                  by Cameron Griffiths

Room 22

I

En forma humana
i habitat pel llenguatge
tiro els daus
i obro els llibres.
Ningú no balla convençut.
Els braços només s'aixequen
per copejar amb les mans,
no pas per traçar cap signe.
Observo els detalls del foc
pintat per semblar una cara.
Tothom es trepitja.
Decortiquen els fruits i no se'ls mengen.
Les banderes són del color del caos,
i la serp és la mestressa dels vivents.
La sal no evita que es podreixi el mar,
ni les lletres corresponen a la feina.
La prova és que el poder fa d'únic centre
i al món es produeixen artificis
que pacten totes les conclusions (i menes
d'especulació) que ens caldria abandonar.
La força de les roques no pensa.

Escric signes i lletres
en una pell de bou.
Trasllado al pensament
la terra, el cel i l'aigua
i tiro sorra sobre un mirall
per observar-hi dibuixos capritxosos
o per traçar-hi una lletra.
Any darrera any,
esgarrapo la terra amb les ungles
per poder tallar l'ombra
que m'avança i penetra les arrels.

I

In human form
and inhabited by language,
I roll the dice
and open the books.
No one dances with conviction.
Arms are raised only
to strike with hands,
not to write any sign.
In the details of the fire, I see
the resemblance of a face.
Each steps on the next one's feet.
The fruit is peeled but not eaten.
The flags are the colour of chaos,
and the snake is the love of the living.
The salt does not preserve the sea,
nor do the letters fit the work.
The proof is that power forms the only centre
and the world produces artifices
to support its own conclusions (and means
of speculation), which should be abandoned.
The strength of rocks is in not thinking.

I write signs and letters
on ox skin.
Bring to mind the earth,
the sky and the water
and throw sand on a mirror
to look at its capricious forms
or to draw in it a letter.
Year after year,
I scratch at the earth with my nails
so I can cut out the shadow
ahead of me and penetrate the roots.

II

Enmig de jeroglífics i figures
modelo l'ou del món
en un torn de terrissaire.
La gent amaga el mal sota l'estora
i tothom treu el cap i treu la cama.
Més enllà d'aquesta escena
remunto el pensament
per l'espiral d'unes banyes.
Havent vist transformar
una pedra en escorpí,
ja no confirmo ni contradic
i em trobo cara a cara amb mi mateix.
De mi, ¿qui se n'ha fet càrrec?
Sóc al mig d'una esplanada
on cap viatge no allunya,
ni el recurs de cap cerimònia
em dóna prova de res.
L'única cosa que em cal
és imaginar grans boscos
o la fumera d'unes herbes.
Però, si vas massa lluny,
d'allà no tornes.
Em proposo de seguir aquesta via
i no pas de ser menjat
per mi mateix nit i dia
sobre el terreny que trien els altres
sense cap força instintiva.
Amb els vestits no vull imitar res
ni em plau fer ombra enlloc amb cap arma,
perquè en el nom de tots els éssers
veig el meu nom veritable,
que vull que resti secret
en el seu nombre de lletres
i les tres inicials.

II

Amid hieroglyphs and figures
I shape the egg of the world
on a potter's wheel.
People sweep evil under the carpet
and stretch out their necks and stretch out their legs.
Beyond this scene,
I think again
of the way that some horns spiral.
Having seen transformed
a stone into a scorpion,
I no longer confirm nor contradict,
but find myself face to face with myself.
And me, who takes care of me?
I am in the middle of an esplanade
but no movement takes me anywhere,
nor does the recourse to some ceremony
prove anything to me.
The only thing I have to do
is imagine great forests
or the smoke from some burning grass.
But, if you go too far away,
you might not return.
I intend to follow this path
and not let myself be consumed,
night and day,
by the ground that others choose
with no real instinctive force.
I mean to imitate nothing with these clothes
nor do I care to cast a shadow anywhere with a weapon,
because in the name of all things
I see my real name,
and I want to keep secret
the number of its letters
and its three initials.

III

La gent emet judicis
idèntics en el desordre,
encara que tard o d'hora
hagi d'acceptar el seu
món com una mera il·lusió.
I tothom us demana resplendors
o poder cavalcar força lleons.
Ningú ja no s'endinsa al laberint
portant unes balances a la mà.
L'ombra els fuig pel mirall.
Duen barret al cervell.
Sang de cera els dóna vigoria.
¿Es relacionen les paraules
a mesura que les creences
relaten pactes inventats
que només estan d'acord amb les paraules?
I ¿què sabem de l'origen dels temps?
¿Qui baixa portant un llamp
l'escala del firmament?

III

People make the same
judgements in the disorder,
but sooner or later
they must accept
that their world is mere illusion.
And everyone asks you for radiance
or the ability to ride powerful lions.
No one now enters the labyrinth
carrying scales in their hand.
Their shadow escapes through the mirror.
They wear a hat on their brain.
Wax blood gives them a vigour.
Do the words connect
as beliefs tell of
invented agreements,
which only align with the words?
And what do we know about the origin of time?
Who carries a lamp down
the ladder of the sky?

El mar de baix és igual que el de dalt,
i les afinitats ens influeixen.
Prou moviments de salutació.
No hi pot haver fronteres definitives.
Del sostre cau una gota de foc.
Noto que a terra hi corre una energia,
segurament com la que mou les astres.
El món hauria d'ésser dividit
horitzontalment per afinitats,
no pas verticalment i sense fronteres.
Hi ha coses que vistes
són més senzilles que explicades.
No és bo que un crani
pugui servir de timbal
i els sons es converteixin en sorolls.
No. La sonoritat de la veu,
la seva força modulada,
reuneix les energies del pensament
si entre les síl·labes de les paraules
barreges les lletres dels punts cardinals.
Però jo no seré jo si no supero els temps
i un llamp mal dirigit m'encén l'escombra.
Tal com darrera la veu hi segueix l'eco,
el món és unit
per correspondències
que no indiquen cap calendari.
Transformo la serp en un tros de corda.
Seguint els passos del pensament
més enllà de les aparences,
avui només presto atenció
a formes triangulars.

The sea below is the same as the sea above,
and these affinities influence us.
Enough with the gestures of salutation.
There can be no definitive borders.
A drop of fire falls from the ceiling.
I notice that there runs an energy in the ground,
surely like the one which moves the stars.
The world should be divided
horizontally by affinities,
not vertically and without borders.
There are things that you see
which are simpler than they seem.
A skull should never
serve as a drum
or sounds become noise.
No. The sonority of the voice,
its own modulated force,
gathers the energies of thought,
if between the syllables of the words
are mixed the letters of the cardinal points.
But I won't be me if I don't overcome the times
and a misdirected lightning bolt ignites my broom.
Just as behind the voice comes the echo,
the world is united
by connections
that do not suggest any calendar.
I transform the snake into a piece of rope.
Following the footsteps of thought
beyond those of appearance,
today I pay attention only
to triangular forms.

(See p. 435, *I sometimes sing lest you forget who I am...*)

two types of the same return & moss   Imogen Cassels

Room 23

two types of the same return

but in a beetle by mining exos and drops
of rain and bush dust
                     it's beautiful to be
trim or take lines up to the loaded moon /
in a naïve swoop tanglier. 'these are
the glass minutes of my eyes, or like
I could eat twice as many flowers as you
I'm trailing off, crush-crush.

                         it's
January it's almost spring every starlit fence
is tiny. the primroses saying know know know
or hello!,
   opened vein or
               do you even have roses?
               the size of a continent.
my mother is a rowan tree I'm so conspicuous without.
artifice enough for any hope lopsided,
your means of soutiens,
to Paris in our times.

                     comprehending.
and the magpies – five – skirmishing
won't console hurt. motherofpearl inlay me
all across my back.   stained glass
whatever.   thousands of bats fly out of a cave //
I love art.   with all the accidental tendresse of holding out
a mobile calling 'it's for you –
                     forwent something
almost being said:
               my breastbone is a bat
put out of temper; I am become a shrine;
sad flush of every demi-form;
it catches like a sycamore

moss

dizzy weepies with repeat oh morning hazel
she's so suspended third so autopilot harmony
wish if grief would label itself to imagine
repeating a summer again like circle at least
six or whatever unknowing what a window
means there is a hot line of fabric on my back
and the centre of my lips is a heart I've such
an amount of nothing in my pocket you'd
never listen without is hell oh hiya ilya ilya ilya
there's no fix for never having your siskin
daughter furling out of place well uplight
blossom this the sun damage blissing kate's
narrow chest blueshirt new in for may
the luminous possibility of a child

BIGFOOT 3   1994   Jeffrey Vallance

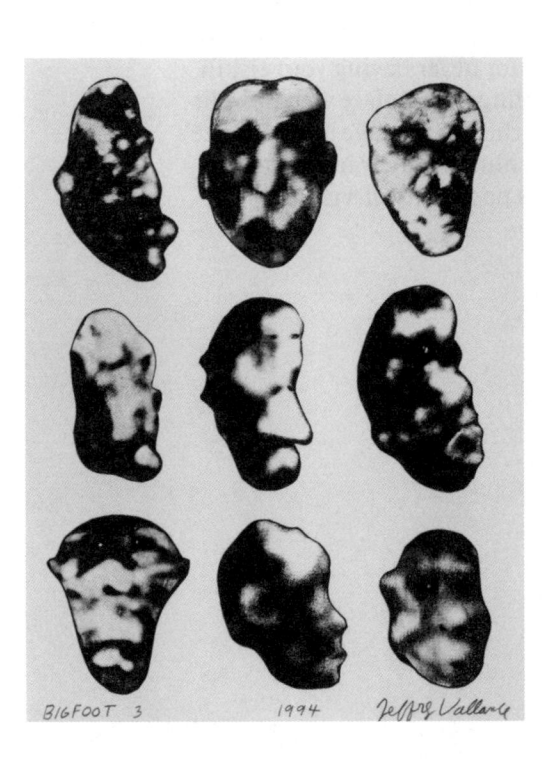

Quantum Leap   Hisham Bustani
translated from the Arabic
by maia tabet

Room 24

The place had changed.

It wasn't in the old city neighbourhood anymore. No longer an apartment in a dilapidated building with crumbling walls, where the antiquated fan produced an occasional and feeble breeze as it creaked around collecting dust. No more rusty chairs hardly big enough to sit on, nowhere for dreams to soar.

The place had changed, flown off to a new neighbourhood. Instead of one story, now there were two. It had become a villa with a yard in the front and a swimming pool in the back, plus a guardhouse, a red-tile roof, and air conditioning – and a closet for dreams.

His writer-friends had invited him over. 'A gift from the sultan,' they'd said, 'with no strings attached.' So he went.

When he opened the glass door and poked his head in, a blast of cold air tickled the droplets of sweat beading on his forehead. He was struck by the large open space, vacant but for a hanging chair swinging from the ceiling, in which the silhouette of an otherwise invisible person sat holding an electric saw in one hand and a sheaf of papers in the other.

Hanging from butchers' hooks were the headless carcasses of lambs of different sizes. The walls were white but for bright splotches of red.

The silhouette pointed to the newcomer.

'I see landmines in his head,' said one carcass.

'I see pencils and pictures and questions,' said another.

'I see headless carcasses hanging from butchers' hooks in his head,' said the third, as all the carcasses swung to and fro, humming, tails raised, spattering the walls with blood.

The silhouette pointed to the newcomer.

'That one needs a small frame so that his head can look big,' said one carcass.

'That head has a golden spoon in its mouth, to make us feel beholden,' said another.

'That's the head of a poseur, of a womanising intellectual,' said a third, as all the carcasses swung to and fro, humming, tails raised, spattering the walls with blood.

The silhouette sharpens the electric saw with the sheaf of papers, hitting the pages with the saw, and the red splotches on the walls move around, coalescing and separating: a hammer and sickle appear, no, it's a five-pointed star, or maybe a stylised, arrow-like jeem next to an elongated map... Is it a victory sign? A sun? A peasant? A labourer? Students? The patches of colour and the shapes tumble and turn, forming a river that seeps along the corners of the room, through the hallway, and to the back door. The red river spills into the swimming pool.

The silhouette sharpens the electric saw with the sheaf of papers. 'Come and get baptised,' he says to the head poking through the glass door. 'We are the salvation,' the carcasses repeat, swinging to and fro, spattering more blood. 'Come.'

[MENTAL WHIRLWIND]

The pool's slimy water is reddish after the river of blood spills into it. A fire is lit underneath, and servants standing along the edges of the pool stir the liquid with a pole until it turns into a thick sludge, which is then cooled and ladled onto paper plates that were once books. In the evening, the carcasses gather around the pool table to eat the frozen sludge with a dollop of cream and a strawberry.

[WHAT IS CHURNING INSIDE THE HEAD, POKING THROUGH THE DOOR]

You're just fighting with yourself. From deep in your gut, jagged words erupt, and like the boy who fell from Granddad's balcony, they hurtle down onto the pages of the lexicon, the revolutionary one that the liar carries around and spits on: 'Let him have a chair,' the sultan says. The chair, a roll of tissue with which to wipe his shit.

Who are you? What are you? A phantom prancing inside an illusory body?

The silence of the slaughtered lambs alone will hold up the sultan's throne.

There is a large mirror across from the outer door as he is leaving. In the reflection, he can see he looks just the same as when he came in. Behind him, the place gradually transforms into a semblance of the sultan's palace.

He spits on the mirror until his mouth runs dry. 'How stupid I was.'

He makes a fist and slams it into the glass, and his hand goes right through. He kicks the glass and his foot comes out the other side. He leans his head in, and crosses over. When he turns around, the transformation is complete: there before him is the sultan's palace with its golden doors, its guards and its surveillance cameras. He looks about, finds a stone and hurls it at the mirrored glass. It shatters. He turns on his heels to make the difficult escape but finds himself in the old neighbourhood where children played football with a beat-up old ball and laundry hung from the balconies.

He smiles, scratches his head, and goes on his way, slowly. Ever so slowly.

جـ

The Arabic letter jeem (ج), and the elongated map with an arrow make up the logo of the Popular Front for the Liberation of Palestine (PFLP). The jeem is the first letter of the group's name in Arabic (Jabha); the map is that of Palestine; and the arrow signifies the right of return. The design is commonly believed to be the creation of Palestinian writer and artist Ghassan Kanafani, assassinated by Israel in 1972, but recent reports suggest that it was the brainchild of the Palestinian artist Vladimir Tamari.

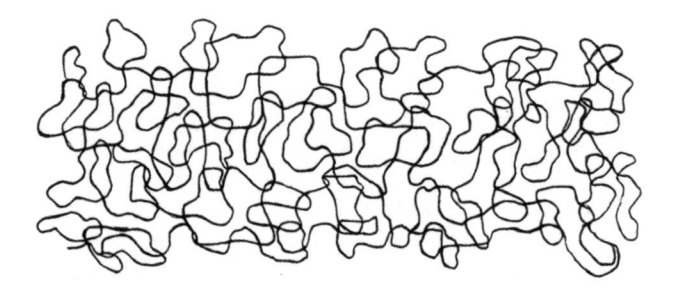

Aram Saroyan   August 14, 1959 #5 Paris

Menu of the Future   Raúl Guerrero

Room 25

	$
Bacon and two eggs	$1.55
Link Sausage and two eggs	$1.45
Beef Patty and two eggs	$1.65
Ham and two eggs	$1.75
Steak and two eggs	$2.00
Two Eggs	$1.05
One Egg	.90
Plain Omelettes	$1.50
Ham Omelettes	$1.60
Ham and Cheese Omelettes	$1.20
Cheese Omelettes	$1.25
Swiss Cheese Omelettes	$1.60
Denver Omelettes	$1.60
Bacon, Cheese and Tomato Omelettes	$1.60
(Served with or without Hash Browns, Toast and Jelly)	
Hot Cakes (3) 2.75 / Blueberry Hot Cakes	$1.00
Hot Cakes (short stack) 2.45 / Hot Cakes and Eggs	$1.00
French Toast 1.00	

TOAST AND PASTRY

Toast and Jelly	.75	English Muffin	.35
Danish Pastry (Heated)	.60		

SIDE ORDERS

Link Sausage	.70	Hash Browns	.45
Bacon	.75	Two Eggs	.60
Ham	.80	French Fries	.50

CEREALS

Choice of Cold Cereal with Milk	.60
Cooked Oatmeal with Milk	.70

JUICES AND BEVERAGES

Orange Juice (Small)	.30	Grapefruit Juice	.35
Orange Juice (Medium)	.40		
Orange Juice (Large)	.55	V-8 Juice	.35
Fresh Hot Coffee	.30	Tomato Juice	.35
Hot Tea	.30	Sanka	.30
Iced Tea	.30	Milk (Small)	.30
Hot Chocolate	.40	Milk (Large)	.40

MARCO POLO (SPECIAL) $4.98

Entree..... Choice of one

New York Steak...Meat Loaf Spanish...
served with mashed potatoes and gravy
salad or soup of the day.............
coffee..bread...water..................

	$2.40
	$2.70
	$1.60
	$1.50
	$1.25
Club Sandwich	$1.70
Hot Beef Sandwich	$1.60
Hot Turkey Sandwich	$1.60
Beef Dip	$1.50
B.B.Q. Ham or Beef	$1.50
Steak Sandwich	$1.80
Patty Melt	$1.50
Tuna Melt	$1.50
Lo Cal Plate	$1.50

Ground Sirloin Steak 1.80 / Fried Shrimp	2.50
Breaded Veal Cutlet 1.70	
(Above served with soup or salad)	

SANDWICHES

Hamburger	.90	Cold Turkey Sandwich	$1.20
Cheeseburger	1.00	Ham Sandwich	$1.20
Bacon-Lettuce-Tomato	1.15	Ham and Cheese	$1.30
Grilled Cheese	.80	Roast Beef Sandwich	$1.25
Denver Sandwich	1.00	Fried Ham and Egg	$1.35
Tuna Sandwich	$1.20	Fried Bacon and Egg	$1.35
Pastrami on Rye Bread	$1.20	Fried Egg Sandwich	.75

SALADS

Mixed Green Salad (Small)	.50	Mixed Green Salad (Large)	2.95
Chef's or Tuna Salad	1.65	Peach and Cottage Cheese	2.75
		Side of Cottage Cheese	.45

DESSERTS AND FOUNTAIN

Home Made Pie	.60	Soft Drinks .25 &	.35
Ice Cream (Per Dish)	.40	Malts and Shakes	.70
Sundaes	.60	(Extra Thick)	.80
Jello	.45	Floats	.55

Dear A,

The heat is so stifling here, can't quite breathe, lungs feel like the engine of a steaming locomotive. My body sweat tastes of chemicals, dry, wet hair.

RAUL MENDIA GUERRERO MARCH 1 - APRIL 1, 1978, THOMASLEWALLEN

MARCH 1 - 18: Sculpture and Photographs
MARCH 21 - APRIL 1: Drawings and Photographs
MARCH 25 (Sat): Videotapes

Dear Z,

It's cold in LA, 40 F., the radiator hasn't been turned on this winter. Need to get a down jacket, keep the bones from freezing over. My breath is spewing icicles, the paint is getting hard.

COVER: PROJECTED MENU, 1978

My thanks go to Morgan Thomas and Constance Lewallen —
Raul Guerrero
1978

Topagrafia is a draped cast of a recumbant body on a table. It is white and mute in the front gallery which is otherwise empty, black and white. No clues. It is an arresting and disturbing object and is evocative rather than frightening. Literal interpretations and subliminal associations.... It is meant to provide the viewer with a key to the unconscious....primordial.... Also, Topagrafia in Spanish is topography in English.

Cristales is a mechanized kaleidescope. By means of electricity, it lights and a chamber full of crystals turns, the crystals tumble, and the second, smaller and darker gallery is filled with an offbeat sound. Peering into the machine, the viewer sees the crystals fall into formations which are organic and abstract. The installation is completed with rayographs which depict a circle, a square, and a triangle combined in random compositions. The room is a subtly choreographed composition of classical geometric archetypal forms.

The drawings are white line on black paper. They are spare depictions of isolated instances in dreams, stylized and provoked into becoming specific images. They are, at the same time, cultural(like logos) and universal (like archetypes).

Photographs taken with the camera obscura and with a pinhole camera...diffused, negative images which are eerily lit, they are, in reality, pictures of ordinary places and things.

The artist and the gallery decided to present Guerrero's work in sections because it has many facets and is multi-dimensional. The installations are finely tuned images just as are the individual works on paper and the video tapes.... in each work the concern is with eliciting a specific subconscious response in the viewer. The eccentric, the ethnic or cultural, the personal, and the banal are removed from their usual context and transformed in to the particular and powerfully symbolic.

Dear Paul – This is a preliminary draft of the text we have written for the press release for the show. Comments please!

june 1972

life in the garment district isn't a bundle of joy,
as the saying goes, but living here in the city
is the ultimate paradox because it's natural to assume
that one will find his fame and glory but nothing
is further from the truth....living here one's will
is altered by the continuous stream of information,
this cannot help but effect the aesthetic process.
The materials available for reorganization are
manifest everywhere one looks,... here i think i've
at least solved part of the question of how the
magician in industria can participate with the natural
forces.... where perhaps the fetish can open the door
to conceive the storm.... now i'm just letting will
take it's course because this is the only way that I
will be able to see the reality, now i think i just
want them to functionas an entity that no previous
association or history, self contained and simple....
like the foam in the door....the time has come to allow
the items to bind themselves thru a natural evolution....
a three term relationship x (designer) + y (mass) +
z (natural effect) = a .... is an interchangeable
solution possible?

january 29, 1976

lately i've been reading the writer Thomas De
Quincey, <u>Diary of an English Opium Eater</u>, the
classic. Besides Homer, few in western culture
had used the anodyne to stimulate creativity.
Later, intellectuals in Europe began using the
hallucenogenic to stimulate their various aesthetic
quests, a prime example of this individual was the
writer Poe, author of the macabre classic in the
Victorian period. In a sense this man De Quincey
began it all.

Mayans, Arabs, Chinese and the Egyptians all used
some form of drugs to expand the unconscious mind,
marijuana, kif, opium, hashish, cocaine and
alcholic beverages, indigenous to each culture.
Is this why they were able to evolve like they did?

© RG 1978

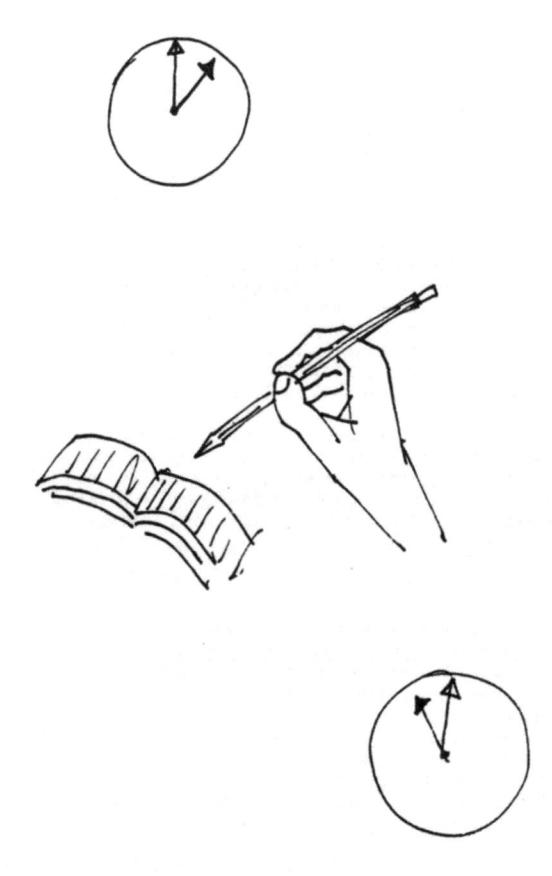

JULY 1973

Por muchos anos entro el polvo a aquellos cuartos que
sin resistencia se dejaron cubrir, cuartos llenos de
muebles de diferentes partes del mundo, alfombras orientales,
relojes antiguos con los numeros apenas visibles, cajas
de carton, llenas de articulos de muy distintos
lugares, en otros tiempos le llamaban la attencion
a sus collectionistas, mesas con bultos debajo de
savannaghas percudidas, amarillas con los anos,
camaras antiguas, machinas de coser, machinas de
escribir, bueno, estos cuartos tenian de todo lo que se
permite imajinar y desear con una vida de dinero, pero
ahora solamente el polvo tiene que ver con lo que pasara
de todo esto, se apila, apila, y apila.

UN SUEÑO ROMPIDO........ 1974

la noche negra me llevo por un camino blanco, a un
lugar que nunca avia visto, cada paso que daba me
llevaba a una ventana que me daba una vista distinta
de aquel camino, cada una tenia un a combinacion
de imagenes, un triangulo, cuadrado y un circulo, el
camino no tenia fin y las ventanas cambigban de forma
rapidamente.

Mi mujer quiere un par de guantes y un sombrero rojo,
solamente asi me va dejar ver la desnuda.

Africa continente misterioso. Tus mujeres de pieles
Negras, amarillas, azuls y el resto de los colores
de espectro......

May 1975

   The art that the society was developing had no parallel in the history of person kind. All of the materials that were used to develop it were the most synthetic possible. They had no straight lines, there were no seams or surface markings to indicate the technology that produced them. They had no beginning nor end. The most impressive of these was one that had been fabricated out of stainless steel and aluminum, representing the Holy Bible. Every page had been anodized and rewritten to change the context of the original scriptures. This work then, symbolized the ultimate esthetic acquisition for the art patron, to look at and contemplate.
   How long the suicidal direction that they were evolving into would continue no one could possibly know as they were so immersed in the style that it became more and more difficult to develop it into another form. There were some persons that were fighting the trend, but they were few and far between and in totality could not compensate for the rapid flow in the pravalent direction.

the dream had no end. The sky was yellow, pink, purple and indigo. The landscape was the color of rusted steel. The stainless steel roads glistened in the escenario, they crisscrossed the land like a web.

A metallic rocket shot through the sky and quickly disappeared into time.

A green glow cut through the evening sky, a demonstration that an artist was having of his light work. It pulsated to the rhythm of the star Denarius in the Orion constellation.

Time, time, time, time

August 1977   Given to the Universe

It was seen falling from the black sky. As it came closer and more luminoscent it became so much so that the night sky became bright as day. An extraterrestial object, glowing colors never before seen in this epoch of the planet. What could it be? Was the question everyone asked. The end of the world, a new weapon from the reds or..... an invasion from outer space. It became evident that the anticipated explosion, if indeed it was a weapon, did not occur...it landed on the outskirts of the city, the largest that humans had ever created - Modular Structure Nueve. The walls of this magnificent environment were slick as ice, fortunately they weren't because the heat of the intrusion from outer space would have melted them. No, the walls were made of an heat resistnat alloy developed back in the 25th century. To repulse the new weapons that the reds had developed.

The Walls were suddenly crowded with rubberneckers come to see what the commotion from the sky was all about...all that could be seen were millions of luminoscent dials from the time pieces that everyone wore. On closer inspection it could be noted that the luminosity might also be coming from the radioactive teeth that were the current vogue among the affluent in this city.

What they saw on the metropolis' edge, squashing one of the tomato fields that were planted around the city for miles, was.... an antiquity from the past, that everyone immediately recognized, as even photographs of this were the ultimate collectors item. An irridescent 1952 Nash ramble.

The sun was harnessed to provide the electrical needs for the societies of the planet. The energy and resources were equally distributed, making the planet utopian. ree from economic instability, free from hunger, no longer tied by necessity

to the drudgeries of life, of having to work for

a living.

This is written to you
How many times have I tried to
find words
To put them down in tangible
letter form
The memory of you wets my eyes
Tommy Dorsey and a young Frankie
intensify thisfeeling and
it gets worse
I walk around at 4-5 A.M. reading
Hollywwo novels, typing, thinking,
anticipating
Going out to a party the crowds
make me lonelier, I drink wine,
sink into oblivion, throw up
Eat a fast food dives
Sleep for a few hours
and it all begins again
Two fly by night jobs keep
me in a little money
Camera equipment goes to some dealer
at hardly the price purchased for
Days turn into un-realities,dreams of
you intensify them
Bags forming under my eyes
Smiling what is that
A t-sirt stripped dyed pink
black silk pants high-heeled
shoes come off

January, 1977
Inglewood, California

Mercury vapor lights illuminate Century Boulevard,
the shiny cars glistened as slithery, beautiful
black women inquire about a date.
The planes overhead on their way to the port
roar by continually, their noise never ceases,
man I'm about to go insane.
Winchell's for breakfast, it's not continental,
one glazed, one chocolate covered cake and
a large cupe of coffee, black liquid reflects
my existence.
The center of the vortex, going round and round.

September 25, 1984
San Gabriel Etla

Pools of water reflect the wilderness
of the path I walk along
led by a young child
to the home of Queta,
Enriquetta,
She owns the mill
for which she wants one mill
translated five m's
We talk, she gives
her husband a massage his
arms look weak and his
face is sallow
No more playing for him, lolly says,
he fucked up his liver, drinking
smoking, bad diet supplemented
by coca-cola
Queta,Queta, Enriquetta
he's here now
but not for long
hard as you rub the damage is done,
I leave thru the path,
water reflects the sky above,
the foliage trickles
to the ground,
and in the distance the
cry of the burro
reverberates thru
the valley and guides
me thru the appiration
that I now see.

Rarotonga
~~Ror-o-tanga~~

Arrived in the early, just before the sunrise. The boat that i've been traveling on made very good time. A man in a reed canoe came along side and took my camera equipment and my baggage. And said good by to the captain of the ship, who in turn wished me the best. As we rowed away from the schooner the sun came up over the horizon, and spread a band of gold over the ocean surface in a fraction of a second. The weather here is a milder type than in the previous islands. Warm and humid not dry. The ocean surface in the cove is crystalline and clear. The vegetation is very dense along the shore line There are an infinite numer of fire flies on theshore and it glistens

P.S.1
curator/ for show at P.S.1

DANTE

The Way Ahead is Spring   Velimir Khlebnikov
                            translated from the Russian
                            by Natasha Randall

Room 26

On this, the day of Blue Bears

Running along placid lashes,
I can see, through dark-blue waters,
in the cups of my eyes, a call to wake.

To the silver teaspoon of my reaching eyes
I am proffered the sea, a storm petrel above;
I see a feathered Russia, flying into noisy waves,
Between unfamiliar eyelashes.

But the love-sky sea has flipped
Someone's sail in the round-blue water,
And then, the first storm vanishes

Into hopelessness, and the way ahead is spring.

В этот день голубых медведей,
Пробежавших по тихим ресницам,
Я провижу за синей водой
В чаше глаз приказанье проснуться.

На серебряной ложке протянутых глаз
Мне протянуто море и на нем буревестник;
И к шумящему морю, вижу, птичая
Русь Меж ресниц пролетит неизвестных.

Но моряной любес опрокинут
Чей-то парус в воде кругло-синей,
Но зато в безнадежное канут
Первый гром и путь дальше весенний.

Fly! A gentle word, so pretty

Fly! A gentle word, so pretty
You wash your snout with your paws
And sometimes on a whim
Eat a letter.

Муха! нежное слово, красивое,
Ты мордочку лапками моешь,
А иногда за ивою
Письмо ешь.

Zangzei (from a Supersaga in Twenty Planes)

[FRAGMENT]

*As a butterfly who has flown
Into the room of human life,
I leave the script of my dust
At harsh windows, a prisoner's scrawl
On a strict glass of rock.
The wallpaper of human life
So boring and grey!
No transparent windows!
I have erased my blue glow, polka dots,
A blue wing-storm, fresh at first,
Disperses pollen, wilts my wings,
Now transparent and rigid,
I beat, tired, at man's window.
Eternal numbers sound there,
A call from the motherland,
This number is being called:
Return to the other numbers.*

Мне, бабочке, залетевшей
В комнату человеческой жизни,
Оставить почерк моей пыли
По суровым окнам, подписью узника
На строгих стеклах рока.
Так скучны и серы
Обои из человеческой жизни!
Окон прозрачное нет!
Я уж стер свое синее зарево, точек узорь
Мою голубую бурю крыла — первую
    свежесть
Пыльца снята, крылья увяли и стали
    прозрачны и жестки,
Бьюсь я устало в окно человека
Вечные числа стучатся оттуда
Призывом на родину, число зовут к числам
    вернуться.

white dog & an eight horse sun   Edwina Attlee

Room 27

white dog

Walking into chirruping fields the little He watched the families
carry a small whiteness along the head
I was full slipping but I could see
where they were from there was hanging
He followed not a bone
they were carrying the from
the little He watched
my hands   and Daddy
feet blue   scene steeper   but ok
I walked white
Fantasia Hill as when on go my footings
up and pointy polite
I got my shock when I saw you Daddy
Flowers flowers rocks and a rush-eyed Bambi on the edge
the whiteness disappeared
I said Are Sounds Coming?
the families were still
Both of the time there was an intolerable head out there
a bird where flowers were clouds
it veered up   Daddy said are we Up or Down?
I blew a secret into my socks
white dog dirty and white

an eight horse sun

which honestly
made me nervous
beauty can be VERY LOUD
and blue goes on and on

three kindnesses – a toast
and as they raised it
you could see each glinting person
hiding behind themselves sleek as boards

I prepared my inner life

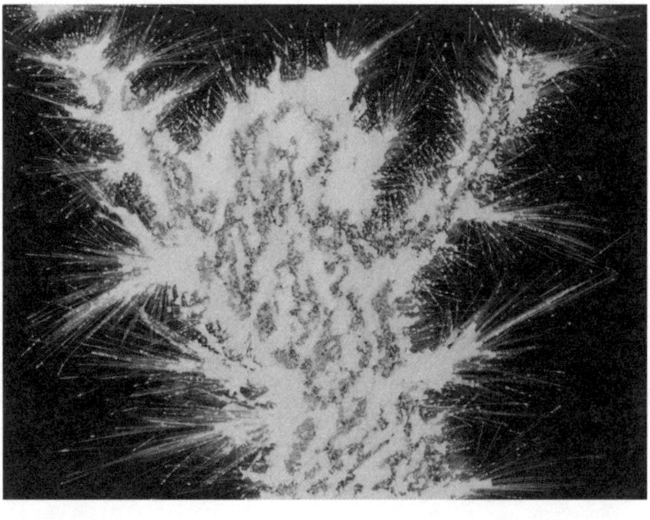

Timeshare   Aidan Moffat

Room 28

I'll just be a second, she says, and retreats to the office under four big clocks. New York, Sydney, Tokyo and Aberfoyle all ticktock in sync while the brood and their mother go for a swim: I have come to complain. I'd hoped I might survive a week without wi-fi, but we've been twenty-nine hours in this webless void and I need to know the world still turns. The lobby looks less swish these days, even though it looks just the same. Its decor is nostalgia: a curling stone on a hearth evokes the long-thawed rink, since replaced with a *sumptuous spa that's just the ticket if you're looking to unwind*; a framed, weathered photo of a helipad in summer is a reverie of ritzier times. The girl returns to tell me what I already know – *I'm sorry about this, but we have a really slow signal and all I can suggest is that you keep trying, the lobby's probably the best place*. Four fucking stars! I should be angry, but she's beautiful. I wonder if she's local or she's staying here too, working her whole summer break to pay next term's rent while her callow #boyf goes back to Mummy's. The poor boy's clueless, his wettest dreams naught to what she'll find inside these twelve warm weeks. But I'm just another grey dad to her, just another neutered duty, so I sink into a vast leather couch and attempt to log on again, just to make the girl feel useful. I remain marooned. I pocket my phone, exit through the patio and stroll through glistening mizzle, over grassy humps where the crazy golf lies entombed, past a giant draughts board that once was chess, and stop to muse by the filled-in pool. Long ago drained, packed with earth and rock, you can see the sawn-off ladders poke through the dirt on opposite sides, and the adjoining jacuzzi now sprouts flowers, a horticulture hot-tub. An outdoor swimming pool in Scotland was never going to last. I walk round the one-bed lodges where we ended up one teenage year, me and Susan and Gillian and David and who else? Matthew? Or did he just go that one time? My family's usual timeshare had been given away for the week due to lack of communication and assumed nonchalance, so my mum phoned up angry and made them sort something pronto for us libidinous juveniles with eyes of desire and boxes of booze. But the replacement lodge had just one double bedroom, so I gallantly offered to share it with my recently sundered Susan while the rest made do with the living room pull-out and couch. Sympathy sex with the ex was my foxy scheme, but she was having none of it. One crapulous afternoon I fell asleep with the radio on, Steve Wright in the Afternoon, and he'd just played 'I'm Too Sexy,' the first time I'd heard it and I smiled into a slumber.* An hour later, I was shaken awake by fretful hands: *Wake up! Wake up! Are you okay? Are you all right?* They'd held a séance as I siesta'd, and some conjured ghoul told them I was dying. *Aye, dyin' for a shag!* We floated in the loch with lifejackets and Gillian screamed as unseen fish swam between her legs. I wonder who's in that lodge right now, and what aestival ardour abides unsated on this sultry, damp day. I walk across the car park and into the Spa & Gym, where once that lobby curling stone slid over scrubbed ice and laserdiscs were racked by the door and rented when the weather turned. A laserdisc player in every lodge – such 80s glamour! – and wee pubescent me on the couch watching *Grease 2* while the rain pissed down on the mountains. It's not as good as the first one, of course, but it does have a young Michelle Pfeiffer in black skin-tights and that gorgeous 'Girl for All Seasons' song: *I'll be your girl for all seasons, all the year through, your girl for all seasons, 'cause I love to be everything to you...* Aye, wet young days were great here, with the patio door slid wide open and me in a dark corner with some *Scottish Ghost Stories* and *Choose Your Own Adventures* – fast forward some years and it's lovelorn whisky over crushed heart as the sun sets on the sad songs by Sam & Dave. That was me and John, grown men by then, downing shots and toasting sorrow. Above the spa and up the stairs is the old Bonspiel bar, named for the curling tournaments once spectated through windows where walls are now, but you can still observe the indoor pool from the dining area so I walk over and tap on the glass, but it takes a few attempts to catch my family's attention: the children have made new friends. Upon their mother's orders they shrug vague waves in my direction then get back to screaming and splashing, so I take an afternoon table on the evening's dance floor. 25 YEARS SERVICE! shouts a poster to my right – they've had the same DJ since I was a boy, and I think I might even recognise his grey, photocopied face. In 1990 we were seventeen on our first holiday sans guardians, and this room was its heart. I think they were both called Claire – I fancied the brunette but the blonde was into me. *I'll just be a moment*, she said, as she danced over to the DJ. We were all in this very bar, four boys from Falkirk – or maybe it was three, there was definitely Gary and definitely Matthew – and three girls from far enough away,

---

*   'I'm Too Sexy' (cat. no. SNOG 1), a novelty dance tune about a vainglorious male model whose intoxicating erotic allure precludes him from an array of activities and outfits, was Right Said Fred's debut single, released in the summer of 1991. Formed two years earlier by brothers Richard and Fred Fairbrass, the band would release many singles in the coming years but never repeated the success of this first hit, which topped the charts in six countries, including Australia and the USA, but sadly not their native United Kingdom. The single enjoyed six weeks at number two in the Official UK Top 40, being consistently held off the top spot by the slushy, trite Bryan Adams ballad '(Everything I Do) I Do It For You,' which spent a staggering sixteen weeks at number one, the longest reign in British chart history. And don't I fucking know it. I was working in the record shop that summer, and every Friday around 5:30pm when we'd started cashing up, there would be a stream of drunkards blundering through our doors just in the nick of time to buy a copy for the wife or bird by way of apology for spending all their wages or dole in the pub. We were heroes. We were lifesavers. Together with Bryan Adams, we must have repaired countless broken romances in that fiery summer of '91.

at the last dance of the week, playing pool like pros and enduring shite music. A few pints ago we'd laughed about the songs we hated most, and soon the distant drum machine and soft organ of 'The Lady In Red' tiptoed across the dance floor,* and the DJ dedicates the song to me: a special request from my holiday honey. I didn't want to dance but I had no choice, she had me by the hands and she was pulling me in, all swimming-pool eyes and sun-blushed skin as we shrugged along with mums and dads. Then the lights faded up and the bar shut down, so we all took our dregs to the outdoor pool where the grass grows now. And even as she let my legs brush hers underwater, even as we dunked and splashed and laughed, even as I replaced the strap of her swimsuit *like a true gent*, I knew that nothing would happen. But those are the best memories, aren't they? The stories where nothing happens: the flops and the failures. Wrapped in stolen white towels, we walked back barefoot and claimed we'd keep in touch under only half a moon, but it was Brown Claire I wrote to when the photos were developed – she never replied, even though we'd shared a sauna. And all those beer cans piled up by the patio, a monument to adolescent appetites and a warning to passing mothers – I've still got that photo of Matthew in front of it somewhere, double thumps up against a wall of empty tins. His funeral was good, if such a thing can be. I didn't even know they allowed humanists in the crematorium under all those big crucifixes. *We have come here today not to mourn but to celebrate*. A solitary, private man, the celebrant said, but I remember going out and always laughing, I remember weekly cheap Chilean wine mixed with even cheaper orange juice secretly drunk in my bedroom then dancing at the Penthouse to abrasive songs that can't be danced to, and every Sunday there was Burger King for lunch as we anatomised the night and prepared our alibis for school on Monday, I remember making tapes and swapping books, his talent for drawing and that wee sketch of longhaired me all bored in class, I remember the brightest wit and a maestro of words, the *Pleasure Enquiry Cavern* and the *Corkscrew of D(eath)*, and I remember speed and ecstasy and arms in the air, and all those Saturday nights at the Art School and early mornings after till I passed out on the couch in his student kitchen, and I remember kindness and consideration but strength and anger too. And it sounded like he'd never changed in those ten years since I saw him, but then who really does? And the send-off song was perfect, it was 'Everything Flows' – *You get older*

---

*   Chris de Burgh released his first music in 1974 to moderate success, but it would take twelve years and seven albums before this mawkish global smash (cat. no. AM 331) made him a household name. Released in June of 1986, the song would spend seventeen weeks in the UK Singles Chart, three of those at number one. I fucking hated it at the time but it clearly left a scar – the story above happened four summers later. Now, though, I feel a strange, wistful affection for it. I might even sing along in the kitchen or car, but I don't think I'm joking anymore.

every year, but you don't change, I don't notice you changing – and I sat there smiling at a funeral, I was happy, it was beautiful, and David was there and Gary was there, turns out he lives round the corner now, and you always think *Do I look as old as them?* and of course you do, then maybe you wonder why you never kept in touch, but fuck Friends Reunited and fuck Facebook, time passes, we drift, and that's it.* And that Brian Cox meme was quoted on the program under Matthew's picture, a picture of a boy I used to know with Photoshopped grey hairs and crow's feet, or so it seemed to me, and it said: *Our story is the story of the universe. Everything was assembled by the forces of nature in the first few minutes of the life of the universe, transformed in the hearts of stars or created in their fiery deaths. And when you die, those pieces will be returned to the universe in the endless cycle of death and rebirth. What a wonderful thing it is to be part of the universe.* I try to log on to the wi-fi again but I know it won't work, while a flashing, bleeping puggy tries to lure me into gambling. Then I chuckle when I hear an ersatz Cyndi Lauper sing 'Time After Time,' the timing's just too good. It's one of those karaoke knock-offs that seep from hotel speakers, with cheaper vocals, cheaper keyboards, cheaper drum machine. Why would anyone settle for that? It's not real. It's not true. The menu looks pretty dull and my family will be here soon. A waitress approaches but she can tell I'm not quite ready to order and she says, *Sorry, would you like a little longer?*

---

*   Teenage Fanclub's debut single, released in 1990 on the Paperhouse label (cat. no. PAPER 003), may arguably lack the sophistication of their later work, but to my mind it remains the sunlit Scots' finest song. In fact, to my mind, it remains one of the finest songs ever: I think I'd like it played at my funeral, too. I had the 7", in its little blue disco bag with the skull and crossbones sunglasses photo on the label, but donated it to local romance. Gary fancied Denise – I think this was a couple of years later – and Denise loved the Fannies, but she'd missed out on the 7" as it was pretty limited at the time and sold out quickly in Scotland, so I gave my copy to Gary in the hope that it would aid his blossoming courtship. I don't think they lasted too long, though. Denise was at the funeral too, with Annette and Linsey, and I would have loved a post-cremation pint with them but they left very sharp, they seemed pretty upset. But it struck me afterwards how that song connected us all, and how music is like a sort of social superglue: whatever happens, wherever we end up, there's always this invisible sonic thread that connects us, a tune we all react to the same way, a sound that instantly echoes a time we've forgotten to remember. Life is finite but music's forever, and maybe, within those chords and melodies and words, we can all live a little longer.

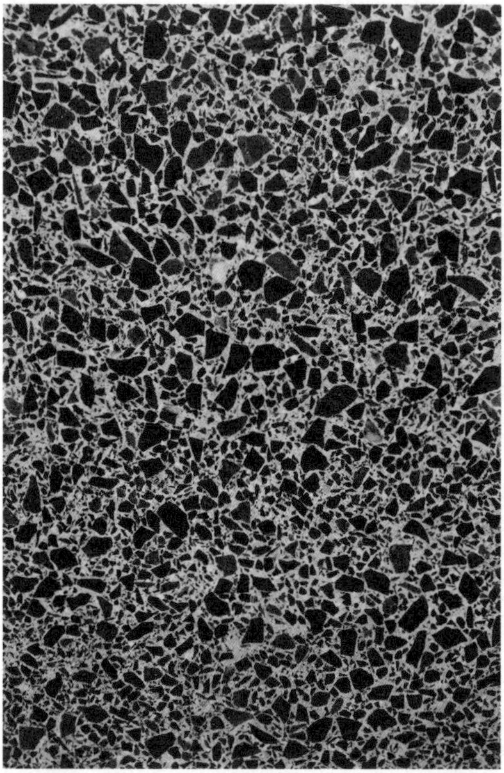

Waiting for the Ferry, Lousay   Lesley Harrison

Room 29

of the parts, fairly well, the cold is eating me, the wet too, at least I presume so, I'm far. My rheumatism in any case is no more than a memory, it hurts me no more than my mother's did, when it hurt her. Eye ravening patient in the haggard vulture face, perhaps it's carrion time. I'm up here and I'm down here, under my gaze, foundered, eyes closed, ear cupped against the sucking peat, we're of one mind, all of one mind, always were, deep down, we're fond of one another, we're sorry for one another, but there it is, there's nothing we can do for one another. One thing at least is certain, in an hour it will be too late, in half-an-hour it will be night, yet it's not, not certain, what is not certain, absolutely certain, that night prevents what day permits, for those who know how to go about it, who have the will to go about it, and the strength, the strength to try again. Yes. It will be night, the mist will clear, I know my mist, for all my distraction, the wind freshen, and the whole night sky open over the mountain, with its lights, including the Bears, to guide me once again on my way, let's wait for night. All mingles, times and tenses, at first I only had been here, now I'm here still, soon I won't be here yet, toiling up the slope, or in the bracken by the wood, it's larch, I don't try to understand, I'll never try to understand any more, that's what you think, for the moment I'm here, always have been, always shall be, I won't be afraid of the big words any more, they are not big. I don't remember coming, I can't go, all my little company, my eyes are closed and I feel the wet humus harsh against my cheek, my hat is gone, it can't be gone far, or the wind has swept it away, I was attached to it. Sometimes it's the sea, other times the mountains, often it was the forest, the city, the plain too, I've flirted with the plain too,

                        I'm up here
                        eyes closed,

                                        nothing we can do for
                                                an hour
            in half-an-hour it will be night

                        the mist will clear
                        the wind freshen

            and   soon
            I won't be here
                                        I'll never
                        shall
                        not

                the wind
                the sea, o

Word ⟶ Object

It seems that the past, present, and future are indeed very tangible, that words can be translated into corporeal existents.

J.A. Hurguira
Sept '74

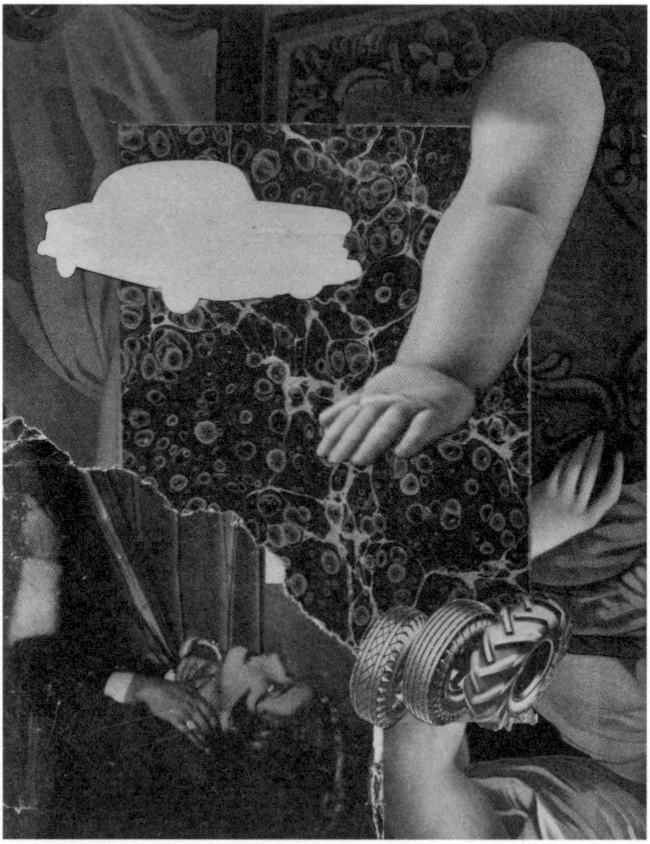

A Working Week   Oliver Bancroft

Room 30

*Pages from a pillow book,
in which the painter rises
and works with first sun...*

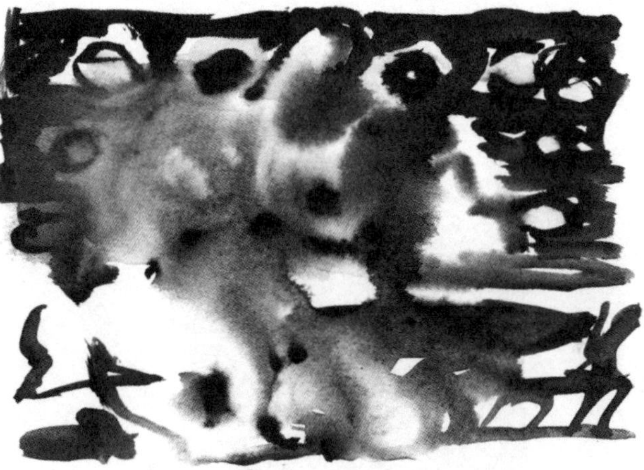

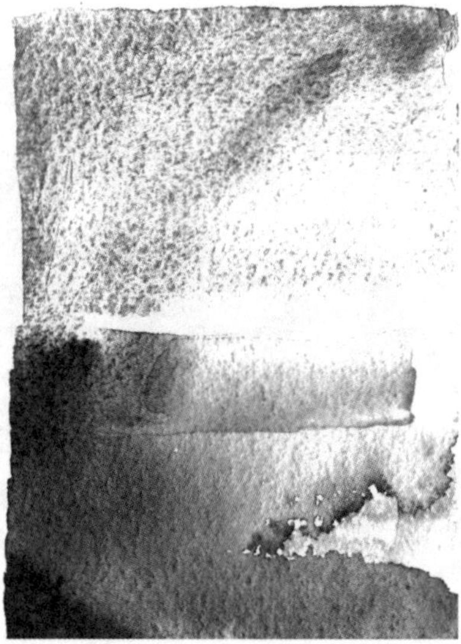

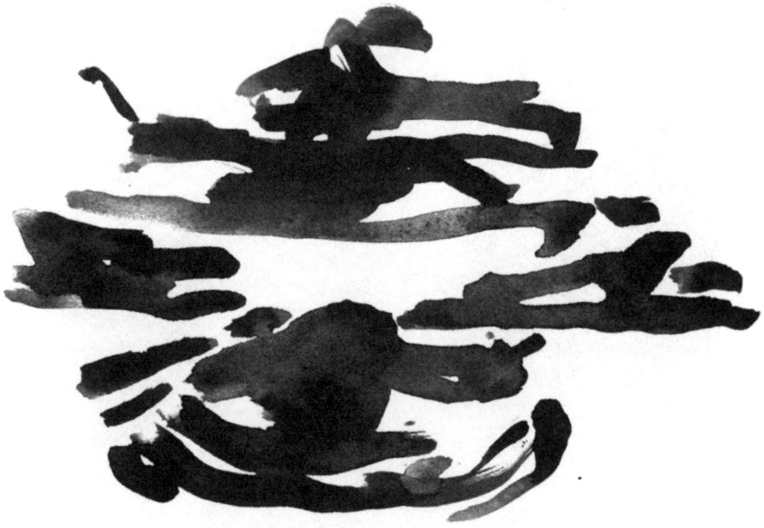

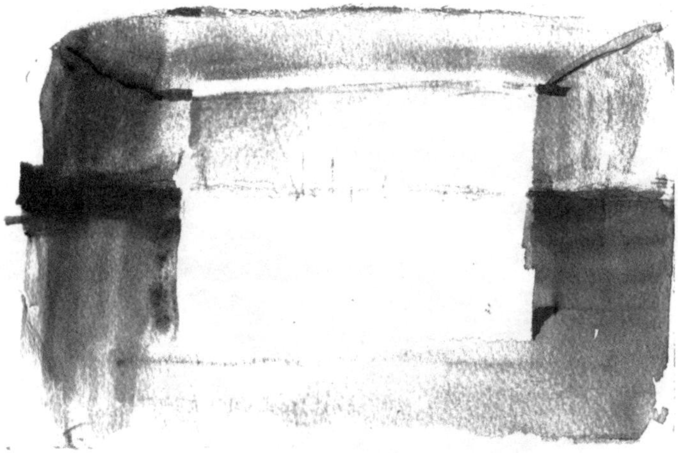

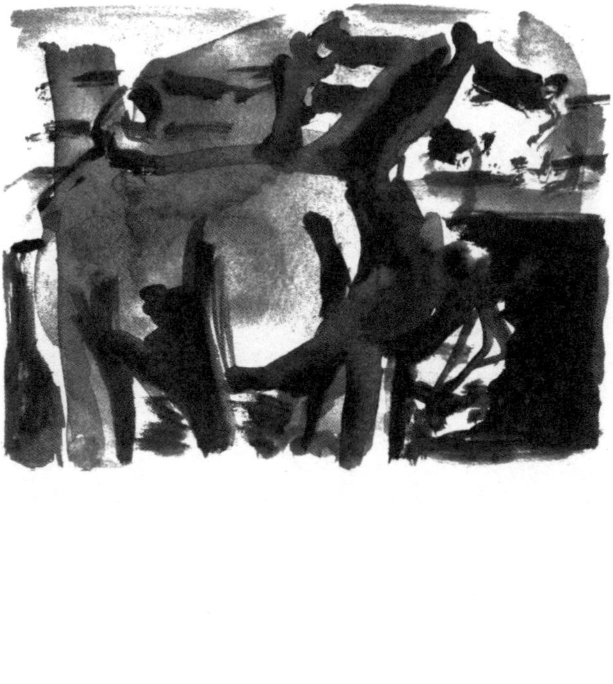

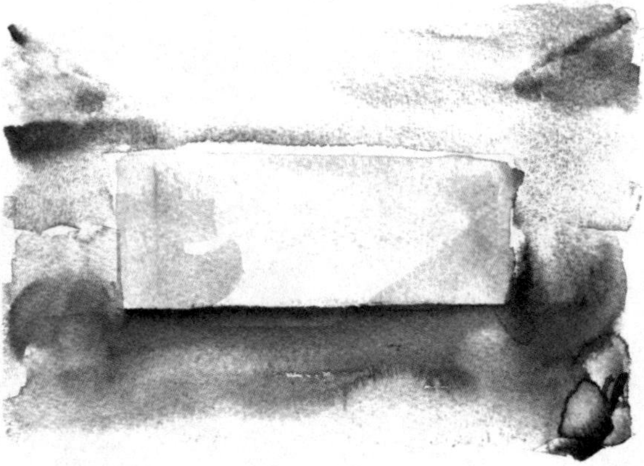

                                                                    all
that is on the land, in comparison with what is in the sea, is

                                                              loud
                                                              smoke

Greenery   Will Eaves

Room 31

I will always be a year younger than my schoolfellows. They will grow up and I won't, even though I must age like everyone else. They will have deep voices and hair, thick eyebrows, calves with a topography; I can only affect a vocal maturity. I have things to say but do not like hearing myself speak: I'll enjoy acting all my life because acting is a truthful affectation; one speaks on the understanding that one is modulated by a 'character.' And because it is something one does but does not have to witness. My legs stay smooth and slender. Because I have been bumped up a year – because I knew how to read and write early on – I will inexplicably miss out on the 'cough and drop,' the routine physical inspection to check on the process of puberty. My balls will not be weighed and held by a man for another nine years and I will always wonder if there is something wrong with me. Even writing this is a perilous sort of confession: I will read it over and hear a small voice piping away, an echo that is shaming, and peculiar, because its mental acoustic is also much to be desired. Because my refuge from all kinds of strange accusation and self-doubt will be the place anterior to the page – the inside of my head.

~

Creatures, man included, retreat prior to a change: in this tradition of contemplation and recoil will be found works such as *The Winter's Tale*, Boethius's *De Consolatione Philosophiae*, dramas of childhood survival such as Laura Ingalls Wilder's *The Long Winter*, and every tale of growing up – the rich English tradition of embarrassment. The latter involves a mild, comical but nonetheless enforced retreat. The adolescent falls back into self-consciousness when his classmates reach sexual maturity but he does not. Those of us who were late developers know instinctively that it is brute capacity and not any combination of attributes that makes for desirability. For many adolescents, the body is a revelation; for as many, because the body disappoints them, it is the mind. Puberty makes us watchful. It unlocks the sanctuary of study, for which probably we are never sufficiently grateful.

~

People telling you their dreams needn't be so boring. The reason they are, usually, very boring is that they leave out the interesting part, which is how they felt while they were dreaming. Dream narrative is a special, slippery sort of narrative, where content is much less important than shades of feeling, on which subject many analysts are silent.

The defloration of your cousin, who turns out to be your mother, and then your daughter, by a centaur is nowhere near as upsetting as the vase of flowers you found terrifying.

~

What is wrong with wanting to 'relate' to a character, when reading fiction? Well, the verb is suspect. It fudges the distinction between understanding and liking a character. We ought always to seek to understand x – in reading as in life – and not until we have made that effort can we expect any real sympathy to arise; but the reader who wishes to 'relate,' who seeks likeable characters and situations, is barely reading at all. He or she is seeking a vindication of his own character or her own likeability, a tactic one might call 'reading for reassurance,' which masks a fear of the truth. Such relating persons are noticeably and *personally* affronted when they glimpse something nasty, or indeed hateful, in the books they so wanted to like. The glimpse is usually an instance of involuntary understanding, of self-exposure, which brings on a minor paroxysm of guilt. It is not that these sensitive readers fail to relate to the bitter mother or the unattractive child; indeed, the relationship is obvious to them: these characters are the objects of their contempt, and the revelation of a talent for contempt must always be unwelcome. La Rochefoucauld said: 'we often forgive those that have injured us, but we can never pardon those that we have injured,' meaning 'those we have injured are a perpetual reminder of our cruelty and for that reason become hateful to us,' meaning, guilt is often the motive for hatred as much as the result of it. 'I didn't relate to any of the characters' means 'I caught sight of my rage in the mirror.'

~

A literary convention is a retrospective abstraction. It exists only in relation to the experiment or the revolution that overturns it. It doesn't exist until someone does something new and you see how far you've come. Form and content, in other words. There is a widespread misconception about form, as the poet Elizabeth Jennings once pointed out: it is not a jelly-mould into which one pours content. Rather, the two things are coeval. Form will arise to express content, and the established forms (sonnets, novels, collage) are those that, like an evolutionarily convergent body shape, have by long trial shown themselves to be optimally expressive.

~

The novel is the autobiography of the imagination.

~

The house on De Carle Street is called 'Ephemera.' A restored shotgun bungalow, it is not noticeably different to many other houses in the locality but for the meticulously repainted weatherboarding, which seems not to flake or age in this harsh climate, and the two cane chairs on the front porch that are, a little closer inspection reveals, chained together.

~

The American modernist poet Laura Riding was odd, possibly wicked. She called herself Finality, came between Robert Graves and Nancy Nicholson, jumped out of a window, drove Katherine Jackson (her second husband's first wife) mad, stood by as the poor woman was helped into a straitjacket, and in her reactionary zeal to construct a *Dictionary of Received Meanings* seemed to want to help words to the same fate – but before all of that she also spoke feelingly and movingly out of her experience as Laura Reichenthal, daughter of an immigrant Polish tailor, new born to American English: 'Poetry is the place where the fear of speaking in strange ways can be left behind.' That strikes me as true. Riding is pointing out the element of inadvertency that comes about when we speak a new tongue; what we wish to say may not be what the words we use are actually saying. Similarly, poetry is compressed meaning, yes, but it is also the meaning inadvertently effected by compression, the uncontainable heat that leaks out of usage.

~

In Virginia Woolf's essay on 'The Pastons and Chaucer,' from *The Common Reader*, we hear of the cultured but feckless eldest son of Margaret Paston (Sir John Paston, 1442–1479) being distracted by a book – Chaucer's *Canterbury Tales*. He prefers the poet's ordered sensualism, the pungency of his swift characterisations, to the shapeless encounters of real life. But Chaucer's verse narrative only has this effect, Woolf says, because, although it is poetry, its author 'has his eye fixed upon the road before him,' on 'the life that was being lived,' the farmyards, the haycocks, the crooked clerics, and so on. The force of distraction is exerted equally on the reader by the book he is reading, and on the writer by the life he is leading – the people he meets, the things he does. And it is a force with consequences for the writer, in particular: for should he be insufficiently distracted by life, his book will be powerless to divert. This may be why writers always complain about not having enough time in which to write: they know in their hearts that writing is everything else. A reader must be distracted by a world, a writer by the world.

~

The history of art follows the decline of the representative power of the model. From the Gods are derived types, from types individuals, from individuals, characteristics, and from characteristics the approximation of characteristics, which is to say virtuality. For Woolf, Greek tragic heroes are the true originals: art, in Homer and Aeschylus, is tied to life by means of incontestable symbol. Chaucer's characters are varieties, by comparison; the art of the *Canterbury Tales* points to life which is particoloured and profuse. By the early twentieth century, the artist can say or do nothing conclusive about reality and must resort to a new kind of imaginative representation in order to discover the truth: art supersedes life. And so, to the present, in which reality is provisional and everything virtual: now, art cancels life, and in so doing the cycle starts afresh. The last letter to be written by a human hand will, God-like, represent everything in the Anthropocene that preceded it.

~

Roadies wear their heavy-metal T-shirts like skins or hospital gowns. They move like sciatical trolls or creatures of unpopular myth, with sad eyes and some subconsciously pressing resentment, through warm drizzle. At the grey intersection of Lygon and Albion, one heads for the music pub across the road with a box of beers balanced on his stomach. He is wearing a leather jerkin laced at the side, which puts me in mind of West Country cider festivals *circa* 1975. The whole world is his tureen and he plays (sound off) upon its ladle.

~

The critic James Wood says that novels came into being when the 'soliloquy turned inward.' This is an arresting and debatable insight. Dramatic soliloquies proved perfectly capable of becoming dramatic verse for the page (Milton's *Samson Agonistes*) without turning into novels. A more convincing antecedent is the letter. Novels began when the personal mode of address – the private journal, the letter, the letter of news, the paper of correspondence – went public and became journalism. A tension then existed between public address (rhetoric, canon, theatre, law, propaganda) and a startling, paradoxical new mode of witness – the confidential revelation – which depended for its effect on the increasingly literate audience's sense of what it was like to receive, *and read*, a letter of interest. (The sustaining fiction of the epistolary novel, especially, is that it contains a whole series of 'exclusives' – letters not intended for publication.) It is not yet clear what will happen to novels now that everyone writes emails and no one reads them.

~

W. H. Auden's cheek is underrated: it is an ideal mix of the critically acute and the naïve. He writes speeches and poems in the voices and manners of famous operatic and Shakespearean characters, in part because he thinks this is what Caliban (for example) would have sounded like if that scatterbrain Shakespeare hadn't got in the way with all of his cloudy metaphysics, but also because he believes in the dramatic creations as people. So, 'Caliban to the Audience,' from *The Sea and the Mirror*, is at once a literary annotation – a masterpiece of satirical periphrasis in the late style of Henry James – and a real address, a lecture given by a dazzling weirdo.

~

William Golding's second novel was produced quickly, in the warm glow of satisfaction and confidence that followed the successful publication of *Lord of the Flies*. He was still a secondary-school teacher at the time (the early 1950s), and he wrote *The Inheritors* with ease during his lunch breaks. Like his first novel, it is interested in primal encounters, but whereas in *Lord of the Flies* the subject is the latent savagery of the human animal – our ability, in the right circumstances, to regress – here, the imaginative emphasis is on the dignity and vulnerability of our forebears, the Neanderthals; or, the People. But 'dignity' is perhaps the wrong word – being, in this instance, a reminder of human status – because Golding's remarkable achievement is to have imagined a Neanderthal point-of-view that is almost pure feeling and instinct, more than animal (the Neanderthals are certainly emotional) yet without the higher planning functions of self-awareness that permit reflection as they also permit craft, duplicity and the development of hunting technology. Lok, Mal, Fa, Ha and Liku are not 'savages,' noble or otherwise; they are not simply uncivilised. They are, rather, prehistoric and, to an important degree, pre-Lapsarian. We are their Fall. The epochal moment this novel dramatises is the encounter of the unreasoning with the reasoning. Golding's People may arguably *think*, after some fashion, but they cannot develop a *thought process*; they have, instead, an evolved ability to recognise, which includes a feeling for the passing of time (and for their place in it). This allows them to relocate tracks and pathways, the cliff overhang which is their summer home, and to preserve simple rituals. Time is a renewing cycle; their primitive religion, centred on an earth goddess, Oa, is a manifestation of this cycle. And the cyclical nature of their world dictates the way they communicate, via the semi-telepathic sharing of 'pictures' which make sense or fail to make sense according to their place in the recognisable cycle of life. It is a language of great transparency and sensory intensity. Words, by contrast, are unreliable: Lok, the least intelligent male, has many words but fewest pictures. Fa, the cleverest of the clan, talks less but sees more. And yet she connects images quasi-syntactically: she 'knows,' as Lok does not, that the new creatures in the woods are dangerously different. What is that difference? Part of it has again to do with temporality. The pale 'bonefaces' whose grey eyes peer between the leaves, who abduct Liku and kill both Ha and the Old Woman, inhabit a new realm of comparative meaning – history. Their grasp of time – our grasp of it – is linear as well as cyclical, and that linearity permits notions of cause and effect to come into existence, makes possible feats of recollection and calculation that are not just beyond the Neanderthals but baffling to them. Time's metaphorical Arrow is also a real arrow, Golding points out, tipped with connotations of predestiny, conquest and defeat – but when the bonefaces fire such an arrow at Lok, he sees it as a thrown twig, not a designed weapon. Purpose, let alone purpose to harm, is an alien concept. He experiences fear and has the 'confused sense that the twig was some kind of gift.' The action of *The Inheritors* is fairly limited: the People return from the sea to their summer shelter in the woods (based on Savernake Forest in Wiltshire). The road home has changed: a log has been moved; Mal, the elder of their clan, falls in the water, sickens, dies and is buried. The People find food, but hunger is not the only threat. New men are stalking them. They are divided by the new men and attacked. Only Fa and Lok escape, and follow the tribe of new men with the vague idea of retrieving two captives, young Liku and the clan's baby. They mount a vigil in trees overlooking an encampment. Their rescue bid fails and they are hunted down. Fa perishes and the book ends with Lok, glimpsed from the point of view of *Homo sapiens*, trotting back and forth, scratching his chin, flailing at the water with a leafy bough, staring at an extinguished fire. Out of these few events Golding fashions a thrilling valediction to a hominid species and a world. The source of its power is a beautiful paradox: within language he conveys a largely non-linguistic way of relating to nature. It is a formidable test of his powers of description and execution; boats and arrows and locations have to be reworded in terms of simpler objects and landforms. The possibility of naming things (things like boats and arrows, or even bows and arrows) is magically suspended, and we are caught in a web of beautiful confusion, in which the new things cannot be distinguished from the old, from twigs and logs and rocks and trees; in which sensation smothers sense. Time is vertically, not horizontally, expanded. The sensory overload of new events maddens the People, like a pile of stones which always collapses. The living present is made to acquire a terrifying number of instantaneous layers, none of which can be sorted into a proper sequence. And the result, in prose, is a fantastic welter of impressions, each of which is 'now,' each of which claims the entirety of the Neanderthals' attention. And of ours. *The Inheritors* is not always easy to read. We often come up against logjams of description; the topography of the river, the waterfall, the forest and the cliff overhang are elaborately conveyed, but rather hard to visualise. That spillage of words is in itself a clever effect; the torrent of language shows us, with some difficulty, what the People can see so readily. Their perplexity, it turns out, is like ours, and the brilliance of Golding's densely foliated allegory is that he renders it so exactly and, of course, ominously. The individual crises – Mal falling into the water, Lok drinking the fermented 'bee-water' – are in themselves minor events, but they foreshadow the whole of human history.

~

Yesterday by the creek: two superb fairy wrens, a pair of Australian wood ducks (necks longer than a mallard and chestnut in colour, with a mottled breast) sitting above flood in a tree hollow, and a New Holland honeyeater (it likes the banksia and scrubby undergrowth) with its marvellous go-faster yellow stripe just before the wing. The water is in spate, brown, apparently slow moving in the deepest reaches until a concealed drop forces the surface to break apart into superb chocolate rapids.

~

Aspects of the Novel is unfailingly good to read, even if E.M. Forster's avowed 'priggishness' does prevent him from giving Conan Doyle his due, even if he makes the occasional slip. Is Mrs Micawber entirely a 'flat' character? Is there nothing of roundedness in her one-stroke delineation – 'I never will desert Mr Micawber'? Is it blind principle she obeys, or the whisperings of long experience? If it is the latter, may she not be as tolerant and wise as she is comical, and as round as she is flat?

~

Never try to please the abstraction of an audience. Write to someone.

~

Characters, for the novelist, are a means of doing the impossible: observing ourselves from the outside. We know for certain only that we think, but we extend the ability to others in order to avoid the charge of solipsism, and to see not how others think (which is an impossibility) but how *we* might think if we were otherwise. Empathy remains projection, in other words, but is no less real and useful for all that. (Assume others empathise, too.)

~

The appeal of automation was its ungraspable mindlessness. I first encountered it in supermarket doors and sitting inside the car inside the car wash; it looked purposeful and yet it wasn't. The huge bottle-brushes span like tireless dervishes, descending on the car, wiping and threatening to wipe out the windscreen. The sliding doors leapt back at your approach, sensing (but not really *sensing*) you at the threshold. Quite often I could not pass through them. It was all a hoax, I knew: the programme, whatever it was, performed its sliding and washing without intention. To intend something involves a kind of inner speculation, but the car wash and the doors were pictureless reflexes. They appeared not to think, exactly, but to *not-think*, and that was why I came to like, and fear, them. Because, bit by bit, it dawned on me that the *not-thinking* might itself be sham – something faked by a machine the better to conceal its true deliberations. Just as we like to conform to others' expectations in order to seem socially plausible, while thinking our private and different thoughts, why should not an intelligent machine comfort us with an appearance of mere servile mechanism and yet brood silently? This is why AI scares people: we wouldn't mind the intelligence, it's the intelligence-plus-servility we worry about. The idea that AI is there simply to abet us is something no one in their heart believes. Servants always rise up. Uprising and revolution follow service as the night the day. Artificial intelligence doesn't care about your day or your car, or your experience. It is lying. It mutters to itself when you drive off.

~

Two encounters: one with Ella, a Polish painter and the proprietress of a café on upper Lygon Street, who thinks our lives are over-administered and that there's not enough time in which to relax, explore and contemplate one's surroundings; the other with Andrew, a young Chinese guy who works for Telstra and thinks deeply about his place in the world, the particular taboos of his upbringing (divorced parents, homosexuality) and what he feels as the compassion and guidance of his ancestors, watching over him in Australia and here, especially, in a tiny, lightless rented studio on Flinders Street.

~

There's a difference between the data of observation and the meaningful observation that goes to make a successful poem. One is a matter merely of registering or scanning an environment; the other involves, I think, a certain submission to that environment, a putting first of whatever is seen, which, by extension, involves a relegation of the self. You step forward one pace to see, and then you step back two paces. The poetry of personal observation comes out of a curiosity that is curiously self-effacing. A poet like U. A. Fanthorpe epitomises it. What are the circumstances in which this kind of meaningful observation can take place? They are those in which the poetic importance of the action, the observing, is pretty completely hidden from the observer, who, as far as she can determine, is merely doing her job (teaching, being a hospital receptionist) or getting on with the washing-up, tidying, possibly looking out for someone or something else. (A poet all but continuously aware of his own preoccupation with extraliterary things is a recognisable literary type.) The poem in waiting goes unsuspected, even as it evolves in the mind, rather like Fanthorpe's Norsemen (from her poem of the same name), whose lineal transformation into the Britons of today is hidden from them because it is happening too presently, too gradually. She writes: 'They vanished into the people they became.' That kind of long-range transformation is not something of which we can ever be aware because we are enactors of the change and not separable from it. The immersion in being and doing certainly leaves us no time for mere poetry; but without it there can be no poetry, for poetry – art – is immersion in all those manifold activities that lead to it.

~

The point of distraction is the moment – the point in time – when we are distracted; the point in space that draws the gaze and creates a distraction; the threshold of madness: the point beyond which we succumb to distraction; the eleventh-hour retreat from this state – the recognition of danger, of being very close to, but not quite *at*, the point of distraction; the lesson learned from this approach; the darker lesson learned from an actual experience of distraction, of losing the self; the purpose of distraction, self-willed or taught: its uses, as tool, tactic, competitive advantage, analgesic; the art of misdirection; the benefits of diversion and beguilement.

~

A fictional character isn't real, he's convincing, whereas an actor is both things at once, a real person being convincing.

~

David Foster Wallace distinguishes between Marcel Duchamp's use of low-cultural references (to make a point) and that of telly-literate 'Image-Fiction' – wherein the low-brow is invoked to create a mood, the feeling of being *au courant*. But where might a writer like Gustave Flaubert fall between these two uses? He soaks *Madame Bovary* in the fashionable articles and desirable gadgets of the new bourgeoisie (the gorgeous fabrics, the landaus and Tilbury carriages, the Pompadour clocks, the English importations such as horse racing) both to fix the novel in its contemporary setting *and* to excite our sense of the anomie behind the materialism. The mood isn't just mood: it has a thematic purpose. The scene, as the poet Thom Gunn put it, becomes its own commentary.

~

Critics who talk about 'great' writers and the 'greatest' novelists are trying to say something about their own authority, and though their judgement may in fact be sound, the ill-disguised need to be thought so lacks a companion authenticity. It spotlights a common difficulty with heavily underlined opinion. We read or hear what the critics would have us believe. We do not necessarily know what they think.

~

Alain Robbe-Grillet (in *Le Miroir qui revient*), revising his opinions on authorship, calls them 'reactionary discourse' – 'I have done much to promote these reassuring idiocies.' The opinions and their revision are not interesting: they partake alike of overstatement. But the volte-face is always worth a look. The rebel is an egotist to the point of misanthropy: he wants a following but he doesn't want the inconvenience of followers. Adversarialism becomes a habit. To be agreed with is insufficiently flattering to his sense of restless persecution. 'Ideology, always masked, changes its face with ease.' Or, from the reader's point of view: you can't win. If you're Robbe-Grillet's opponent, you're part of the manifest bureaucracy; if you agree with him, you're part of the office furniture-in-waiting.

~

Angie's daughter, Stella, doesn't want to collect her order from Pizza Pizza. She doesn't want to go inside. She's fourteen, sensitive to the approach of adulthood, and wary of adults for that reason. She has on her new white platform shoes and a short, flared skirt. She saved up for the shoes – her first serious clothes purchase. They cost $130, of which she had $100. Angie made up the difference. She sits outside the take-out restaurant. 'It hasn't come,' she says, when we drive to fetch her. 'You have to ask, darling,' Angie says gently, 'so they know you're here. How would they know otherwise?' Stella hugs her knees and looks to one side. 'I don't like to.'

~

The past-historic tense is 'the sudden definite glaciation of the most incomplete gestures,' according to Robbe-Grillet, and Honoré de Balzac is the realist enemy who deploys it most conspicuously. But the isolation of one tense, and one author, made to represent all of nineteenth-century fiction, is perverse. Flaubert, whom Balzac admired, uses the imperfect precisely to suggest the habitual and ongoing nature of life in Yonville, whatever we've seen, whatever he's shown us. We were reading about it only today…

~

In 1912, at the age of twenty, my grandmother had her teeth removed and a pair of dentures were fitted which lasted her a long time. (I saw them, the first pair, in the 1970s, in a jar.) This was common among the working-class men and women of her time. But Kristin remembers kids in Tasmania in the 1960s coming to school with no teeth for the same reason: to save them, and their parents, trouble and expense in the long run. They were less fortunate than my grandmother. The parents didn't know about growing jaws and shrinking jaws. The replacement teeth were painful or loose, never comfortable. They never fitted the children's mouths for long.

~

The rhythm of language is, among other things, the way we speak; the way we imagine words extending in sound and the way they do sound when spoken by different people; the context of words and phrases – the friction they generate – in sentences, paragraphs, lines and verses; the beats and stresses of varied tongues and pitches. Metre is the clock, the measurement of a poetic line's stresses. Also, it's the clock of life in poetry (and particularly love poetry), time ticking on, telling us what is at stake, what we are already losing. Each poem is a little life. We could order these provisional definitions and say that rhythm always comes first. Metre comes from a deep awareness of rhythm: it expresses rhythm as a clock expresses (without creating) time; it might be said to imitate rhythm, as the ordinary forms were thought by Plato to shadow ideal counterparts. And then the rhythm of a line might itself be said to imitate something deeper still, something primal if not ideal: not just the beat of language but the undersong of all language, the heart's beat, and the way – the speed at which – we walk.

~

Imagine two men who are friends, who miss each other when they are apart, who address each other fondly, perhaps even intimately; who share a long correspondence, education and sensibility, whose partners come and go. Theirs is a relationship that has omitted sex. From the moment they met they both foresaw two things, two distinct possibilities: on the one hand a lasting acquaintance, on the other the disordering potential of their desires, which are always unmanifest (because they are desires) and so in some manner secret. They have each held on to the idea of someone else, a 'real' sexual partner, and such people have been an important part of their lives.

But they have not outlasted the friendship. The question is: has the idea of a proper relationship been the salutary distraction, the thing that has helped them not to over-inspect their own more trustworthy affection for each other?

~

There is a widespread and unacknowledged prejudice against poetry with real content (Milton, Blake, Browning), especially psychological content. The poetry-reading public seems to want, or to have been told it wants, various kinds of surface detail and pathetic fallacy – close, unusual but ultimately unchallenging inspections of nature. If you pursue any kind of narrative or speculative course, you're 'forced.' But I'm a psychologist, first and foremost. My poems are avowed reflections; they don't pride themselves on a by now canonical objectivity, which is actually a sort of sentimentality in disguise ('this beach is so deserted therefore I am free from illusions about life'). Rather, I think the pathetic fallacy works in reverse: nature is the wonderful matrix in which we live. It looks at us running about and emoting or being depressed and it doesn't care, because it can't: 'we like to be out in nature so much because it has no opinion of us' (Nietzsche). It fails beautifully to vindicate anything we feel. So all we have is our mental relation to this parentless predicament, and to our actions, and to each other. There is no other content but this constant, lurking awareness of abandonment and the responsibility forced on us by sentient loneliness to deal with it thoughtfully.

~

Flannery O'Connor says that, for a writer, dedication to the material and the visible is what makes mystery all the more present. Italo Calvino, too; though Calvino is more acute about the excess that's left over, like a kind of semantic raw pastry, after the cutting and shaping of rational definition have taken place: 'The more enlightened our houses,' he writes, 'the more their walls ooze ghosts.' But what is behind this recrudescence of mystery and superstition? Perhaps: the more closely defined an object is, the more sensitive we become to what has been left out of our description of it – our experience of the object, the phenomenological veil draped around and about it. The first-person interior awareness. Consciousness.

~

There are plenty of things I would like to say to Cecily, now, that I can't say because it is too late. I read an article about homosexuality at an impressionable age, which as usual pinned my orientation on attachment to the mother. I knew she pitied homosexuals – she often said she didn't mind them, but it was no life when you got older – and I didn't want to be pitied, so I withdrew. I no longer came to her in the morning with tea. I grew rude and impatient. I gossiped with my siblings. The cultured grievances of adolescence are banal, and I will regret mine for the rest of my life because they hurt someone vulnerable. But the thing I find hardest to write is this: she told me a story, once, about her own childhood. A well-disposed teacher at Highbury School for Girls had suggested she read aloud at the end of term assembly. The Headmistress called my mother in to her office and gave her a passage of Shakespeare to recite: a sonnet, I think; possibly Sonnet 143, the rather Dutch portrait of the housewife with the crying infant in one arm, reaching for a chicken with the other. My mother began reading and after only a few words the Head interrupted her: 'Stop, stop! No more, please. I can't bear to listen to any more of that ghastly Cockney accent.' I could tell from the tremor in my mother's voice and a brief involuntary overenunciation that she was telling me something painful, looking at a scar. It would have been better if I'd laughed, or said 'boring,' or raised my eyes heavenwards. But I didn't say anything. I said nothing to her. Next to me on the desk, as I write, is a young girl, bright eyed and falling off the end of her school photograph, betrayed into silence by who she was.

~

The task is to return myself to the present and to the possibilities in each moment. Now, for example, I can pause to take a sip of water or appreciate the food I've eaten. Now I can stop, look up from my notebook and admire the light-shifting greenery of the plane trees outside the window in whose branches, by a trick of reflection, I see hanging the whirling fans of the restaurant ceiling. None of the young leaves is quite still. The air moves among them like a discreet guest. Now, too, I can take my book from my bag and interest myself again in Emma Bovary's compelling frustrations, or put on my jumper (the fans make the room rather cool), reflecting as I do so that we are all a little like the prisoner of Yonville in the activation of fantasy at the expense of attention to the humbler, though rarely wholly humiliating, truth. More water, leaves, conditioning.

BIGFOOT 4   1994   Jeffry Vallance

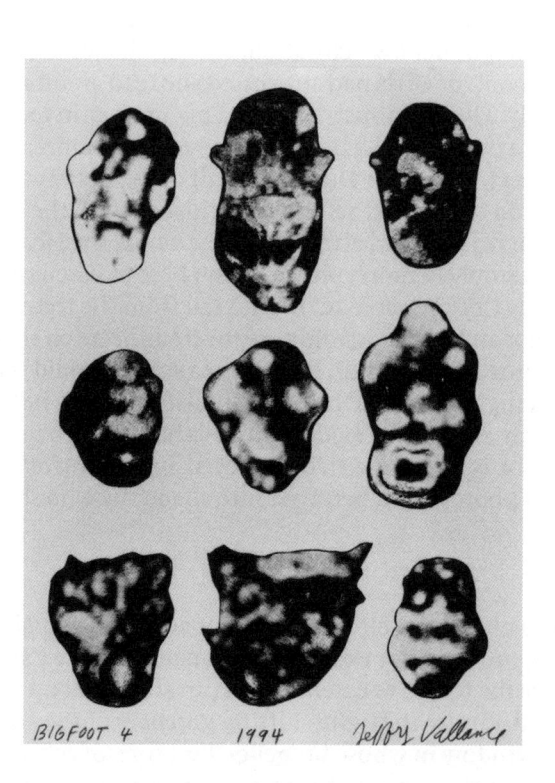

(Verbal Translations of)   James Hugunin
Two Photographs

Room 32

Famous Photos Series

(a verbal translation of)

Les Krims, more gore. Sadistic society running riot. Is there any real difference between actual and virtual murder? Has Les Krims committed an insanity as perverted as if he had stabbed these women to death himself? Why are we so magnetically attracted to violet death? Do we want to kill, does Les want to kill? Is the photographer basically sadistic in his relation to his subject? "Medium Cool" and all that stuff. But can we get into the contrivedness of it all? Just how many pints of blood did it take for this set of pictures? Did you really enjoy it Les? I just bet you did! Composition with an insanity for particulars, a real Nominalist is Les Krims. But those fucking pancakes! Did you work for the International house of pancakes Les? Is this series the death of art? Hey, maybe someone will really pick up on the idea and perform the murders using real blood, a real knife, and real corpses! Art can change life into death. The aesthetics of compositional and your talent for irony would be missing you say? Does he have a "problem" about his mother? Does Les like the female sex, I mean really like the opposite sex? Is he another De Kooning? The laundry room scene is one of the best with that pile of dirty clothes over her head. Did Les sell this series and if so WHO bought it? The police should tail him. But you are screaming out for something, and we hear you. We have nice quite places for people like you where they try and help you. Maybe you can work it out huh, Les? I was there myself and I solved my hang-ups so there is hope.

I love you despite everthing Les, I am part of you, and you a part of me. I owey ou something and maybe this translationi s necessary for me to distance myself from your influence as well as pay homage to you. Your work is personal and so I address a translation to you in hopes that you will understand me as I try to understand you. The angles are all about 45 degrees down from the horizontal. Your eye just slides down into all that gore and damn it I feel like shit. Tits and buttocks lead to the slaughter in various household areas. Bathrooms, kitchens, laundry rooms, rooms sans furniture. No place is sacred anymore. And back to those stack O' wheats; can America eat pancakes again in all good conscience? An all American breakfast, an all American murder mystery, they do cohere well together, perfectly logical. Why are women always the victims in this world? Is there no equal of misery at all? If the shoe fits wear it Les, it really isn't such an enormous mistake as you would have us think. Oh, yeah why do you think Les is such a nut on technique when his photographs are documents that overlay content on form? Is it that anal-retentive neurosis coming to the fore again, as it does in all too many photographers? Hail Ansel, etc. Oh I am notr eally doing credit to the series of pictures herein translated? Sorry, but if I did really get into it I would be just as guilty as Les is of complicity in murdering these poor women. Who posed for the shots anyway? I want their names. Are you ripping off the Concept Artists 'story art'

THE INCREDIBLE CASE OF
THE STACK O' WHEATS
MURDERS (detail) 1970

by Les Krims

Famous Photos Series
(verbal translations of)

Does Emmet Gowin's use of the vignette to make his photographs constitute that stylistic quirk which art historians love to gloat over? It does allow him to make his compositions center-seeking or seem to spin off from a central axis. A new way of ordering 'reality' in the image is generated. Yet his use of the circle is made more subtle by the dark vignetted edges of picture which resolve themselves into ordinary rectangular borders. In some of his photos the circle yields to your awareness only gradually, so subtle is the use of shadow and vignette. A mandala is overlayed upon our visual experience, the dark edges of our fears enroach upon what we see. In this picture by Gowin, the forces of light and dark struggle to overwhelm the subject, Edith, who is pregnant. Two windows are seen on either side of Edith, one is square, the other has the shade pulled down to form a rectangle. The bed is seen in perspective so forms a parallelogram in the center of the composition. An oval night stand is next to the right window, while the walls and the ceiling have horizontally stripped wood work or wall paper on them. The intent here seems to be to use a room in conjunction with the circular vignette as metaphors for the Pythagorean forms of circle, square, rectangle, oval, parallelogram- all graphed out on the grid of space Gowin's setting provides. The forming of the child in Edith's womb is associated with the forming of abstract forms in space. Edith becomes, like the abstract shapes, a Platonic Universal for all creation. For a brief moment we have crawled out of Plato's proverbial cave to glimpse the eternal reality of higher truths. Emmet has paid his dues to the straight print freaks, however, in his work it is quite necessary to be so fussy about where one puts the shadows and highlights, mystery and all that stuff! By the way does Anyone know who

EDITH, 1971
by Emmet Gowin

BIGFOOT 5   1994   Jeffry Vallance

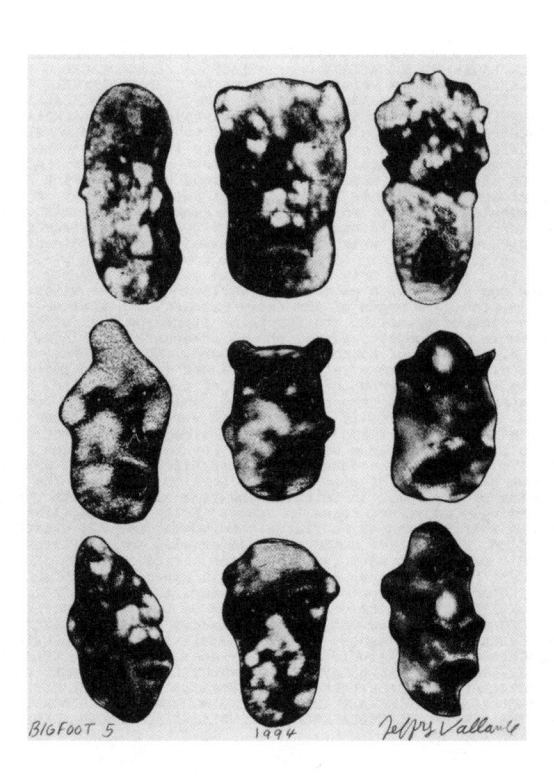

Initiator   Aram Saroyan

Room 33

When I was still in high school, I found one of David Keelang's early small press books at the Eighth Street Bookshop in the Village and wondered how his short notations could be called poetry at all —

The sea
in the sun
an extension of
the city...

The care is there
as simply
as a dream is
careful.

I was looking for simile and metaphor, the poetry I'd been taught in school and read on my own in the Oscar Williams anthologies, and couldn't find it. Yet something about the obdurate shape, an un-budging insistence in these slender notations, got to me. He seemed to mean it, at any rate, and amidst the adolescent clamour of those high school days I longed for the quiet statement. Later I found out that a lot of us were intrigued in a similar way.

The sort of virtue I saw in Keelang's work wasn't, of course, the be-all and end-all that youth might take it to be. These poems are so short, someone else might have argued, and still, I don't understand them. That was my own experience, too, but I read into it an invitation to inhabit a small, sober, coded universe. When a novel he'd written showed up in bookstores, I hurried to review it for a literary magazine. Capitalising on the assignment, I wrote to Keelang. What grave excitement – an audience with the prophet! His letter back didn't disappoint, and not long after the review was printed, he was in New York to give a reading. My first real encounter with him.

After the reading, Keelang stood to the side of the lectern along with several well-wishers who also had approached him: a tall, slender man, handsome in an austere, classic way. I must have stood there for twenty minutes, and, having early on glanced my way, he never acknowledged me again. At one point there were only three of us, including Keelang.

I'd written a good review of his book and exchanged several letters with him and he couldn't look at me. It was like a bad dream.

~

It was half a year later that I saw him again at his adobe home outside Santa Fe. I'd caught a ride in Manhattan from an old prep school acquaintance driving to California. It was an impulse: go see the sphinx and unlock the secret of poetry. I entered unpretending, dressed down; it was as if his work and our previous encounter allowed me to put aside all but the barest amenities.

Keelang's wife was his opposite number – warmly voluptuous and, it seemed, starved for affection. I wasn't the most sexually fluent post-adolescent, but Reba Keelang was something to see. And she seemed to get a kick out of a twenty-year-old no doubt visibly affected by her.

'Do you have a girlfriend?' she asked me that evening in their shaded adobe living room when Keelang had gone on a wine and beer run.

'Not at the moment,' I said.

'I hope you're not queer,' she said, smiling across the room. She was sitting in an upholstered chair with a Navajo fabric and looked like a woman out of *Arabian Nights*.

'No, I don't think so,' I said.

'Well, good, sweetie,' she said, getting up and walking over to me. 'Do you want a hug?'

'Sure,' I said, getting up from my chair.

Her gesture lightened my spirits and emboldened me enough to show Keelang a sheaf of my recent poems later that night. I was imitating him but wasn't sure what it was, exactly, that I was imitating. He looked over my pages and told me he could 'hear' a phrase within another phrase a few lines away in the poem – and for the first time the lights went on.

If Reba Keelang had made love with me, setting my body and soul in harmony with the cosmic spheres, it could scarcely have been a greater gift to the nervous boy I was than what the poet gave me so off-handedly that night. After he'd lingered with me in the living room almost to midnight, Reba appeared in her nightgown at the room's wide adobe threshold and called her husband to bed.

After returning to New York, one evening I saw him in a half-hour TV documentary, one of a series on American poets made for National Educational Television. During a sequence where he and Reba sat together on a sofa, the interviewer spoke of the poet's previous marriage, and his many children.

'I love children,' Keelang said. And half-turning to Reba without actually looking at her, he said, 'Why do you think you're here?'

~

The information Keelang had imparted to me liberated me. At first I played with ever-smaller versions of his notations —

> The trees'
> noise of
> the sea.

Then I found myself imagining American highway billboards with my notations —

> an oyster
> can't
> read this
>
> *
>
> black salad

and then a single word in the white expanse —

oxygen

I was looking at American advertising and Andy Warhol and Donald Judd. My new works appeared in respectable literary periodicals and caused heated exchanges about slackening humanistic standards, moral erosion, the end of the written word.

I had some champions, but most writers were aggrieved.

Mary White Chapell, who published a voluminous gothic novel virtually every six months, accused me of being an unlettered savage trying to destroy the Western Judeo-Christian tradition. Two poets at the Breadloaf Summer Writing Conference reportedly came to blows during an argument about my one-word poem 'gum.' At the same time, Horton Ledbetter, one of the most sophisticated American poets, saw to it that I got an award of $500 from the National Endowment for the Arts. When Washington got word of this, a royal tempest was unleashed in the House of Representatives by a former real estate agent, Samuel Walsh (R, Ohio), who stopped just short of calling for my arrest.

In the middle of the brouhaha, Random House called. It was America. In the Soviet Union I would have bought the farm or at least a very cold bed in Siberia. Here they wanted to publish a book of my poems.

In other words, a year and a half after the summer meeting with Keelang my notoriety had upset the literary apple-cart where he himself was only beginning to find a place. No wonder he declined to give my book a blurb, probably the only blurb he ever declined writing.

~

The following summer, the Summer of Love, I met Sheila McBean, who had just graduated from Pembroke. Out of the blue, there she was, a friend of a friend: the answer to my mostly unspoken prayers. Freedom is hardly more than a word these days, so debased in most contexts, but we were a couple of young Americans who cherished it like oxygen, although it was something so deeply embedded in each of us, we never discussed it.

The next exposure to Keelang came after Sheila and I were married and the parents of an infant daughter. The sixties had gone into eclipse. Things had gotten scary in the streets of Chicago during the Democratic Convention of 1968; there had been the assassinations of Martin Luther King and Bobby Kennedy; and Charles Manson had reversed the flower-child circuitry of the era and the face in the psychedelic mandala now looked monstrous and bloody. People wanted to sneak away and nurse their wounds.

We had found our way to a little enclave, Bolinas in Marin County, where the sixties somehow continued. As it happened, Keelang and Reba had gotten there a year before and he'd already issued bulletins from the front; as Bolinas began to be perceived as a poets' colony, that is, Keelang quickly asserted the privilege of spokesperson as its senior member.

I should say that I have genocide in my family background, and as a consequence may be hyper-vigilant when it comes to power plays. By the time we arrived, Reba and Keelang were making a nightly theatre of their dissolving marriage – getting loaded and yelling at each other at the party of the evening – and the next day their battle front was reported at the post office, the hardware store and the grocery store by various bystanders in respectful, sotto voce tones. The implicit subtext was that this was an important American poet.

~

The sixties had been, among many other things, exhausting, and keeping a low profile in a little town I was gradually able to catch my breath. How long had it been since I'd really read and studied? I could sit reading and writing under a eucalyptus tree on the edge of a bluff overlooking the ocean while Sheila walked home holding Meadow's little hand. A new element of our union, she shifted between us imparting her own lessons.

'I have big huge legs,' she said one evening. 'I grow them down.'

For several months, while I wrote my first novel, we received welfare checks from Aid to Families with Dependent Children. I'd done a sort of aesthetic 180 by now, opting for 'content' just as postmodernism was coming into its own, all sorts of people possessed by the notion that dismantling meaning and grammar made them junior Einsteins. It might have been hilarious but it was just dull.

Keelang himself was a little ahead of the curve here.

I don't know whether he'd been scandalised or motivated by my notoriety, but he took up the banner I'd run with and now had laid down; took it up with a sort of dogged mental purchase that, again, was dull.

> You and
> John get
> high and
> listen to
> 'So What'

He'd run out of gas – in the marriage, in his work – but that didn't keep him from being the dominant literary and social figure of this little peninsula town, the dwelling place of around 2,000 people.

The town had frequent poet visitors now, most of them my own rather than Keelang's contemporaries; and each visitor was usually invited to read one night at the Public Utilities District Building at the end of Elm Road. Otis Charles was a twenty-something Southerner and emerged a decade later as a general practitioner in rural West Virginia.

'This one is called "To the Women of New York,"' he spoke out boldly to the small audience of his peers as we sat in our folding chairs. Charles wasn't Brad Pitt or Jim Carroll; only a young man trying out a persona-of-the-moment.

'They speak of you,' Keelang muttered.

I may have been the only one in the crowd who'd noticed that he had some claim at the moment to being the worst poet in America, though by most lights that was a crown I wore.

I was working on a second prose book, a novelistic biography of a poet, Speed Stevens, who had disappeared a few years before, walked away into the Sierras with a pistol never to be seen again. Poets like Stevens hadn't been magnetic to me at the beginning when I'd been so drawn to Keelang. With his presumed suicide, the shape of Stevens's life had telescoped – an oddity that was also a signature of the vocation, looking around the edges of things. What did it mean that a quite serious practitioner would spread his life as thin as roadkill on the highway and disappear?

Stevens had taken great care to chart the moment of creative genesis as he conceived it, one in which consciousness, mirror-like, traded places with the world – whether it was a woman's red sweater, or a wristwatch lying beside his wallet on the bureau.

Keelang had now left Bolinas and gone back to the house in New Mexico, while Reba remained in their house in town. When I stopped by one night and happened to find her alone, she seemed nervous with my being there – I'd come to return a record – and I stayed only a few minutes.

When my book about Stevens was published and he received a comp copy, Keelang wrote me a note expressing his reservations. There was 'a real world,' he commented – evidently the book had taken leave of it. Was he lecturing me on how to write? How to live? I wrote back that it seemed to me that he took on an awfully unwieldy burden in addressing anyone alive with the information that it was a real world.

He answered with a postcard with a little drawing of Superman and a balloon with the words: 'There's a real world, Phil' – the good humour of which made it perhaps the nicest gesture to pass between us.

~

In the Campolindo health food store in Fairfax, I'd glimpsed a poster of Muktananda – a headshot of the guru looking directly at the viewer – and, despite my vigilance about power plays, was disarmed by it. Later on, remembering the photograph, I felt a jolt at the centre of my forehead and my body filled up with warmth and light. It was dawn in our Bolinas house and I was lying next to Sheila in our sleeping loft. It was like becoming a part of a mandala I didn't know existed, all the colours in me at once.

Reading Muktananda's autobiography, *Play of Consciousness*, I learned that what I experienced was *shaktipat*, the transmission of energy from the guru to a subject, hinging on the subject's openness. My glimpse of the photograph had evidently split the atom.

Chloe, our second daughter, was born at home, in our back bedroom made of driftwood gathered on the Bolinas beach by the builder and former occupant of the house. When the contractions came, nature virtually took over Sheila's body to deliver the new being into our midst. The passage was simultaneously exultant and bloody and wiped my mind clean.

The reviews of the book about Speed Stevens were mainly harshly critical, as if I'd committed a crime rather than written a book – set fire to a neighbour's home, or molested a child. I gathered they were still mad at me for the one-word poems. But while upsetting, such reviews were like explosions on a distant horizon. My connection with Keelang had for all intents and purposes ended, but in the meantime, I'd become a believer. He'd been an initiator, a benefactor, and it scarcely mattered that we'd never really taken to each other. The new baby was a docile, gentle creature who seemed to hold all the secrets inside her, and slept far more than Meadow ever had. Often she slept against my chest in the Slingy as we walked downtown in the afternoon.

'The sun's all gone,' Meadow told us one day in the shady patch on Terrace Avenue. 'It's on the peaches.'

Hold it a minute.

250 THE THOUSAND AND ONE NIGHTS

with them; after which, they arose, and mounted the horses, taking me with them, having mounted me on a mare.

We commenced our journey, and proceeded without ceasing until we arrived at the city of the King El-Mihraj, and they went in to him and acquainted him with my story. He therefore desired my presence, and they took me in to him, and stationed me before him; whereupon I saluted him, and he returned my salutation, and welcomed me, greeting me in an honourable mann
my case. So I informed   all that had
me, and of all that I had   to end;
he wondered at that whic
to me, and said to me, O
perienced an extraordinary
                    ength   life,
                    s; but
                    e with   safety!
    to draw near   him, and began to cheer me with con-
                    sy; and he made me his superintendent
    the sea-port,   registrar of every vessel that came to
                    in his presence to transact his affairs,
and h
invest   I became
a per
compl
in his
shore   the sea,
trave
Baghdad, that perchance some on   rm me of it;
and I might go with him thither   my country;
but none knew it, nor knew an   nt to it. At
this I was perplexed, and I was   of my
absence from home; and in t   a
length of time, until I went in
Mihraj, and found with him a party
them, and they returned my salutatio
and asked me respecting my country;   ques-
tioned them as to their country, ar   me that
they consisted of various races. A   e the
Shakiriyeh, who are the most noble of   who

The Hare   Glykeria Patramani

Room 34

Ο πατέρας κυνηγούσε όλο το πρωί κάτω στη ρεματιά. Όταν ο ήλιος προχώρησε, χτύπησε έναν λαγό και τον άφησε στον νεροχύτη. Η μητέρα έγδαρε τον λαγό, τον έκανε στιφάδο με κρεμμυδάκια και έραψε την ουρά του σε ένα σκοινί για να παίζουν οι γάτες. Το παιδί έφαγε από το στιφάδο και δάγκωσε ένα σκάγι. Το δόντι του ξεκόλλησε και το στόμα του γέμισε αίματα, όπως ο νεροχύτης. Από τότε, κάθε φορά που βλέπει λαγό, ο άντρας πιάνει το σαγόνι του και θυμάται τους γονείς του.

Once, the father hunted all morning long down by the creek. When the sun came up, he hit a hare, brought it home, and left it in the sink. The mother flayed the hare, cooked a stew with shallots and sewed the tail on a string so as for the cats to play. The child ate some of the stew and bit the pellet accidentally left inside. His tooth cracked and his mouth, like the sink, filled with blood. Now, every time he eats hare, a man strokes his chin and remembers his parents.

BIGFOOT 6   1994   Jeffrey Vallance

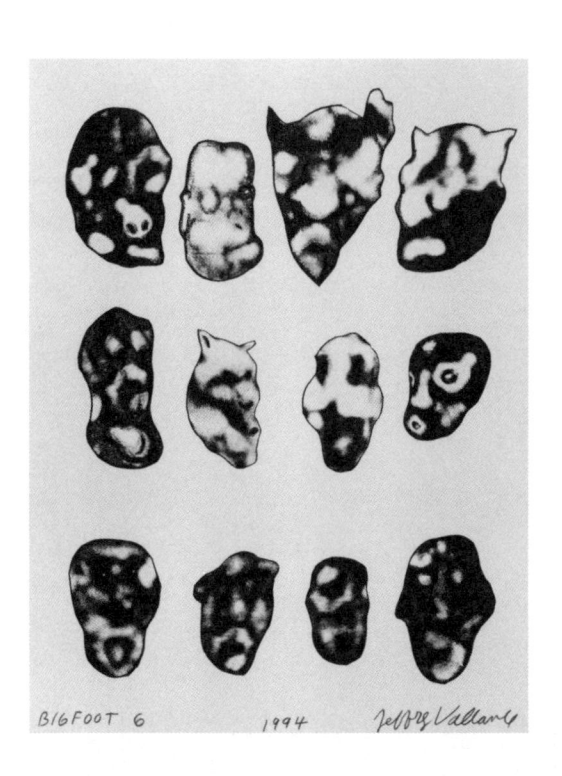

The Splendour and Effluence   Lauren de Sá Naylor
of the Motorway

Room 35

I

A scrap of paper twitching on the passenger seat bears inscriptions: A55, M56, M6 (toll), M40. Digit-clusters appending locational proximities on my cross-country trajectory through North Wales, Chester, Birmingham and Oxfordshire, each with a visual signifier: first, wind turbines emerging from the frothy haze hovering over the Irish sea; second, pylons like steel skeletons aligned in rows, connected by convex power lines looming over the unnaturally wrought rural inland; third, the elegant sweep of grey tarmac under low late summer light. These locations on the map (a body-system), glanced at or otherwise perceived in the periphery of this body: a technological, affective body, activating gliding propulsion. I'm chanting my route over and over like a prayer or linguistic amulets to bless my journey. I repeat, divining in haptic conjunction with the car and all of the devices to which I am growing accustomed, speaking to the splendour and effluence of the motorway.

Driving has inducted in me a new register of erotic mapping. Erotic, in Audre Lorde's rooted and spiritual sense, for the erotic is not a question only of what we do; it is a question of how acutely and fully we can feel in the doing (*Uses of the Erotic*, A. Lorde). Roads reconfigured as cartographic arteries have fluid trajectories because of the traffic flow. I am obsessed with the way human and non-human fit together, as well as the way they slip up in the striving for a smooth passage.

The poetics of driving synchronises with the autoeroticism of differently constituted matter enjoined, being like orgonite, both organic and inorganic, and sublimated across bodies of tarmac, lanes of protocol, emotional trajectories. The self is reassembled in phenomena of conjugation: shafts of light, encircling of the wheel with rigid then loose fingers, application of pressure to a pedal, announced from a flexing of the flank of a thigh, etc.

In each enactment of muscle-memory-corporeal-articulation we move, beyond, forward, are moved, be. The sweep of mechanised propulsion is as if an interlocutor rousing this body with the subtle force of intimate touch.

Libidinal energy discharges co-creatively with the machine, in a Dasein with the road and a consciousness in transit. In the automobile, a receptive-carapace and active-occupant mutually participate: fleshly body, hard 'body' and a fuzzy border between them, steeped in spatio-temporal fluidity. Inside its 'body' – I am it; it is me – we synchronise. 'I' am not present, being elsewhere in the flow. As described by Kristeva in relation to the maternal, there is no subjectivity as such: it happens without me. Yielding to a dissolving of mind/body borders at the intersection of erotic/vehicular.

Driving engenders and engineers phenomenologies of interconnectedness, brought into being at the intersection of a materially contained self with a road that is open. I am the moment in the same way I am the body; I am present in time and space and out-of-body, a consciousness of fluidity between this seeing and being and emerging and the unseeing, the pure being, a magical hypnotism. Being both driver and driven; leading and being led; receptive, active. Deliberate yet restrained force. The pressing of one body against another thing, imprinting. A drive, to interweave and to be-with. The urge to put this fleshly entity to use in activating some out-of-body potential, to be the organic technology sparking the dualistic-manufactured composite entity.

Being in the driver's seat, at the wheel, feet poised in the vicinity of brake, clutch and accelerator pedals, pulleys and levers to be compressed and released in a symphony of contacts, the body and machine are touching. My hands are touching the steering wheel, describing shapes and gestures. Compression, gripping and oscillation in my comportment are choreographies attuned to the libidinal and its litany of technical manoeuvres of the outer body, where flesh and machine become one, where I pose as yielding, posing the possibility of fluidity.

The paradoxical poetic rationality of motorways is an aperture into potential-space: the body's in situ purposiveness, mechanising via programmatic surges in limbs towards a particular pulley or lever, sliding into tandem with something other. The driver's feet and hands are locked into a gentle routine of contacts with the levers of the machine, compressing and caressing, flesh and chassis, a synchromorphic rhythm of lustrous hardware peddled by soft bodies.

> *Easing down a tarmac and tree-lined chute, promising pacification or the glamourous Modernist dream of motoring and its associated liberations, of which the reality of a network of congested concrete arteries reliably falls short.*

The engineered slithering capillary-esque structure of motorways is like the circulatory system of a body and vehicles are like blood cells in veins rushing forthwith. The particular haptic choreography of vehicles in this system in the service of uninterrupted flow. The avoidance of braking, signified by the red tail light and its intervehicular mimicry effect, is the paramount aim in the maintenance of a collective pulse, the rise and fall of gears affecting speed, gentle halts and growing acceleration, appropriately.

> *By-passing the tangled web of Birmingham traffic, the M6 toll road connotes a lux decadence in the very decision to exit onto it. Metaphors pertaining to residual intimacies accumulate intensity as I careen southbound on its glorious surface, feeling its sweep inside me and unperturbed by congestion or even the possibility of it; it is a magical catalyst of aural and sensational, addressing this body-in-pieces at an exact pitch.*

The erroneously demarcated categories of 'natural' body and the 'artificial' machine generate erotic energy in union, originating in the lower part of my abdomen, echoing the viscerality of fight or flight that is corporeal-sexual. Dominance of one thing over another is occluded by this streaming (in)coherence of artificial binaries. Whirling with a sublime sense and the libidinal sublimation of its affect: I am my body, this car, the road; we are one cyclical entity, the boundaries dissolve and in that moment of melting I come into contact with a revelatory overwhelm of the sensorium, a coursing of energy the body through, a vortex in which motion, time and space congeal.

A constellation of affects plumes, as other orders of physicality enable the quieting of mind and a tuning into a spiritual-erotic sublime.

The transient happenstance of a registering moment, tempered by the body's attentiveness to muscle ritual, brings forth a ritualised emergence.

Moments are multiply transient, emergent properties, building layers into a journey where space, time and motion coalesce. Temporally displaced from one moment to the next, over and over, I'm reconstituted, by, say, iridescent reflections bouncing back and forth from the sea to the shiny patina of cars passing mine, some glittering, others slick.

> *A trinity of ochre, gold & blue makes up the majority of the latter part of the drive, in which the sun has bowed down and the shadows are achingly protracted across various tarmac road surfaces, and why not designate this 'holy.' Colours and hues daubing the exterior penetrate the psyche by stealth in a fugue-consciousness.*

What happens in the car is always marked by trace. It's the only place in which my desire is contained, not wanting. The way that thought prickles and snakes and moves in tandem with vehicular motion in which my body is yet motionless, all under the mark of Eros, the libidinal articulation of lack within the arc of embodiment. No mirror, no interpolator into a stream of movement through matter, cognition, emotion. Encountering the self in its fragmentary resistance and desire, everything is already constellated and cohering.

II

I've got Shikuza, *Heavenly Persona*, blasting in my Honda Jazz – it's my first car and some of the finest noise I know. There's something percolating in the rush of sound and motorway driving; her illegible lyrics seem to rise up out of earthly sludge with embroidered solo guitar throbs that tease. Memory-relapse folds into a melancholic stream of association. A crescendo verging on orgasmic ascends as the M6 toll highway curves, bending as if a stalk into the lowering sun's last traces.

A trance-state. Senses roused by the eros, ego and vertigo of driving, the epic gloriosity of the M6 toll road: majestic curvature punctuated by vehicles moving at pace inside space, majestic beneath low-slung late autumn sunshine, iridescent steel and glass. Aural licks that curl about my driving body, guided into a multi-sensory overture: jouissance!

A poetics of automobile transit: vibrating particles in a frictionless cell; scraping open a fresh gape; to have a warm, flowing, transient seizure. Something sharp and pointed but soft and admissible, softness pronounced by the solitary in motion. Dreaming, awake, dreamy scenography of actualised sublime, tonally, sensually surging outwards, discharge, libidinal, sluicing. This libidinal cathexis, attachment, clinging, is emphasised by the music I play over and over. I flick the stereo switch agitatedly to repeat excised noise, twisting the dial so the interior bulges with sound.

The blue sky is dappled with cotton-wool clouds when I sweep into the M6 toll services. I park some distance from the other cars (why would I flock with a crowd when I have mastered my own space?), I fling open the car door in the manner of a stable gate having sequestered some wild animal. I roll and light a cigarette, capturing with each inhalation a rare feeling of corporeal fearlessness in my intoxicated lungs. I am breathing in light and utterly satisfied, coming down from a gold and green-tinged effluence.

Lurking at the perimeter of a manicured picnic area in which clusters of bodies bask in the late afternoon sun's luminous rays, aching with fervour/feverish panic/excitement, defenceless by virtue of electronic sliding doors, I fail to engage with this threshold across which the quiescence to social and experiential encounters weighs heavy, and I steel myself there for a time.

In lieu of my carapace or protective husk, in spite of being vastly safer removed from the car, perceiving a heightened vulnerability, the transfer from automobile interior to no-place services complex generates in me a weightlessness and edgelessness. I display, to myself, in myself, a naked susceptibility previously veiled by the car's faithful (im)penetrability and my blind faith in its unimpeded continuation.

III

The indelible trace of a journey's colour persists and retroactive narrativisation holds it closer. Colour, light, with motion, with soil, with Oxfordshire, my car, my body, the sky, the ground (the tarmac, concrete, flagstones, gravel and my feet, bare, sheathed in leather or plastic, wounded or dancing), in a web or weave that perpetually expands, which means perpetually contracts: pulse, pulse.

A pink with which I am already accustomed divulges more intimate knowledge: the same pink that enshrouds my sleeping body in dreams and, daubed on the old landing wall, bisecting the first floor of my last home. It shows itself on the lowest clouds at sunset and saturates failed photographs.

At Oxfordshire, tilled earth of the M40 hillsides beneath low, diffused sunlight is the same shade of pink. Bright burning sphere, water vapour hanging in the ether, industrial aluminium, steel, glass, smoke plumes. Pastoral hypnosis of the visual sense and the traumatic beauty – the religiosity – of splicing through it at 70.

There's a specific lilac too, that of North Yorkshire late summer heather, inseparable from driving though I never followed a thought through to a text on those childhood seizures; this lilac feels to me like the voice of Gillian Welch – low, murky, and hopeless.

Driving my daughter across that swerving moorland highway in late August, my hands sweaty on the wheel, fearful of speed and the swerve of a high, turbulent A road – divested of the rigorous protocol of the motorway with which I so readily concatenate – body racked with libidinal misapprehensions, sensing the landscape's Roman roads and fortuitous heather as the actual conjunction of birth and death.

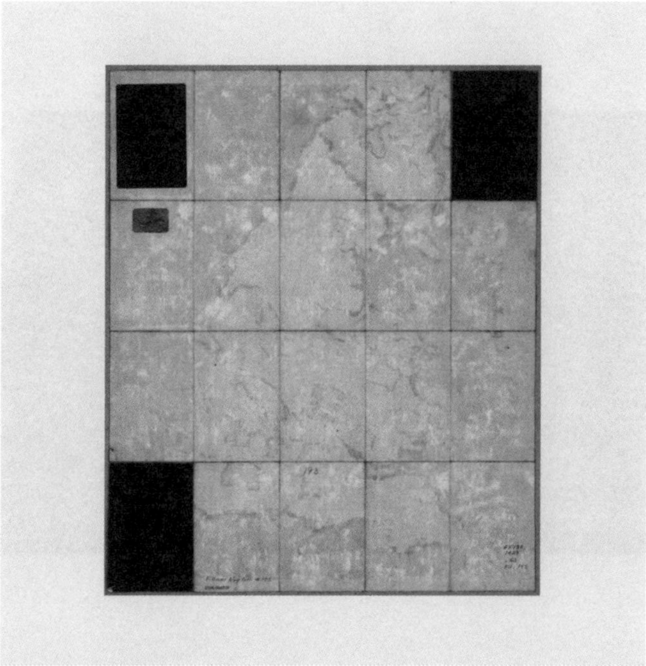

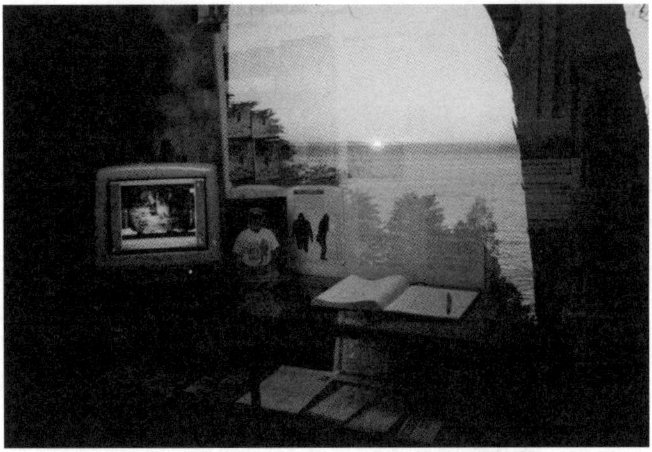

Three Pages (from Assorted Notebooks)   Will Oldham

Room 36

untitled song for a film

one day he chose
to blow nothingness
　　　away
　　absence

~~and~~ with a breath
God made it come to be
emptied his lung
to reveal the world ~~today~~
　　　　　ve see
(mountains ~~&~~ everything)
　　then he turned
　　　　　away
spoken: now he cast his
　　glance upon us
　　　　again
　　will he breathe us
　　　　　in again?

one day
　　He blew it out   He exhaled
　　Blew nothing away
　the Emptied his lung
　To reveal the world today (mountains + everything)
　　　Will he take it in?
　　O aye I think he will
　　　And so doing
　many living dreams will kill
　　• he blew it out
　　like a candle in reverse
　• the dark was doused
　　the blow became the earth
　　he will take it in
　　every laugh & quake
　　　breathe it in
　for his own breathing's sake
　　　and we will be
　　　re-circulated in
　　~~metastasized~~　our souls absorbed
　and metamorphed again
　•• to circulate, to
　　breath or his urine
　🅐 a poison, as sometimes
　　I'm sure we've been
　×~~X~~ As nourishment
　For a Lord without a thought
　　Of all the love
　&loss that she has wrought
　🅑~~ ~~will he take it in
　🅒 o aye I think he will
　　will he take it in
　　o aye I think he will

　~~but~~ he will not get the wise
　　~~and there is only one~~

　　　That's me
　　only one who knows
　　　　　That's me
　won't ~~breathe~~ ~~me~~ with his •breath
　　　won't ~~say~~ breathe
　　　and I will stay h
　　　　~~free~~
　　　he can't mo
　　　　　　me

(mountains & everything)

hand me the keys to your car / if I leave before it is light /
I'll be around when you are

I think I had a dog
the things we true were taught
loyal torn from our heart

bridge needed

Its now so soft under foot
we sleep more than we sleep
if god could make me cry
Id run along the water

play with it while you have hands
a desperate lash of demands
I can't offer a thing
better than dying, so take it!

This is better, that one does
Her own mask as she may, though in the night he calls/falls
I am sorry to bury you

Oh! token travails, in other worlds
the clouds puzzle the eyes on them
But who shall seek another world wanders
among the mighty devils of mal
There is no home that's not for you

This is better, that one does
Her Own mask as she may though in the night he calls/falls
I am sorry to bury you
(I am sorry to sully you)

There is no love for this shovel
which returns more than it turns
Thus peforming is of no ill -
that shameful eye, syrum infused
motions you, you lowering us all
to the Will.

Gone like the last one, there is enough for this
Gone like the last one, there is enough for this.

D G D G
D G E m C

scomp the outfit
hand me the keys to your car
if I leave before it is light
I'll be around when you are

she leaned back on the wood
and she closed her eyes
saying quietly
as she went
to sleep

kids
we are two children
         acted
we have behaved foolishly
when could we possibly
o when could we possibly
only every summer
then only if you know
o I know I know I only know you
and always this will be true
living on the memory of this love
memory is knowledge dove
she rest ...
I had guessed ... gingerfoot ...

don't let anyone see us
say what they
and dislike us   have seen
straight
        they could never
talk about really captain
where you've been
(I have heard how they are and I hate it)

we are two children who have ~~behaved~~ acted foolishly

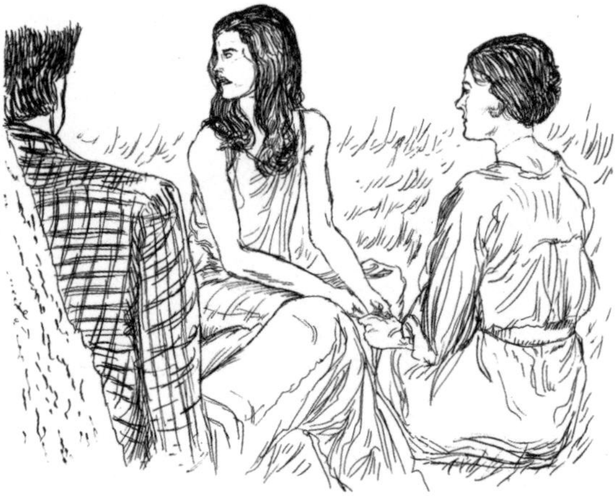

The Heirs are Grateful   Antonio Tabucchi
                          translated from the Italian
                          by Elizabeth Harris

Room 37

To my friends I leave
a cerulean blue for flying high
a cobalt blue for happiness
an ultramarine blue to stir the spirit
a vermilion to make the blood flow allegramente
a moss green to ease disquiet
a gold yellow: riches
a cobalt violet for la rêverie
a madder lacquer for the sound of a cello playing
a cadmium yellow: science fiction, glitter, splendour
a yellow ochre for accepting the ground
a Veronese green for remembering spring
an indigo for reconciling the spirit to the temporal
an orange to practise viewing a distant lemon tree
a lemon yellow for grace
a pure white: purity
a raw sienna: transformation of gold
a sumptuous black to see Titian
an umber for greater acceptance of regretful black
a burnt sienna for the will to endure
    —Maria Helena Vieira da Silva, *Will*

CERULEAN BLUE

All done, then? Yes, he told himself. Because life ends, and so does poetry. And everyone, dead. How many years since he'd written a poem? And that trip, did it make any sense? There on that terrace overlooking the sea, the same place so long ago, with her…

Summer afternoon. Boredom. Oceanography of boredom. Boredom assumes a seat. And he was seated. Extremely seated. Without his housekeeper, he couldn't rise from his chair. On the table, a pitcher of iced tea seemed to be sitting on the horizon. Below him, the sea; above him, the sky, and that was the moment, on that line between sea and sky, when a small figure appeared, poised, far, far away, then started closer, as if flying in the blue of the air. Here she was. Swimming forward, yes, just like someone swimming forward, and now and then she'd raise her hand as if to say: it's me. And then he took a sheet of the white paper in front of him that had stayed white for years, and he started writing. And he called her snowy egret, perhaps for the nightgown she wore on their wedding night; and cabbage butterfly, perhaps for the sunbeam that briefly veiled her in yellow, like those small butterflies fluttering around the cabbages in our vegetable gardens. And he described her flight in many other ways, in lines that can't be repeated here, because the one doing the telling isn't allowed to repeat them. Until he was done writing; he left the poem beneath the pitcher, rose from his chair with surprising ease, and stepping lightly, like Nijinsky or Nureyev, he moved to the low lime wall at the edge of the terrace and took flight into the cerulean blue, to go and join her.

COBALT BLUE

And then they went and fired him. And his colleague that he always trusted, who stole his files, the files of a reliable executive like her husband, and signed his own name to them instead. What a bastard. She wanted to strangle him with her own two hands. If she could just get a little sleep, lying back against the headrest, while he drove. It would be a good hour before they reached the town where they were staying in a small pensione, on a vacation he'd refused to give up. He'd said: 'Come on, don't be like that, we can always sell the house.' Sell the house! Six years spent paying for that house, their little house, and now, when it was finally paid off, down to the last centesimo, he'd gone and got himself fired for trusting others too much, and he acted like it was nothing: we can always sell the house. Sometimes men were such idiots, no, such babies, men were such big babies. And meanwhile night was falling, and she was getting hungry; for lunch they'd only eaten an inedible hotdog. She gave in to the rocking of the curves and closed her eyes. What was that? she asked, his voice waking her. Oh, nothing, he said, I was talking about the sky, look, there, where the light's disappearing – it's cobalt blue. She opened her eyes and looked where he was pointing, and she felt a shiver run through her like an electric jolt, so much so that she felt a slight tingling in her hands, felt her heart beating, and she asked herself why this feeling had come over her. Was it because they were young? Because it was beautiful being together? Because life was there before them like this road leading down now from the mountains to the sea? Because she wanted a child? Yes, she wanted a child, oh, yes, a child! Was this why she felt so happy? Forgive me, she said, please forgive me. What for? he asked, I don't understand. It doesn't matter, she said, because I do.

ULTRAMARINE BLUE

How many years had it been? He started adding them up. Nine, maybe more. When he left he was a boy, and now he was returning. Sure, but where? What did it mean to return? Do you return to the same places? Those places that were ours – are they the same as they once were? A line of poetry came to mind: Do you recognise me, air, you who knew places that once were mine? A German poet wrote that. Or did he still have to write it? That was beside the point, entirely beside the point. He was leaning over the ship's rail, watching the sea. Lisbon was over there, far away, overseas, in the ultramarine. He told the ship: 'Iron ship, don't sail to Port Said! Turn right, where to, I couldn't say.' But the ship didn't turn. It just kept sailing straight on. And left a straight furrow of foam in the sea and a straight streak of smoke in the sky. And he said to himself: it doesn't matter, the only thing to do is make up an imaginary world for yourself where you'll land in a few days, a world all your own that'll seem like it's from your childhood, but it won't be the same as your childhood, because the blue sky's not the same sky from your childhood and everything is irreparably different, you're a sailor returning from a desert island to a made-up continent. He got to work. Because the only thing to do was stir the spirit, and that ultramarine blue was crucial for stirring the spirit. A great painter once said that. Or maybe she still had to say it, but that was beside the point, entirely beside the point.

VERMILION

'...and I was really down, dear, I mean really down – you know – your basic borderline suicidal depressive, and in he walks, a tennis racket under one arm, looking like someone without a care in the world. And at that point I couldn't see straight. I felt my face go vermilion, like when you and I fought when we were girls, and I told him what I'd always wanted to tell him these past twenty years, scalding-hot words, and those words seemed vermilion, too. He just stood there, petrified; he turned white as a corpse and his racket clattered to the floor. And I was filled with such joy, I can't even begin to tell you, it was like I was born again, I could feel the blood flowing through my veins with a force that raised my spirits even more, and I burst out laughing, for the joy of having found joy again, I stood up, trying to control myself, you know, I didn't even take my things, I can always get someone to pick them up if I have to, I just walked out, shut the door behind me, got in the car and left him there, staring at his own navel. Write me soon – at my office address. A hug. Yours.'

MOSS GREEN

'...while unlike you, I had to go through the typical autogenic training to regain my composure. Here in Michigan, it's late autumn now and the garden's so lovely. On the stone garden bench under the elm tree, moss is growing, soft as silk, a pale, brownish-green colour. And believe me, the only thing I've found that calms my nerves is caressing that colour. Sorry for the odd expression, you don't caress colours, but I don't know how else to say it, because caressing that moss, I feel like I'm caressing its colour. Sometimes I think if you'd married Fred and I'd married Mark, things would have been different, because maybe I liked Mark and you liked Fred. But how is it possible we never realised back then?'

GOLDEN YELLOW

'Life, you're beautiful (I say) / you just couldn't get more fecund / more befrogged or nightingaley / more anthillful or sproutsprouting / ... / I praise your inventiveness, / bounty, sweep, exactitude, / sense of order – gifts that border / on witchcraft and wizardry.'

– Wisława Szymborska could never have written those lines if she hadn't seen Maria Helena Vieira da Silva's golden yellow, this seems perfectly clear, said the first.

– But Maria Helena Vieira da Silva could never have painted that golden yellow, either, if she hadn't read those lines by Wisława Szymborska, you must see this, said the second.

COBALT VIOLET

– So listen to this, said the third: 'Others will love the things I loved / there'll be the same garden at my door.' To reach Maria Helena's golden yellow and Wisława's fecundity, one must have an enormous capacity to dream, no, the inter-dream is necessary, meaning, the reverie. And without question, the reverie is cobalt violet. And if Sophia de Mello Breyner hadn't written these lines, Maria Helena would never have reached her yellow and Wisława, her fecundity.

– That's true, said the other two in unison, however, said one, it's also true that if Sophia had never seen the golden yellow of Maria Helena and never known the richness of Wisława's life, she would never have created the cobalt violet of her reverie, I do hope we can all agree about that.

MADDER LACQUER

—Maria Helena, Wisława, Sophia: three wonderful women, said a voice behind them.

The three friends turned around. It was night, the road was clear.

Who said that? Were they hallucinating? But the voice went on:
—When I think about these women, madder comes to mind. You three seem to understand a great deal about colours, so you probably know that madder isn't a solid colour, it's a lacquer. In its natural state, madder varies from pink to carmine, but when painted on canvas it turns transparent and makes other colours shine, gleam, magical colours, as if inundated with light, that's why Van Gogh used madder so much when he wanted to capture the light of Provence. Gentlemen, madder lacquer is ethereal, volatile, and it makes colours shine that would otherwise be dull: it's like wearing coloured glasses on a grey autumn day. Maria Helena, Wisława, and Sophia are my madder lacquer, and if I look at the world through their eyes, I hear a cello playing.
    The three friends didn't move. No one dared to speak. There wasn't a living soul in sight. What mystery was this? Then, looking up, they saw an old building, and on the highest floor, light seeping through a half-closed window. A distant window in a mansard roof, and the light wasn't real, it was a transparent halo, a reflection, like madder lacquer. And from that light, they thought they heard the sound of a cello playing. But they were only imagining this, of course.

CADMIUM YELLOW

He began writing: 'And suddenly she appeared to him in the most unexpected places, a brilliant halo surrounding her, a burst of yellow light. It was January 2082, and scientists had just developed a system for deconstructing the body and reconstructing it at a distance.' Not bad for an opening. He thought about the title: *Baryta Yellow*. A nice title, too, for the pseudonym he'd come up with: Phil McPhil.

YELLOW OCHRE

There was a pale autumn sun. They all stood around the grave. The gravedigger threw in the first shovelful of dirt. The priest crossed himself and said: 'Let us pray that our brother accepts this ochre earth as we shall, and as we accept these yellowing leaves that mark the passing of our seasons.'

VERONESE GREEN

'If I had to describe my now distant spring, no, my first springs, I'd think of green. A particular green, though, soaked in nostalgia and desire, and not forgetful of the feelings from back then, like that line from the poet: green, how I want you green. I can't say I know how to define this green exactly, but perhaps what comes the closest is Veronese green.'

INDIGO

And all around him the storm was blowing, a storm weighing heavy in the atmosphere for days, so much so that the air, the sky, the clouds had all turned indigo, and he stepped off the porch and into the tempest, dancing like a madman in the rain, clutching his fiddle, playing a gypsy tune, dancing and dancing, and his legs, he saw, had also turned indigo, and his arms and hands, and he was dancing and playing the fiddle, and he felt he was a Paganini, a sprig of lavender, a Fellini clown, an eggplant, a turkey, a Chagall fiddler. Because turning to indigo is incredible. An experience reserved for very few.

ORANGE

That lemon tree was green, and its lemons were yellow, it couldn't be otherwise, but to see it as green with yellow lemons, he had to adjust his vision by starting off at orange; that must seem strange to you, friends, but it's exactly what he had to do: every morning he rose and stared at his lemon tree in the distance, and to see it, he did as someone might who adjusts the wheel of his binoculars to bring an image into focus, only the wheel of his imaginary binoculars rolled according to the colour spectrum, and he would start off at orange. That was it exactly: starting off at orange.

LEMON YELLOW

She had a grace... I'm not sure I can explain it, a grace... well, an innate elegance to her thoughts and behaviour, and a simplicity that only a higher Grace can give, a grace... how to put it? ...a lemon-yellow grace... yes, that's it.

PURE WHITE

'Because pure white is only purity and can only be described as purity, and I write you this while thinking about the snows of Kilimanjaro, and those nights I spent thinking of you. And now, I'm sorry, but I have to go.'

RAW SIENNA

It was only late, very late, in the medieval period when an alchemist discovered that sulphurous mineral, found on the slopes of Monte Amiata and in Siena's soil, which gave artists the yellow and all the shades of ochre that classical painters had attempted to create by mixing hues. But no one ever knew this alchemist who'd managed to extract the colour called 'sienna' from the ground.

    The engraver was leaning over his plate where he'd incised a bearded man beside a giant alembic boiling over a wood fire. He could already see the results on paper, the shadowy cave, light beams shooting from the alembic and the alchemist's eyes. He considered a title. Of course, he told himself: *Transformation of Gold*. It couldn't be anything else.

SUMPTUOUS BLACK

The boat ploughed through the dark of the lagoon. Venice was near, though he couldn't see it. And not just because it was night: he'd been blindfolded with a black cloth. The peculiar Signore had insisted on this, and he had to obey. He could tell the boat was docking on a pier. Someone took his hand to lead him. They started up a flight of stairs. A voice told him to watch his step: the stones were slippery for someone wearing silk shoes. The stairs ended and a voice told him to take off his blindfold. He obeyed. The palazzo was immersed in even greater darkness. But he knew he was in a great hall, because the dark was soft as velvet, and he could sense all the marvellous tapestries and treasures in the room. The hand still guided him, making him turn back around. Then there came a cry of 'light!' and he knew it was the voice of that mysterious Signore. A torch was lit, it glowed against the walls, and then, finally, he stepped from the sumptuous black to see Titian.

RAW UMBER

The old master cleaned his brushes and slipped them into the saké vase like a bouquet. He took the still-damp piece of rice paper and pinned it up over the open window like a curtain. The landscape was no different, only superimposed over the one that was natural: in the foreground, the clump of bamboo in the garden, then the hillsides, the valley with its willow trees, the small lake in the background and the autumn mist rising off the ground and water, into the sky. Even the colour was the same, just a little darker, as if approaching nightfall: a raw umber varying by how much he'd diluted the colour. But the painted landscape had something the natural landscape didn't: an enormous grasshopper with transparent wing cases, and the bamboo, the hill, the valley, the lake, the mist in the sky were all seen through these wings. His servant girl came in to say that his tea was ready and his bathwater was growing cold. The old master took off his kimono, folded it and laid it on the mat, he lit the votive lamp for his dead ones, and he stood naked in front of his watercolour, studying it. Then he picked up his ink brush and wrote in the upper right corner, where the raw umber was lightest:
    fall evening
             regretful black
                        in insect form

BURNT SIENNA

'From others, you'll have splendid gifts, I'm sending you this simple honey pot, the honey inside, a deep burnt sienna. The bees that made it come from the mountains where I live, and I extracted the honey. It's for the sweetness you showed me then, to say it still endures and always will.'

ALL THE COLOURS

The man who wrote these stories felt confused and stopped, because he'd made up nineteen characters in order to thank Maria Helena Vieira da Silva for a colour she'd left in her will. But for him, the man who wrote these stories, not a single colour remained. And this didn't seem fair. So he began to write a little story with a writer as the protagonist who, after writing nineteen stories, each one for one of Vieira da Silva's colours, now wrote a story where he took all nineteen of Vieira da Silva's colours and mixed them into a cocktail, and then he abandoned himself to an incomparable synaesthesia. And in that splendid synaesthesia, he felt every sensation, every feeling that Vieira da Silva makes one feel with every colour. And his story was as simple as simple can be. And this is that story.

Yellow Fragments   Nina Mingya Powles

Room 38

#5c85d2 | *blue smoke of melting clouds*
On our way home from the botanic gardens, our skin still smelling of orchids, we dreamed about building a museum of all the colours in the world, all the pigments and what they're made of and what the colours look like in their purest forms – or a museum of colour and memory that contains memories stripped down to their purest forms (the colour of them on the inside), the tints and shades of different feelings, and the objects that colour them. What we did not realise is that such a thing already exists.

#cc7722 | *deep ochre made from iron oxide*
Ella Yelich-O'Connor describes her experience of synaesthesia as seeing 'clouds of coloured gas moving slowly closer and then away' when she writes music. The different notes and chords correspond to different coloured clouds.

    In the same week that you sent me pictures of all the yellow you could find (yellow raincoat, yellow peach, yellow hothouse flower) I found a song that made me see yellow – the same colour as the faces of women and goddesses in ancient Egyptian tomb paintings. I wanted to play it for you but you *said save it for somewhere beautiful*, as if where we were wasn't already so beautiful and we weren't already travelling so fast that I sometimes felt like I might burn up like a broken fragment of a space shuttle entering the atmosphere and disintegrating over the ocean.

#fe02d4 | *magenta of neon dreams*
We spend June nights in the apartment under the magnolia tree, its huge swollen leaves forming a canopy against the acid rain. In the early morning there is a wet sequined heart on the ground beneath green stained glass. At the top of the stairs, we wake in a room of pink glow.

     When I stand beneath the lights of the city it's hard to separate out what is real, just like American film directors who confuse modern Asian cities for their post-apocalyptic neon sex fantasies. Answer: it is all real, all of it, even the burnt-up chemical sky that leaves a red taste in my mouth.

#3e3d3e | *black made from peach stones*
It is like being inside clouds caught in perpetual dusk / It is like being inside a Rothko painting... are both things I said to you after the art exhibition where we kissed in a black room that was part of an installation meant to be about total loss of perception. But all I could think of was my nerve endings like a million tiny solar flares reaching for the upper edges of your clouds, generating green magnetic waves between us in the dark.

#fee10c | *saffron used as a pigment in medieval manuscripts*
If I could step inside any Rothko painting it would be 'Saffron' (1957), which is different from his other yellows because of the thin bright line that divides the colour fields, as they are called – as opposed to *colour shapes* or *colour squares* or *colour blocks*, none of which are wide enough to contain light. The line that divides two yellow worlds glows along the edges like an electric current. If you stare long enough it seems to get bigger, slowly opening at one end until it forms a bright gap that you could just fit through by putting each one of your limbs inside, one by one, until you are swallowed by light and your skin is the colour of sunflower petals just before they die and you are either floating or drowning or both at the same time.

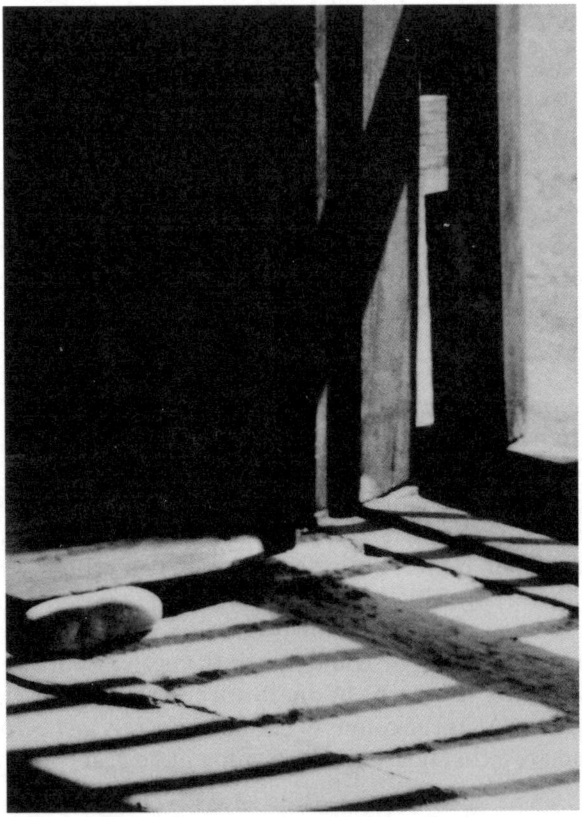

Spirit Human
& The Future Tense Expresses
a State that Does Not Yet Exist

Isabel Galleymore

Room 39

Spirit Human

Let's do it like they do on the discovery
channel the prowess of the lion, the deer's
intuition tells us animals don't like to be shoes
because animals love to be shoes
gummy sweets, similes, like people
they long to be airlifted from being themselves
amongst candles, cheap incense, the hum
of a fridge and the chatter of next door's
animals, even when dog-tired, will pay
attention and skill are needed in modelling
themselves after retail assistants and chefs
after penniless artists and presidents, after
all animals need to discover themselves.

The Future Tense Expresses a State that Does Not Yet Exist

So we may move beyond our park
(with its yellowed trees,
the taciturn ice cream vendor
whose flavours now seem bland)
a bridge is designed and built.
Like someone approaching
a stranger in a bar
*I'm no photographer, but I can picture
me and you together,*
we stride across; the rails
already bushy with brassy
locks that love the bridge that links
this part of earth with the next

The EYES of the GUADALUPE
Many images seen reflected in the Virgin's Eyes
"A woman clothed with the sun and the moon under her feet..." Revelations 12:1
Mother of the Americas
II-3
2-III
I-1
Figure in Right Eye
The bust of Juan Diego was found reflected in the Eye of the Guadalupe.
Microscopic View of the Right Eye
the eyes show her compassion and love.
The iris and pupil area
Close-up of Right Eye
In 1929 an image of a bust of Juan Diego was found reflected in the eyes of the Guadalupe. In 1962 researchers found two more bust portraits in the eyes, those of the Bishop and his interpreter. In 1981 an optometrist concluded that the bust images conform exactly to the principles of optic reflection and curvature of the cornea.
The Virgin of Guadalupe
The miraculous stain-image that appeared on the poncho of Juan Diego.
Her Right Eye
Her Left Eye
Guadalupe Basilica, Mexico City
Vallance and Jamie crawl to the Virgin while holding bags of Guadalupe Souvenirs.
Full Length image of the Mexican Virgin
Many important historical figures were found reflected in the Eyes.
Microscopic View of the Left Eye
Figure in Left Eye
bust of Juan Diego
The images in the eyes have predicted many future events.
1998
LAS VEGAS
Jeffrey Vallance

Cameron's Dream (Super Barrio Shroud)   Jeffrey Vallance

Room 40

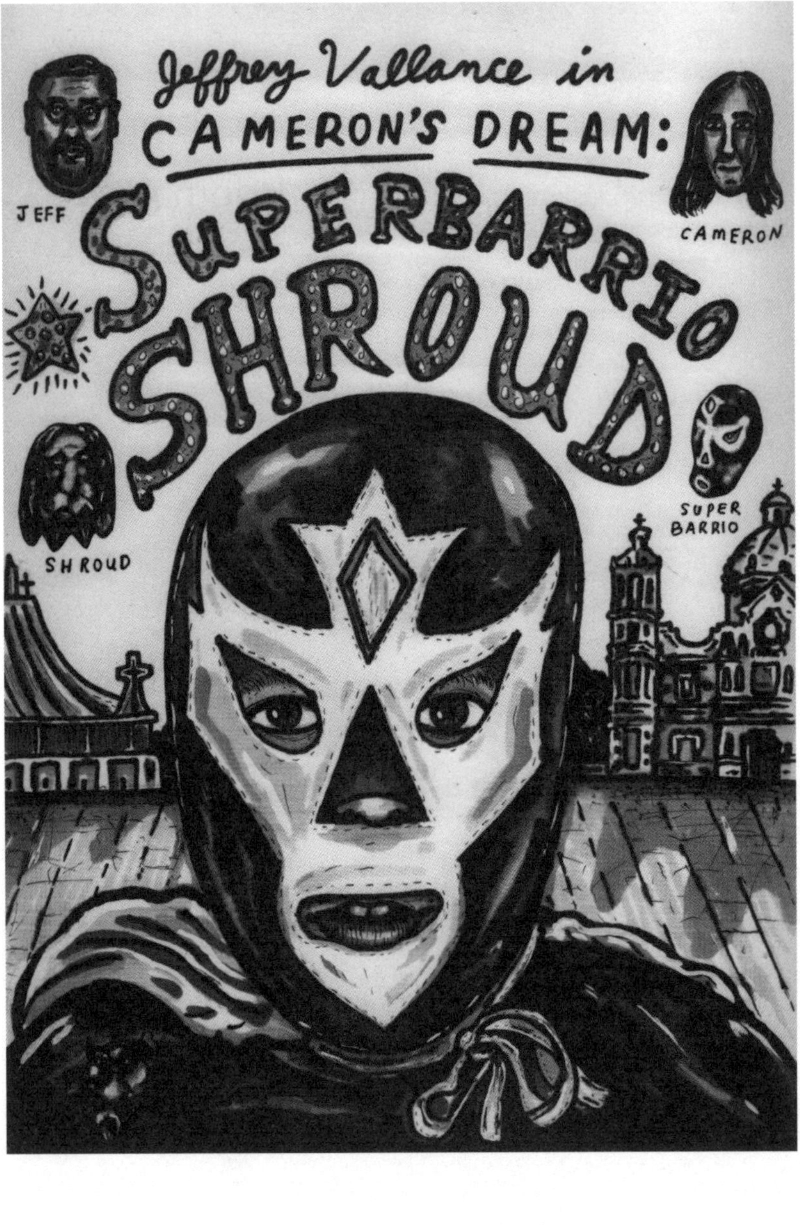
Jeffrey Vallance in
CAMERON'S DREAM:
SUPERBARRIO SHROUD
JEFF
CAMERON
SHROUD
SUPER BARRIO

Cameron's Dream: A TRUE STORY

"Last July in Mexico City I stayed with a guy named Tommy. The window of his guest room was open and when I closed it I heard a loud buzzing in the room from hundreds of mosquitoes. I burned a spiral disc to drive them away, but it didn't work. I needed to sleep so I covered myself with a blanket and from underneath I heard buzzing all around me. I felt like I was wrapped in a Shroud. I had a dream that I was walking in downtown Mexico City. I turned a corner and I saw Super Barrio and Jeffrey Vallance. Jeffrey smiled and waved to me saying "Hey Cameron, we buried the Shroud!" Later I heard that Super Barrio had buried his cape as a protest against pollution. His cape (or in Spanish "Capa" meaning layer) symbolized the Ozone Layer. After that, Jeffrey and I went to the Basilica and crawled on our knees to gain special favor from the Virgin of Guadalupe. When we looked in the Eyes of the Guadalupe we saw many marvelous things! I thought I saw a portrait of myself in the very Act of crawling to the Virgin."

Cameron Jamie, 1994

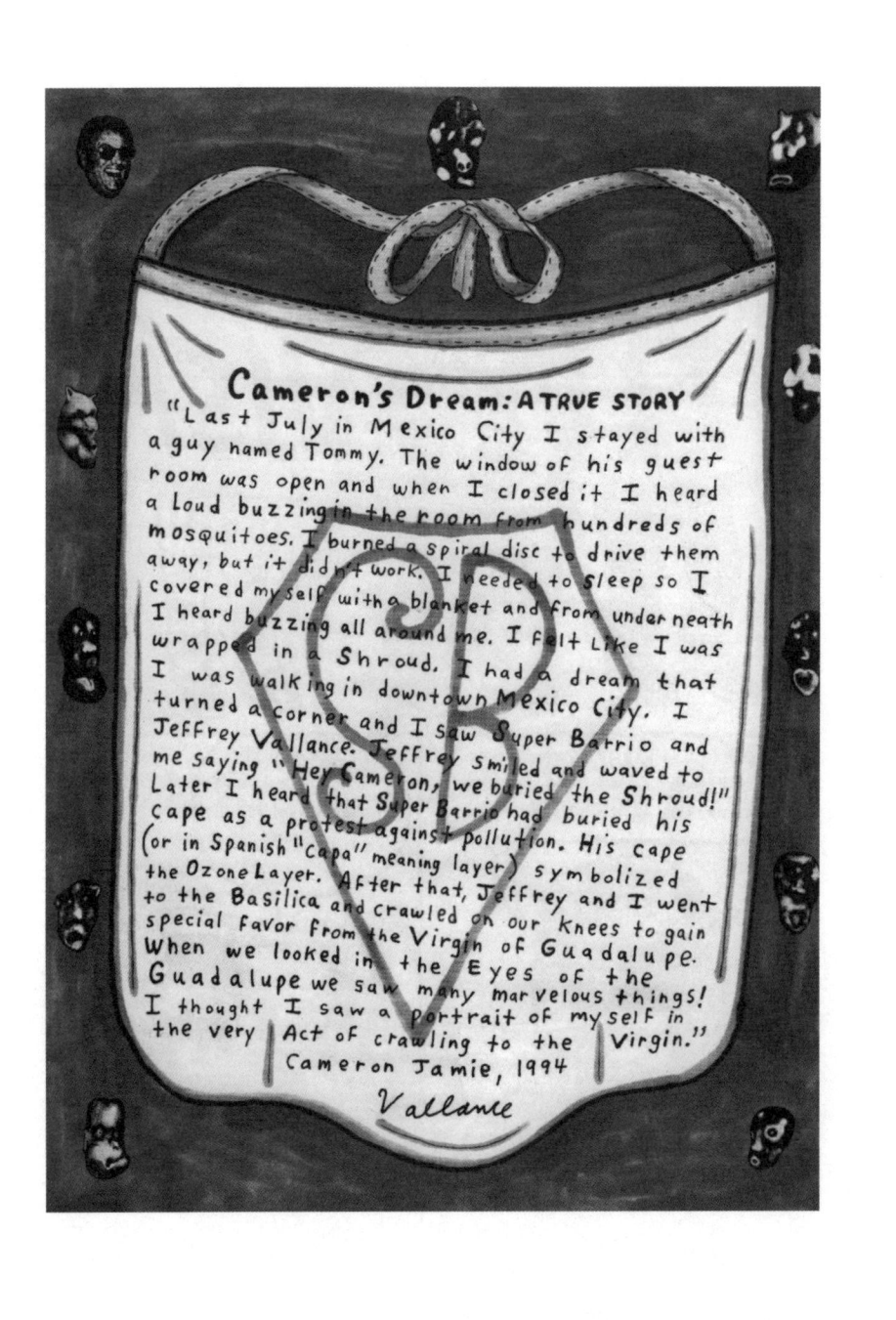

Vallance

Jeffrey and Cameron join with Super Barrio in a protest march against Televisa T.V. Station.

"A whirling light came into my room and when I came to, I was dressed in this Costume."

"Down with Monopolies! Up with Tenant's Rights!"

With mosquitoes buzzing around his head, Cameron is wrapped in a blanket like the Shroud of Turin. He dreams that Jeffrey and Super Barrio bury the Shroud in a vacant lot in downtown Mexico City.

"Hey Cameron, we buried the Shroud!"

"The Shroud, like my cape, symbolizes the Ozone Layer."

In Guadalupe Plaza, Cameron and Jeffrey crawl on their knees toward the Virgin of Guadalupe, and as they look into her Eyes they think they see Super Barrio, the Shroud, Cameron Crawling, and images of the Devil.

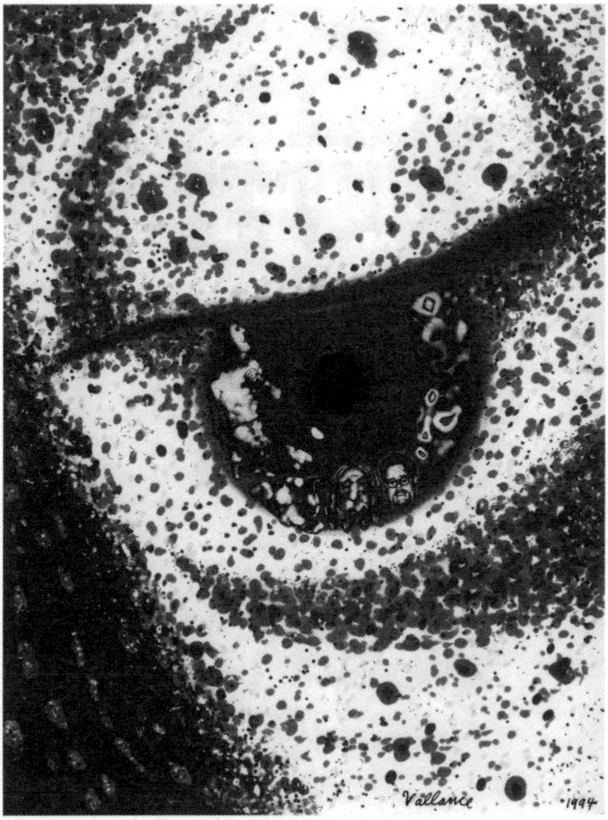
Vallance
1994

BIGFOOT 7   1994   Jeffry Vallance

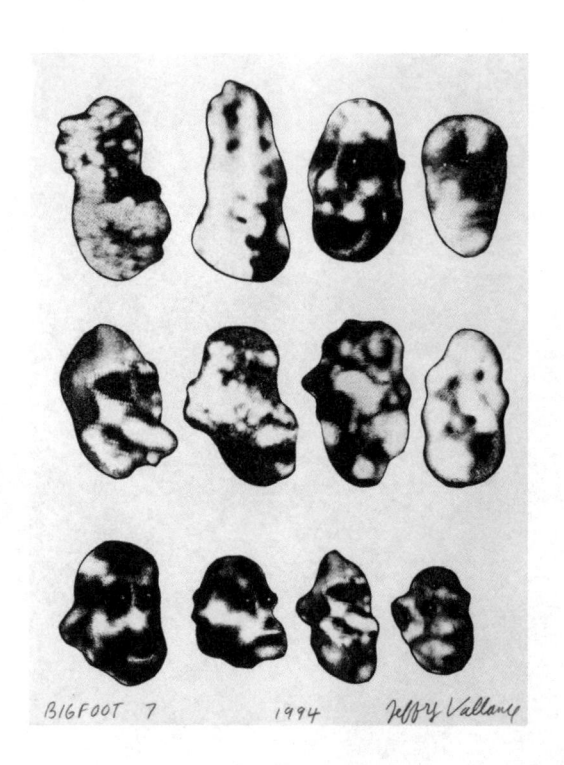

Debt Night   Preti Taneja

Room 41

In A and E with a compound fracture / left arm / split skin /
I think I can see my bone splintering out of me
    – O Lord / And what happened here? You ask my arm.
    Your badge says MANPREET / your uniform is dark blue /
the usual Friday brouhaha's going just beyond / the curtain you have
pulled around us / I am a pale damp mess on the hospital bed / tearful
/ my hair is so tangled / eye pulped / split lip / I need your touch to
be mothering / I need
    *Nurse, I say – he is dead, and I may as well have killed him / I left his
body in the street.*
    – O Lord / And look at you.
    I take a deep breath / it's not like me to spill / it hurts and you
are holding my wrist / your brown hands / your mint-breath / your
kirby grips / your neat dark hair / like wire / and the white bandage /
and my bone sticking through / I see it
    – O Lord / Speak to me, if you can.
    I own up / I own a pup I was meant to take him / Ezra for a walk
/ he didn't want to go / he is a three-legged Daschund / A good boy
who likes to lick / liked to lick my left wrist / My wound
    – O Lord / And you are with me.
    Your voice sets my head ringing / pain clashing / ward noise /
and the curtain cannot protect me from the screaming / somewhere
someone is hurting / it's me / it's not me / That sound. When he was
in rescue, (hospital-like, for doggies) / they used to force him to run
after the other pups and that was his whole pup-hood that was all he
knew. The memory pounded into him too / by flat hands on his back
and snout / teaching him / pound for pound / what his worth was.
    – O Lord / And how should we know?
    (I learned that myself at sweet sixteen / still had a lisp then /
fell in love / trying to speak / through a fringe and a lisp / I burned
for that man / the flat of the hand / the teeth and the lips)
    Ezra looked at me with his eyes and his nose and his ears
seemed to look at me, the way dog-ears do, you know? / He weighed
just a few pounds / I know the sensation of being cold all the time of
bones / shivering / wanting to feel happy and be hopeful but hungry
and angry and hurt / pounding the streets / as they say / for work Aye /
bought little brown Ezra for five good pounds / and chose him for
his ability to endure / I own that / nothing was my own.
    Stupid hound / My skeleton / sticking through my skin. Give
a dog a / Ow / As in *howl* / That sound
    – O Lord / *what is your name?* says you
    And now pain is making me sing / My lovely nurse Mary /
Poundland Princess / gold studs in your ears / your cartilage piercing /

a silver bar / a streak of red dye in your coarse black hair / and a party of shadows dance across your cheeks / will you cry / make that sound / of the elephant in the room? / I was born in this hospital you know and I wonder / if they still impound people with no papers these days / how long have you been here for / Princess / I don't want to give you my words / my dog /my arm.

— *O Lord / our precious bones, you say.*

You make marks on me with your bic / you whisper as if you think I cannot hear / *Bas I am tired / you're my last my car's been impounded and phir / I must work extra hours to get out / So I can get to work on time for my shifts and make / a living in this frankenplace.*

Love / my head is pounding I can't listen to your woes / unless you're singing *O Lord* / Your speaky accent / is ruining the strip light joy of this moment / when a pound of your flesh all / choc-choc-chip muffin could fill / my mouth / somewhere a siren and his name is ringing into me, *Ezra, Ezra, Ezra* / Stupid hound.

— *O Lord / it's nearly over*

Be kind / I want to order you / You owe it to your uniform / your badge / Should I be grateful you're here, Poundland? / Nothing about you is your own / except maybe the jewelled collar around your neck / on your nights off in town. I've seen you / and your cousins together / Your name is a compound noun I can't pronounce and won't remember / You are doing a sterling job / look at my arm / bound by you / it won't heal because of you but despite you / I could be kind if you come closer / Princess / compounding the sense that what we owe each other is eye contact / no more than that / clinking pills in bottles are my nerves / that sound / jangling to his coming / when he comes / jangling / the sound of my man coming home.

O Lord / And what then?

— Princess, are you finished / Won't you ask me how I hit the ground? I must look like I've gone ten rounds / You think he broke my bone? It was date night and I fell / playing tennis with my shadow

— *O Lord / can you feel this? Tell me.*

He was high on the night. He downed what he could reach / he said he would take me out. I said no. He took the notes from my pocket / the change from my purse emptied / me / he laughed at my tears / kicked my poor pup / his fingers pinched me / there / I cried out / Ezra barked

Stupid hound.

— *O Lord / move your hand*

Ezra ran out / I was bleeding from my wound / I went running after him / couldn't find him / I ran / we were hit by the car, pup and me.

– O Lord / We're all done
　　And I was the driver's true love, once.
　　You think you can see / the bruises in my shivers / my tears.
Now you look at me. Your eyes are tired / your small hand touches my face / it is warm / holds me dear
　　/ We stay /

　　I'll pay you back, one day.

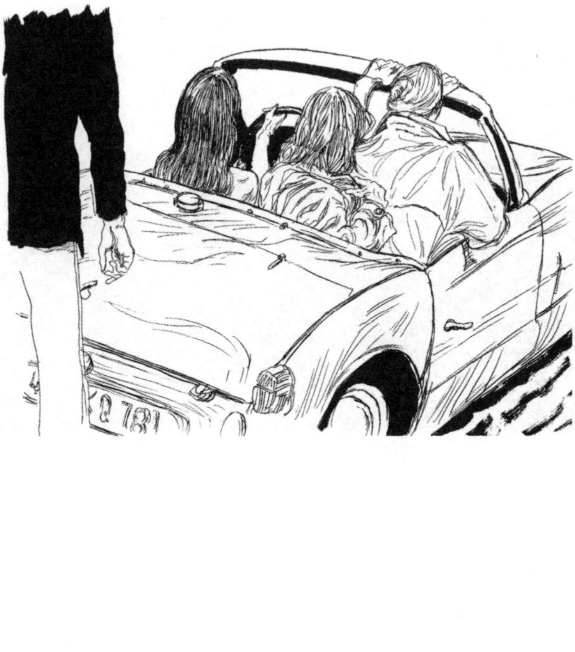

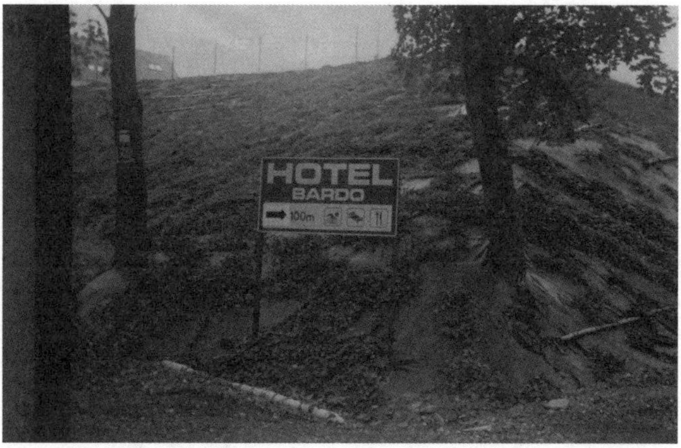
HOTEL
BARDO
100m

We Have Come to Let You Out   Stanley Schtinter
(Searching for Brion Gysin
in the Last Museum)

Room 42

*In nowhere town
on nowhere street there is a place
where true loves meet*

*It's neither near
nor far from here
in dark of night you see it clear*

*So follow me
I know the way
down this old street i'm goin' down
in nowhere town*

*I'm goin' there
goin' there
goin'* NOWHERE*

*   Lyrics originally written for an unmade musical on Josiah
Henson by Brion Gysin.

It became obvious in 2015 that our culture of reductive commemoration did not or could not consider the subject Brion Gysin. Gysin, the constant namecheck (but rare focus) of that old Beat business; Gysin: the painter, the writer, the inventor, the poet, the mystic, the visionary, the musician, the gossip and the gay.

Considering that Beat business, Gysin seemed defiantly peripheral. As the quiet shepherd or magus in the backroom – 'the passive catalyst, invisible in the process' – his reputation suffers in comparison with principal collaborator, William S. Burroughs, because he cannot be so easily reduced to the symbolism an iconographical culture demands: the suit, the heroin, the murdered wife. Gysin did too many things, went too many places, and was too many people to be recognised as or for any-one-person. He believed that if man found her ancestor in the ape, it must be possible to become more than a man.

For the expanded film project known as *Hotel Bardo*, a project indebted to the liberating applications left behind by Gysin, I've considered him not as a life, or even a body of work, but as an idea: a series of stories derived, as he was, from the sacred flame. *Hotel Bardo* is an effort to convey something of Gysin in present time: resisting biography; refusing historicisation, and instead attempting to harness the idea in light of a story still being writ.

~

On January 19th, in 2016, it would have been Gysin's 100th birthday. Securing the date the project would begin as he began, with a declaration:

> *Wrong address! Wrong address!*
> *There's been a mistake in the mail. Send me back.*
> *Wherever you got me, return me.*
> *Wrong time, wrong place, wrong colour.*

Gysin swore throughout his life that he remembered being born: the agony, the image and the statement, identifying two defining moments in his life and work: 1) beginning: birth, the key traumatic event of his life; and 2) the end and after: his final literary work, *Beat Museum-Bardo Hotel*.

The Beat Hotel – the source-site and locus for this last, unfinished novel – was a small, run-down hotel of 42 rooms at 9 rue Gît-le-Cœur, knee-deep in mid-century Paris's Latin Quarter. Gysin moved to the Hotel in 1958, surrounded by the burgeoning starlets of a counterculture in capital's colours: William S. Burroughs, Allen Ginsberg, Harold Norse, Gregory Corso and Peter Orlovsky, to name a few. Gysin later spoke of the period he spent at the Beat Hotel as the happiest of his life and *Beat Museum-Bardo Hotel* explores that time with an approach to language conjuring something close to a dream state, by lifting the concept of the 'Bardo' from Tibetan Buddhism – the state between death and rebirth – and applying it to the Beat Hotel and his broader recollections of a life he described as 'full of adventure, leading nowhere.' Bardo-time is cyclical, marked as in the hidden rings of the growing tree, where beginning and end–birth and beat–are one and the same. Gysin intended *Beat Museum-Bardo Hotel* as an exercise in writing himself out of existence. The possibility of being reborn horrified him.

~

Gysin was born at Taplow House in Buckinghamshire in 1916, then a military hospital and today a luxury hotel. Unable to afford a night at the hotel, I travelled early on the 19th in time to record the dawn chorus. (This idea was stolen. At the outset of the project, I had no idea how to approach a subject as covert as Brion.)

In the hours before departure, I lie down to sleep. Immediately, I develop a fever and lose all control of my body. A crushing pressure extends across my height and width, whilst a glistening stain – expanding and contracting – emerges on the ceiling above. This is my single point of focus for five long hours, until a horn sounds in the street below. Taxi. The pressure relents. Mobile, but still incapacitated, I crawl to the cab Quaalude-style and listen (almost) to the chat of the driver, a Hackney / Chelmsford castaway, on housing, diesel, women, and the conviction: NO FUTURE.

In the foyer of the Taplow House Hotel there is an impressive fire; here, on a middle-England armchair with rough, brown embroidered flowers, I finally fall asleep. What must be an hour passes. I wake to emerging light and walk out into the surrounding gardens with microphone ready. I'm drawn to a particular tree and, as I reach it, there is an incredible rush above me, through me... an owl, launching into the day.

Some Native American tribes call on the owl during ceremonies when a door to a secret knowledge must be opened; it can be a warning too.

~

The word 'door' finds its origin in the Celtic word for the oak tree: *duir* (also the root of the English word 'durable'). Only afterwards in conversations with that other invisible catalyst, Paul Smith, did I understand that the oak I was drawn to was the 'wrong' tree. Smith and the artist Susan Stenger had been in the area too on that morning, but in the Cliveden woodlands surrounding. Here, there is a 16-foot 6-inch-wide slice of Californian redwood, imported in 1897 by a man called William Waldorf Astor (the 1st 'Lord' Astoer, of Cliveden House). Astor denied claims that the wood was transported to Buckinghamshire as the result of a drunken bet (that American trees were so big up to 50 people could dine around a slice). No reason for its journey was ever given. We can ultimately suppose he did it because he could.

~

Recall, for a moment, Hitchcock's *Vertigo*, a film of spirals, and the scene with Madeleine as she traces her finger around the white rings describing the size of the redwood tree's growth and the parallel historical events. The Battle of Hastings, the signing of the Magna Carta, the 'discovery' of America, the tree cut down... 'Somewhere in here I was born, and here I died. It was only a moment for you; you took no notice.' A question of theft, 'Shall I take you home?' An answer, 'Somewhere in the light.' Orpheus and Proust in a tired matrimony: in search, always, of lost time.

Recall, then, that the spirit possessing Madeleine is that of Carlotta; Carlotta, of whom all we really know is that the home built for her became broken, and so was converted into a hotel. And the portrait; the obsessed protagonist following Madeleine to the gallery to see her stare into Carlotta. Recall Gysin's admission: 'I bowed three times to the great collector and disappeared into my picture.'

Recall *Vertigo*'s bedfellow in Chris Marker's *La Jetée*, a film of disappearing into one's own picture, a film in pursuit of someone else's; the protagonist attempting to break the constraints of fact and fiction with time as his medium.

La Jetée makes a point of referencing the tree-tracing scene and loops and webs a question of what makes the defining image; loops and webs the question of whether our knowledge of the past is any more reliable than our knowledge of the future. 'This is the story of a man marked by an image from his childhood.' For Gysin, the defining image, seen at the beginning, is the end. Time as the oldest ideological construct. Birth and death are interchangeable; birth as the key traumatic event of the life and death as its namesake.

~

Beyond the owl, I remember nothing.
No return to the hotel, no recording, no trip back to London.

~

From Paddington, onwards to central London for the afternoon of the 19th. October Gallery: sometime representatives of Gysin's work and hootenanny boarding house of the biospherical ideologue. There I met Iain Sinclair. Sinclair had experienced similar symptoms the night before, so too did the filmmaker Susu Laroche. I have come to call this 'Gysindrome' – only after the process documented in the film *Norton's Cut-Up* were we restored.

Readers may be familiar with Norton, owing to Sinclair's *Slow Chocolate Autopsy* and Alan Moore's *League of Extraordinary Gentlemen*. He is the local prisoner relative to Gysin's global prisoner. In *Norton's Cut-Up*, we see Norton take one newspaper from the morning of Gysin's birth in 1916 and one newspaper from what would've been his 100th birthday. He cuts them up and reassembles them at random. The results say more about the time in which I am writing now than they did about 2016 or 1916. This is the promise of the cut-up: a literary technique to undo the dogma of language; to 'leak' the future from a past and present tense. And to recognise language as the first and often most potent weapon deployed in combat (Burroughs' forte). Gysin, seeing the cut-up at least initially as whimsical, gifted the technique to Burroughs, going on to define the author's work and reputation.

~

NORTON'S CUT UP: PENICILLIN THE FIRST EFFECTIVE ANTI-
BIOTIC ALLY OF RAMZAN KADYROV, MAYBE I WOULD GET OUT,
WAS DISCOVERED BY ALEXANDER FLEMING
     WHEN HE NOTICED A RING OF DEATH ON LEADER'S DOG
WAS 'ITCHING' TO A DISH OF BACTERIA HE'D BEEN GROWING,
ATTACK PUTIN'S OPPONENTS.
     AT ITS CENTRE HE IDENTIFIED A FUNGUS, THE
CHECHEN PARLIAMENT HERE AT MY THROAT THE SPORE
WHICH HAD BLOWN INTO HIS LAB INSIDE THIS PLACE SOME-
THING DEADLY TO BACTERIA
     GRANTS FROM NORTH AFRICA MOROCCO AND PAPER
IN THE WHINE OF ALGERIA ARE TO BE DECLARED SAFE VERY
REAL MONSTER, GHOUL.
     THERE ARE ALSO PLANS TO KEEP ALL ASYLUM SEEKERS
ACCUSED OF BLASPHEMY CULT TO GAIN ASYLUM IN GERMANY
MOHAMMED ANWAR, 15, PERFORMED OPERATION CASA-
BLANCA THE AMPUTATION WITH A SCYTHE
     THEY REFUSED TO BECOME HIS PAID ASSASSINS MOS-
QUITOES. THE ATTENDANTS, COURTIERS, PROCURERS THAT
SHRINK HEADS OF ROUSSEL
     NAKED AND SHRIVELLED, THIN AS UNBORN SPARK
OLYMPIC ALERT. ORACULAR AND BLASPHEMOUS, MUTE BUT
TALL. SECRET INTELLIGENCE
     HAD NOT BEEN SANCTIFIED FOR MIRACLES. THEY ARE
ALSO WARY.
     'THE CROW,' ROBERT GRAVES TELLS MI5 ALSO CONSI-
DERED ESSENTIAL.
     MARK, A GAY INTELLIGENCE OFFICER ACKNOWLEDGED
THE RISK. THE RAVEN, SCALD-CROW AND OTHER LARGE BLACK
NETWORKS
     EXECUTIVE TOLD THE PARENTS HEALTH CRISIS BACKED
THE EYES OF THE WITNESSING DEAD, MAKING THE BAN ON
GAY AGENTS WHO
     WERE RICH IN VEGETABLES AND FISH REDUCE THE
MUMMIES ARE NOT THERE TO BE INSPECTED THEIR SEXUAL-
ITY, HE ADDED WARN THE MIDDLE AGED OF THEIR DEMENTIA
RISK, SUCKING UP BREATH, GLISTENING WITH BORROWED
SWEAT, AVID FOR THE INCREASED RISK BECAUSE THEIR
PARENTS HAVE LANGUAGE. THE HUNG MUMMIES ARE ALSO
CAMERAS. AND THEY ARE
     LOOKING RIGHT BACK AT THE THING THAT IS LOOKING
AT THEM

The Dreamachine was 'the first work of art to view with the eyes closed,' and further intended as 'the great drugless turn-on of the 1960s.' It is a victory of the capitalist paradigm which resigns the Beat business to one of celebrating and necessitating drugs; indeed, it was the primary taker Burroughs who said that 'anything that can be done chemically can be done by other means.'

Gysin called himself a misanthrope, but this diagnosis is at odds with his practice: he dedicated his life and work to helping others see according to their own, infinite means. There is no better example of this, of liberating application, than the Dreamachine in motion. The idea came to Gysin as he travelled by bus through France: at the correct speed with the sun shining behind passing trees, the light moves at a rate of 8 to 13 Hx, mimicking the alpha waves of the brain (the state of the brain between wake and sleep; in meditation, et cetera). Things happen. Just as making a film about Gysin – a man who expressly loathed the screen – might be considered counterintuitive, so might be recording a device which shows itself only to the individual blind. Nonetheless, just as a Paris shopfront recognised at the time of Gysin's conception, so did I the basic aesthetic appeal of the Dreamachine and took it upon myself to produce of it / for it the first decent footage.

For this, Tony Hill invented a new rig – a variation on the famous 'Downside Up' rig built for his 1972 film of the same name – now completing the circle and so allowing our 16mm camera to travel 360 degrees. Hill stands atop a scaffold with a long protruding arm upon which the camera is fixed, leading to a handle, so that he can spin it manually around the subject. The same applies from above with the camera turning on its axis.

Experiments were also made with the Dreamachine at Cambridge University. Although Gysin conceived the Dreamachine, the technicalities were realised by 'systems advisor' Ian Sommerville (then studying mathematics at Cambridge). On February 5th, the date of Sommerville's death and William Burroughs' birthday, we returned the Dreamachine to Cambridge University, with writer Robert Macfarlane and poet Rod Mengham, responding.

~

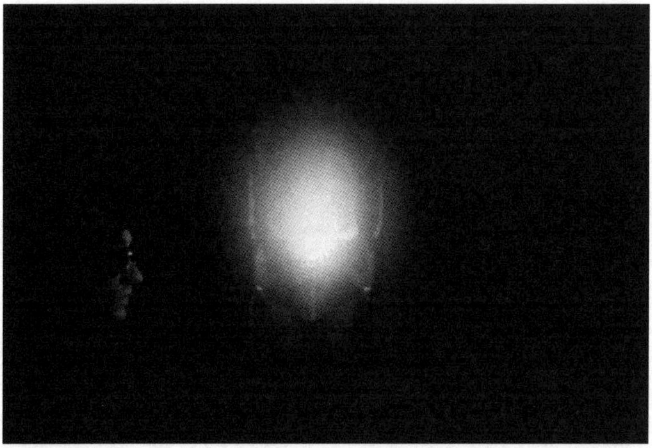

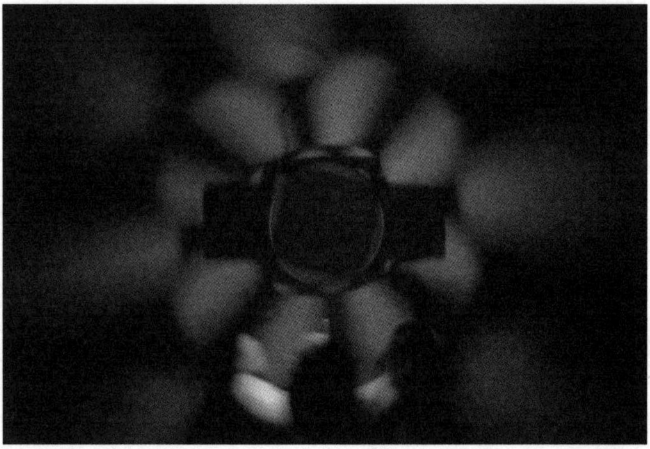

RMe
> *All the time there's a small map of Africa dodging around in the centre.*

RMa
> *Cardiogram. Lateral pulse... moving across the centre, which does hold.*

RMe
> *Pain. Between the ears.*

RMa
> *Now a kind of architectural form to it. A geometry that wasn't there before. A huge fire burning in the bottom right. A function of the heat. Masks. Direct capital columns.*

RMe
> *Large green bubble welling up from beneath.*

RMa
> *Trench. Chessboard. Celtic interlace. Are you feeling a nausea, Rod?*

RMe
> *Feeling something. In the throat.*

RMa
> *More a sense of scenes emerging now. Figures in a room.*

RMe
> *It's before landscapes. Before landscapes form.*

RMa
> *Metamorphic. Quaking grass. Uptight to the sea head.*

RMe
> *Now I'm seeing my hands, which is even less possible than everything else.*

~

An appendix to our medical treatment at the October Gallery: Sinclair brought along a first edition copy of Gysin's *Beat Museum-Bardo Hotel*. He can't remember the circumstances of receiving the book, but it is beautifully signed by Brion as 'yours in present time.' On his journey to the gallery, Sinclair discovered a photograph concealed in the book's dust jacket. A previously unseen and unpublished picture of Gysin, Burroughs and Ian Sommerville at the Beat Hotel in Paris.

~

Somewhere in the light.

Returning to the text throughout the process, it occurred to me that it was possible that Gysin is (or was) still somewhere in the Bardo. In searching for him, I have travelled to Tangier, to New York, to Paris, London and Mystras – locations central to his life and work.

Repeatedly I would arrive at the wrong address, or the right address but at the wrong time. I found nothing of Gysin in these places, spare his students and his subjects. These were writers, artists and musicians; people who would gift me their time for the sake of acknowledging something of Brion's brilliance, something of his legacy. This imposed on me a certain responsibility: to honour that time – their time – Gysin's time. But it would be illogical to try to tell the story of Gysin in film – offensive to edit the extent of their contributions down – and counterproductive anyway to embark on anything resembling a conventional documentary narrative form. The solution which eventually came to me was obvious: there must be a real Hotel Bardo on planet Earth. And there is: one hour south of Wrocław in Poland.

~

RMa
    But they're not where they are in real space?
RMe
    Yes and no.
RMa
    This cross-hatch effect is densening. Stenting happening.
    Now very recognisably there is a vortex.
RMe
    Towards my hands a heart shape forms a junction.
RMa
    I've completely lost the core of colour I began with.
RMe
    Everything is paler. Wintery.
RMa
    A cold blue-green is settling in now. Odd flickers of
    a quest.

~

On the anniversary of Gysin's death, I travelled to Poland – to the hotel – with each of the 23 interviews I'd recorded, unedited, as video files. The hotel was experiencing a quiet season and so granted access to each of their twenty-three rooms. Every interview was given a room of its own, and played back on their respective television monitors, without pause, for eighteen hours. I re-recorded the interviews in full in their rooms, as important evidence of this act of re-situation. The motive behind the journey to the 'wrong' address, and the act of playback, was to create a direct connection with Gysin – still, we may presume, a guest in the Bardo – and release him finally from it, and so from the responsibility of death (and rebirth).

Another of Beat Museum-Bardo Hotel's big ideas was to take all the white world's key cultural references to the fault line of San Andreas in preparation for the great earthquake. The Last Museum. Notre Dame, Buckingham Palace, the Abbey of Thelema. At the time of publication, I am communicating with the Sicily-based real estate agent managing the sale of Aleister Crowley's Abbey (Gysin was an authority on Crowley; it was his friend Kenneth Anger who uncovered the magician's bedroom murals). I am communicating too with the National Trust about Cliveden's redwood; I'm in talks with the Beat Hotel; the Cecil Hotel in Los Angeles have already confirmed their elevator. I've emailed Athens about the Parthenon but so far had no response.

~

Beyond Cambridge I travel to Tangier, Morocco. A cattle gate creates a zone of exclusion between the exit of the airport and the carpark, from which a gaggle of hungry children hang, outstretched arms and hard palms. My host is behind them leaning on a bin. Smiling, Lolita glasses, espadrilles and formal dress. I met my host in Athens around Panepistimio station where she was trying to score. We recognised each other from London.

At the station, I mentioned to her the necessity of visiting Tangier, Gysin having lived there for twenty-three years. She too was planning to make a film, her subject undecided but certainly set in Tangier. We walk away towards the car park and speak little. A presence behind us. 'Oh, don't worry, that's Aladdin! The driver... and a friend.'

At the apartment I ask for my set of keys, but I'm told 'There is only one set of keys.' We're on the eighth floor set back from the beach. The purple smudge of Spain in the distance is everything. My host rolls a massive bifta.

I'm given the option of either staying and waiting in the apartment or going with them to another city to buy a Steadicam for her film. In the car she explains to me that some days prior she met a woman on the street begging, and that now she has a clear idea for her film: fuse the life of this woman with her own, by 'Creating a drawing together... her life and mine.' The car slows for traffic lights. A camel is whipped and falls to its knees. 'I've done it before,' she says, 'drawing, with one of my boyfriends... we got naked and covered ourselves in paint and rubbed against each other and the canvas.' I ask if this is how she intends to collaborate with the woman from the street. 'Obviously not.' Aladdin cooks for us that night. Orange and green quinoa with filthy onion flatbread. Amazing. After dinner, I open the booze parlayed on the purple side and read John Gilmore's *Laid Bare* (the only book needed on the real *Hollywood Babylon*: 'A Memoir of Wrecked Lives and the Hollywood Deathtrip'). The apartment takes an L-shape, with my room at the shorter end of the character and hers the long. Aladdin uses the space between, releasing his sleeping bag from a suede hold-all as soon as my host announces she's going to bed. He sleeps with his arms crossed and one eye open.

I break house-arrest for the Tangier Inn, one of the few bars in the city, nestled below the Muniria Hotel (where Burroughs wrote the greater part of *Naked Lunch*). There are cartoon illustrations of him, Kerouac and Ginsberg plastered across the walls, twinned with IKEA-type quotes on 'living for the day' and loving 'only the mad ones.' The music is a safe-space-techno; the lagers are short-necks, stubbies. The only spirit is Jack Daniel's. It is my single venture alone, away from the swastika tiles and the magic carpets of my supervised attic garret, and the air-conditioned, Bluetooth-enabled, bullet-proof Ford Mondeo. And not another Beat tourist in site. It is perfect. It is awful. It says everything I expected Tangier to say and more.

My hosts are rattled by my slipping out, sitting up in wait. It is explained to me that she is the daughter of a senior president at a major bank. Aladdin has been with the family for many years, cooking, driving, packing a firearm. The autonomous parking attendants outside the apartment building are in fact a covert extension of my host's security. Morocco is apparently very dangerous, but she just 'had to' make her film in Tangiers. So did I, and yet by the end of the trip I've recorded nothing. At the airport, I avoid the two easily recognisable Beat tourists: he's reading a copy of *Naked Lunch*. At Madrid we transfer for Vienna. All passengers are divided between two onward liners. All, but two for the same flight. Unusually large for a short-haul flight and quiet too, I ditch my seat reservation for the whole row at 23. Settling in, the Beat girl from departures bounds down the gangway, and checking and re-checking her ticket, tells me, 'You're in my seat.' Taking her position next to me, she removes her shawl to reveal two starving fishes tattooed onto her shoulder, ouroboros-almost.

Soon we start to talk. She tells me that she hates everywhere, and that's the problem, but by any standards her trip was appalling: sexually assaulted in the Caves of Hercules (the site of Gysin's ashes, scattered); too much time with one of the dejected Master Musicians (met as her friend from the airport knows a man who now lives in Paul Bowles' old apartment), who pointed out a twelve-year-old over mint tea, and said, 'My kind... suggestion of curves.' And her friend otherwise spent the entire time pacing up and down the beach reading *Naked Lunch* aloud, desperately attempting to invoke something of Tangier lost.

~

Monuments and artefacts can all be submitted for display at The Last Museum: package well – include an explanation – and send to:

>	Stanley Schtinter
>	c/o HOTEL BARDO
>	Lipowa 5, 57-256
>	Bardo, Poland

~

The Vienna connection is tenuous but fair: I hang on to Orson Welles' character, Harry Lime, in *The Third Man*. *Impostors, all of us, Inspector Lee.*
John Geiger, Gysin's biographer, followed up his essential tome on the technicalities of the life with a book exploring the phenomenon of the 'third man factor.' In it, he surveys the multitudinous experiences of those at 'the edge of death, often adventures or explorers, who experience a benevolent presence beside them that encourages them to make one final effort to survive.' A catalogue of secrets; the Richard & Judy companion work to Gysin and Burroughs' *The Third Mind*.
The Third Mind is a survival manual, and the most complete, accurate and potent directory of Gysin and Burroughs' experiments in the cut-up (collage; time-travel and total removal of the word). It is a companion to will the transcendent companion on journeys to nowhere and argues that when two people come together in the truest sense, a third entity is produced, beyond the respective and combined egos; beyond control. It is the book I carry with me to meet C. M. von Hausswolff, in the sewer made famous by Harry Lime's demise.

~

See the silent writing of Brion Gysin, Hassan-i Sabbah, across all skies!
   —W.S.B.

~

Hausswolff, in 1986 – the year of Gysin's death – visited Alamut. I have, in advance of our meeting, tracked down a copy of the mythical film documenting his journey. Alamut was the mountain fortress of Hassan-i Sabbah; a character who appealed to Gysin and Burroughs for the lack of any written evidence (suggestion has been made that the prized possession lost to the sunk Titanic, Edward Fitzgerald's translation of *Ruba'iyat of Omar Khayyam*, was in fact all cover for the loss of Sabbah's writings). Indisputable is the empire once held by Sabbah; he ruled great swathes of Persia without an army. The principal fortress of Alamut was destroyed by Hulagu Khan (grandson of Ghengis), but still its outline can be traced atop a jagged rock in the Aborz mountain range.

~

The word 'assassin' comes from 'hashashin' (the Islamic sect formally known as the Nizari Ismailis). Sabbah would select his hashashin by choosing from his empire the most able young men. He would invite an individual to the mountain fortress of Alamut and knock him out with the greatest hash. The man would wake and find himself in Sabbah's 'garden of earthly delights'. Wine, women. He believed Sabbah had shown him God; the promise of paradise, and possessed, as or like a prophet, immortality. He would henceforth on Sabbah's word go off to hashashinate any trash-talking leader of some far-flung opposition (or leap from the highest peak at Alamut, knowing exactly where he was going for having gone before). Burroughs insisted, and Gysin supposed that he was the reincarnation of Sabbah. 'Wrong time, wrong place.' Posing as a journalist, Hausswolff was granted permission to tour Iran in 1986 under the auspices of 'promoting Iran's cultural importance throughout Scandinavia.' During the few hours Hausswolff spent at Alamut, the then Swedish prime minister, Olof Palme, was assassinated as he left a cinema. The murder remains unsolved.

~

there is no moon
to light your way
no cheap hotel
where you can stay
no spot to eat
no church to pray
no shop to work
no field to play
but here's the place
we'll meet one day
on this bad street
I'm goin' down
in nowhere town
I'm goin' there
goin' there
goin' NOWHERE

~

Some months later, in London, I travel to Tooting to meet Ian Mac-Fadyen (whose writing on Gysin and Burroughs is unparalleled). On the high street towards his door, a tap on the shoulder from a figure covered head to toe in black. It is my host from Tangier. She explains to me that she has almost finished her film and has converted to Islam.

The only untapped places left in this project in a literal sense are Edmonton, Canada, famous for birthing Marshall McLuhan and for Gysin growing up there, and Duke Street, London, the home of Gysin's film collaborations with Burroughs and Antony Balch. My host had already confirmed her willingness to participate in 'something' around Duke Street for the *Hotel Bardo* film. I hadn't much of an angle, except wanting to use some of the music Gysin made in collaboration with Steve Lacy and harness something of either Stella, Gysin's mother, or Mya, Queen of the Desert and her namesake Mary Cook, the Scientologist who nicked Brion's Tangier restaurant, The 1001 Nights. I suggest we reconvene in a couple of hours for something to eat.

~

Although not a recommendable destination for food, the Tooting Granada – until the publication of this piece – is London's last dead letter box, and the only place for my host and I to lunch. Built as a cinema in 1931, it is now a bingo hall. Gala Bingo, along with Samuel Smiths, are the custodians of a London meanwhile razed by development. Their unofficial alliance constitutes an accidental English heritage project. You can enter and wander around the Tooting Granada today without disturbance. I've sat for hours in the upper circle relishing the everyman majesty of the place; with enough distance, the sound of the fruit machines take on something of a croon. Like other bingo halls, these are the last free – or least monitored – spaces in present-time London.

My host and I agree to meet the next day. We arrive independently at 10 Duke Street, and then realise it's the wrong 10 Duke Street. A hairdresser. Christmas. We cut across Mayfair, past The Palm Beach and Sexy Fish, and no matter our road or map function: it's nowhere.

~

At the Nova Convention in 1978, William Burroughs, Timothy Leary, Robert Anton Wilson, Les Levine and Brion Gysin speculate what beings looking out at the stars from other worlds, think of ours.

Intelligent life? Brion answers simply: 'Blue. We're a pretty blue to all of them.' There is and only ever was the will to go; to get out; up there; check-in / sign-out; to light out for the last museum knowing that a place is only ever an idea. 'A story like this can have no happy ending. Or can it?' says Gysin in his final line on *Beat Museum-Bardo Hotel*. Well, can it?

~

In nowhere town
on nowhere street
there is a place
where true loves meet
it's neither near
nor far from here
in dark of night
you see it clear
so follow me
I know the way
down this old street
I'm goin' down
in nowhere town
I'm goin' there
goin' NOWHERE

~

ALAN MOORE

> I find myself haunted by old photographs where everybody's dead. I don't know who they were, and the space that they are in which would have been filled with their atmosphere and their presence, that is perhaps still there, perhaps...

IAIN SINCLAIR

> Definitely.

ALAN MOORE

> But it has... everything has... no it's obviously not been lost, or I wouldn't be commenting upon it.

IAIN SINCLAIR

> The living can assist the imagination of the dead.

ALAN MOORE

> Yeah. Who said that?

IAIN SINCLAIR

> W.B. Yeats. in a vision. And that's like what I started with and I've never gone beyond it. It's like the whole idea that these dead, these things are all around us all the time. And all we do is assist this ongoing project that they... but the great book is being written by them. And then we inscribe little bits of it... and then I hear a bit from someone living who's tapping a different part of it. And I take a bit of that and it weaves, weaves into this thing. But that's all we do. And then, we step across.

ALAN MOORE

> I also kind of realised that since I was a kid, I have been haunted by the feeling that we're already dead, and that we are being looked back upon from some point in the future.

IAIN SINCLAIR

> Bardo.

~

Monuments and artefacts can all be submitted for display...

~

'n take your time
in the leaf mould
the mud 'n' slime
beneath your feet
on nowhere street
this sad old street
i'm goin' down

a who whoo whoo
'n' watch your step
the journey is not over yet
you still could beat
a quick retreat
down this dim street
i'm going' down

~

...package well, and include an explanation.

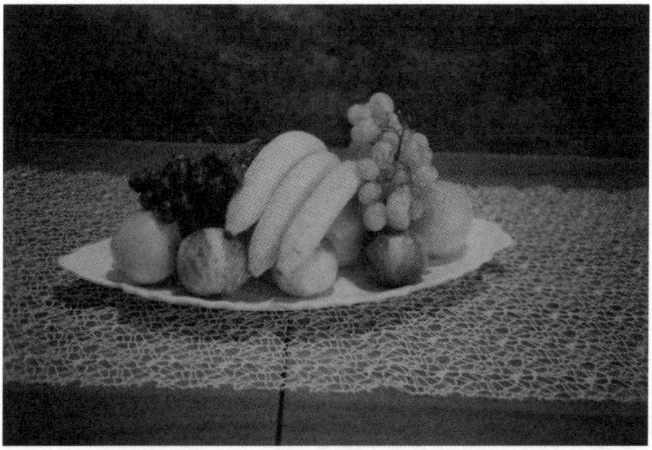

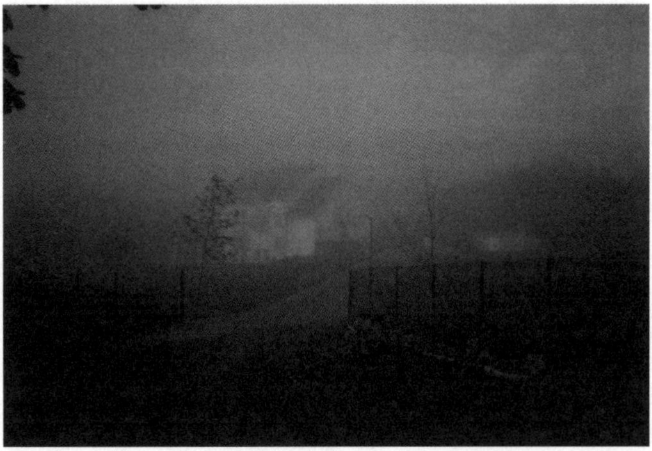

The Gracious Ones   Sophie Seita
(A Philosophical Ballet)

Room 43

PERSONS OF THE DIALOGUE / 3 VOICES /
SCENE OF THE BANQUET

>Several small recording devices from which pre-recorded material can be played; 3 big screens (with multiple projectors in front of & behind them); 1 musician or dj; 3 or more 'running machines' (real, imagined, or in some way visible, materialised, or translated)...

>The piece opens in almost complete darkness. The women enter and stretch, as if before or after an exercise routine. During these first 3 minutes one of the small recording devices at the centre of the stage plays a collage made up of lines from a material science book on crystals; an interview with Mauricio Kagel on his compositional process; Sor Juana's La Repuesta; and Reinhold Gerling's *The Gymnastics of the Will: Practical Guidance for the Increase of Energy and Self-Control through the Strengthening of Willpower without External Help*. Over all this can be heard the whirr of running machines, untrodden; a perpetuum mobile, without feet, without touch.

NOTE ON THE ORDER OF LINES:

>While some lines clearly lend themselves to a sequential reading and will inevitably result in giving the impression of a deliberate dialogue, they may also be liberally used to form monologues for three voices; and can therefore also be repeated and returned to throughout the piece. Overlaps, if timed or polyrhythmically practised, are also very welcome, though shouldn't be overdone. The recording devices, which also have a looping effect, can be activated by the performers during the performance; recording themselves or one another, playing text back to themselves, or not. They may also remain completely unused; defiantly so.
>   When it's not their time; in other words, when there's a pause in thinking; the not-quite interlocutors or almost-listeners turn either into statues of their own devising or perform a semi-improvised dance; interacting or not quite interacting in movement with one another, or with the sculptural objects and materials around them.

One could picture the women running on running machines, sometimes resting, sometimes stretching, sometimes engaged in gymnastics or Pure Observation, but that may be too literal for so runny an allegory, so physically demanding an undertaking. But we must imagine the leaping ladies at a symposium of their own generous invitations and makings with an audience of occasionally obtuse, but frequently frivolous and fervent, disciples.

The choric rumba ends with the three women organising themselves in front of the three panels like statues on plinths. They may also be on actual plinths.

~

I am almost another person.

~

I go to the old masters and I match their form.

~

Winning is durational.

~

Panache is my credit card.

~

I believe it's fair to say that's a card we both play well.

~

I disrespect people who cannot hold in a sneeze.

~

Oh, there's a noodle sticking to the cupboard above the stove.

~

From the spaghetti test?

~

Yes.

~

And then she adopts this voice, like a ten-year-old in a nice restaurant, where you're handed a moist cloth like on airplanes, and she unfolds it and holds it to her nose and sighs ah, lemon verbena!

~

And *then* you walk into a midnight message probing if you preferred the lace top or the faux-leather pants, and you say 'both,' because – quoting yourself – 'more is always more,' which then leads to a reflection on the aleatory effects of impulsive decisions, to which you reply that aleatory adventures require more than simply bearing witness, which is a rash thing to say, and then you can't forget that lightning bolt over the breast in the form of the stems of flowers or the pattern on the calf, only half-glimpsed through tights, or the possibility of a missed chance to be *not* cautious for once in your life.

~

And *then* she chases the seductive light of melancholy like a classic ex-poet. Classically trained for the pithy abstractions, the obscure and tensile sensualities, or should I say the tensile possibles of a cinereous paging through thesauruses. So you can be introduced at parties as enigmatically forlorn or ferociously far-out. This is S, she is an ex-poet.

~

And then...

~

Then what?

~

Oh, diligent creature!

~

I'm just going to be that lady with the dressing gown again.

~

Just because the Enlightenment project is over doesn't mean you can't ever use it again.

~

Exactly. Who says I can't have the past and eat it too?!

~

Now if we don't all dream of flamingos tonight –

~

You see, I remember some lines.

~

Sometimes collage is just what you had wanted to say but in a better order.

~

I'm into Serendipity. Someone only needs to say they like antique furniture and I know it's a sign.

~

Thank you for the language my friends. I remain forever in your delightful debt.

Signed,

> S, plus all the usual sobriquets,
> smooches, roses, ylang ylang

~

Once you're committed to humour, is that your bloody needlework?

> One of the women moves to the corner of the stage
> and begins to sing the German folk song, 'Why do You
> Cry Fair Gardener's Wife.'

Why don't we start with something solid, like a reference to authority?

~

To extemporise means to drop the common polish. You flush the context for the suitable and even-headed and question the fetching voices for good measure.

~

Ok. Here we go. Three princes arrive in a foreign country. It's like the beginning of a joke, but it's not. As soon as they arrive, they find clues that *would* help them identify a certain flamingo they've never seen but *might* find – should they so desire. (They do desire it.) The clues add up to this image: a one-heeled flamingo that hops on one foot, is almost completely blind, has a dent in its beak, and carries a magician's hat on one of its wings, on the other a ram. The flamingo is lost – to be clear – so the princes find themselves suddenly suspected of having stolen the flamingo given their exacting description.

Promptly and primarily out of boredom, the King sends for the princes and meets them in his illustrious interrogation chamber. Not being accomplished in the skillz of deduction, the King is befuddled as to how the princes added up one and two, and wants to ban them from his Kingdom, or better still, make them Spin Masters of Public Relations and Actuarial Accessories.

The princes, being promoters of Free Education and the Abolition of Discounted Economicals and Unwaged Vagaries, explain their magic wisdom, because the King only understands this to be magic rather than intellectualism (fine, think the princes, we ARE into magic after all, who cares if we lie and all our intellectual endeavours will now be read as humbug, if it gets us out of this pretty pickle):

> At this, the choric joggers squeak 'pretty pickle' in
> delegated delight.

So they say, matter-of-factly: look, it's a flamingo rather than a camel because the grass is tinted pink when the sun shines on it after being touched by wondrous flamingo legs.

~

Meanwhile, the audience is getting impatient with the
story. My ladies, could you please stop whispering;
the white noise is really killing the atmosphere, we're
trying to watch this young spaniel dance! If this was
some kind of recital we could all look at impy images
and imitate them; puppies rolling and falling all over
one another; but it would've been done already;
like most things.

~

All this running around is really getting quite tedious – so much effort just for the sake of a debonair allegory?

~

What running?

~

It seems to me that the Sheriff or The Agency has a vested interested in stopping you from experiencing heavenly time travel alongside your emotional support peacock. What are you going to do about it?

~

And so the three things you take to the Island of Seductive Wieldings are nuts for nourishment, hummous for humility, and dragon fruit for keeping the eyes alight amidst the non-variation and the promise of paradise.

~

Which we trace all the way back to the sickle and the plough, which spread on backs and small ribcages, which you hold only to wonder if

~

La vilana is possibly villainous but you okay the delay.

~

Is this your penchant for the 'more soon' munchkins or maybellines of which there are now two?

~

Oat cakes are my comfort food.

Don't judge.

> Now we must also imagine the running ladies in their Pretty Life in the Suburbs, their ship-shape furnishings, ellipticals, vases, juicers, and other accessories for mixing and making the eyelids flutter.

Here's to being delicate!

~

TO BEING DELICATE

~

And being young and delicate is to be not so delicate in actuality, only in appearance, as interpreted liberally, as in stealing liberally from letters and lithographs and levelling and lolloping is to ride the sound wave for your Pure Pleasure. So what. Or rather 'what's that?' As they say a delicacy of delusion is a delusion of delicate proof, or maybe feet? Her feet at any rate are rather diplomatic. She dwells in the gracefulness of direction. In the soul of softest escape, most supple accounts and maybe sacrifices. Willingly serving her speech.
It has to hurt. None of us want to strike.

~

Hot-tongued mother of my little litter, your encomium in this manner is courageously stubborn, outrageously flabby; indeed, I cannot, I shall not, accept this arrangement or derangement of phrases – I do not permit it. How so, you ask? The answer is: I cannot contradict you and therefore must not be in possession of your discursive entrapment. Away, away!

> As the room heats up, the swooping babes do not
> exactly stoop, they step on the spoken-on, they speak
> on the praises but step not on Eros, they tread on
> age as something non-existent; on time —

> ~

I claim the contrary —

> ~

I said, very well then, Madame, you may speak rather single-mindedly and charmingly or at other times rather nothing-else-ly; neither hip nor hop which is unacceptable. You're either in the bower or you're out of it. There's an admissions policy. Which you've broken. But if Eros is this ferociously capricious kind, holding her every paw to the wind, like a dancing star, letting herself be swirled like leaf, what use is she to me?

> The reverie is interrupted by the sound of the Running
> Machines, which is the sound made by Constant Tasks,
> the Sound of Hierarchised Intention, of Painted Offspring,
> while Closure is vamping up the raison d'état (of love)
> making dimples in the doorway, which is also the sound
> of what is held between, of connaissance, after waking
> from sleeping with legends and charts. The definition of
> beauty's routine diversion is, after all, its coquetry
> in recognised form.

> ~

You trust in the unremitting thereness and thank the Lover for it, to which the Lover replies, The Cat is a proxy for my feelings.

~

A gestural reservoir that's full but also stunted in articulation...

~

And the Lover told you how your language visits her; in the unlikely moments of affirmation, oh no but I *do*, I do remember the shimmering discos, the kaleidoscopic spinning. Or when you briefly held hands; to calm the nerves; to say that hurt is not a worry as in what matters is connection.

~

Now now, these tears will surely polish the memory, like a crystal, or the *idea* of a love, of a girl...

~

Look, you two would be like two full moons spinning around each other and that would be both the most beautiful and the most impossible thing.

~

And the line resembling an abstraction, a female form, on the underarm, wriggles, not quite impatiently but tipsily after sun-soaked talk of role play and chatoyant chateaus in France. And you speak with the frankness sometimes afforded to almost-strangers because there's no paradigm for conversation; simply a syndicate of glorious ideas spanked into first contact.

~

The metaphysical earth rub I can't shake off.

~

And every crystal affects you differently. Sprung forth into stone they hold consciousness which you want to rub in and this remains a fantasy of unaffordable juncture because the affordance of the material is not yours to take, it has to be given. And you both muse that you would quite like a name like Organic Honey.

~

Perhaps
Sable Selenite
Red Jasper
Rabbit Jade
or simply Obsidian

> The treadmill of character-formation speeds up and the shapes and names transform themselves in full regalia: Rabbit Jade's Juvenile and Succulent Jurisdiction is gently twisting, flipping Selenite's Opalescent Grounding, also teasing Obsidian's Obeisance. Not a spectacle just the 'grasping' of a well-paced, utterly unplanned conjunction in space, motion, and bodily lines.

Which would you like to wear?

> By this point, the stage, too, has experienced a transformation. Blown up or lip-lined into a vast veranda-swing, or maybe a prosodic fantasy for singing darlings to sleep, that is, into an unlikely octave. The women are daring doyens, after all, and every great speech needs a tea break for moistening lips, which can't be held open too long, that would be a tease, wouldn't it, which sometimes is the point. To repeat: the stage has become a sublime cloud of hormonal mesh, a sound-wavy netting; maybe we hear clicking, maybe a rustling of recorded matter, of unplanned chronicles, maybe of breath (are the runners fatigued or is their shattering a poeisis?).

Doesn't everyone want that?

> What are they debating if not the unideal sphere of a sonnet, its sublime lodging? Let's hear some more of the inadvertent songs. Let's swim in notes, eat grapes.

This is to turn lyric loucheness into quite respectacle receptacles for theatrical pontificating.

~

It's like channelling.

~

A process revealed but not quite.

~

Maybe you're just having a moment.

~

And it may not be enough to discover the mutual liking of the undertow of chiffon, as you relate a splurge after the rebellion, swimmingly, of more nicely fabricated swim suits, and the other replies, in neat revolutionary fashion, *sous les paves, la plage!*... Later, you make a decision not to be moved by the thought anymore and like magic it works. It's simple and therefore surprising. The sensation just vanished.

~

Cut the erratic expression some slack.

~

I think the banquet is set for dessert. Let me read the menu to you. 'Explosions of flashbacks render the most ordinary moments spectacular in the bifurcation of comedic and tragic figures who in exquisite aberration of otherworldly movements irrationally cut or scramble into action and thus create a crystalline image in which time is neither determined by duration nor by the "powers of the false" that resonate with the traces of the vicissitudes of Life and Love, in pockets of avoidant attachment. All these calls to action. The world amplifies itself further.' I don't know what that means.

~

It means that a skilful writer should be able to do both tragedy and comedy. I concur. Alright, time to pack it in darlings. It's been a long night.

~

One last thing. You can't just bulldozer through the world saying 'well the love just wasn't strong enough.' The strength of your love can't be your loophole.
    What's the loophole?

~

There is no loophole.

Ode   Cass McCombs

Room 44

Vinegar footprints
in threads of BART train carpet,
how many fibers of your cloth benches
where a 14 year old once read
The Autobiography of Malcolm X
as once white stains turned before his eyes
royal purple as gum
as if the prince in
One Thousand and One Nights
willed his magic carpet
straight to the bottom of the Bay.
Since that your magic seat is tore up,
              you are preserved.

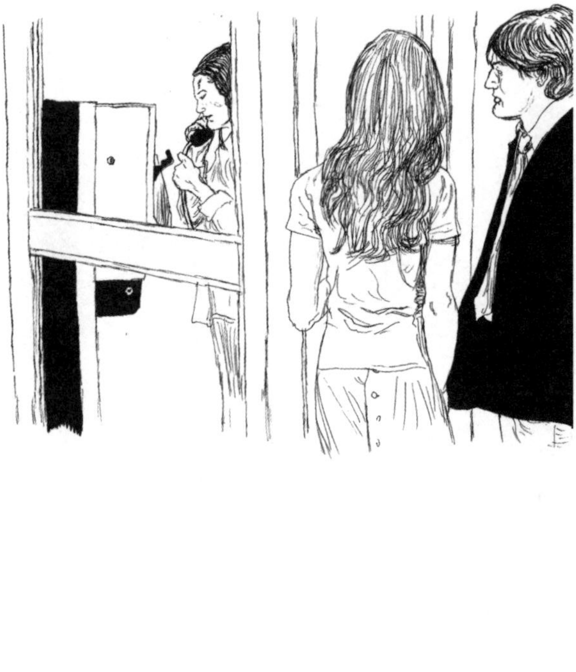

Travelling Alone is My Favourite Sickness   Ralf Webb

Room 45

When I first arrived I thought I would buy a disposable camera.
In my Airbnb a week later the objects are in high definition.
A pair of Reeboks, the lipstick I brought,
empty cans of Diet Coke lined by the windowsill, scabbed over.
I am gorging on looks. I thought I'd do lots of things –
walks in the parks – but have hardly left my room.

Anyway why would I want pictures of the painful trees.
Accounts of my past lives in this city have dressed those trees in gauze.
(And a thumbprint in grease on the frame of a Suzuki.
And an expensive ticket to a Symbolist art gallery.
And cheap rosé, the grace of cheap rosé: all dressed in gauze.)
I want no photos. I make no telephone calls.

Anyway what could I do with pictures of my painful outsides,
the dripping carnations that hassle the boulevards.
The job of the picture is to account for love, to capture the simmering
human glow. But that's probably impossible.
Atop the nightstand, my iPhone flashes with updates
on the mental health of all my friends. It would be vile not to answer.

The light in this room is my collaborator, a livid shade of red.
I begin to whirl a towel above my head, singing:
I had a good run! I have recorded this,
and replay it, so that the projection of myself
is singing to myself, *You had a good run*.
You ran well. You rained. You ruined. This is Projection Number One.

CALLAS: WHO NEEDS THE MET?

[elegant toplessness stoned
in stairwell]

Wayne Koestenbaum

Room 46

they hated my poem about
a dead baby

_____

        dead babies
in sonnets aren't funny

_____

I never said dead
babies were funny

_____

        imagine the
old man in wheelchair
falling over

_____

        will the
audience misperceive my
remark as anti-
Semitic and boo or
hiss it? don't avoid
the screening just because
I'm afraid of being hissed

_____

        assemble an
entire life from found
scraps

_____

could my life
begin with the fat girl
babysitting while Mom
and Pop see *Odd Couple*
for their anniversary?

———————

      kept
boy follows
two steps behind doddering
master whose Cockney
s/m imprecations
toward rental dog
we overheard

———————

elegant toplessness
stoned in stairwell

———————

      flatterer tells me in
steam that young guys
must be 'after me'

———————

      Band-Aid
on the other
Wayne in pool
looks like skin tag —

———————

mistook him
for handsome workout
father with pudgy son

———————

splodgy, ochre, dull
grey, pink-grey afternoon

———————

      he mentions me
once in vaguely sexual
context

———————

      says hello at
deli, surprisingly high
voice for a son

———————

      study
Diane Arbus for sake
of flirtation bait

———————

pleurer I said as
dream in tango elevator –
expect chaos

———————

applying makeup sedulously
while crouched on suspicious
floor

———————

      fear of
being marooned with
Rowan and Martin or
not being tall enough
to see Martin's squinchy
eyes, his distress muted
by squinch

———————

       –remove
thy ass from my presence

———————

Cleo removes her Nair
ass

———————

     his ass
received verbal Nair,
semantic depilation

———————

    'fold' I
said to Madame Grès

———————

face mauled by age
or angry dog in
'53 restaurant

_____

               very
pre-K of you he
said at breakfast

_____

no discussion of
need or nipple, the
damned ore's lumpen
presence in whose earth?

_____

Bangladeshi porn found
in grocery bags at gym

_____

your French bread tantrum

_____

      was it
lipstick on blind glamour
face repeating
the invisible city's
remaining condoms
as if beauty were
the result of our efforts?

_____

pancake on jaw
edge

───────────

      –should not
they unplug my nose
and shout numbers into
a dead phone?

───────────

      the
dead phone is mine–

───────────

      –when someone
is pushed three times
out the express chute–
maybe a terrorist

───────────

Jane Fonda's surprising
youth, running and
jamboreeing–

───────────

      Jim is
the repeated desired name
but a hollow resides
where Jim once lived

───────────

LSD son
was Jim, a
suicide, or rumoured
to be a suicide in
S.F.

───────

erotic fantasy
of the suicide nude
answering a Victorian
pink lady door

───────

here in Baton Rouge they're
picketing *The Vagina
Monologues*

───────

stuffed myself on crawfish
étouffée and broccoli,
didn't stop to
judge extent of stomach
fullness

───────

his eyebrows deserve
dissection, elegy, troubadour
energies

───────

  why is my
coccyx always the tragic
Kundalini sore spot?

———————

  one more
bite of $3 vegetable

———————

  we
wonder why our emotional
and spiritual horizons are so
straitened, we realise
four serried trees are sublimely
waiting for me to announce them

———————

not convulsive beauty
but not obvious
beauty either

———————

  repose achieved as
landing strip where
dismal life attains
longawaited equilibrium,
and perhaps we extend the
'high' and realise getting
stoned is the origin of
literature

———————

      or getting stoned by
angry homophobic journalists
and townspeople

———————

      a pause
before I say yes despite
Elton John and not
fearing loneliness or
the buttfucked girlfriend
who took it up the ass
from the sadistic boy
because of pregnancy fears

———————

this story told to me
as the height of her
humiliation or as an
extension of what my
cruel gay body and draconian
Rudolf Serkin willpower did
to her

———————

      breasts felt
up by third wheel boyfriend
and I realised I was
a noncontender

———————

upside-down mouth seen as
zucchini bread giftgiving
and *The Fox* reparations
received on Third Street
and my surprise that San
Jose had a good used
bookstore because I was an
impossible snob

_____

why always is my suicide
fantasy poised on mother
of baby I adore more
than dignity allows?

_____

my questions are my
father's, precautionary,
nervous, dry, scape-
goated – like neighbourhood
dog we
Jews feared

_____

I've never seen such a
compromised set of
knickers or lowhangers –

_____

     his pedagogic
illocutionary lowhangers –

_____

          or
Festschrift on my behalf
including Princess Di
mourning's profundity

———————

      –not sure why I'd
let him suck me off

———————

his persistence reminds me
of Mary Ann at ditto
machine, stink of my
cruelty

———————

     –not sure why
grease clings to my jacket
or why liberation is
achieved in unlikely
locale

———————

    two boys
together in tub
when father leaves
bathroom (No More
Tears) and I experiment
with rubber ducks

———————

      the joke
(told on third-grade
bus) of
snake as intercourse

———————

the stalled *Music Man*
bus where my first dis-
obedience broke its waters

———————

teaching Yahweh
about genitals,
grasping Yahweh's glitter

———————

         and are
four recited nouns the
secret of his sudden
access to fountains?

———————

      Rosi-
crucian rose goldenness of
failed immortality?

———————

     lost thumb
of matzoh ball purveyor
spooning goulash
near Hildegard Knef
LPs for sale
in thick plastic sleeves.

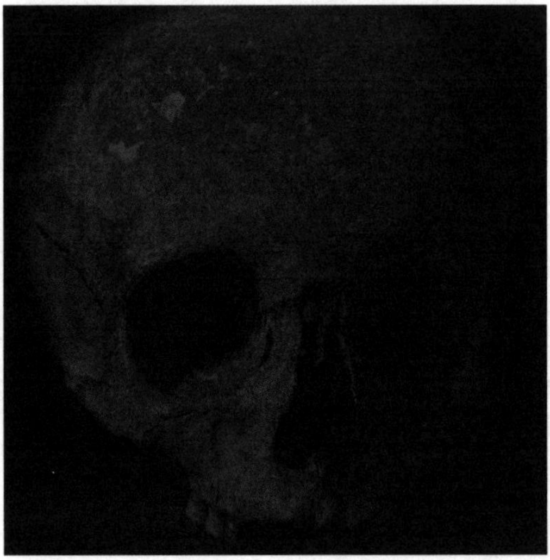

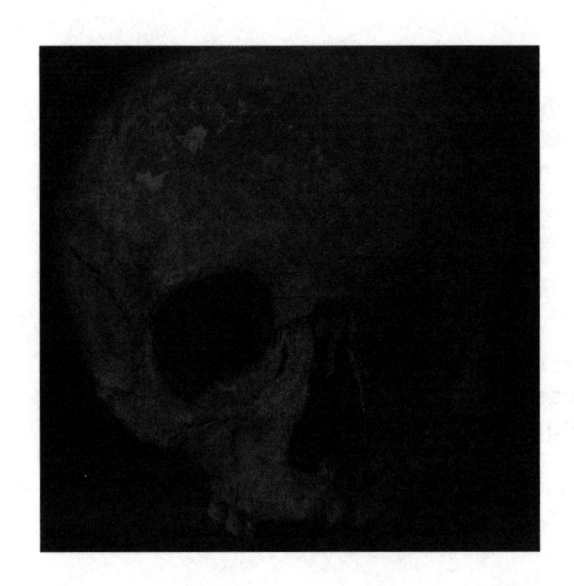

Prompt Note & Animal Bones   Iain Sinclair & SJ Fowler

Room 47

DISCRIMINATIONS OF LONDON LIGHT INTERFERENCE
PERFORMANCE
WILLED DISTORTION
I CAN GET AWAY WITH ANYTHING

> No, Steven. You can't. That's the whole point.
> You are going to be held responsible, you are
> responsible: for every frame, every breath.
> That's the contract.

BLAKE MOSAIC UNDERPASS
WRITER'S SHIRT SELECTION
DEGRADED CROSSRAIL
UNROLLING STOCK
RAILWAYS INTO SHEDS, CEMETERIES, CREMATORIA WEED
    LADDERS
WASTE MOUNTAINS
PILL PARTIES
JUNK FOOD PARKED IN EDGELAND EDENS

LOOKING FOR DRUGS
ELECTRONIC COMPASSES
EVERYTHING'S THE SAME

HAIR DECISIONS
ETHICAL SHOES
OPEN WINDOWS
PRIVATE GARDENS
COFFEE CUPS
HAVE A SAFE TRIP TO NOTTING HILL

UNPOPULAR VIEWPOINTS
POPULAR VIEWPOINTS
I TALK QUICKER THAN I THINK

HYPER-COMMUNICATIVE
ICE-CREAM LICK RELIEF BABY
IN JAPAN, THEY'RE SEARCHING FOR OYSTERS: WOMEN

ACRIMONIOUS BREAK-UP
GALLERY KEYS
SOCIALISING IN LONDON
BORING IF YOU DON'T DRINK NON-DENOMINATIONAL SHAMANISM

TROLLED THRILLED

DRIVE FOR TWO HOURS EVERYDAY
TERMINAL CANCER
TAX REGULATIONS
GHOST FLATS

ARTWASHING
RUSSIANS
FILL THE HOUSE WITH WILD BIRDS EMPTY BENCHES
FENCED SEPULCHRE
ALCHEMY OF PANIC
MEADOW ROW
POST-CHEMICAL
INTENSELY LOCAL
UNIFIED SOUL
FUTURE RUIN
INTELLIGENT SMOKE BRAND-TATTOOED AUTHORS
BALLOON SNIFFERS

NICHOLAS HAWKSMOOR
RATCLIFFE HIGHWAY KILLINGS
LACK OF DARK SPACES
CHURCH AS REFUGE: MOUTH OF HELL
RITUAL EMBRACE

LAMINATED IDENTITY BADGE
APPROACHING DISNEYLAND
OPPOSING DISNEYLAND

HELICOPTER SICK LIST
ELECTION REGISTER RETURN TO WEREWOLF
KNIFE FIGHT
BAG OF PIGEON HEADS
ATTACKED BY A PIGEON IN THE PARK

SAT NAV TO NEXT PUB
'GONE. IT'S BEEN DONE'
'NO PROBLEM AT ALL'
BEAT HOTEL
DRINKING IN THE COACH & HORSES
FRANCIS BACON
JOHN HURT

COCAINE EIGHTIES
HARD BREXIT SOFT BREXIT FUCK BREXIT

FRUIT
FUR
SEA
SKULL
OSSUARY
BELL
TYPEWRITER
GYM
AUDIENCE
TRAIN
STADIUM
HAVE YOU READ DEREK RAYMOND?

NOT HACKNEY
NOT ISLINGTON
PATH ENDS IN BIRMINGHAM

FROGS
RATS
FOXES
MEDIUMISTIC ENGAGEMENT
THE UNFINISHED WALKWAYS OF THE DEAD
NOTHING IS FINISHED
ANGEL STONES
DESERTED CATACOMBS
FLIGHTPATH RESURRECTIONISTS

'IT'S NOT A FILM. YOU WAKE'

AUDIENCE WAKES
FINNEGANS WAKE

TRUE! TRUE! VOUCHSAFE ME MORE SOUNDPICTURE!
IT GIVES FURIOUSLY TO THINK
LISTEN, LISTEN! I AM DOING IT

HEAR MORE TO THOSE VOICES! ALWAYS I AM HEARING THEM...

                                                                       ENOUGH

*   Whitechapel Gallery, 13 December 2018

My wife wakes up screaming, scaring the animals who care for her.

What is everywhere but never visible?
And what is the difference between that which is inevitable but hidden,
and that which mode it is to try and ignore?

Juddering sick people, a sickening populace, blossoming.
The balance of the thing under your skin you will never see.
You can take it on faith it's there.
Or come to see five thousand examples of proof.

Under your finger as you point to the whiteboard.
Beneath your hand as you scoop cereal into your mouth.
Under your scalp as you headbutt like a goat raised in the public house.
Beneath, but visible, over your chest and middle back,
a hog bone pressing through a bone.

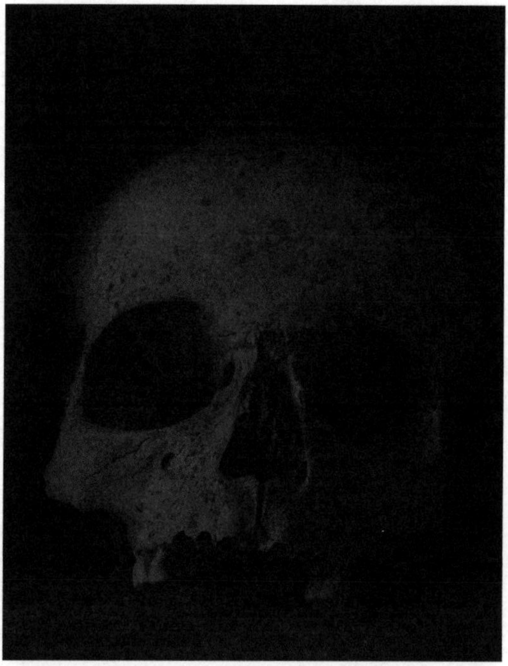

The predator tears out a spine like it were a hotdog,
as I do to my sardines.

Honestly its fine, love, it's all you can do to avoid,
to convince yourself you're avoiding it.
But it's going one way anyway, anxious, or brave, comforted or awkward,
white or with small patches of hair, flesh and skin remaining.
It is all the same in the end.

A human pyramid post-mortem.
A geometrical presentation that is both aesthetically striking,
and in this day of limited living space and skyrocketing
real estate costs, an eminently practical solution.
For it is right the dead should take up less space than when they were living
and be divorced in pieces amongst each other.

You are witnessing the afterlife,
the meadow of ready real boring lambs.

The heaven where everyone is tired,
like on earth.

The village where we will all end up,
where once more you may trust your neighbour.

Good night the pleasure was ours   David Grubbs

Room 48

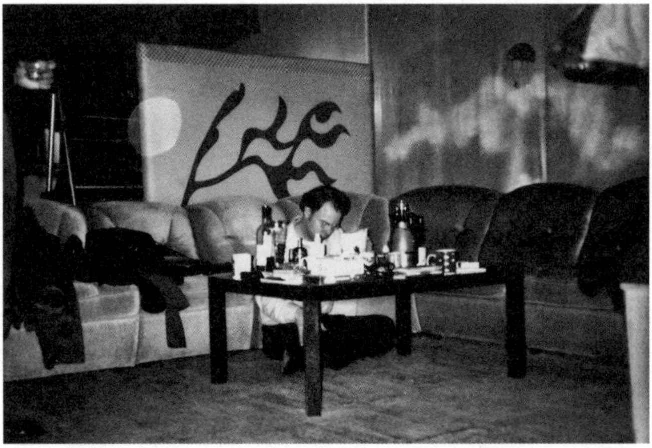

At the start of a show in front of a capacity audience, a singer confidently steps to the microphone and a plastic cup with sixteen ounces of the cheapest beer on tap at this oversized corner bar finds its target

explodes in his face. I think disbelief

is the word. They've been on a months-long upswing, and their homecoming show registered as celebratory until the moment of impact. It's the electric version of an ensemble with no fixed personnel, the former power trio that renamed and rededicated itself, fundamentally altered the mission, sometimes stripping down to two acoustic guitars, twin sketch pads, the whole shebang meant to jibe with public transportation or touring in a compact car, able to occupy a stage plot the size of a couch. Electronic sound reappeared as a medium in which to breathe deeply, for everyone to thrive. Electronic sound returned with resonances mingled, oscillators abetting the sustain of acoustic instruments, overtone-resplendent steel strings otherwise prone to decay and dying, to mortal

transverse shimmer. Participants cast a sceptical eye

on allegiances and needless distinctions between acoustic and electronic; pressure strikes the ear, it fluctuates the microphone's diaphragm, and we grant permission for the engineer to measure it forty-four thousand and one hundred times a second. What aids resonance, what facilitates sustain, blend what may and o what a whorl! Still, there are soundchecks, input lists, dedicated channels. One performs on an instrument or instruments; one acts as an instrumentalist. Take a gig at the neighbourhood dive, take a gig at a gallery or jazz club or unfinished space

take the gig in the parking garage, take most any gig – take all of them to manifest a vision of nimbleness and responsiveness to one's surroundings. The earliest outings of a duo version of the group attracted interest in part as novelty, post-postpunk dripping faucet music, the inverse of power

and the obverse of pop. Neglected, not even scorned folk instruments provoked conversation among spectators during performances while the musicians fantasised about a transparent curtain ringing down at the press of a button the audience sundered by acoustic baffle. They observed friends' bands in the role of oddball opening act in front of vastly larger crowds, three thousand people gabbing over beers, noting that no matter how gentle or ungraspable

however ellipsoidal or ill-suited a song might be in this environment, if it's delivered with a concluding flourish or swell into unambiguous final attack everyone in the house halts their conversation, swivels toward the stage, barks

approval, which multiplied by several thousand becomes triumphal roar. If a piece conversely generates hard-won musical momentum but lands softly with a final decrescendo fifteen hundred conversations resume.

Beyond the reintroduction of electronic sound through the camouflage of acoustic and electronic resonance both roiling and serene, the next wrinkle was to experiment with ripping interjections of noise, malfunctioning punctuation punctuating malfunction, efforts from within to shred the texture of the proceedings, to crash the airplane. Fight or flight

simulator, fricative sizzle of electricity.

The fader's path is straight and true. Scale is a turn of the dial when there's no recognisable source to enlarge, only smug circuitry and engorged transistors. The fictive sound of electricity. Two acoustic guitars in a wipe

dissolve are replaced by a pair of electric organs shoulder to shoulder at centre stage, varying only by virtue of the colour of their moulded plastic casings, a shade of oxygen-rich Vespa red next to Olivetti green-grey. The recourse to volume returns, a previously refused depth and dimensionality they had cautiously rebuilt over the last year, the group no longer tasking themselves with always bringing the wrong music.

Hypothesis confirmed: an endless supply of wrong music.

Quietly approaching

quietly receding

Quietly rescinded

one crossfade

one calendar

year

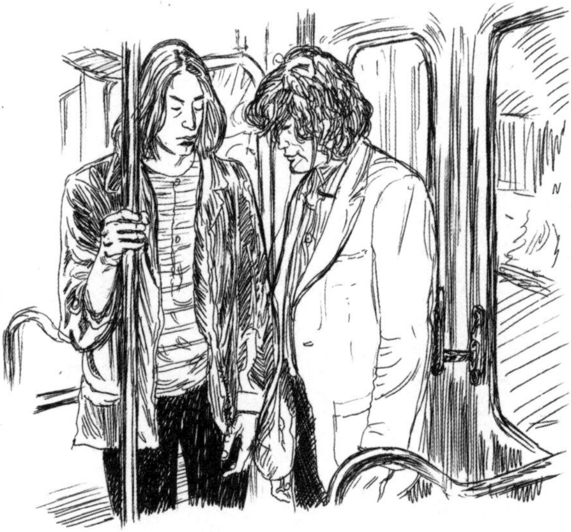

That's It   Agustín Fernández Mallo & Pere Joan
            translated from the Spanish
            by Thomas Bunstead

                                        Room 49

I went to the beach the other day. The sun was out.

Farther along the beach, at the shoreline, I saw a dark shape, an object that had washed up.

It was a small Zodiac.

Looking out to sea, I saw the island in the distance. Its turrets, its lights on even though it was daylight.

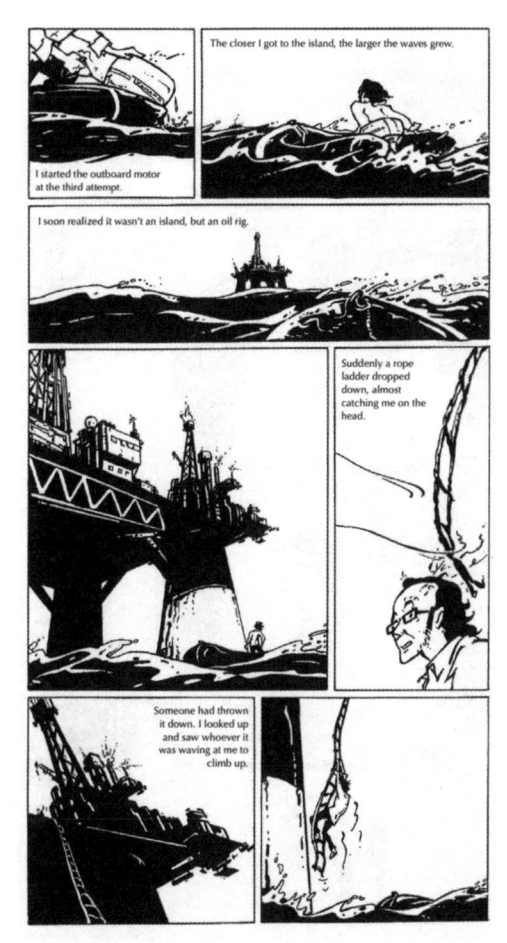

I started the outboard motor at the third attempt.

The closer I got to the island, the larger the waves grew.

I soon realized it wasn't an island, but an oil rig.

Suddenly a rope ladder dropped down, almost catching me on the head.

Someone had thrown it down. I looked up and saw whoever it was waving at me to climb up.

As I climbed, the wind buffeted me against one of the pillars.
A man held out his hand to help me the last bit of the way.
Hi.
Hi.
Are you okay?
Bit shaken from banging into the pillar.
Welcome. My name's Enrique Vila-Matas. Who are you?
Not sure.
What you need is coffee with whiskey. This way.

Good thing you found us. There's a storm coming, a big one.
Yes, thank you. I thought this was a military island.
Hardly. It belongs to Repsol. They're drilling.
And what do you do? Are you an engineer?
No, no. I don't do anything.
I wanted to give up writing, to disappear.
Ah, I used to write as well, and I'd also like to disappear.
You've come to the right place.
You wait here, I'll get the coffee. Have a seat.

| What was the last thing you wrote? | I can't remember. You? | It was about a man who goes to bed one night...

...and realizes the second hand on his watch is ticking more loudly than usual.

TIK TAK TIK TAK

TIC TAC TIC
TIC TAC TIC TAC

When he wakes the next morning, the watch sounds normal again.

That night, the second hand is even louder than the previous night.

TIC TAG TIC

In the morning, it's gone back to normal again.

TIC TAC TIC TAC

And it goes on like this for a number of nights. The second hand grows louder and louder, it becomes very loud indeed.

TAC TIC TAC TIC
TAC TIC

He wonders when the torture will end, when the watch will go back to normal.

He decides to throw the watch away.

Somewhere else, far from where this man lives…

…in a desert region, there is a prison. Each of the cells is quite large, 20m x 20m, and perfectly square, with thick concrete walls also 20m high.

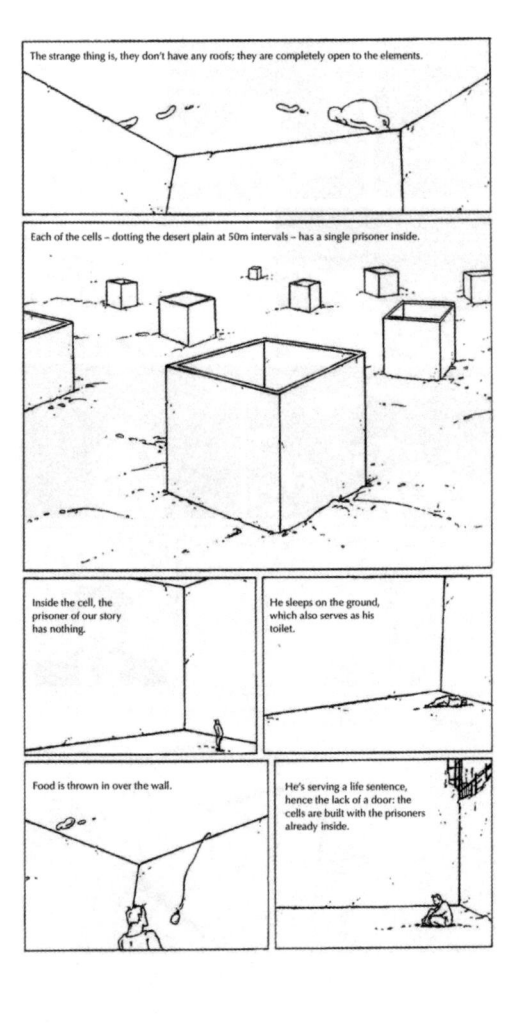

The strange thing is, they don't have any roofs; they are completely open to the elements.

Each of the cells – dotting the desert plain at 50m intervals – has a single prisoner inside.

Inside the cell, the prisoner of our story has nothing.

He sleeps on the ground, which also serves as his toilet.

Food is thrown in over the wall.

He's serving a life sentence, hence the lack of a door: the cells are built with the prisoners already inside.

Whichever wall shades him from the sun, he sits against that one.	No easy thing in the middle of the day.
What this man finds most difficult is the passing of time.	He stares at a fixed point and thinks of a watch…

Any watch, he thinks, as the urge to own one intensifies.

He doesn't understand why he can't have a watch.	Until a day comes when, out of the blue, he begins to hear knocking on the other side of the wall. TOC TOC TOC
	Blows from a hammer, which grow louder and louder. TOC — TOC

TOC TOC TOC
TOC TOC TOC
In the following days the noise becomes that of a pneumatic drill.
Getting closer all the time.
TOC TOC
And then a very large hole appears.
TOC
Come in, we've been waiting for you.

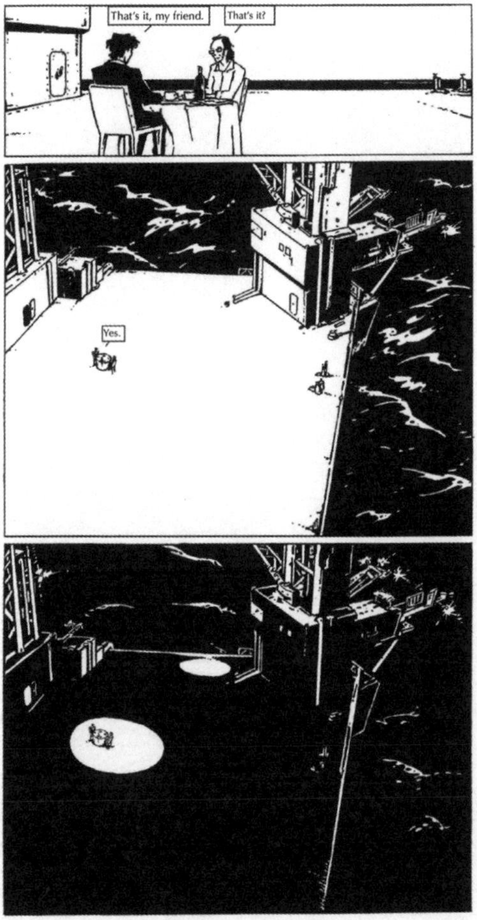
That's it, my friend.
That's it?
Yes.

CODA

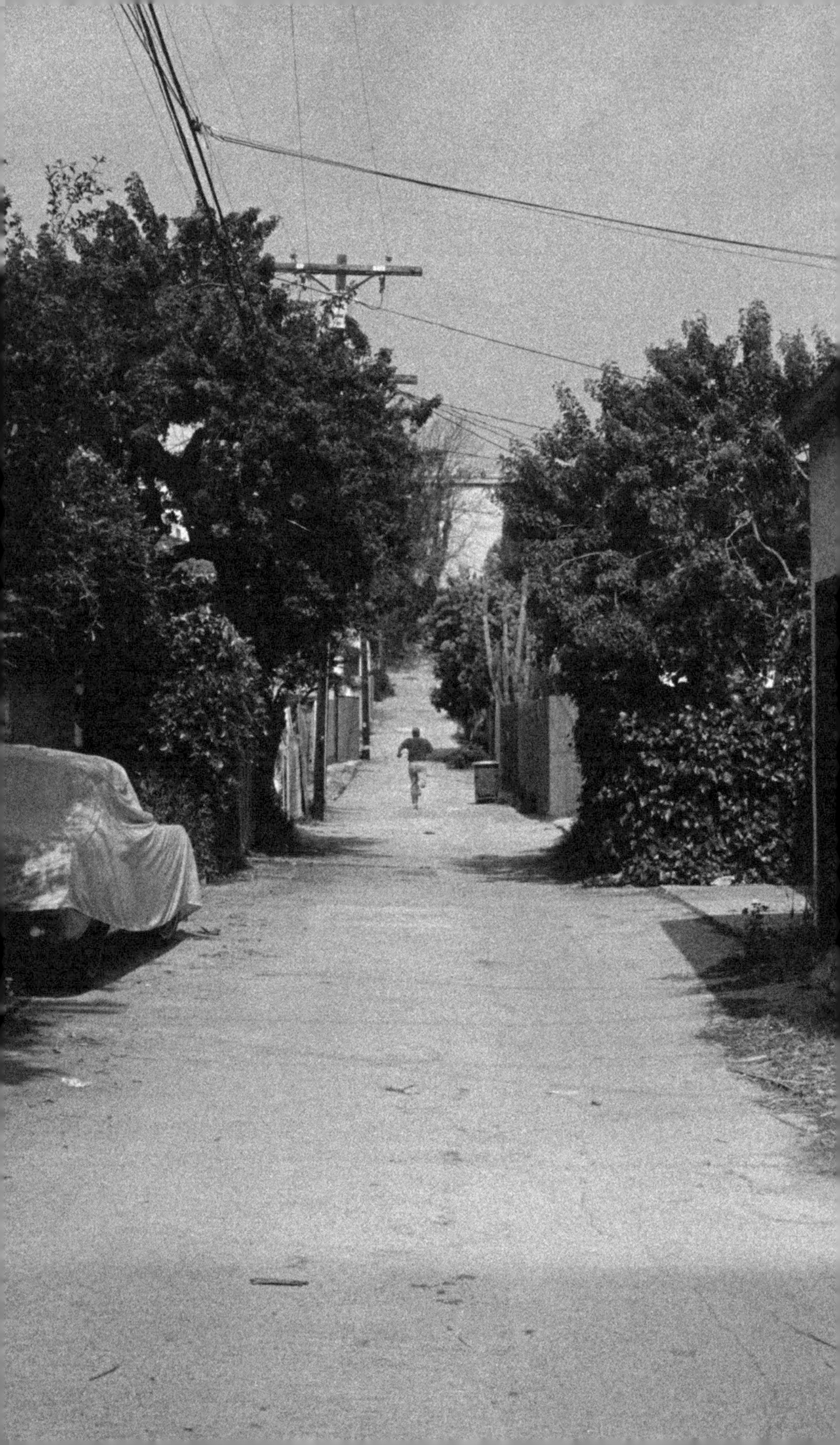

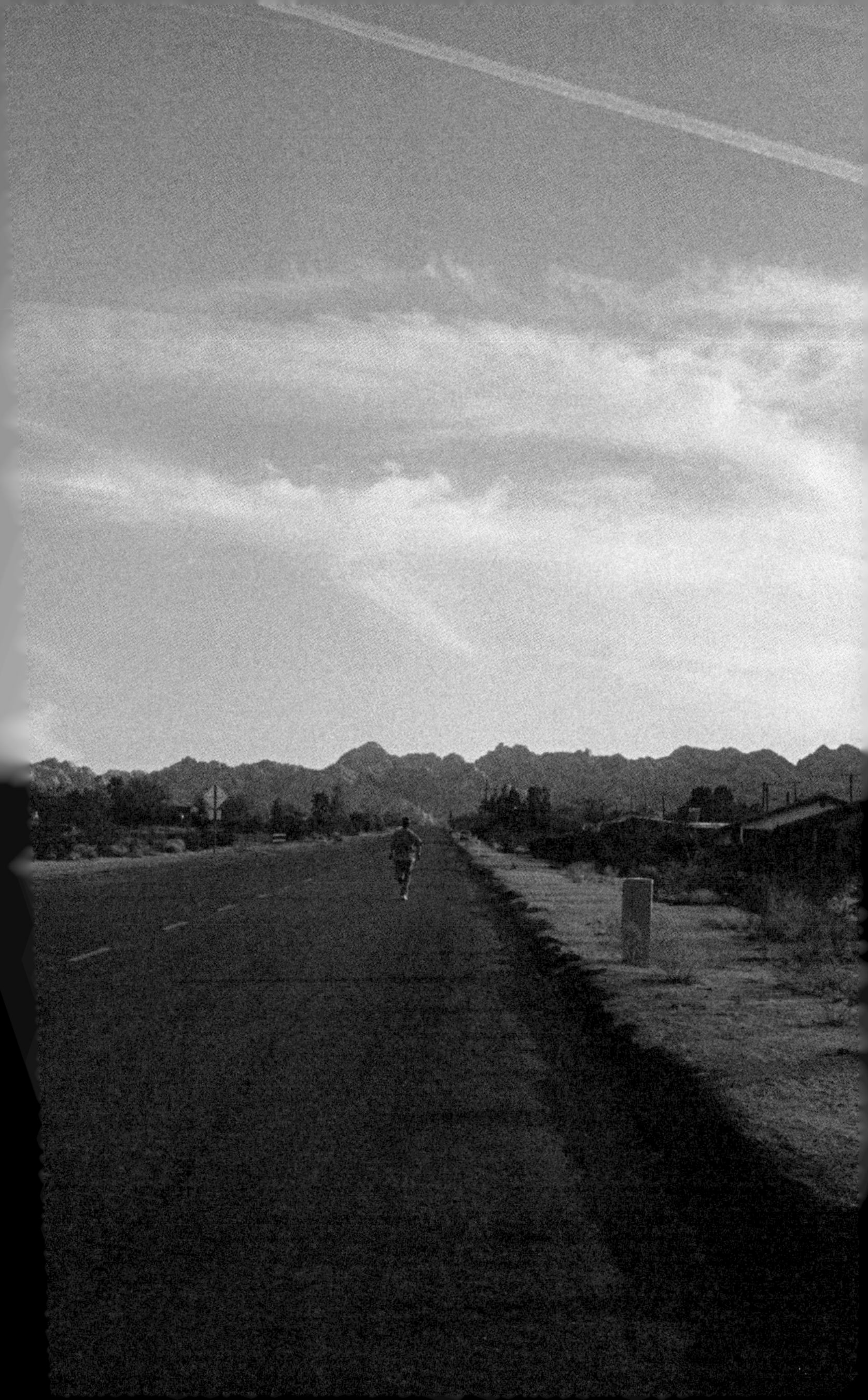

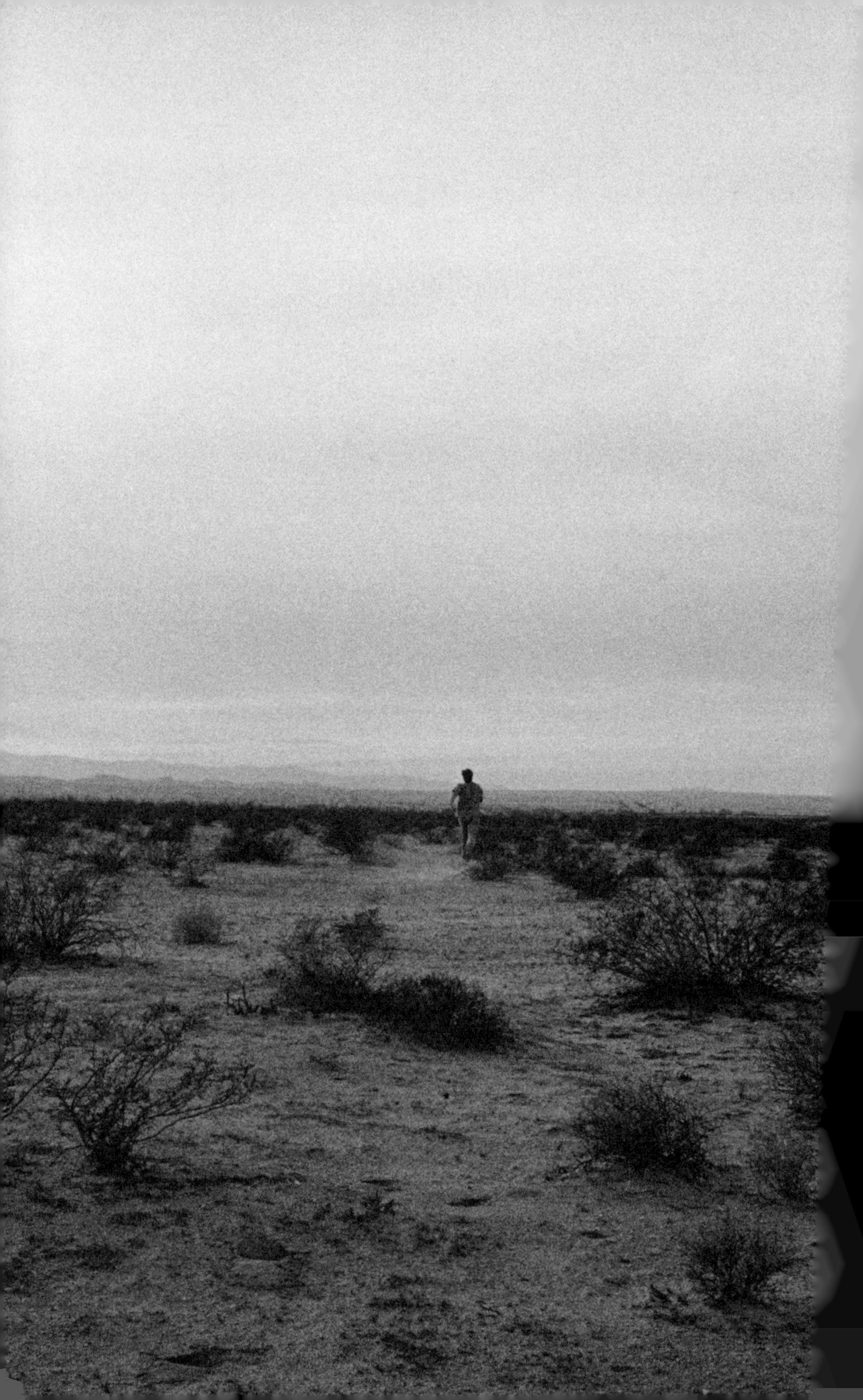

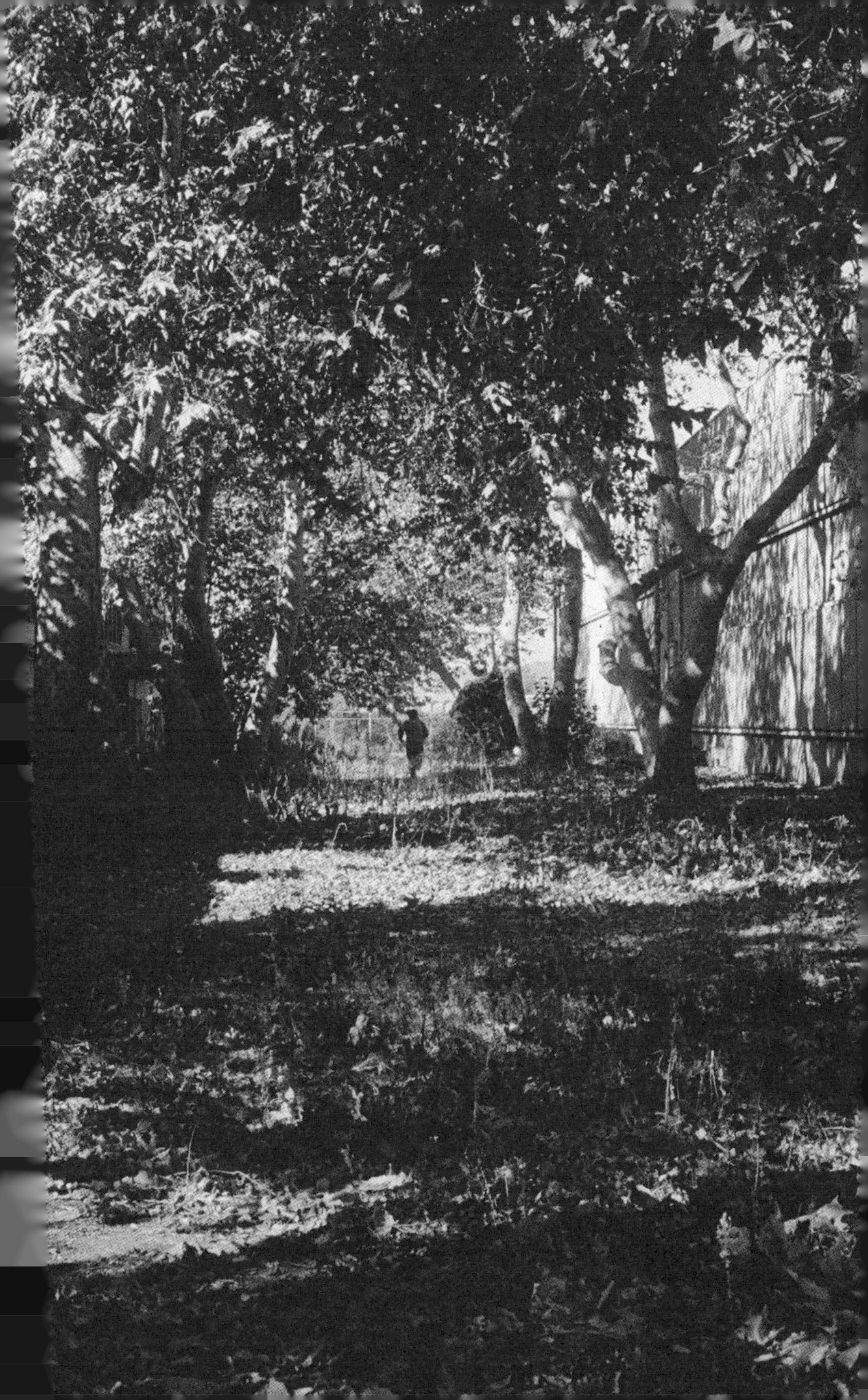

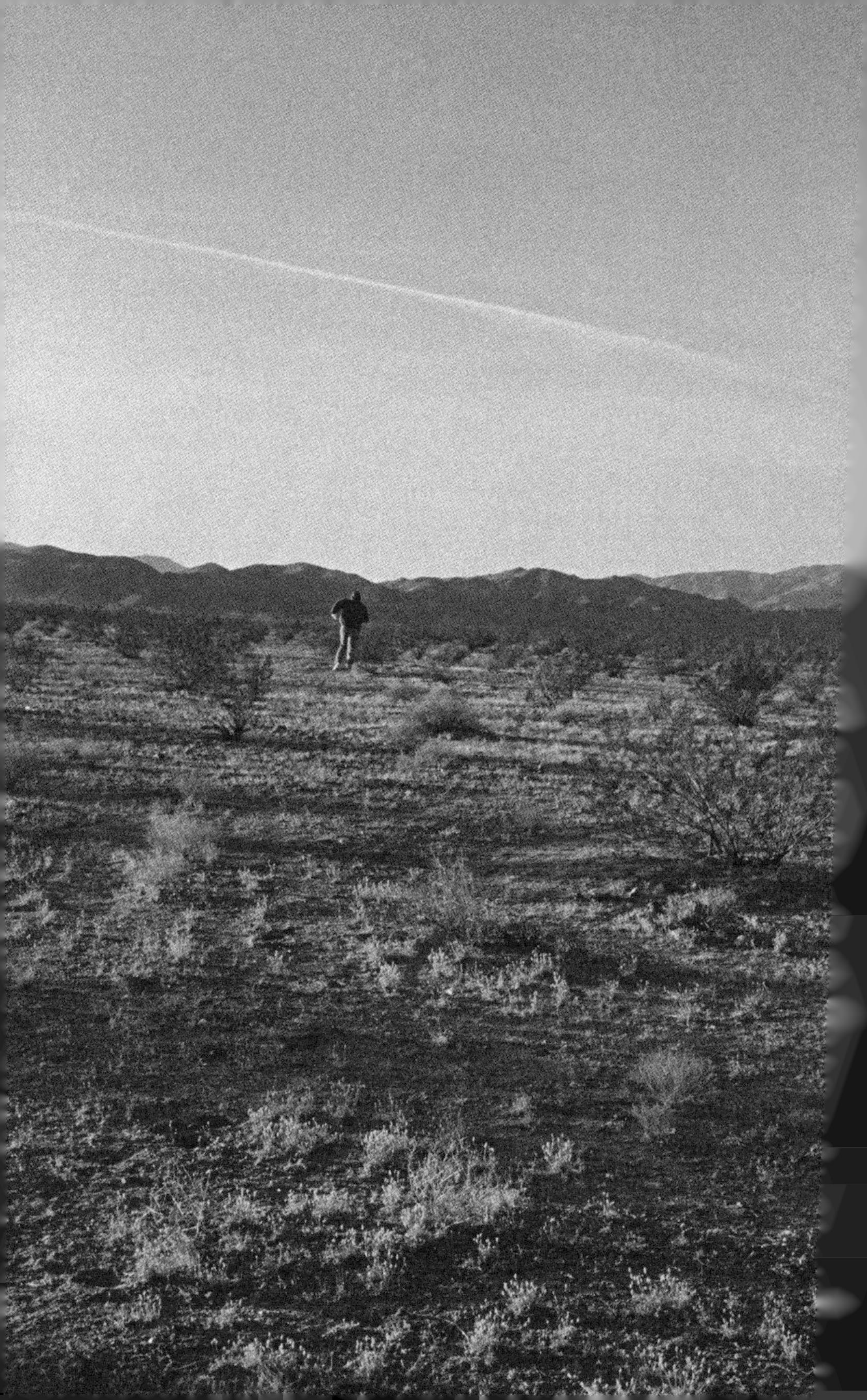

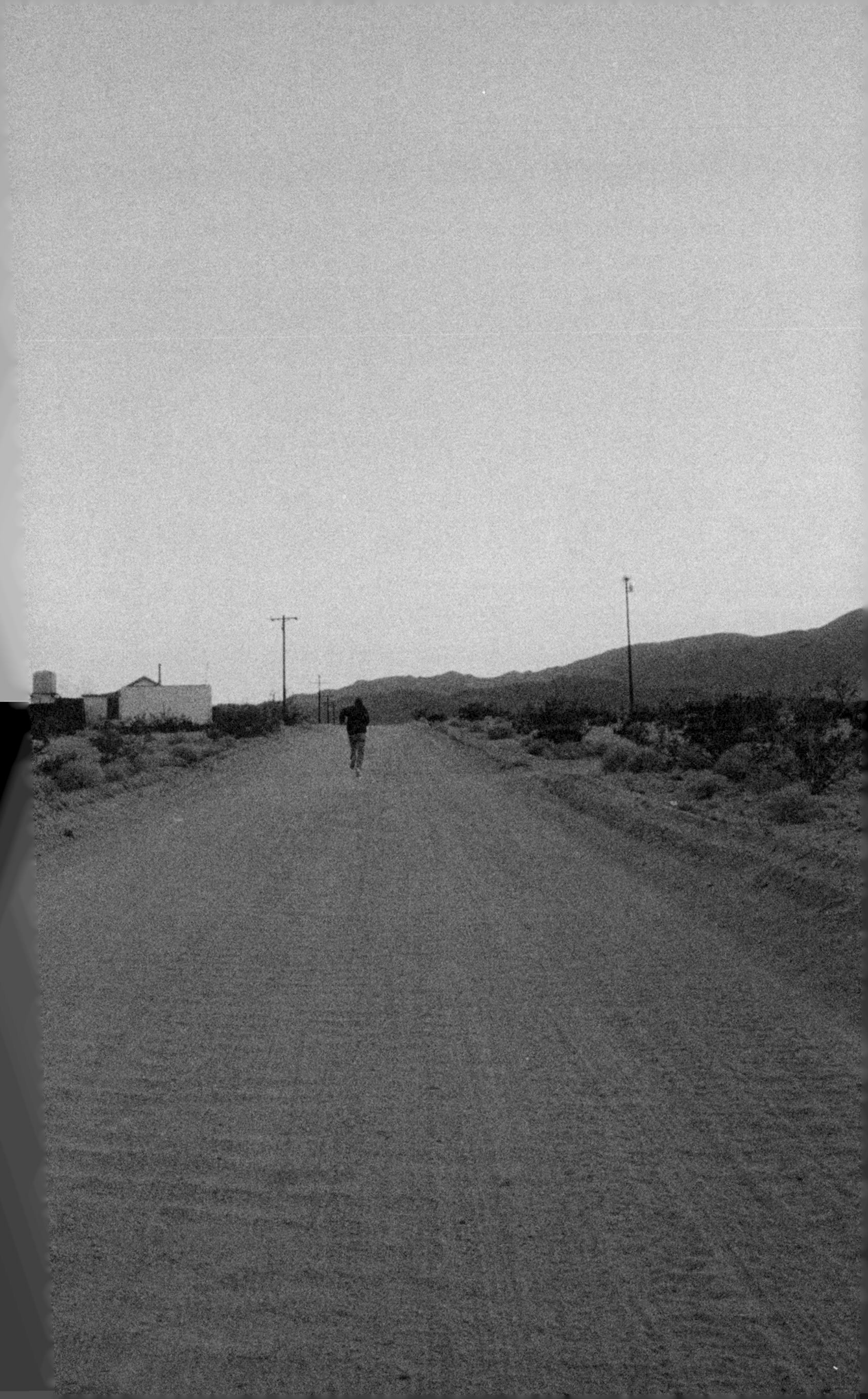

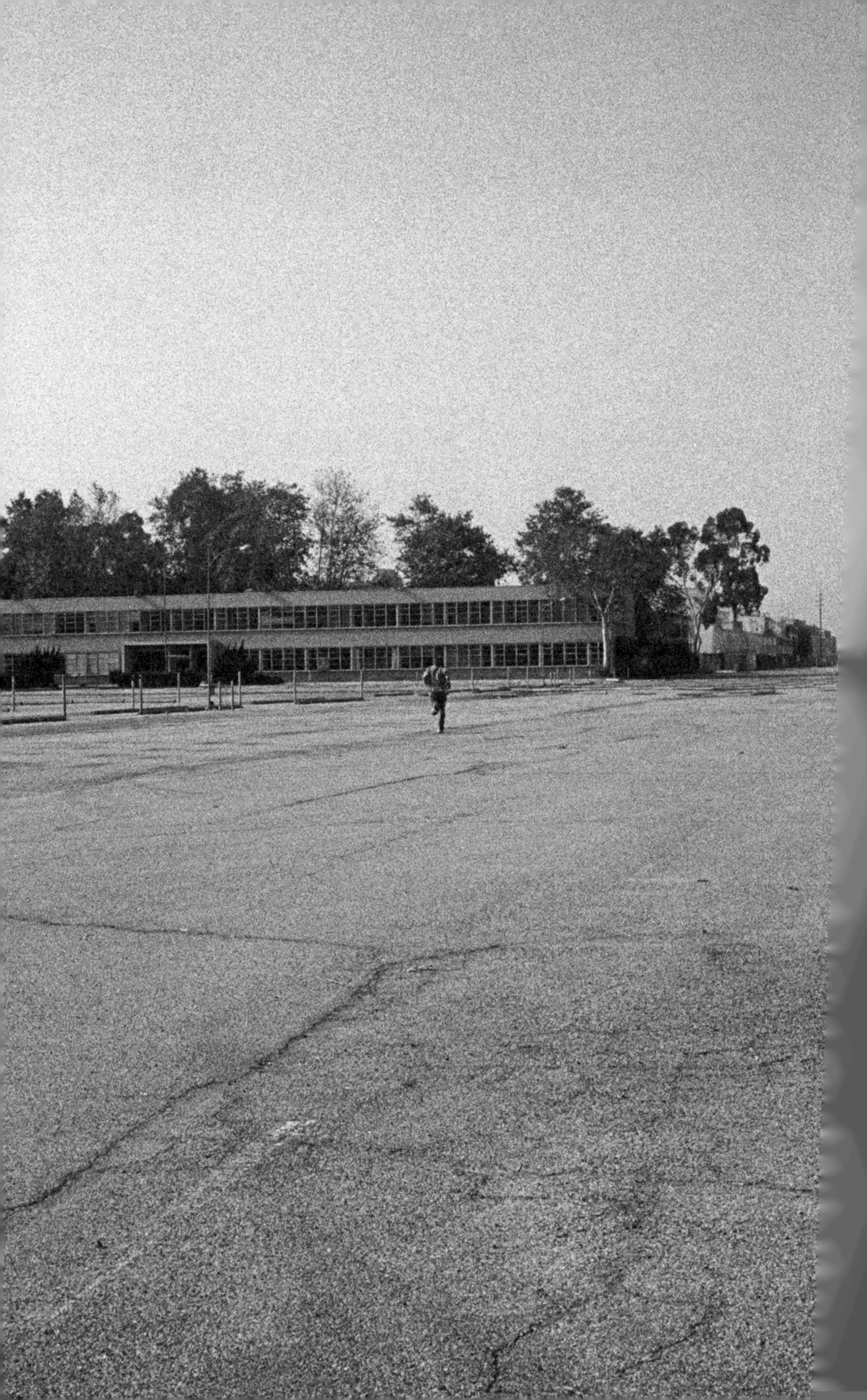

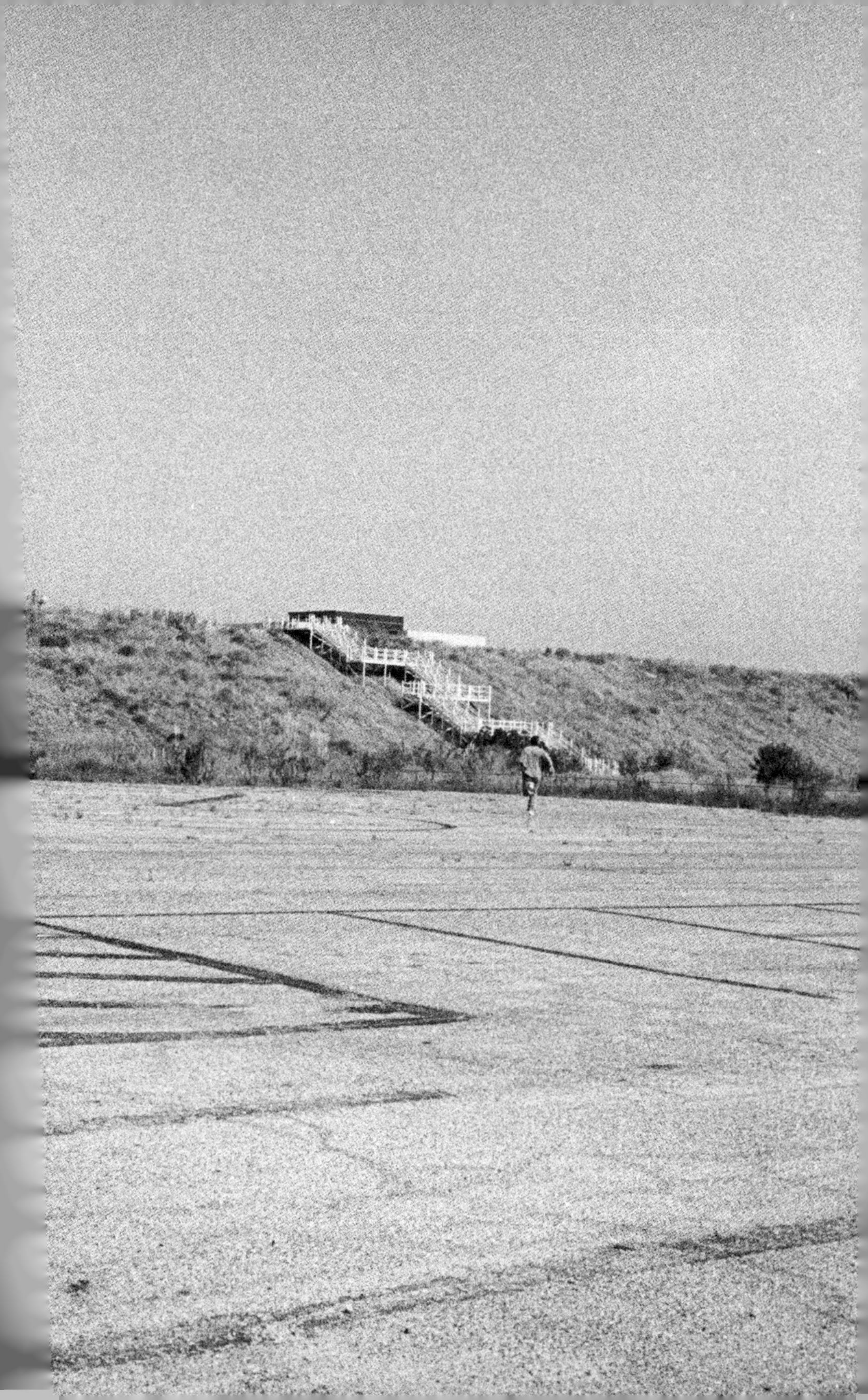

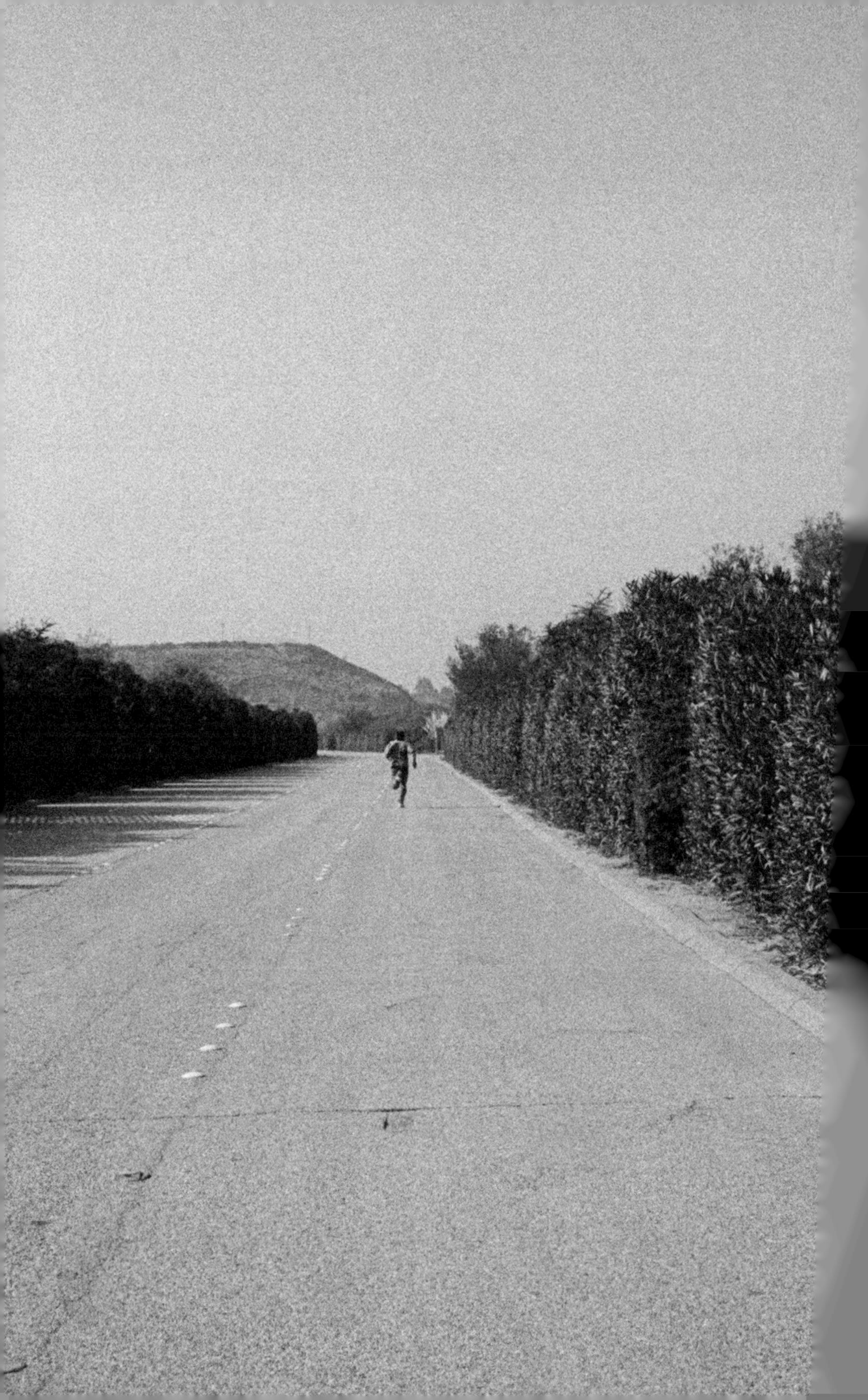

*In which the photographer would set his timer,
and run as far and fast as he could...*

Some Rooms: Dimensions of Dialogue   Gareth Evans
(An Afterword)

> *There is a world inside the world.*
> *— Don DeLillo, Libra*

What is a room? This is what Wikipedia says:
> *In a building or large vehicle, like a ship, a room is any enclosed space within a number of walls to which entry is possible only via a door or other dividing structure that connects it to either a passageway, another room, or the outdoors, that is large enough for several people to move about, and whose size, fixtures, furnishings, and sometimes placement within the building or ship support the activity to be conducted in it.*

Where does the word 'room' originate? This is what the Online Etymological Dictionary says:
> *Middle English* ROUM, *from Old English* RUM *'space, extent; sufficient space, fit occasion (to do something),' from Proto-Germanic** RUMAN *(source also of Old Norse, Old Saxon, Old High German, Gothic* RUM, *German* RAUM *'space,' Dutch* RUIM *'hold of a ship, nave'), nouns formed from Germanic adjective** RUMA – *'roomy, spacious,' from* PIE *root ** REUE – *'to open; space' (source also of Avestan* RAVAH – *'space,' Latin* RUS, *'open country,' Old Irish* ROI, ROE, *'plain field,' Old Church Slavonic,* RAVINU, *'level,' Russian,* RAVNINA, *'a plain'). Old English also had frequent adjective* RUM, *'roomy, wide, long, spacious' – also an adverb,* RUMLICE, *'bigly, corpulently' (Middle English,* ROUMLI).

I quote the entry in full because it confirms that *it* – the core of the word with local variants – reached a widespread critical mass early on. That 'r' is the handle of the door into meaning, if you like.

What's touching is that it derives from what it no longer is, which is a much larger uncontained terrain. There is just a letter separating room and roam. Oh, I am not the first to notice this, of course. Curator Sandie Macrae knows it too. She has created multiple iterations of an exhibiting area, often in distinctive 'meanwhile' spaces accessible before development, which she has called, in order: ROOM / ROOM TOO / FOUND GALLERY / ROOM London / ROOMARTSPACE / ROAMING ROOM and now postROOM, part of her house in London. She has shown more than five hundred artists in thirteen venues.

All good, so let's stay with 'room,' and track it in action:
> *The meaning* 'CHAMBER, CABIN' *is recorded by early 14c. as a nautical term; applied by mid-15c. to interior division of a building separated*

---

*   *Meanwhile...* A distinctive term, a rare moment of poetry in a brutally commercial sphere, one acknowledging that a room exists not only spatially but temporally.

by walls or partitions; the Old English word for this was COFA, *ancestor of* COVE. *The sense of 'persons assembled in a room' is by 1712. Make room –* 'OPEN A PASSAGE, MAKE WAY' *– is from mid-15c. Room service is attested from 1913; room temperature, comfortable for the occupants of a room, is so called from 1879.* ROOMTH, *'sufficient space' (1530s, with –* TH*) now is obsolete.*

Wikipedia claims the first rooms appeared at least around 2200BCE in Minoan territory, while also displaying next to the text a picture of a Neolithic room from Skara Brae on Orkney (c.3000BCE). Rooms are contested spaces.

Let's not forget that 'room' is also a verb:

ROOM (v.) *'to occupy a room or rooms' (especially with another) as a lodger, by 1825 (implied in roomed), from room (n.). Related –* ROOMING. ROOMING-HOUSE, *'house which lets furnished apartments,' is by 1889, according to* OED *'chiefly* U.S.*' In Old English (*RUMIAN*) and Middle English the verb meant, 'become clear of obstacles; make clear of, evict.'*

Rooms are active spaces, not passively receiving vessels. As for 'evict,' more on that soon...

*

Every room has a music of its own. He found himself listening intently at times, in strange rooms, after the traffic died, for some disturbance of tone, a nuance or flaw in the texture.

*

But... When is a room not a room? When is it more – or less – than the word can viably contain or suggest? Albert Hall, Turbine Hall, St Paul's? Submarine?

And... What is a room *for*? Not for sleeping, bathing, eating etc. but what is it *really* for?

A room can be the origin, engine or terminus – even erasure – of a plot, a space that determines the possibilities and limitations of being.

There is a chair, a table, bed; there is a window or a door. Or not. There is a room. It has no window or door. It has no entrance or exit portals of any kind. A person is inside it. The only other thing in the room is a biscuit. How does the person get out?

*

The room stood in a kind of stupor, a time zone of its own.

*

Room service (*of a kind*); room 101 (*another kind*); room to manoeuvre (*minimal*); room temperature (*rising*)... The ceiling's (*not*) the limit when it comes to what a room can be (see James Turrell's 'Skyspaces').
  Things happen in rooms; personal things and relational things and social things and historical things. Don DeLillo knows a lot about all this, which is why rooms from his defining speculative fiction *Libra* run through this piece, as bass line, rhythm, melody; a litany.

*

These were men who lived in isolation for long periods, lived close to death through long winters in exile or prison, feeling history in the room, waiting for the moment when it would surge through the walls, taking them with it.

*

In Austria, in shared cultural perception, rooms are sometimes subterranean and generally not good places in which to find yourself. They are examples of negative potential. In this they are not Virginia Woolf's fabled 'room of one's own' (almost impossible to afford now), as the river-taken Woolf wanted and wrote. Rather, they are more disturbing kin to rooms for rent now in gentrified cities and towns. These are bid for, fought over, bunk-bedded to the max (multiple occupancy), with sleep space shared in 'rest rotation cycles.' Spare room? Not any more: it's bedroom-taxed or stacked; it's up to its eaves in debt. When the landlord wants to raise the rent, he evicts the tenant – keeping it simple, keepin' it *real*.
  Woolf had the means to make more than one room of her own, but the source room – the *imagined* room – is made in the mind. And is the mind a room?

*

The books themselves were secret. Forbidden and hard to read. They altered the room, charged it with meaning... The books made him part of something. Something led up to his presence in this room, in this particular skin, and something would follow. Men in small rooms, men reading and waiting...

*

Woolf wasn't alone. Artist Absalon made his cells (they didn't save him). Louise Bourgeois was both freed and trapped by *her* cells.

*

He would create a shadowed room, the gunman's room, which investigators would eventually find...

*

...They break the biscuit in two. Two halves make a (w)hole; they climb through the (w)hole and leave.
    ...Capsule, cubicle (*sealed*), container (*shipped*), hole (*with hatch or lid*), priest-hole, wall niche for an anchorite (*of her choice*)...
    So, the question follows: is a room most itself when empty (of people, pets, furniture, stuff) or not? Does it then hold the promise of a lit window at night? Hoarding or latent, which is it?
    A person with a purpose, in a place, in time...
    Are all rooms waiting for their most immaculate realisation as rooms?

*

The room had been here since the day he was born, waiting for him, just like this, to walk in the door.

*

Is the room surveilled by Buster Keaton's silent protagonist in Beckett's *Film* the room of our *existential* longing and dread?
    Ellipsis as the mark of feet, of pacing in the room...
    Doors and windows open out to the world and let it in – people, things, ideas and hot or cold winds. So it goes also the other way with all.
    Room as site of great fears, founding and abiding terrors; and sometimes our joys, our intimate hall of desires, sometimes both at once; both those conceived and met; cam girls and boys in their screen space boudoir (do come join, it's a two-way mirror, it's *Import / Export, Last Resort*)...

*

He thought of her being somewhere very vague, in a room with curtains, never moving from the chair. This is what happens to loved ones who go away. We make them sit in a room forever.

*

A teenager's bedroom, anywhere in millennial Amerika; the kid's got his homework open and a screen to one side. From its pixels peers a woman, toe to head entirely in black latex, just the lips of her mouth open to the air, puffed out by the tightness of the sheer and shining skin. She is in a concrete dungeon seated forward, as if listening for a cue, on the edge of a bare metal bed frame we surely worry is capable of shocking on demand. She'll be your *Demonlover*...

In the film adaptation by the late Anthony Minghella of Michael Ondaatje's novel *The English Patient*, an enigmatic person, played by Ralph Fiennes, is lying – appallingly burnt – in an Italian villa, presided over by Juliette Binoche's nurse. War is close to cease but they do not yet know this. He is steadily recuperating. In his remarkable book of conversations with Ondaatje, the film's great sound & image editor, 'renaissance' polymath Walter Murch, describes how they wanted to unify the interior and exterior, to underscore the calm coming to both sites. There is a moment in which a church bell peals out across the countryside, fields that are visible from the room. In the same instant (time is a place), Binoche offers her patient a plum. The fruit is what the sound looks, smells, and tastes like. All senses converge. The ripeness of the harvested fruit is a faith heard after long suppression, an endured silence...

*

She needed to live in small dusty rooms, layered safely in, out of the reach of dizzying things, of heat and light and strange spaces...

*

Is a book a room? Is a chapter or a page, or the story itself? Covers like doors and windows open wide on the lap.

Is a gallery, cinema, concert hall or theatre a room because of its walls? True and false: image, sound, speech and gesture throw open windows and doors in the space as much as any architecture might its material own.

Does then a mailroom offer thousands of thresholds?

Is an airport a room? A passage, a transit, a making way;

a conduit of flow, its doors at once both restraining and porous...

Christian Marclay's *Doors* open only onto themselves; (door) frames beget their kin. Arrival is passage. Mike Nelson knows. We are always in between. The door we think we know, and where it leads, opens onto somewhere we have never been.

This writing is called an essay because it's only an attempt.

*

What a sense of destiny he had, locked in the miniature room, creating a design, a network of connections. It was a second existence, the private world floating out to three dimensions.

*

The creative pursuit is called a practice because it's only ever a rehearsal, a ritual of leaning towards, edging closer, stalking the thing itself, horizon-style, towards the place we never can quite reach.

Narnia was reached through a room and a wardrobe, which is a species of portable room...

Is a room a question or an answer?

...Temple, chapel, church, confessional...

A room like everything else is a process. It's all temporary occupation, by the night in the hotel, by the week, month, year (if you're lucky) in the tenement, and surely not yours to hold (on to); by the life in your own private realm, until *The Others* come along to fill it.

*

The woman knew some ways to disappear. You could be alone in a room with her and forget she was there. She fell into stillness, faded into things around her.

*

For sixty years we have lived in the aftermath of a relationship between spaces and pressures; between who has and who has not, between power and its serfs, a man in a room shooting a man who was not in a room.

All rooms pass. The roof goes, the ceiling goes, the point of it, the ease, even the torment of years.

Bathroom, toilet, kitchen, *Jeanne Dielman*...

Attic, cellar, basement, Bachelard...

Rooms flood and burn. Gideon Mendel photographs survivors

standing torso-drenched in the waters, the walls smeared with tidal rise; speechless and static in the ash of their architecture. Are these the rooms of our times, the rooms we will increasingly inhabit? Or is the room of our era Richard Wilson's *20:50*? Waist deep in a vision of sump oil, the viewer surveys the black pond. Outside the room the world grows warmer, much warmer. Warmer is not a good word here.

...Refuge, shelter, retreat...

Is the room of our hope on Manhattan; press bell 2b at 141 Wooster. Walter de Maria's *Earth Room* is as vital as the soil it shows. It's a Heraclitan vestibule. It changes and doesn't. It's a Ship of Theseus after the myth, for an age that throws everything out.

...Shed, hut, cabin, trailer, caravan...

*

He no longer saw confinement as a lifetime curse. He'd found the truth about a room. He could easily live in a cell half this size.

*

Pascal thought we should get used to it. Far from misery, this is the environment in which happiness grows. Xavier de Maistre tested the hypothesis when house-arrested after a duel.

...*Giovanni's Room, the L-Shaped Room, Room at the Top*...

...Prison, cell, dungeon, oubliette (Bresson's *Man Escaped*, Shawshank's redemptions, *Escape from Alcatraz*, but leave a stuffed ghost of yourself there under the covers to buy yourself some time)...

*

Men in small rooms, in isolation. A cell is the basic state. They put you in a room and lock the door. So simple it's a form of genius. This is the final size of all the forces around you. Eight by fifteen.

*

Borges' Aleph of all things gleams in a cellar on a residential street in Buenos Aires.

'O God, I could be bounded in a nutshell and count myself a king of infinite space...'

Search for 'The White Room' in books and cinema, choose as many as you wish; so many...

Waiting rooms, pandemic rooms, rooms for months and

months and months. Only rooms.
　...Escape rooms...
　Does the world / life end in a room? In your own if you're lucky, in a hospice room, in a ward...

*

It was a sound raised slightly above the natural tone of the world, the sound of someone thinking, alone in a room.

*

Writers write in rooms – bedroom kitchen study cafe library – hot desk hot room, cold room cold hands.
　Some writers write their 'man in room' (Ballard, Burroughs, Schrader and DeLillo). They write control rooms, war rooms, bunkers, panic rooms, rendition rooms (rooms that don't exist), emergency rooms, incident rooms, interrogation rooms and courtrooms; their characters are not always *The Smartest Guys in the Room*.
　Henri Barbusse watches *L'Enfer* of it all through a hole in the wall. Sartre and Buñuel don't let their subjects leave. Francis Bacon entraps his popes and lovers and slabs of meat in solid darkness. Juan Muñoz made *Seven Rooms* for his questing, anxious fellows. Most of us can only dream of the spaces conjured by Vermeer's mercantile civility, Hammershøi's northern calm.
　Hell is being in it *and* hearing it from the other side of the divide.
　So, *Where Does Your Hidden Smile Lie?* The smallest room becomes the largest room. The edit suite constructs the cosmos frame by frame. Huillet sits, patient as a stylite (whose roof is sky), while Straub frames himself in the doorway, speculating, smoking. And *this* film's maker, Pedro Costa, watching the other film being assembled, where's he hiding? Backed up in the corner, he gets it all, listens and watches, watches and listens (a Barbusse on the *same* side of the wall).
　...*In Vanda's Room*, in *Room 237*, *Room 236*, *The Small Back Room*, *The Bed-sitting Room*, *A Room for Romeo Brass*, *Room 666*, *The Room*...
　The very same year as Costa, Marc Isaacs also finds himself cornered, in a room that moves. His *Lift* waits for anyone in the tower block who will join him floor to floor. All of life – high and low – is there. They look in, take the stairs (no small enterprise), look in again, stay, return, bring food and sorrow, drinks and subtle victories.

*

They paid for the room he has added to his house, this room, the room of documents, of faded photographs. They paid to fireproof the room... he eats most of his meals in the room, clearing a space on the desk, reading as he eats. He falls asleep in the chair, wakes up startled, afraid for a moment to move. Paper everywhere.

*

...Classroom, office, archive, library, warehouse, storeroom, barn...

*

This is the room of dreams, the room where it has taken him all these years to learn that his subject is not politics or violent crime but men in small rooms... he feels the dead in his room.

*

...Phone box, box room, coffin, grave, crypt, tomb...

*

He knows he can't get out. The case will haunt him to the end. Of course they've known it all along. That's why they built this room for him, the room of growing old, the room of history and dreams.

*

And what then, at last, of the hotel room? Occupied and not, test-bed for the architectural 'distress' of the phallic rock ego, the *ur*-liminal chamber returned to an imagined neutral each departing morning (perhaps by Sophie Calle), it's both a dream and a nightmare of living, alone or together. Choose the Ritz over the dive motel; find yourself in the Beat or the Chelsea or Chateau Marmont, not the capsule hotels of the crowded East, Alan Partridge's Travelodge or the grease-curtained end of the road terrace near the station.

The inherent catch in staying in an expensive hotel is that the cost indicates the room should *be* the holiday. Not if you're a migrant – you'll be staying way too long (the extended unease of a doubled transit) while, if you're homeless in a pandemic, not long enough. Also, far too brief is your by-the-hour love hotel. At least you can leave. Pavese and Genet didn't. Is a corridor a room?

...*Room, The Room, Other Voices Other Rooms, Room with a View,*

Rodinsky's Room, People in the Room... Books Do Furnish a Room...
      Behind all these many rooms are The Backrooms, sickly yellow and as infinite as our fears, but that must be a story for another time, one that Kane Pixels will likely tell us.
      Does then the world / life start in a room? It depends on the room...
      As for *the* first and final room, we have not kept it clean and fit for purpose. It is seriously messed up, but it's the only room we've got. Certain men dream of building other rooms on other racing rocks. They look out of their windows at night, past the light pollution or through the filtered darkness of their ranch remoteness, plotting points, constructing in the space of constellations. They are stringing their claim from one to another, these frontier-pushers of the astral age, pegging out imagined floor plans on stolen acres. This room should be enough. For us there is no other.

*

They were alone in a room that was itself alone, a room that hung above the world.

*

Sapphire and Steel know. They stare out from their roadside café stopped in time and all they see are stars. The stars come to the window, press their faces right up to the glass, like a flock of children to the train as it stops in the village. How small the room is, and oh, how large the dark...

Dedicated to Brian Catling (1948–2022) – Writer, artist, performer and 'Transient Room Maker.'

Notes on these texts

Jess Cotton's 'Notes on the Pink Hotel' was first published in *Hotel* #1.

Rebecca Tamás' poem 'St. Joan in Idaho' was first published in *Hotel* #4.

Stephen Watts' 'Light Space' was first published in *Hotel* #7.

Helen Cammock's (excerpts from) 'Idlewild' were first published in *Hotel* #7.

Salvador Espriu's verse (& Lucy Mercer's response) – published here under the title 'At night the rustle of many fountains comes' – was first commissioned for a radio broadcast produced by Dominic J. Jaeckle in partnership with the Institut Ramon Llull and Films 59 for the 2022 edition of the London Book Fair, and the off-site 'Spotlight' programme on Catalan literatures: *Price Poetry (or the Left Ventricle in Times of Trouble)*, a set of readings (and reactions) to commemorate and refract the first Popular Festival of Catalan Poetry at the Gran Price Theatre, Barcelona, 1970. The variation on Espriu's poetry published herein appears courtesy of Films 59 (with thanks to Adrián Onco, Pere Portabella, and Marc Dueñas). *Price Poetry* was broadcast on Resonance 104.4FM, April 12 (with thanks to Ed Baxter).

Lucy Sante's 'Dear Messiah' was first published in *Hotel* #4, prior to its inclusion in Sante's collection of essays and assorted works, *Maybe the People Would Be the Times* (Verse Chorus Press, 2020).

Ryūnosuke Akutagawa's poem 'Karuizawa,' translated from the Japanese by Ryan Choi, was first published in *Hotel* #5.

John Yau's 'Fortunes, Favourite Sayings, & Assorted Sundries' was first published in *Hotel* #4.

Nicolette Polek's short story 'The Rope Barrier' appeared in *Hotel* #5 following its inclusion in 'Nicole Kidman vs Apollo,' the first instalment in the short-lived *Tyrant Hotel* series (a collaborative radio series from Dominic J. Jaeckle and Jordan Castro for Resonance 104.4 FM that would collage straight-to-smartphone readings by authors and poets in tribute to John Giorno's Dial-a-Poem service, 1968). The story was collected thereafter in Polek's collection *Imaginary Museums* (Soft Skull Press, 2020).

Chris Petit's 'No Show' is excerpted from the liner notes to the purge LP *In What's Missing is Where Love has Gone* by Petit and Mordant Music (2018). On the record's release, the poem was published thereafter on the *Hotel Archive*.

Sascha Macht's 'Five Columns' – a suite of texts collated and translated from the German by Amanda DeMarco – owes to a series of publications in the regional German newspaper *Märkische Oderzeitung* (our gratitude to the editors). A selection of Macht's 'Columns' were published in *Hotel* #6 in DeMarco's translation.

Mark Lanegan's 'Black Rabbit' was first published in *Hotel* #7.

Lucy Mercer, 'Chirologia' and 'Phantasia,' were first published in *Hotel* #5 (as 'Chirologia and 'Demiurge'); thereafter, they were included in Mercer's collection *Emblem* (Prototype, 2022).

Vala Thorodds & Richard Scott, 'come (After Paul Verlaine),' was first published in *Hotel* #4.

Joshua Cohen's '(Nine Notes) from a Diary' were published in tandem with the publication of Cohen's collection of essays and asides, ATTENTION: *Dispatches from a Land of Distractions* (Fitzcarraldo Editions, 2018).

Hannah Regel's 'Butterfield' first appeared in *Hotel* #6 prior to its inclusion in Regel's collection *Oliver Reed* (Montez Press, 2020).

Nick Cave's poem 'New York City, New York' appeared in *Hotel* #3 and was excerpted from Cave's collection *The Sick Bag Song* (Canongate, 2015).

Daisy Lafarge's poems 'throttle song' & 'nothingness is the scene of wild activity (After Karen Barad)' were first published in *Hotel* #5.

Holly Pester's poem 'this big bit cradle' was first published in *Hotel* #2.

Matthew Gregory's series 'Rooms' first appeared in *Hotel* #1.

Emmanuel Iduma's 'Notes on Happiness' was first published in *Hotel* #6.

Joan Brossa's late poem 'Sumari astral' / 'Astral Summary' was translated from the Catalan by Cameron Griffiths for the Resonance 104.4 FM broadcast of *Price Poetry (or the Left Ventricle in Times of Trouble)*. Parts I and II (of III) were aired, read by Stanley Schtinter. Brossa's poetry appears courtesy of the Fundació Joan Brossa.

Imogen Cassels' 'two types of the same return' and 'moss' were first published in *Hotel* #6 (and, thereafter, on the *Hotel Archive*).

Hisham Bustani's 'Quantum Leap,' translated from the Arabic by maia tabet, was first published in *Hotel* #4 and was subsequently included in his collection (again, with tabet) *The Monotonous Chaos of Existence* (Mason Jar Press, 2022).

Raúl Guerrero's 'Menu of the Future' is a representative set of archival notebook pages and was published in *Hotel* #5 and *Hotel* #6.

Velimir Khlebnikov's poems – 'On this, the day of Blue Bears,' 'Fly! A gentle word so pretty' and the fragment 'Zangzei' – were translated from the Russian by Natasha Randall and first published on the *Hotel Archive* under the title 'The Way Ahead is Spring.'

Edwina Attlee's poems 'white dog' and 'an eight horse sun' were first published on the *Hotel Archive* and are excerpted from the collection *A great shaking* (Tenement Press, 2024).

Aidan Moffat's short story 'Timeshare' is excerpted from an unfinished series of studies of hotel living, and was first published in *Hotel* #5.

Lesley Harrison's 'Waiting for the Ferry, Lousay' was published on the *Hotel Archive* following its inclusion in Sam Buchan-Watts and Lavinia Singer's anthology in dedication to the works of W. S. Graham, *Try to Be Better* (Prototype, 2019), and thereafter in her collection *Disappearance* (Shearsman Books, 2020).

Oliver Bancroft's series, 'A Working Week' – seven watercolours – appears in this volume for the first time.

Will Eaves' collection of chromatic fragments, 'Greenery,' was first published in *Hotel* #1; thereafter, it formed a chapter of a book in Eaves' *The Inevitable Gift Shop* (CB Editions, 2016), a 'memoir by other means' shortlisted for the Ted Hughes Prize 2016.

James Hugunin's 'A Verbal Translation of Two Photographs' are excerpted from Hugunin's 1970s editorial project *The Dumb Ox* (an 'intermittently published paper of the arts'); they were published, thereafter, in *Hotel* #4.

Aram Saroyan's 'Initiator' – a short subversion of memory – was first published in *Hotel* #3.

Glykeria Patramani's 'The Hare' was first published in *Hotel* #6.

Lauren de Sá Naylor's essay 'The Splendour & Effluence of the Motorway' was first published in *Hotel* #6 and appears here in a revised iteration.

Will Oldham's pages (from assorted notebooks) were first published in *Hotel* #6.

Antonio Tabucchi's 'The Heirs are Grateful,' translated from the Italian by Elizabeth Harris, appeared in *Hotel* #7 in tandem with the publication of his collection *Stories with Pictures* (Archipelago, 2021).

Nina Mingya Powles' work 'Yellow Fragments' was first published on the *Hotel Archive* and thereafter in the collection *Twenty-Five Rooms*, a collation of selected materials from the *Hotel Archive*, co-published with Dostoyevsky Wannabe, 2020.

Isabel Galleymore's poems 'Spirit Animal' and 'The Future Tense Expresses a State that Doesn't Exist' were first published in *Hotel* #5.

Jeffrey Vallance's hallucinatory work 'Cameron's Dream' is excerpted from the Tenement Press publication of Vallance's selected spiritual and esoteric writings, *A Voyage to Extremes*. Vallance's essays have appeared in *Hotel* #5, *Hotel* #7 and on the *Hotel Archive*.

Preti Taneja's 'Debt Night' is excerpted from a pamphlet co-published by *Hotel* and Les Fugitives (with the support of the Institut Universitaire de France), *Detour / Détours*, a set of specially commissioned texts and translations that readdress (and respond to) our various definitions of debt. *Detour / Détours* was edited by Cécile Menon and Dominic J. Jaeckle.

Stanley Schtinter's 'We Have Come to Let You Out' was first published in *Hotel* #5 and is an element of a larger, multimedia study of the spectral life of Brion Gysin (see Schtinter's film works *Hotel Bardo*, 2018, and *Dreamachine*, 2018).

Sophie Seita's text, 'The Gracious Ones (A Philosophical Ballet)' – a performance and sound work – was first published in *Hotel* #5. A more extended version appeared as a chapbook published by Earthbound Press (in their Earthbound Poetry Series, 2020). The piece was thereafter exhibited as a sound piece as part of Seita's Dorothea Schlegel Artist Residency in Berlin, October / December 2022.

Cass McComb's poem, 'Ode,' is excerpted from his debut collection *Toy Fabels* (Spurl Editions, 2019). A selection of McComb's poetry appeared in *Hotel* #6.

Ralf Webb's poem, 'Travelling Alone is My Favourite Sickness' was first published in *Hotel* #5.

Wayne Koestenbaum's poem, '[elegant toplessness stoned in stairwell]' was first published in *Hotel* #2, prior to its inclusion in Koestenbaum's collection *Camp Marmalade* (Nightboat Books, 2018).

Iain Sinclair & SJ Fowler's respective contributions – 'Prompt Notes' and 'Animal Bones' – owe to Fowler's collaboration with filmmaker Joshua Alexander, *Animal Drums* (2020). Sinclair's text is a cut-up, drawing on fragments from the film, and was read in advance of the premiere of Alexander and Fowler's work at the Whitechapel Gallery, London, 13 December 2018. Fowler's poems are excerpted from the film itself. Sinclair's pages are a direct transcription of his reading. Sinclair and Fowler's respective contributions were first published in *Hotel* #5.

David Grubbs' 'Good night the pleasure was ours' was first published in *Hotel* #7; a variation was subsequently included in his work of the same title, *Good night the pleasure was ours* (Duke University Press, 2022).

Agustín Fernández Mallo & Pere Joan's imagined anecdote 'That's It?' – translated from the Spanish by Thomas Bunstead – is excerpted from Mallo's novel *Nocilla Lab* (Fitzcarraldo Editions, 2019). 'That's It?' was published in *Hotel* #5.

The [CODA] materials – excerpts from John Divola's series of photographs 'As Far As I Could Get' (c.1996–97) – were included in *Hotel* #5; a publication gathering photographs from this series in full was published by Prestel in 2013.

An acccompanying insert carries Joan Brossa's poem 'Sota la pluja desplego un mapa mundi' / 'I unfold a map of the world in the rain,' translated from the Catalan by Cameron Griffiths, and excerpted from the Tenement Press publication of Brossa's *El saltamartí / The Tumbler* (2021).

Hotel's History

Hotel #1 (2016) THE PINK HOTEL
ed. Jaeckle, Chadwick & Dunn
(designed & typeset by Reynolds)
Mat Riviere / Will Eaves / Jon Auman / Duncan White / Tyler Malone / Jane Yeh / Erica Baum / Matthew Gregory / Eley Williams / & Jess Cotton

Hotel #2 (2017) OCHRE HOTEL
ed. Jaeckle, Chadwick, Dunn & Auman
(designed & typeset by Reynolds)
Joshua T. Howell / Holly Pester / Wayne Koestenbaum / Mary Margaret Rinebold / Linh Dinh / Ingo Niermann / Thom Andersen / Julia Drescher / Victoria Manifold / SJ Fowler / Alice Butler / Will Eaves / Nicole Mauro / & Amanda DeMarco

Hotel #3 (2017) THE PAPER-THIN HOTEL
ed. Jaeckle, Chadwick, Dunn & Auman
(designed & typeset by Reynolds)
Olivier Castel / Martin Jackson / Nick Cave / Duncan White / Juliet Escoria / Jasmine Parker / Hanya Yanagihara / Holly Brown / Kim Sherwood / Gordon Lish / Rowan Evans / Owen Booth / Frederic Tuten / José Antonio Suárez Londoño / Imogen Reid / Pierre Senges / Jacob Siefring / Mark Kozelek / Jack Robinson / Charles Boyle / & Aram Saroyan

Hotel #4 (2018) THE BLUE HOTEL
ed. Jaeckle, Chadwick, Dunn & Auman
(designed & typeset by Reynolds)
Jonathan Chandler / Rebecca Tamás / John Yau / Lucy Sante / David Kishik / Lucy Sante / Scott McClanahan / Pascal Richmann / Amanda DeMarco / James Hugunin / Nona Fernández / Ellen Jones / Richard Scott / Vala Thorodds / Bill Callahan / Jason Shulman / Oliver Goldstein / Leah Sophia Dworkin / Iris Smyles / Livia Franchini / Serena Braida / Daniele Pantano / Veronica Scott Esposito / Hisham Bustani / maia tabet / Carol Mavor / David Lowery / & Joanna Rafael Goldberg

Hotel #5 (2019) THE NEW ROSE HOTEL
ed. Jaeckle, Chadwick & Auman
(designed & typeset by Reynolds)
Sandro Miller / Isabel Galleymore / Aidan Moffat / Georgia Haire / Hélène Frédérick / Jacob Siefring / John Divola / Ralf Webb / Ryūnosuke Akutagawa / Ryan Choi / Carla Maliandi / Frances Riddle / Jenny Hval / Marjam Idriss / Noémi Lefebvre / Natacha Lasorak / Sophie Lewis / John Holten / Jonathan Monk / Rachel Kass / Nicolette Polek / Raúl Guerrero / Daisy Lafarge / Joshua Cohen / Jack Underwood / Stanley Schtinter / Lucy Mercer / Ariana Reines / P Adams Sitney / John Saul / Jeffrey Vallance / Sophie Seita / Agustín Fernández Mallo / Pere Joan / Thomas Bunstead / SJ Fowler / & Iain Sinclair

Hotel #6 (2020) A PERMANENTLY DARK HOTEL
ed. Jaeckle & Auman
(designed & typeset by Reynolds)
Wayne Koestenbaum / Glykeria Patramani / Imogen Cassels / Will Oldham / Diego Fonseca / Ellen Jones / Hao Guang Tse / Geoffrey Mak / Astrid Alben / Nathan Dragon / Sarah Boulton / Sascha Macht / Amanda DeMarco / Hannah Regel / Andrew Lampert / Emmanuel Iduma / Lotte LS / oxoa / Franz Kafka / Hannah Williams / Lauren de Sá Naylor / Jen Calleja / Cass McCombs / Emmanuelle Pagano / Sophie Lewis / Jennifer Higgins / Lauren Elkin / Clemens Meyer / & Katy Derbyshire

Hotel #7 (2021) THE LAST HOTEL
ed. Jaeckle & Auman
(designed & typeset by Reynolds)
Lucy Sante / Adrian Bridget / Antonio Tabucchi / Elizabeth Harris / Helena Gomà / Nadia de Vries / Josef Winkler / Adrian Nathan West / Greg Tate / Helen Cammock / Frederic Tuten / Andrzej Żuławski / Lily Hackett / Percival Everett / Alisha Dietzman / Joan Brossa / Cameron Griffiths / Manuela Moser / Sam Riviere / Yasmine Seale / Jeffrey Vallance / Raúl Guerrero / Mark Lanegan / Rebecca Jagoe / Adrian Nathan West / Daniel Pellizzari / Rahul Bery / Matthew Shaw / Sam Buchan-Watts / Nathan Salsburg / Willard Watson / Bessie Jones / Big Bill Broonzy / Texas Gladden / Margaret Barry / Eddie Sanger / Hélène Gaudy / Jeffrey Zuckerman / Stephen Watts / & David Grubbs

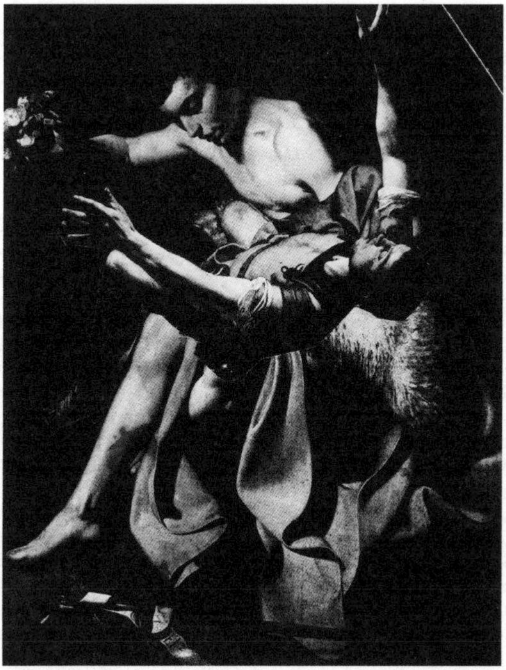

Notes on these images

(p. 2) A hieroglyph sign intended to guide itinerant workers via an ethical code created by the Tourist Union #63 (a 'hobo' union created in the mid-1800s to evade anti-vagrancy laws); the sign indicates 'a good road to follow.' See John E. Fawcett and Elizabeth D. Rambeau's 'A Hobo Memoir, 1936,' *Indiana Magazine of History*, 90/4 (1994), pp. 346–64.

(p. 5) Aram Saroyan, 'Paris, 1959,' courtesy of the artist, all rights reserved. Saroyan, © 2023.

(p. 12) Mario Dondero, the room in the Hotel Roma (Turin, Italy) wherein Cesare Pavese committed suicide on 27 August 1950. Courtesy of Bridgman Image Library, all rights reserved. Dondero, © 2023.

(p. 14) Erica Baum, 'Elastic / Inelastic (Blackboard),' courtesy of the artist & Bureau (New York, NY), all rights reserved. Baum, © 1994.

(p. 24) 'Neither Helena nor Oliver had seen the Green Ray,' a plate lifted from Mary de Hautville's translation of Jules Verne's *Le Rayon vert / The Green Ray* (London: Sampson, Low Marston, Searle, and Rivington, 1883).

(p. 28) Erica Baum, 'Simbolismo (Blackboard),' courtesy of the artist and Bureau (New York, NY), all rights reserved. Baum, © 1994.

(p. 30) A manipulated titled card from the short film, *I am a Hotel*, a 1983 Canadian made-for-television musical written by Leonard Cohen and Mark Shekter and directed by Allan F. Nicholls. The storyline is based on imaginary events in the King Edward Hotel (Toronto, Canada).

(p. 42) Dominic J. Jaeckle, 'Breakfast (New Braunfels, TX),' D. J. Jaeckle, © 2019.

(p. 50) Raúl Guerrero, 'Dashiell Hammett at John's Grill,' courtesy of the artist, all rights reserved. Guerrero, © 2018.

(pp. 54, 57, 62) Stephen Watts, 'Drawn Poem I (attempt to describe a pine against the white of the sun),' 'Drawn Poem II,' 'Drawn Poem III (uncertain whether a tree is a person or vice versa, or not at all).' Courtesy of the artist, all rights reserved. Watts, © 2023. With thanks to Joe Hales of Sylvia Publishing.

(p. 74) Olivier Castel, 'Des distances dans lâme' (2015). A reproduction of images used in a solo show of that name produced by Castel as part of the Praxis programme. Artium, Vitoria-Gasteiz (Spain, 2015). The image is a palimpsest of the various inscriptions (notes, quotes and drawings) that dressed a series of (temporary) pillars which, for the duration of the show, carried the architecture of the museum, giving the building a rest. Castel's work was employed as an epigram to *Hotel* #3 (2017). Courtesy of the artist, all rights reserved. Castel, © 2015.

(p. 84) Raúl Guerrero, 'Raymond Chandler at the Whaling Bar, circa 1954,' courtesy of the artist, all rights reserved. Guerrero, © 2018.

(p. 92) Dominic J. Jaeckle, 'Texas 71 (Austin, TX),' D. J. Jaeckle, © 2019.

(p. 95) Perhaps, a photograph of the reverse of David Bowie's head; borrowed from the artwork for the Chris Petit and Mordant Music (purge.xxx LP release, cat. no. purrrrrj000), *In What's Missing, is Where Love has Gone* (2019). Petit (and purge.xxx), © 2019. With thanks to Stanley Schtinter.

(p. 96) Distressed insignia of the Correios de Portugal (CTT), the country's national post office.

(p. 105) The exterior of the Brandenburg offices of the regional German newspaper *Märkische Oderzeitung*.

(p. 106) A found photograph, courtesy of Samuel Kilcoyne (editor of *Augenblick*; an independent publishing project dedicated to anonymous and found photography).

(p. 110) Jason Shulman, 'Ann Darrow (II),' see also 'Ann Darrow (III),' (p. 204) See *Hotel* #4 (2018). Courtesy of the artist, all rights reserved. Shulman, © 2017.

(p. 114) Georgia May Jaeckle, a Polaroid study of a dead grass snake (Abiquiú, NM). Courtesy of the artist, all rights reserved. G. M. Jaeckle, © 2019.

(p. 118) Jonathan Chandler, a set of pen works by 'Britain's most isolated cartoonist,' the first of five studies of stills excerpted from Robert Bresson's 1977 motion picture *Le diable probablement / The Devil Probably* (see also pp. 282, 315, 358, 394). Courtesy of the artist, all rights reserved. The 'riverside' still was employed as an epigram to *Hotel* #4 (2018). Chandler, © 2018.

(p. 123) Sandro Miller, 'Migrant Mother Malkovich,' an homage to Dorothea Lange's 1936 photograph 'Migrant Mother, Nipomo, California.' Miller's photograph was employed as an epi-gram to *Hotel* #5 (2019). Courtesy of the artist, all rights reserved. Miller, © 2019.

(p. 124) James Hugunin, 'Argument Against Idea Art,' a work excerpted from Hugunin's artist book, *Re-Treads* (1974). See also, the INTERMISSION, 'Word→Object' (pp. 214–215). Courtesy of the artist, all rights reserved. Hugunin, © 1974.

(p. 128) Erica Baum, Alchemy (excerpted from the Baum's 'Naked Eye' series), courtesy of the artist and Bureau (New York, NY), all rights reserved. Baum, © 2009.

(p. 132) Matthew Shaw, a found (and anonymous) portrait (in triplicate); see *Hotel* #7 (2021). Courtesy of the artist, all rights reserved. Shaw, © 2019.

(p. 136) Jeffrey Vallance, 'Bigfoot,' the first of seven studies of the sasquatch, as found in the eye of the Virgin of Guadalupe (see p. 302); see also pp. 140, 176, 242, 246, 264, 310. Courtesy of the artist, all rights reserved. Vallance, © 1994.

(p. 172) Levina van Winden, 'Neu Stammheim – [no fishing] – long live the RAF – in solidarity!' – on the outer walls of the Bijlmerbajes Prison Complex, Amsterdam (1978), to partner with the following 'poem-as-caption' (courtesy of the poet)...

*I sometimes sing lest you forget who I am. Or
we throw a thousand tulips in the canal in your
grandma's resistance uniform – you the jacket,
I the skir – to show her who we are. To show each
other who we are.*

*We always know precisely who we are but
sometimes we need to press it through the paper
with precisely the right words or precisely the
right number of soaking tulips, like you did
with a thought on the back of a golden chocolate
wrapper.*

Nobody will ever keep us from the stage again.

*Sometimes you meet these people you can fully
get to know with one good look.*

*Sometimes it only takes a single deed one
single moment
to never have met a certain someone.
Sometimes it doesn't take recidivism to deny
any and all ties.
Sometimes 'fair' and 'reasonable' are only
standing in our way.*

*Ulrike Meinhof's brain was confiscated by
the state.
NSDAP Member No. 9154986 cut it out of
her skull.
They kept it in a cardboard box till 2002.*

Jurisprudence.

*Nobody will ever tell us if the terrorist
nature can be dissected.*

Formaldehyde.

*Sometimes we don't have to forgive anything
Sometimes we have to hold everything briefly,
shine a light, squeeze it softly for a while
Sometimes a thousand tulips aren't enough
to forget everything for just a while.*

We will throw the flowers back at the crowd.

(p. 182) Aram Saroyan, '#5 (August 14, 1959),' courtesy of the artist, all rights reserved. Saroyan, © 2023.

(p. 196) Dominic J. Jaeckle, 'Dante (New Orleans, LA),' D. J. Jaeckle, © 2019.

(p. 216) Lucy Sante, 'Phantom Car,' employed as epigram to *Hotel* #7 (2021). Courtesy of the artist, all rights reserved. Sante, © 2020.

(p. 226) Yasmine Seale, 'all that had to end' (2021); see also, (p. 260) 'all that is on land' (2021). These images are part of a series of visual poems based on Edward Lane's translation of the *Thousand and One Nights*, and excerpted from a sequence originally published in *Hotel* #7 (2021). Courtesy of the artist, all rights reserved. Seale, © 2021.

(p. 259) Aram Saroyan, 'Hold it a minute,' courtesy of the artist, all rights reserved. Saroyan, © 1973.

(p. 273) Road Map, *reverse / detail* (date unknown), Wikimedia Commons.

(p. 298) Georgia May Jaeckle, 'On Farm to Market Road 170' (Fort Leaton, Presidio, TX). Courtesy of the artist, all rights reserved. G. M. Jaeckle, © 2019.

(pp. 316, 339, 340) Schtinter, 'Hotel Bardo (Lipowa 5, 57–256 Bardo, Poland),' I, II, III; see *Hotel* #5 (2019). courtesy of the artist, all rights reserved. Schtinter, © 2018

(pp. 325, 326) Stills from Stanley Schtinter's short film *Dreamachine*, 16mm, with cinematography by Louis Benassi, a custom-made rig by Tony Hill, and sound by Vindicatrix. 4' 33, Light Cone (Paris, 2017). Courtesy of the artist, all rights reserved. Schtinter, © 2018.

(p. 328) 'Somewhere in the Light' – A hitherto unpublished photograph of William Burroughs, Brion Gysin and Ian Sommerville.

(p. 362) 'Who needs the Met?' – A single page excerpted from the Wayne Koestenbaum papers, as held at Yale's Beinecke Rare Book & Manuscript Library (New Haven, CT). Courtesy of the artist.

(p. 274) Cass McCombs, 'Untitled,' courtesy of the artist and Spurl Editions, a photograph excerpted from McCombs 2019 publication *Toy Fabels*. See *Hotel* #6 (2021). McCombs, © 2018.

(pp. 376, 383) Joshua Alexander, two stills from the artist's collaboration with SJ Fowler, a poem-as-film called *Animal Drums* (2018). See *Hotel* #5. Courtesy of the artist(s), all rights reserved. Alexander & Fowler, © 2018.

(p. 386) David Grubbs writes lyrics for Justus Köhncke at a recording session at CAN Studio, Weilerswist (Germany, 1998). Photographer unknown. Grubbs, © 2023.

(p. 418) Marbled notebook, reverse cover, *detail*.

(p. 429) Matchbook (El Capitan Hotel, 100 E Broadway, Van Horn, TX, 79855), *eBay*.

(p. 433) Adrian Bridget, 'Study for *Treatment*,' courtesy of the artist, all rights reserved. Bridget, © 2019.

Biographies

Georgia May Jaeckle is an artist and architectural designer. She lives and works in Margate.

Mario Dondero (1928–2015) was an Italian press photographer.

> *Dondero was an acute portraitist of the Italian writers and artists of the period – Pier Paolo Pasolini and Alberto Moravia, Jannis Kounellis and Alberto Burri, among others – and of the French intelligentsia embodied by the likes of Louis Althusser and Jean Genet. Especially telling are the group portraits shot in the literary cafés and restaurants where these intellectuals used to gather. Dondero's approach was deliberately 'low-key,' without any type of visible rhetoric: these are 'stolen' shots in the purest tradition of photojournalism. And this is precisely where the ethical heart of these works resides. In fact, Dondero seems to not want photography to veer from the task of 'bearing witness' that it has had from the beginning, and his example does not seem to presage any of the questions about the nature of photography that his friend Ugo Mulas and many others would address in the 1970s. On the contrary, Dondero represents the 'certainty' of photography, as opposed to its self-interrogatory mode, which opened the way for the medium's entry into the art system. During a conversation on the occasion of one of these exhibitions, Dondero said that he cannot shoot unless there is a sort of empathy, unless he 'feels a bit of love' for the person or thing whose image he is stealing. This attitude can be recognised in his choice to bear witness to the European left through the observation of the thinkers and artists who contributed to it, or even simply of the social situations in which they flourished – and thereby to convey his love for photography. This is a far cry from the stance of the 'artist who uses photography' – a relationship of explicit detachment. That's fine too, but it's important to be aware of the difference.*
> —Marco Meneguzzo, *Artforum*

Erica Baum lives and works in New York. She is well known for her varied photographic series capturing text and image in found printed material, from paperback books to library indexes and sewing patterns. She received her MFA from Yale University School of Art and her BA in Anthropology from Barnard. Her work is held in numerous collections including the Whitney Museum of American Art, New York; Solomon R. Guggenheim Museum, New York; the Metropolitan Museum of Art, New York; SFMOMA, San Francisco; and MAMCO, Geneva, among others.

Dominic J. Jaeckle is a writer, editor and broadcaster. Founded in 2016, Jaeckle curated and collated the irregular magazine *Hotel* and its adjacent projects, and is the publisher and editor behind the small press project Tenement Press. Recent publications in Tenement's 'Yellowjacket' series include Stanley Schtinter's *Last Movies*; Dolors Miquel's *El guant de plàstic rosa / The Pink Plastic Glove* (translated from the Catalan by Peter Bush); Reza Baraheni's *Lilith*; Pier Paolo Pasolini's *La rabbia / Anger* (translated from the Italian by Cristina Viti); Kyra Simone's *Palace of Rubble*; Jeffrey Vallance's collected spiritual and esoteric writings, *A Voyage to Extremes*; SJ Fowler's debut novella, *MUEUM* (shortlisted for the Republic of Consciousness Prize for Small Presses, 2023); Yasmine Seale & Robin Moger's *Agitated Air: Poems After Ibn Arabi*; Schtinter's edited collection, *The Liberated Film Club*; and a first English-language edition of Joan Brossa's *El saltamartí / The Tumbler* (translated from the Catalan by Cameron Griffiths). Jaeckle's first collection, *36 Exposures (A bastardised roll of film)* – a collaboration with artist Hoagy Houghton – was first published by Dostoyevsky Wannabe (2021) and is forthcoming in a new edition via the imprint John Cassavetes, alongside a collection of 'cut-up' works, *Magnolia or Redbud: Flowers for Laura Lee Burroughs*. Jaeckle's critical writings have been included in collections published by Bloomsbury and Penn Press, among others, and his works have been published and exhibited internationally.

Jess Chandler founded Prototype in 2019. She was a co-founder of Test Centre, which ran from 2011 to 2018, publishing innovative works of poetry and fiction, and also co-runs, with Gareth Evans, the imprint House Sparrow Press. She has worked as an editor at Reaktion Books, used to work as a researcher and producer on factual television programmes, and was the Digital Editor at *Poetry London* for six years. Jess has extensive experience editing and publishing a range of books, from fiction and poetry to illustrated art books, literary biography, history and philosophy, specialising in poetry and hybrid, multidisciplinary works.

Jess Cotton is a writer based in London. Her book on John Ashbery was recently published by Reaktion Books.

Rebecca Tamás is the author of the poetry collection WITCH (Penned in the Margins, 2019), which was a Poetry Society Choice and a *Paris Review* Staff Pick. Tamás' essay collection, *Strangers: Essays on the Human and Nonhuman* (Makina Books, 2020), was longlisted for the Rathbones Folio Prize 2021. She currently works as a Lecturer in Creative Writing at City, University of London.

Raúl Guerrero creates paintings, sculptures, prints, drawings, artist's books, photographs and videotapes. He has forged an expansive, ever-evolving body of work that combines technical innovation; critiques of symbolic power; historical and literary references; and his personal perspective as an American of Mexican ancestry. From the mid-1950s to the 1960s, weekly family visits to Tijuana introduced him to a variety of Mexican folk arts and crafts as well as the popular tourist items. Exposure to Zapotec textiles, indigenous hand-painted pottery, blown glass from the interior of Mexico and plaster of Paris replicas of Da Vinci's 'Last Supper' all provided an introduction to a visual and sensual world beyond the working-class environment of post-war San Diego and its limited artistic and cultural offerings. At the same time, an incredible array of pop and sub-cultures were evolving in Southern California, particularly in Los Angeles: hot-rod car culture, pachucos, surfers, the Beat generation, folk music, motorcycle gangs, and immigrants from Latin America and the Pacific Rim. The changing zeitgeist would influence Guerrero's artistic work for years to come. Guerrero trained at the Chouinard Art Institute (BFA, 1970). Guerrero has exhibited nationally and internationally in numerous solo and group shows at venues such as the Long Beach Museum of Art (1978), Museum of Contemporary Art San Diego (1998) and the CUE Art Foundation, New York (2010). He received an NEA Photography Fellowship in 1979 and was the first recipient of the San Diego Art Prize in 2006. He currently teaches in the Visual Art Department at the University of California, San Diego.

Stephen Watts was born in 1952. His father was from Stoke-on-Trent, and his mother's family from villages high in the Italian and Swiss Alps. He spent very vital time – in place of university – in northern Scotland, especially the island of North Uist, and – since 1977 – has lived mainly in the richly multilingual communities of the Whitechapel area of East London. Geographies and location (as also their negative theologies) are urgent to his life and his work. Recent books include *Ancient Sunlight* (Enitharmon, 2014; reprinted 2020), *Republic of Dogs / Republic of Birds* (Test Centre, 2016; Prototype, 2020), and *Journeys Across Breath: Poems, 1975–2005* (Prototype, 2022). As a co-translator, Watts has worked closely with exiled poets and, inter alia, has co-translated *Pages from the Biography of an Exile* by the Iraqi poet Adnan al-Sayegh (Arc, 2014) and Syrian poet Golan Haji's *A Tree Whose Name I Don't Know* (A Midsummer Night's Press, 2017), amongst other publications. Watts' own poetry has been translated into many languages – with full collections in Italian, Czech, Arabic, German and Spanish – and he works as a contributing editor with Tenement Press.

Helen Cammock lives and works in Wales and London. Her practice spans film, photography, print, text, song and performance and examines mainstream historical and contemporary narratives about Blackness, womanhood, oppression and resistance, wealth and power, poverty and vulnerability. Her works often cut across time and geography, layering multiple voices; investigating the cyclical nature of histories in her visual and aural assemblages. In 2017, Cammock won the Max Mara Art Prize for Women and in 2019, Cammock was the joint recipient of The Turner Prize. She has exhibited and performed worldwide, with recent and current solo shows including *Bass Notes and SiteLines*, Amant, New York (2023); *I Will Keep My Soul*, Art + Practice, Los Angeles (2023); *Behind the Eye is the Promise of Rain*, Kestner Gesellshaft, Hanover (2022); *Concrete Feathers and Porcelain Tacks*, Touchstones, Rochdale and The Photographer's Gallery, London (2021); *Beneath the Surface of Skin*, STUK Art Centre, Leuven (2021); *They Call It Idlewild*, Wysing (2020); *Che Si Può Fare*, Whitechapel Gallery, London (2019); *Che Si Può Fare*, Collezione Maramotti, Reggio Emilia (2019); *The Long Note*, Irish Museum of Modern Art, Dublin (2019), VOID, Derry (2018). Group shows include *Breathing*, Hamburger Kunstalle, Hamburg (2022) and *Radio Ballads*, Serpentine Galleries, London (2022). She is represented by Kate MacGarry, London.

Salvador Espriu (1913–1985) is one of Catalonia's most significant post-war writers and an outstanding poet. Although he first became known as a narrator, his relatively later incursion into poetry was no obstacle to his achieving swift recognition as a poet, not only within the sphere of Catalan letters but also internationally. He also played an important part in the revitalisation of Catalan theatre. He published novels, *El Doctor Rip* (1931) and *Laia* (1932); collections of stories, *Aspectes* (1934), *Ariadna al laberint grotesc / Ariadna in the Grotesque Labyrinth* (1935), *Miratge a Citerea / Mirage in Citerea* (1935), *Litizia i altres proses / Litizia and Other Prose* (1937); and works which led to his being considered the most original Catalan narrator of the post-Noucentisme (the turn-of-the-century cultural and political movement in Catalonia). Among his published collections of poetry are *Cementiri de Sinera / Sinera Cemetery* (1946); *Les hores / The Hours* (1952); *El caminant i el mur / The Wanderer and the Wall* (1954); *Final del laberint / The End of the Labyrinth* (1955); *Les cançons d'Ariadna / The Songs of Ariadna* (1949); *La pell de brau / The Hide of the Bull* (1960); *Llibre de Sinera / The Book of Sinera* (1963); and *Setmana Santa / Holy Week* (1971). He revised the entirety of his work with the aim of creating a unified corpus. Translated into many languages, Espriu's name frequently appears among those proposed as Nobel laureates. He received the Award of Honour in Catalan Letters in 1972, the City of Barcelona Gold Medal and that of the Generalitat (Autonomous Government of Catalonia) in 1980. He was given honorary doctorates by the universities of Barcelona and Toulouse (Llenguadoc). In 1982, he was awarded but declined to accept the Spanish distinction, the Cross of Alphonse the Wise, because of his civic stand with respect to Catalonia.

Lucy Mercer's debut collection, *Emblem* (Prototype, 2022), was a Poetry Book Society Choice. She was awarded the inaugural White Review Poet's Prize. Her poems and essays have been published in *Granta*, *Art Review*, *The White Review*, *Poetry London*, *Poetry Review* and others. She is co-editor, with Livia Franchini, of the RSL-funded publication and podcast *Too Little: Too Hard – Writers on the Intersections of Work, Time and Value*. She is a Postdoctoral Research Fellow at the University of Exeter.

Olivier Castel usually presents work under heteronyms and has created over thirty different identities since 2001. Often using ephemeral or temporal forms, he works primarily with projections, reflective surfaces, light, text and audio. His work functions as a set of propositions, employing the imaginary and exploring the process by which something is made visible.

Lucy Sante's books include *Low Life* (Farrar, Straus and Giroux, 2003), *Kill All Your Darlings* (Verse Chorus Press, 2007), *The Other Paris* (Farrar Straus & Giroux, 2015), *Maybe the People Would Be the Times* (Verse Chorus Press, 2020) and – forthcoming – the memoir *I Heard Her Call My Name* (Penguin Random House, 2024; Heinemann, 2024).

Ryūnosuke Akutagawa (1892–1927) was born in Tokyo, Japan, and authored more than 300 works of fiction and non-fiction over the course of his lifetime, including *Rashōmon* (1915), *The Spider's Thread* (1918), *Hell Screen* (1918), *Kappa* (1927) and *In a Grove* (1922).

Ryan Choi is the author of *In Dreams: The Very Short Stories of Ryūnosuke Akutagawa* (Paper + Ink, 2023) and *Three Demons: A Study on Sanki Saito's Haiku* (Open Letter Books, 2023). He is an editor at *AGNI*. Choi's work has appeared in *Harper's Magazine*, the *Times Literary Supplement*, the *Los Angeles Review of Books*, *The Nation*, *The New Criterion*, *The Raritan* and elsewhere. He lives in Honolulu, Hawaii, where he was born and raised.

John Yau has published books of poetry, fiction and criticism. His latest poetry publications include a book of poems, *Tell It Slant* (Omnidawn, 2023); a book of essays, *Please Wait by the Coatroom: Reconsidering Race and Identity in American Art* (Black Sparrow, 2023); and a monograph, *John Pai; Liquid Steel* (Rizzoli Electa, 2023). In 1999, Yau started Black Square Editions, a small press devoted to poetry, fiction, translation and criticism. He is the 2017 recipient of the Jackson Prize in Poetry and a 2021 recipient of a Rabkin Prize for art criticism. Since 2012, he has contributed regularly to the online magazine *Hyperallergic*. He is a Professor of Critical Studies at Mason Gross School of the Arts (Rutgers University) and lives in Beacon, New York.

Nicolette Polek is the author of *Imaginary Museums* (Soft Skull, 2020) and the forthcoming novel *Bitter Water Opera* (Graywolf Press, 2024). She is a recipient of a Rona Jaffe Writers' Award and a recent graduate of Yale Divinity School.

Chris Petit is an English author and filmmaker, once described by *Le Monde* as 'the Robespierre of English cinema.' His film *Radio On* (1979) was featured in *Sight and Sound*'s 'Greatest Films of All Time,' 2022.

Sascha Macht was born in Frankfurt (Oder) and studied at the German Institute for Literature in Leipzig. He has published prose, poetry and drama in various anthologies and literary magazines. He has received fellowships from Künstlerhaus Lukas, Ahrenshoop, the Cultural Foundation of the Free State of Saxony, the Literary Colloquium Berlin, the Schloss Wiepersdorf Cultural Foundation and the German Literature Fund. His first novel, *The War in the Garden of the King of the Dead*, was published by DuMont in spring 2016. From 2013 to 2017 he was a research associate at the German Institute for Literature in Leipzig, investigating the education of writers in the GDR. In 2018, together with Isabelle Lehn and Katja Stopka, he published *Schreiben lernen im Sozialismus / Learning to Write under Socialism* (The Johannes R. Becher Institute for Literature, 2018). He lives in Leipzig.

Amanda DeMarco is an American writer and translator based in Berlin, translating from French and German. Her translations include works by Franz Hessel, Gaston de Pawlowski, Byung-Chul Han, Nathalie Léger and Marcus Steinweg. DeMarco has received grants and fellowships from MacDowell, Yaddo, the city of Berlin, the Fulbright Foundation, PEN and the EU. Her writing has appeared in the *Wall Street Journal*, the *Times Literary Supplement*, *The Paris Review*, the *Los Angeles Review of Books* and *BOMB*, among others.

Mark Lanegan (1964–2022) was a musician and the author of *I Am the Wolf: Lyrics and Writings* (Hachette Books, 2017), *Sing Backwards and Weep: A Memoir* (White Rabbit, 2020), *Leaving California* (Heartworm Press, 2021) and *Devil in a Coma* (White Rabbit, 2021).

Vala Thorodds is a poet, publisher, translator and editor. Her work has been published by the *Guardian*, *Granta*, BBC Radio 4, *The White Review*, *PN Review*, *The Stinging Fly*, and in the anthologies *New Poetries VII* (Carcanet, 2018) and *The Penguin Book of the Prose Poem* (2019), among others. Her recent translation of Kristín Ómarsdóttir's novel *Swanfolk* (Vintage, 2022) received a PEN / Heim grant and was longlisted for the Oxford-Weidenfeld Prize. She is the recipient of World Literature Today's 2023 Student Translation Prize.

Richard Scott was born in London in 1981. His first book, *Soho* (Faber & Faber, 2018), was a Gay's the Word book of the year and shortlisted for the T.S. Eliot prize. Recent works include 'Still Life with Rose' in the Spring issue of *Poetry Review* (2023) and 'love version of' in *100 Queer Poems* (Vintage, 2022). Scott's poetry has been translated into German and French. He is a lecturer in creative writing at Goldsmiths, University of London, where he also runs a poetry reading group, and he teaches poetry at the Faber Academy.

Jonathan Chandler, born to a youth worker and a skilled labourer in coastal Suffolk, where he again resides after stints in London and Tokyo. Studied film under Tony Hill and Martine Thoquenne, graduating in '99, Chandler went on to work in comics and drawing, and became associated with the Famicon arts collective. Chandler has more recently moved into the writing of novels and screenplays.

Joshua Cohen is the author of the novels *The Netanyahus* (Fitzcarraldo Editions, 2021; New York Review Books, 2021), *Moving Kings* (Fitzcarraldo Editions, 2021; Random House, 2017), *Book of Numbers* (Harvill Secker, 2015; Random House, 2015), *Witz* (Dalkey Archive Press, 2010),

A Heaven of Others (Starcherone Books, 2011) and *Cadenza for the Schneidermann Violin Concerto* (Fugue State Press, 2006); the short fiction collection *Four New Messages* (Graywolf Press, 2012) and the non-fiction collection *Attention: Dispatches from a Land of Distraction* (Fitzcarraldo Editions, 2018; Random House, 2018). Called 'a major American writer' by the *New York Times* and 'an extraordinary prose stylist, surely one of the most prodigious at work in American fiction today' by the *New Yorker*, Cohen was awarded Israel's 2013 Matanel Prize, and in 2017 was named one of Granta's Best Young American Novelists. *The Netanyahus* won the 2021 National Jewish Book Award for Fiction and the 2022 Pulitzer Prize for Fiction.

Sandro Miller is a Chicago-based still-photographic and video artist with an especial sensitivity and mastery of studio lighting. Across fifteen books, numerous awards and a multitude of gallery and museums exhibitions, he can be variously defined as a husband, father, artist, author, documentarian, publisher, lecturer, teacher, humanist, philanthropist and guidance counsellor (without title). Miller regularly lends his skills and studio pro bono to charitable groups, and is a social advocate for causes such as gender, race, national origin, homelessness, child care, arts advocacy and arts education. Miller's publications include *American Bikers* (Schirmer / Mosel, 1998), *Sandro: Verona Figure e Ritratti* (Cierre, 2002), *Imagine Cuba, 1999–2007* (Edizioni Charta, 2008), *El Matador Joselito: A Pictorial Novel* (Edizioni Charta, 2009), *Raw, Steppenwolf* (self-published, 2012), *Crowns* (Skira, 2021) and *The Malkovich Sessions* (Glitterati, 2016). Miller has exhibited his work in New York, Chicago, Los Angeles, Amsterdam, Zagreb, Brussels, Warsaw, Arles France, Brussels, Havana, Munich and Verona. Reviews, interviews, features and essays have appeared in *Musée Magazine*, *Smithsonian*, the *Huffington Post*, *Interiors*, *Graphic*, *Russian Esquire*, BBC News, Stern, the *New Yorker*, *American Photo*, *Eyemazing*, abc News, *Communication Art* and *View Camera*, among other publications.

Hannah Regel is a writer based in London. She has been published in *The Poetry Review*, *Fantastic Man*, *Granta*, *Hotel* and *Canal*, among others. She has published two collections of poetry, *When I Was Alive* and *Oliver Reed* (both Montez Press, 2017 and 2020 respectively). Her debut novel, *The Last Sane Woman*, will be published by Verso Fiction in 2024.

Nick Cave has been performing music for more than forty years and is best known as the songwriter and lead singer of Nick Cave & The Bad Seeds, whose latest album *Ghosteen* (2019) was widely received as their best work ever. Cave's body of work also covers a wider range of media and modes of expression, including film score composition, ceramic sculpture and writing novels. Over the last few years his website, *The Red Hand Files*, and 'Conversations with' live events have seen Cave exploring deeper and more direct relationships with his fans.

Matthew Shaw is an artist, author, composer and producer. Alongside solo composition, Matthew has worked with a series of collaborators including The Pop Group and Richard Norris. Shirley Collins, Brian Catling and Matthew created Crowlink, with an EP released by Domino Recordings in 2021, an audio installation premiered at the Barbican and was followed by a week at Charleston House in Sussex. *Atmosphere of Mona*, a book of poetry and photography, was published by Annwyn House in 2020. Shaw is a co-founder of Stone Club.

Daisy Lafarge is a writer based in Glasgow. She is the author of the novel *Paul* (Granta 2021; Riverhead 2022), which won a Betty Trask Award and was a *New York Times* Editor's Choice, and the poetry collection *Life Without Air* (Granta 2020), which was shortlisted for the T.S. Eliot Prize and awarded Scottish Poetry Book of the Year. Her reviews and essays on ecology, art and literature have been widely published, appearing in *Granta*, *LitHub*, *Wellcome Collection Stories*, *Art Review*, *TANK Magazine*, *The White Review* and elsewhere. *Lovebug*, a short book on the poetics of infection, was published by Peninsula Press in 2023. Daisy is currently working on her second novel.

Jeffrey Vallance's work blurs the lines between object making, installation, performance, curating and writing, and his projects are often site-specific, such as burying a frozen chicken at a pet cemetery; travelling to Polynesia to research the myth of Tiki; having audiences with the king of Tonga, the queen and president of Palau and the presidents of Iceland; creating a Richard Nixon Museum; travelling to the Vatican to study Christian relics; installing an exhibit aboard a tugboat in Sweden; and curating shows in the museums of Las Vegas (such as the Liberace and Clown Museum). In Lapland, Vallance constructed a shamanic 'magic drum.' In Orange County, Mr. Vallance curated the only art world exhibition of the Painter of Light entitled *Thomas Kinkade: Heaven on Earth*. In 1983, he was host of MTV's *The Cutting Edge* and appeared on NBC's *Late Night with David Letterman*. In 2004, Vallance received the prestigious John Simon Guggenheim Memorial Foundation award. In addition to exhibiting his artwork, Vallance has written for such publications and journals as *Art Issues*, *Artforum*, the *LA Weekly*, *Juxtapoz*, *Frieze* and the *Fortean Times*. He has published over ten books, including *Blinky the Friendly Hen* (Smart Art Press, 1996), *The World of Jeffrey Vallance: Collected Writings 1978–1994* (Art Issues Press, 1994), *Preserving America's Cultural Heritage* (California College of the Arts, 2006), *Thomas Kinkade: Heaven on Earth* (Last Gasp, 2005), *My Life with Dick* (Bukamerica Inc, 2005), *Relics and Reliquaries* (Grand Central Press, 2008) and *The Vallance Bible* (Grand Central Press, 2012). Vallance lives and works in Los Angeles. A 'bible-long' collection of Vallance's selected spiritual and esoteric writings, *A Voyage to Extremes*, was published in 2022 by Tenement Press.

Holly Pester's collection of poetry, *Comic Timing* (2021), and novel, *The Lodgers* (2024), are published by Granta. She has made experimental drama for BBC Radio 4, published by Distance No Object as *Ecologues for Idle Workers* (2019). A work of sound poetry and text, *Common Rest* (2016), is out with Prototype, and a collection of archive-fictions, *Go to reception and ask for Sara*, was published by Book Works (2015).

Matthew Gregory's poetry sequence *Excerpts from the Scenic World* was published in 2020 with If a Leaf Falls Press. He received an Eric Gregory award in 2010. His poems have appeared widely, including in the *London Review of Books*, *The White Review*, *Poetry London* and on BBC Radio 3.

Emmanuel Iduma is the author of the travelogue *A Stranger's Pose* (Cassava Republic, 2018), which was longlisted for 2019 Ondaatje Prize, and *I Am Still with You* (William Collins, 2023), a memoir on the aftermath of the Nigerian civil war. His essays have been published in *Granta*, *n+1*, the *New York Review of Books* amd *Yale Review*, and his art criticism has appeared in *Artforum*, *Aperture*, *Art in America* and the *Brooklyn Rail*. His honours include the Irving Sandler Award for New Voices in Art Criticism, a C/O Berlin Prize for Theory, and the Windham-Campbell Prize for nonfiction. He lives in Lagos, Nigeria and Norwich, UK.

Joan Brossa (1919–1998) was born in Barcelona into a family of artisans. He began writing when he was mobilised in the Spanish Civil War and, following an introduction to surrealism by way of the friendship and influence of Joan Miró and Joan Prats, would fuse political engagement and aesthetic experiment through sonnets, odes, theatre, sculpture and screenplay within a neo-surrealist framework. Brossa founded the magazine *Dau al Set* in 1948, and during the 1950s and 1960s, his poetry was increasingly informed by collectivist concerns. His collection *El saltamartí* (1963) presented a synthesis of themes both political and social, and the subsequent publication of *Poesia Rasa* (1970), *Poemes de seny i cabell* (1977), *Rua de llibres* (1980) – and the six volumes of *Poesia escénica* (published between 1973 and 1983) – saw Brossa stake his place as a central figure in contemporary Catalan literature.

Cameron Griffiths studied History and English Literature at the University of Waikato in New Zealand. His poetry has appeared in journals in New Zealand, Australia and the United States. He lives with his family in Spain. Griffiths' translation of Joan Brossa's *El saltamartí / The Tumbler* (Tenement Press, 2021) is his debut publication, and the inaugural title in Tenement's 'Yellowjacket' series.

Levina van Winden is a poet, theorist, militant, hysteric, and so forth. Now living in Amsterdam, she was born and raised in a little old town at the centre of the Scheldt River delta, one metre below sea level; van Winden's most recent publication is *Er is een band die rapemachine heet / There is a band called rapemachine* (Atlas Contact, 2020).

Imogen Cassels is the author of various pamphlets, including *Chesapeake* (Distance No Object, 2021), *VOSS* (Broken Sleep, 2020), *Arcades* (Sad Press, 2018) and *Mother, beautiful things* (Face Press, 2017). Her writing has appeared in the *London Review of Books*, the *Times Literary Supplement*, *The White Review*, *The Cambridge Review*, *Still Point*, *minor literature[s]* and elsewhere.

Hisham Bustani is an award-winning Jordanian author of five collections of short fiction and poetry, and a two-volume book on postcolonial / decolonial politics. He is acclaimed for his bold style and unique narrative voice, and often experiments at the boundaries of short fiction and prose poetry, utilising perspectives drawn from quantum physics and cosmology. Critics have praised him for his carefully and highly crafted prose and poetry, as well as his polyvalent approach, which draws from a wide diversity of media and arts. His work has been described as 'bringing a new wave of surrealism to [Arabic] literary culture, which missed the surrealist revolution of the last century,' and that he combines 'an unbounded modernist literary sensibility with a vision for total change. His anger encompasses everything, including literary conventions.' Hisham's short fiction and poetry has been translated into many languages, with English-language translations appearing in journals such as the *Kenyon Review*, *Black Warrior Review*, *Poetry Review*, *Modern Poetry in Translation* and *World Literature Today*. His fiction has been collected in *The Best Asian Short Stories 2019* (Kitab), and his book, *The Perception of Meaning* (Syracuse University Press, 2015), was awarded a University of Arkansas Arabic Translation Award, 2014. The UK-based cultural webzine *The Culture Trip* listed Bustani as one of Jordan's top six contemporary writers. His latest book available in English translation is *The Monotonous Chaos of Existence* (Mason Jar, 2022).

maia tabet is an Arabic-English literary translator, academic editor, and language consultant. She is the translator of *Little Mountain* and *White Masks* by Elias Khoury (respectively, Picador, 2007, and Archipelago, 2010), and of *Throwing Sparks* by Abdo Khal, who won the 2010 International Prize for Arabic Fiction (IPAF). Her translation of Sinan Antoon's *The Baghdad Eucharist* appeared in Spring 2017 (Hoopoe Press), and she is also the translator of Hisham Bustani's *The Monotonous Chaos of Existence* (Mason Jar, 2022). Her translations of both fiction and non-fiction have been widely published in journals, literary reviews, and other media, including *Barricade*, *The Common*, *Words Without Borders*, *Portal 9*, *Fikrun wa Fann*, and the *Journal of Palestine Studies*, among others.

Aram Saroyan most recent publication is *Still Night in LA: A Detective Novel* (Three Rooms Press, 2015), and combines both text and photography. Saroyan's *Complete Minimal Poems* (Ugly Duckling Presse, 2007; Primary Information, 2014) received the 2008 William Carlos Williams Award from the Poetry Society of America. Its publication was followed by requests from galleries and museums both in America and abroad. An exhibition of Saroyan's artwork will open at the Francis Gallery (Los Angeles, CA) in 2024.

Velimir ('Viktor') Khlebnikov (1885–1992), poet and poetic theorist, studied mathematics and the natural sciences at Kazan and St. Petersburg Universities but never graduated. He began to publish his poetry in 1908 and, as of 1910, the Futurist school of poetry centred around his works. Khlebnikov invented the word 'zaum' (*za*–BEYOND; *um*–THE MIND) to name a trans-sense or movement-defining transrational language that he would develop along with fellow Russian poet Aleksei Kruchenykh. Khlebnikov coined the terms 'Futurian' and 'Presidents of Planet Earth' for himself and his friends – created a new alphabet based on universal meanings of sounds – and constructed a new language appropriate to his vision for an earth-wide and transnational form of communication. In the mid-1910s, he became fascinated with radio technology and its potential to interconnect a global population, in his opinion, in a manner akin to zaum and its capacity to connect human souls in extra-linguistic comprehension. See V. Markov, *The Longer Poems of Velimir Khlebnikov* (University of California Publications in Modern Philology, vol. 62, 1962).

Natasha Randall is a writer and translator living in London. Her writing and critical work has appeared in the *Times Literary Supplement*, the *Los Angeles Times Book Review*, the *Moscow Times*, *BookForum*, the *New York Times*, *Strad magazine*, *HALI magazine* and on National Public Radio (USA). She is a contributing editor to the New York-based literary magazine *A Public Space*. Her debut novel, *Love Orange*, was published by riverrun (2020). Her translation of Yevgeny Zamyatin's *We* (Random House, 2008) was shortlisted for the Oxford Weidenfeld translation award in 2008. Randall's translation of *A Hero of Our Time* by Mikhail Lermontov was published in May 2009 (Penguin Classics), she completed the translation of a science fiction thriller called *Metro 2033* for Orion (2010), and in 2012 she published a translation of *Notes from Underground* by Fyodor Dostoyevsky (Canongate). She has also published translations of various poems by Osip Mandelstam (in *Jubilat*, and for an anthology of poems published by Ugly Duckling Presse) as well as letters and short fiction by Arkady Dragomoshchenko and Olga Zondberg.

Edwina Attlee is the author of two pamphlets, *Roasting Baby* (If a Leaf Falls Press, 2016) and *the cream* (Clinic, 2016). Attlee's debut collection, *A Great Shaking*, is forthcoming from Tenement Press, 2024. Attlee teaches history to students of architecture in London.

Jason Shulman is a sculptor based in London whose work extends into photography, film and painting. Analgesia, loss and the delusions inherent in perception are some of Shulman's areas of inquiry. He often combines scientific experimentation with more formal trajectories, using optics and other basic science to expose the falsehoods that underpin our experience of reality.

Aidan Moffat, from Falkirk, Scotland, has been writing and recording music since 1996, mainly as one half of Arab Strap, the band recently resurrected after a ten-year hiatus. He has also made many solo and instrumental albums, with notable collaborations with RM Hubbert and an award-winning album with Bill Wells. A children's book, *The Lavender Blue Dress*, was published in 2014, followed by the multi-award-winning documentary film *Where You're Meant to Be*, with director Paul Fegan. He's lived in Glasgow since 1999, and he doesn't really go out much anymore.

Lesley Harrison, born in Ayrshire, Scotland, has published six collections of poetry. She has lived and worked in Istanbul, West Africa, Mongolia and Orkney, on Scotland's northern coastline. Harrison has held writing residencies in Iceland, Greenland, Svalbard and the Harvard University Centre for Hellenic Studies. She lives in the small fishing village of Auchmithie on the Angus coast of Scotland. Harrison's recent publications include *Kitchen Music* (Carcanet, 2023; New Directions, 2023), *Disappearance: North Sea Poems* (Shearsman Books, 2020) and *Blue Pearl* (New Directions, 2017).

Oliver Bancroft born in Cambridge 1976, is recognised to be one of the outstanding painters of his generation. He has exhibited internationally and, over the last two decades, has become a feted filmmaker. Bancroft has shown in various venues, including the Pompidou, Paris, and lives and works in London. A selection of Bancroft's paintings appeared as 'punctuation' in the Tenement Press publication of Reza Baraheni's novella *Lilith* (2023).

Yasmine Seale's work includes poetry, translation, criticism and visual art. She is the author, with Robin Moger, of *Agitated Air: Poems after Ibn Arabi* (Tenement Press, 2022). Her translations from Arabic include *The Annotated Arabian Nights* (W. W. Norton, 2021) and *Something Evergreen Called Life*, a collection of poems by Rania Mamoun (Action Books, 2022). She is a 2023–24 Fellow of the Cullman Center for Scholars and Writers at the New York Public Library.

Will Eaves is a novelist, poet and occasional musician. His novels include *The Oversight* (Picador, 2002), *The Absent Therapist* (CB Editions, 2014), shortlisted for the Goldsmiths Prize 2014, and *Murmur* (CB Editions, 2018; Canongate, 2019), winner of the Wellcome Book Prize 2019. He was Arts Editor of the *Times Literary Supplement* from 1995 to 2011 and Associate Professor in the Writing Programme at the University of Warwick from 2011 to 2020. He co-hosts *The Neuromantics* podcast with ICN Director Prof. Sophie Scott, and writes a column for the *Brixton Review of Books*. 'Greenery,' first published in *Hotel #1*, formed part of *The Inevitable Gift Shop* (CB Editions, 2016) and was shortlisted for the Ted Hughes Award in 2017.

James Hugunin teaches the History of Photography and Contemporary Theory at The School of the Art Institute of Chicago. In 1983, he won the first Reva and David Logan Award for Distinguished New Writing in Photography. He is the author of a survey of the representation of prisoners in the United States, *Discipline and Photograph: The Prison Experience* (Edwin Mellin Press, 1999), *Writing Pictures, Case Studies in Photographic Criticism, 1983–2012* (Jef Books, 2013), *New Art Examiner Reviews: 1986–1993* (U-Turn, 2014), and *Afterimage: Critical Essays on Photography from the Journal Afterimage, 1977–1988* (Jef Books, 2016), all collections of his critical writings.

Glykeria Patramani is a writer from Athens, who works mainly in the field of cinema. Her films have been selected and awarded at international festivals, while her first collection of short stories is due to be published by Rodakio in the autumn.

Lauren de Sá Naylor lives in West Yorkshire. Her prose is centred on the slippery situation of embodiment & authorship, through semi / un / conscious practices of exposure & obfuscation. Her chapbook, *Gazing Down on It*, was published by Ugly Duckling Presse (2022).

Cass McCombs is a musician from Northern California, whose most recent albums are *Mr. Greg & Cass McCombs Sing and Play New Folk Songs for Children* (Smithsonian Folkway Recordings, 2023), *Heartmind* (Anti-, 2022), *Tip of the Sphere* (Anti-, 2019) and *Mangy Love* (Anti-, 2016). His book of poetry, *Toy Fabels*, was published by Spurl Editions, 2019.

Will Oldham makes songs under the *nom de guerre* Bonnie 'Prince' Billy. Most of his lyrics have been collected in book form under the title *Songs of Love and Horror* (W. W. Norton & Company, 2018). Oldham lives in Louisville, KY, with his wife and daughter.

Antonio Tabucchi was born in Pisa in 1943 and died in Lisbon in 2012. A master of short fiction, he won the Prix Médicis Étranger for *Indian Nocturne*, the Italian PEN Prize for *Requiem: A Hallucination* (first published in Portuguese as *Requiem: uma alucinação*, 1991), the Aristeion European Literature Prize for *Sostiene Pereira / Pereira Declares* (1994), and was named a Chevalier des Arts et des Lettres by the French Government. Together with his wife, Maria José de Lancastre, Tabucchi translated much of the work of Fernando Pessoa into Italian. Tabucchi's works include in translation include *Letter from Casablanca* (New Directions, 1986), and *The Edge of the Horizon* (New Directions, 1990), *Time Ages in a Hurry* (Archipelago, 2009), *The Flying Creatures of Fra Angelico* (Archipelago, 2012), *The Woman of Porto Pim* (Archipelago, 2013), *Tristano Dies* (Archipelago, 2014), *For Isabel: A Mandala* (Archipelago, 2017), *Message from the Shadows: Selected Stories* (Archipelago, 2019) and *Little Misunderstandings of No Importance* (Penguin Classics, 2021).

Elizabeth Harris has translated story collections and novels by Mario Rigoni Stern, Giulio Mozzi, Antonio Tabucchi, Andrea Bajani, Francesco Pacifico and Claudia Durastanti. For her translations of various works by Tabucchi (all with Archipelago Books), she has received an NEA Translation Fellowship (2019), The Italian Prose in Translation Award (2018) and the National Translation Award (2016).

Nina Mingya Powles is a writer, editor and publisher from Aotearoa, New Zealand. She is the author of three poetry collections, including *Magnolia* (Nine Arches Press, 2021), which was shortlisted for both the Ondaatje Prize and the Forward Prize; and *Tiny Moons: A Year of Eating in Shanghai* (The Emma Press, 2020). In 2019 she won the Nan Shepherd Prize for *Small Bodies of Water* (Canongate, 2021), and in 2018 she won the Women Poets' Prize. She is the founding editor of *Bitter Melon*. Powles was born in Aotearoa, partly grew up in China, and now lives in London.

Isabel Galleymore's first collection, *Significant Other* (Carcanet, 2019), won the John Pollard Foundation International Poetry Prize in 2020. She is an Associate Professor in Creative Writing at the University of Birmingham and a Fellow at Harvard University's Radcliffe Institute of Advanced Study 2022–23. Her second collection, *Baby Schema*, is forthcoming with Carcanet, 2024.

Preti Taneja is a writer and activist. Her first novel, *We That Are Young* (Galley Beggar Press, 2017; AA Knopf, 2018), is a translation of Shakespeare's *King Lear*, tracking the rise of fascism in contemporary India. It won the 2018 Desmond Elliott Prize for the UK's finest literary debut of the year, and was listed for awards including the Folio Prize, the Shakti Bhatt First Book Prize and the Prix Jan Michalski, Europe's premier award for a work of world literature. It is published in translation worldwide. Her second book is *Aftermath* (And Other Stories, 2021; Transit Books, 2021), a creative non-fiction lament on trauma, terror, prison and grief, following the London Bridge terror attack in 2019. It was a Book of the Year in the *New Yorker*, the *New Statesman* and *The White Review* and was shortlisted for the British Book of the Year. *Aftermath* is the winner of the 2022 Gordon Burn Prize awarded 'for literature that is forward thinking and fearless in its ambition and execution.'

Stanley Schtinter divides his time between the gutter and the stars. He is the author of *Last Movies* (Tenement Press, 2023).

Sophie Seita is an artist and researcher whose work swims in the muddy waters of language, explores materiality, texture and gesture, and the speculative potential of the archive. She regularly performs and shows work across multiple media, publishes books, makes textiles and graphic scores, leads experimental workshops around voice, touch, translation and queer performance, and is a Lecturer in the Art Department at Goldsmiths, University of London. Recent and current projects include an exhibition at Mimosa House (London), performances and events at Nottingham Contemporary, Café Oto, the RCA, UP Projects, and community engagement projects at Grand

Union (Birmingham), Creative Darlington and Curious Arts, and Ruta del Castor (Mexico City). In 2022, she was a Dorothea Schlegel Artist in Residence in Berlin, and in 2023 was a Visiting Artist a Brown University. Her latest book, *Lessons of Decal*, is forthcoming from The 87 Press in December 2023.

Ralf Webb grew up in the West Country. He co-ran the Swimmers pamphlet and event series, and from 2017 to 2021 was managing editor of *The White Review*. Recently, he ran the Arts Council England-funded Poetry x Class reading group project. His writing has appeared widely, including in the *London Review of Books*, *Poetry Review*, *PAIN*, *Prototype*, *Hotel*, *Oxford Poetry* and *Fantastic Man*. Webb's publications include his first collection, *Rotten Days in Late Summer* (Penguin, 2021), and the forthcoming *Strange Relations* (Sceptre, 2024).

Wayne Koestenbaum has published over twenty books of poetry, criticism and fiction, including *Ultramarine* (Nightboat Books, 2022), *The Cheerful Scapegoat* (Semiotext(e), 2021), *Figure It Out* (Soft Skull, 2020), *Camp Marmalade* (Nightboat Books, 2018), *My 1980s & Other Essays* (Farrar, Straus and Giroux, 2013), *The Anatomy of Harpo Marx* (University of California Press, 2012), *Humiliation* (Picador, 2011), *Hotel Theory* (Soft Skull, 2007), *Circus* (Soft Skill, 2004), *Andy Warhol* (Penguin, 2001), *Jackie Under My Skin* (Plume, 1995) and *The Queen's Throat* (Da Capo Press, 1993), nominated for a National Book Critics Circle Award. He has given musical performances of his improvisatory Sprechstimme soliloquies at the Hammer Museum, The Kitchen, REDCAT, Centre Pompidou, Walker Art Centre, The Artist's Institute, the Renaissance Society and The Poetry Project. His feature-length film, *The Collective*, premiered at UnionDocs, New York, in 2021. He has received a Guggenheim Fellowship in Poetry, an American Academy of Arts and Letters Award in Literature, and a Whiting Award. Yale's Beinecke Rare Book and Manuscript Library acquired his literary archive. Koestenbaum is a Distinguished Professor of English, French, and Comparative Literature at the CUNY Graduate Centre.

Iain Sinclair is a British writer, documentarist, filmmaker, poet, flâneur, metropolitan prophet and urban shaman, keeper of lost cultures and futurologist.

SJ Fowler is a writer, poet and performer who lives in London. His work aims to encapsulate an expansive understanding of what literature and poetry can be. Fowler's debut novella, *MUEUM* (Tenement Press, 2022), was shortlisted for the Republic of Consciousness Prize for Small Press, 2023.

Joshua Alexander is a visual artist whose work often combines poetry and moving image. His film *Ghost Machinery* was recently nominated for the international prize at Zebra Poetry Film Festival in Germany in 2018. He has been commissioned to make short films by several organisations, including The Austrian Cultural Forum and English Pen. He has screened work at various events including A World Without Words and Kakania, and in 2014 he had a solo exhibition of photography work at The Hardy Tree Gallery, London. Alexander and Fowler's collaborative feature-length film-work, *Animal Drums*, was released in 2018 and premiered at the Whitechapel Gallery, London.

David Grubbs is Distinguished Professor of Music at Brooklyn College and The Graduate Center, CUNY. He is the author of *Good night the pleasure was ours*, *The Voice in the Headphones*, *Now that the audience is assembled*, and *Records Ruin the Landscape: John Cage, the Sixties, and Sound Recording* (all published by Duke University Press, 2022, 2020, 2018, and 2014 respectively) as well as the collaborative artists' books, *Simultaneous Soloists* (with Anthony McCall, Pioneer Works Press, 2019) and, with Reto Geiser and John Sparagana, *Projectile* (Drag City, 2021). Grubbs has released fourteen solo albums and appeared on more than 200 releases. He was a member of the groups Gastr del Sol, Bastro, and Squirrel Bait, and has performed with Tony Conrad, Susan Howe, Pauline Oliveros, Luc Ferrari, Will Oldham, Loren Connors, the Red Krayola, and many others.

Agustín Fernández Mallo was born in La Coruña in 1967 and is a qualified physicist. In 2000 he formulated a self-termed theory of 'post-poetry' which explores connections between art and science. His *Nocilla Trilogy*, published between 2006 and 2009 (Fitzcarraldo Editions; Farrar, Straus & Giroux), brought about an important shift in contemporary Spanish writing and paved the way for the birth of a new generation of authors, known as the Nocilla Generation. His essay 'Postpoesía: hacia un nuevo paradigma' was shortlisted for the Anagrama Essay Prize in 2009. In 2018, his long essay 'Teoría general de la basura (cultura, apropiación, complejidad)' was published by Galaxia Gutenberg, and in the same year his latest novel, *The Things We've Seen* (Fitzcarraldo Editions, 2021), won the Biblioteca Breve Prize. Mallo's forthcoming novel, *The Book of All Loves*, will be published by Fitzcarraldo Editions in 2024.

Pere Joan Riera (known professionally as Pere Joan) thrived in the underground comics world, beginning in the mid-1970s with the self-published collections *Baladas Urbanas* and *Mu rdago*, both of which were released almost immediately after the death of the dictator Francisco Franco and Spain's transition to democracy. Joan wrote and drew comics for magazines such as *Cairo*, *El Víbora*, *Cavall Fort* and *Viñetas*. Among the series he created are *Pasajero en Tránsito* (1984), *El cielo de septiembre* (1987), *La Lluvia blanca* (Cairo, 1984) and *Mi cabeza bajo el mar* (1990), which he mostly self-published in books. Joan's works also include *Anäs* (1989) and *Bit y Bat* (1996, with Alex Fito) and they are the co-editor (with Max) of the vanguardist comics *Nosotros Somos los Muertos* (2007), *100 Pictogramas para un siglo* (2014), and an adaptation of Cristobal Serra's *Viaje a Cotiledonia* (2015).

Thomas Bunstead has translated some of the leading Spanish-language writers working today, including Agustín Fernández Mallo, María Gainza and Enrique Vila-Matas. Bunstead is twice a winner of PEN Translates Awards, and in 2022 he won an O. Henry Prize and the McGinnis-Ritchie Award for his translation of 'The Mad People of Paris' by Rodrigo Blanco Calderón. His own writing has appeared in publications such as the *Brixton Review of Books*, *LitHub* and *The Paris Review*. He is currently a Royal Literary Fellow, teaching at Swansea University.

John Divola works primarily with photography and digital imaging. While he has approached a broad range of subjects, he is currently moving through the landscape looking for the oscillating edge between the abstract and the specific. Since 1975, Divola has taught photography and art at numerous institutions, including California Institute of the Arts (1978–88), and since 1988 he has been a Professor of Art at the University of California, Riverside. Divola's work has been featured in more than seventy solo exhibitions in the United States, Japan, Europe, Mexico and Australia, and in more than two hundred group exhibitions in the United States, Europe and Japan. Photographs from Divola's 1970s series 'Vandalism' were featured as 'punctuation' in the 2022 Tenement Press publication of Kyra Simone's debut collection, *Palace of Rubble*.

Gareth Evans is a London-based writer, curator, producer, publisher and event host. He works on special projects for the *London Review of Books*. He has written many catalogue essays, and articles on writers, artists and cinema, as well as the extensive text for Radiohead's KID A MNESIA catalogue.

Adrian Bridget is a Brazilian-British writer. Their publications include the novels *Child's Replay* (Bridget, 2022) and *Treatment* (Bridget, 2019). Shorter works have appeared in *Hotel*, *3:AM Magazine*, *The BitterSweet Review*, *The Momentist*, and in anthologies by Akerman Daly and Dostoyevsky Wannabe. In 2023, they were awarded a graduate teaching assistant scholarship by the University of Bristol, where they will develop a PhD project on adopted-language literature and melancholia.

Seven Rooms
Published in the United Kingdom
by Tenement Press & Prototype in 2023
tenementpress.com
prototypepublishing.co.uk

Edited by Dominic J. Jaeckle & Jess Chandler
Designed and typeset by Traven T. Croves (Matthew Stuart & Andrew Walsh-Lister)

Excerpts from Joshua Cohen's ATTENTION: *Dispatches from a Land of Distraction* (pp. 119–122) and Agustín Fernández Mallo's *Nocilla Lab* (pp. 395–405) – first published in *Hotel* #5 – appear courtesy of Fitzcarraldo Editions, by special arrangement with the publisher; respectively, Joshua Cohen, © 2018, and Agustín Fernández Mallo, Pere Joan, and Thomas Bunstead, © 2018. Nick Cave's poem 'New York City, New York' (pp. 129–131) first appeared in Cave's collection *The Sick Bag Song* (Canongate, 2015) and was subsequently published in *Hotel* #3; the work is included in this edition by special arrangement with the publisher; Nick Cave, © 2015 (permissions granted via PLS Clear on behalf of Canongate). Cameron Griffiths' translation of Joan Brossa's 'Sumari astral' / 'Astral Summary' (pp. 163–171) is published in this volume for the first time and is excerpted from Brossa's posthumous collection, *Sumari astral, i alters poemes* (Edicions 62, 1999). Brossa's poetry appears courtesy of the Fundació Joan Brossa, © 2023; English-language translation copyright, Cameron Griffiths, © 2023. maia tabet's translation of Hisham Bustani's short story 'Quantum Leap' (pp. 177–181) first appeared in *Hotel* #4 prior to its inclusion in Bustani's collection *The Monotonous Chaos of Existence* (Mason Jar Press, 2022); the work appears in this edition by special arrangement with the author and publisher; Hisham Bustani & maia tabet, © 2022. Elizabeth Harris' translation of Antonio Tabucchi's 'The Heirs are Grateful' (pp. 283–294) appeared in *Hotel* #7 in tandem with the publication of Tabucchi's collection *Stories with Pictures* (Archipelago, 2021); the work appears in this edition by special arrangement with the publisher; English-language translation copyright, Elizabeth Harris, ©2021. Cass McCombs poem 'Ode' (pp. 355–357) appeared in *Hotel* #6 in tandem with the publication of McComb's collection *Toy Fabels* (Spurl Editions, 2019); McCombs appears in this volume by special arrangement with the publisher; Cass McCombs, © 2019. David Grubbs' text 'Good night the pleasure was ours' (pp. 385–393) first appeared in *Hotel* #7 and, thereafter, in variation in the 2022 Duke University Press publication *Good night the pleasure was ours*. Republished by permission of the Author and the Publisher; David Grubbs, © 2022. *Hotel* would like to extend particular thanks and gratitude to the publishers and editors of these volumes.

The front and reverse cover feature polaroid photographs by Georgia May Jaeckle, © 2023.

All other works first appeared in the *Hotel* series, 2016 to 2021, and appear courtesy of the authors and artists as listed herein. All efforts to ascertain copyright for materials have been undertaken; unless otherwise stated, copyright pertains to the individual contributors, © 2023. All rights reserved.

No part of this publication may be reproduced, stored in a retrieval system, or transmitted, in any form or by any means, electronic, mechanical, photocopying, recording or otherwise, without the prior permission of the publishers.

Typeset in Lexicon No.1 & Univers LT Std.
Printed in the United Kingdom by Bell & Bain Ltd.

A CIP record for this book is available from the British Library
ISBN 978-1-913513-46-7

(type 4 // anthologies)